THE
CATCH

**ALSO BY
YRSA DALEY-WARD**

*The How: Notes on the Great
Work of Meeting Yourself*

bone

*The Terrible:
A Storyteller's Memoir*

THE
CATCH

A Novel

YRSA
DALEY-WARD

Liveright Publishing Corporation
A Division of W. W. Norton & Company
Independent Publishers Since 1923

For information about permission to reproduce selections from this book,
write to Permissions, Liveright Publishing Corporation, a division of
W. W. Norton & Company, Inc., 500 Fifth Avenue, New York, NY 10110

For information about special discounts for bulk purchases, please contact
W. W. Norton Special Sales at specialsales@wwnorton.com or 800-233-4830

Manufacturing by Lakeside Book Company
Book design by Lewelin Polanco
Production manager: Anna Oler

ISBN 978-1-324-09251-3

Liveright Publishing Corporation, 500 Fifth Avenue, New York, NY 10110
www.wwnorton.com

W. W. Norton & Company Ltd., 15 Carlisle Street, London W1D 3BS

1 0 9 8 7 6 5 4 3 2 1

For my mother, who blessed me with the dark.
You don't get more lovely than that.

She was frightened for her daughters and frightened of herself. She would love them so fiercely, so *truthfully*. They might not survive it.

—EVIDENCE, CHAPTER TEN

THE
CATCH

AN EVENING WITH
CLARA MARINA KALLIS

It is hot. Too hot for the twenty-fourth of June.
(or) It's too hot. Wrong for the twenty-fourth of June.
(or) It feels hot (and wrong) this twenty-fourth of June
(and) how can anyone *breathe* right now, anyway, the world becoming what the world is becoming; the world being how the world has always been? My thighs are slippery where they meet. The back of my neck, wet slick. Somewhere out ahead, I hear my name and a swell of applause. Emma grins at me from the sidelines.

"Go get 'em," she says, nodding her small, pink head.

"Go get 'em," she says, as if anyone speaks like that.

I gather my breath and arrange a smile. Once I spent money on porcelain veneers, I was never the same again. My mouth was suddenly set differently; the alignment of my face altered. Something seemed improved, but only I knew what was gone, never to be known again. The end result was pretty, though in a tamer, more regular way. Since I fixed my teeth I have become a large-smiling structure.

My shoes are crushing my toes at the sides, causing this terrible pinch. Across the hardwood stage I stride, stopping ahead of the mic on the chalk-marked *x*. Beyond me, a gallery of keen, open faces. The cameras are positioned at multiple angles to get in today's top-to-bottom look; all pieces on loan, in season and shoppable. These shoes, though torture, pronounce my calves. It'll be worth it for the video assets. You don't often get this turnout for a book event, especially as a first-time novelist. My previous books swam along quite nicely—nothing outstanding, but all respectable enough. The first was an anthology of prose and poetry from women of African descent, and the second was an anthology of selected essays by Black British writers of the last century. Both books did well in colleges and libraries and mostly kept me afloat, along with the odd brand deal or speaking engagements. This novel, though, shifted genres, shifted everything.

I called the book *Evidence*. Things were happening that no one would believe, so I wanted to have somewhere to harbor the facts. The book-sellers are calling it *autofiction*, which is a laugh. Early reviewers said the plot was about time travel, which was, again, missing the point. It helped create buzz, so I didn't argue. I had planned to write a splashy, commercial story with a deft political message, a prize-winning thing lauded by critics, but the dark material arrived at my feet, dressed and ready to talk, hijacking all other possibilities. You have to let the spirit in, even if she's frightening. Even if she bursts rudely onto the scene, threatening to drown you. I resisted at first, but she won out. After nineteen months of drafting, it was as though the person in the story and I had always been together and there was nothing new or strange about it. I wrote day in, night out, because I needed to get her out of my body—she was heavy in my gut. When I was done, I congratulated myself in the mirror. The fragments of my life felt rearranged, complete, even. I took myself out for dry martinis, feeling somber and accomplished, then looked up Janine Arterton of Holzer Literary in the *Writers' and Artists' Yearbook*. You're supposed to shop around, send your samples out to a few relevant names, and wait to see who might be interested, but for me there was no other contender. Janine is in her forties—and tall, like me, with a pro-nounced hero's jawline. All her authors are wealthy and fame adjacent. They've all had books optioned for movies or twelve-part HBO shows. They show up legs crossed in the front and second rows at London and Paris fashion week. This was precisely what and whom I was destined towards. There was nothing to do but go for it. The book was burning a hole in my head, and I needed Janine to take a look at things.

It didn't happen the way I wanted, what does? Janine, who claimed to be taking on no more new authors at the time, skimmed the manuscript and palmed me off to her assistant, Emma West, who appeared, from a Google search, to be the youngest person at the boutique agency.

Emma-Louise West; petite and tattooed with pink, unserious hair. Exactly the kind of person who, Janine surmised in her intro email, *might be hungry for a "diverse" nonlinear tale. And all about women!* According to Janine, I ticked all of Emma's boxes. I was more than a little disappointed, having my heart set on Janine's wisdom, guidance, and—let's be honest—*name*, but Emma was hungry, I'll give her that. She read my pages and immediately wrote me for more. Then she went silent for two weeks, during which time came the sharp, intrusive fear that what I had spent the best part of two years writing might be unreadable crap. Then I got a reply, subject matter,

!!!!!!!!!!!! WHAAAAATTT??? SCREAMING!!!!!!!!!
THE WORLD IS NOT READY, GUUUURL!!!!!

Success. The mess that had pooled its way out of me and onto the pages was decent. Not only that, it was working, spreading. Emma was so excited by the book that we went for a seven-course taster menu at the best fusion restaurant on the South Bank, and all the chilled skin-contact wine I could drink, which is too much.

I was wary of Emma from the beginning. All the exuberance and uncomfortable overfamiliarity—traits that I, growing up the way I did, have been taught to suspect. But she was very *now*, and knew how to schmooze. She wasn't Janine, but she *was* Holzer Literary. Here was an entry point overseen by Janine herself. If I had to make nice with Emma, well, fine. I signed the dotted line. I applied her eager notes to the text, embellished wherever I was encouraged to, removed what was suggested. The story grew a new neck. We made it sexier, darker, more titillating. There was a five-way bidding war on the budding, twisting story. We chose the hottest publisher in the draw. I, in turn, received a healthy advance.

I was right. Janine had been right. Emma was right. Just shy of a year later, *Evidence* is currently number seven on the *Sunday Times* bestseller list and has been sitting between there and number three for seven and a half weeks. The book is hot pink for optics and marketing. On its back cover is a picture of me, sitting against a textured concrete wall, lit and airbrushed to heaven.

••

I wait for the clapping to die. I show the even white plates in my mouth again and make a small joke about the venue. Ahead of me: a gallery of curious faces, bodies and hands. The booze I swallowed in the green-room is dancing its way down, lighting me up like the city at night, shifting me into glittering performance. My voice warms the room. Everyone is laughing in their seats. The joke, whatever it was, worked. I begin to read from page 55, the moment when the prettier, more successful twin sees their long-lost mother for the first time. The catch is this; the mother and the daughter are both eight years old. Both at the same time. I get a startling rush of something cruel, or smothering.

Here it is again, this fog, this near-blue thing. But it is dimmer than blue, more solemn than blue. It is heaving and formless, filling me to the eyes. It is trying its best to sink me, and there is no help anywhere, nothing vaguely resembling land. All I can see for miles is the pink, pink book. A person in a rust-coloured hat is speaking at the mic, moving their hands a lot. I try to focus in on their face, but the room appears to be darkening.

"Can I ask about your mother?" they say with a careful tone. "Can I ask about yours?" I shoot back, and everyone laughs. "Only joking," I tell them, grinning with these teeth.

"What of the daughters in the novel?" a different person with a Scottish accent is asking. "Is that part largely autobiographical, or—"

"No," I cut them off. "The girls were metaphors."

"I want to talk about *words*," says someone else, who is close to tears. "I am a new mother, and mothering brings me purpose, but not enough to function. I am called to write and make art so that I do not feel as isolated as I do, but I'm stuck. I can't get started because of this growing lack of connection to myself—to anything these days. Like you, or, sorry, like the woman in the book, the ordinary feels so uninspiring, so monotonous. I don't know how you managed to record this experience so precisely. Either way, you seem to have the answers."

I don't have any answers.

I open my mouth to say this, but the person carries on.

"Writing is what I want to do—what I always expected to find myself doing—and I've always taken it for granted that I'd *somehow* make it into a career. I'm not sure how it happens, but these days I don't have the words. The world is burning. I feel it. I feel so demotivated, like an imposter of sorts, as though nothing I create will be real, because I am not in fact real, and as I give all daily motivation up to domestic chores and caregiving, I'm scared I might be getting farther away from anything that is only mine. Even though what I am actively doing— keeping a child alive—feels like the realest task, the only necessary task, *I* don't feel real anymore. I don't belong to me anymore. That's it—I don't feel *mine*. Every night, I say to myself, *Tomorrow you'll start. Tomorrow you'll exist enough to trust your work*; but for now someone needs me and I can't remember to think about myself. How can a person who cannot prove themselves real produce anything of resonance, anything of note?"

This person is *intense*. The audience is dead quiet. I need an answer, but I'm coming up short. I want to say, *I don't know, how can anyone know what is real?* and *don't you know we're made up of dead and dying things and that's all we are?*

But you don't have this option when you have somehow been named someone who knows something about some things. This happens when you write a book and said book does well on the charts and all that. It feels like a racket, an ominous trick.

"Sorry. That was quite long-winded. Sorry," the woman says, returning the mic to the usher and taking her seat, looking very much like a person who exposed too much of themself in public. I move it along by saying some practiced sentence about feeling your feet on the ground; about looking around yourself, returning to your breath, taking note of the people places and things that you know are, in fact, *Real*. But the cruelness is upon me again. I say, "If you really were called to *start*, you would have *started*." The woman nods her head, goes into her book bag, pulls out a pen and paper and begins to take notes, and I suddenly feel a recognizable heaviness. I cannot hear my voice so much anymore, but I think I say a thing that I might want to hear. I say that even when you go into a room and leave, the air has changed because you were there; *are* there, forever. I talk about how the air around us bends, how every person changes the shape of the living world.

"Write about *not* having the answer," I hear myself say. "Write about the imposter body, or the harrowing, unpleasant nature of parenthood, and how nothing is as you hoped. Write about not knowing." Then the mouth that I am using makes another joke that makes everyone laugh a little more. I call the sad mother back to the mic. The sad mother puts away her notebook and pen. I ask some questions, gently teasing until her cheeks flush. When we are done, she flops back down onto her chair, self-aware but high on the attention, I think.

I'm sweating by now, because of the sudden threat of colour, clinging off the beams above our heads and resting on the seats in the hardback chairs. The worse-than-blue has been hanging around for weeks, taunting me because tomorrow is my birthday. Tomorrow is our birthday, and I don't want to talk about it.

I glimpse my profile in the side monitor. We decided on a dress that is not my colour at all but has a magical cut. Ordinarily, you couldn't pay me to wear purple, but this is somewhat short of it, indigo in the shade, the unmissable hue of forget-me-nots under the hot lights. The designer is one to watch, and I have never worn anything that has held me together so well. It is the kind of dress that makes people pay attention. My hair is wavy today, blown out and decadent. My face is contoured, gorgeously lit, smooth as a mannequin's. I look like the thing with eyes on the back of the book.

It must be time to stop talking, because the host is motioning to me from the stage curtain. Another burst of applause happens, and as I move backstage again, I feel the damp gathering at my armpits beneath the silk of the material, the parted mouths of two small rivers. Emma passes me my drink again for a sneaky little sip, before the hosts lead me toward the signing desk where I sit with a pitcher of ice water. By the time the signing part is over, I am vibrating, running off some manic, exhausted fervor. I am ready to throw it off at the door, to retire the bad act. That, and these unbearable shoes.

Oh, but then, I see a *beauty*.
A fish in the sea, see.

The man is leaning on a pillar in the back wall of the room. He looks fairly bored, standing by a redhead who asked me a very uninteresting question about how long it takes to draft a book. She is touching his hair, touching his arm, talking at his face, talking away at the dead space around them. The man is as bronzed and contoured as me, so flawless that he seems a little unreal, a little filtered, fuzzy around the edges— almost photoshopped into the atmosphere, a mirage of sorts. From the dim place where I am sitting, I find his eyes. His stare is the shade of the feeling I cannot name, whatever is loose inside me.

The redhead skips across the room to ask for a selfie. Emma tells her to join the signing line. I say it's fine for them to cut in—it'll only take two minutes—and right before posing for the picture, I pull Emma to one side and tell her to make it happen. I notice a glimmer of judgement in her eye, but she gets on with it. As I pose with the red-haired girl for no fewer than six selfies, I see Emma approach the bronzed man. He takes in what she is saying and is careful to temper his reaction. After a beat or two, we catch each other's eyes and he almost nods, but not quite.

••

An hour and a half later,
the sky is pink.

Emma, the man, and I are out of there and sitting in the car in a
kind of bleak, awkward silence. It is one of those large, electric limou-
sines with a glass panoramic roof, boasting a view of the trees overhead.
I stare at the leaves, all accents and manners of green. There is more
breath available to me now. The evening feels looser around me. Emma
is chattering away at both of us because she doesn't know how to sit there
and shut up. As we pull away, he is responding to her, but I tune them
both out in favor of the music. I sip on the brandy in my flask and make
a clear point of not engaging. Outside the windows, the streets and fields
whip by like deer.

Unfortunately, because of Emma, the odd word is slipping through,
so I also learn that a) the man is an actor, an actor who is sometimes on
the TV and most of the time not, and b) his Christian name is *Cristian*
(with a CR).

The chatter is destroying my buzz, and things are turning worse. Up
close I can see that, yes, those are highlights in his curls. Also, his skin is
a little sallow and I'm sitting just a little too far away to confirm this for
sure, but I suspect he might be wearing coloured contact lenses. These
sudden details cause a swell of alarm in my chest. I could open the car
door right now and roll out to safety. I could be blood and other materials,
parts left here and there. It *could* be delicious, a shocking way to end—but
I am a coward, and it is late in the day. Late in the journey. Too late to turn
around or drop him off at the tube and say that I made a mistake.

"Turn it up, please?" I call out to the driver, feeling a little desperate. Ambient techno fills the space in the back of the car and I exhale, a
touch soothed. I pass my guest the flask so that he can get on my level
if he needs to be. He takes it with both hands and without meeting my
eye, takes a swig. It is a tentative movement, so obedient and erotic that
my body immediately begins to respond. *That's it*, I think. *That's it*. The
brandy is stroking the backs of my knees and I am starting to feel quite
charged, even while Emma talks on and on and—God help us—on. But

her voice is no match for the music, no match for the deepening scene. Cristian has gone quiet now, apparently taking my cue. He squints out of the side window at something imperceptible. Thankfully, Emma-Louise West gives up, and once we finally approach Canary Wharf tube station, zips out of her seat. I almost think she is going to say the two words of doom as she leaves the car, but my birthday slips her mind, I think, and I thank the heavens, the bruised sky.

Now that he and I are alone, I can be whatever I want to be, whatever the moment calls for. I can sense that he is stuck trying to make conversation, which pleases me. To fuck him up a little more, I mumble what I want to do to him. The driver looks ahead, pretending not to hear. Cristian tenses but makes no eye contact, breathes out of his mouth. Then he brushes a hand across his smooth chin, and I watch his lips, considering every place I want to feel them, all my breaking points, all my dreadful gaps. When I am no longer sure I can bear the strange, delightful tension, we pull into my driveway.

Right away, Cristian takes stock of my house. I made an error in judgement here, perhaps, and maybe ought to have chosen a hotel. We get out of the car and he places a hand on my waist, and I hate it. Once in the house, I have to ask him twice to remove his shoes. He keeps on complimenting the furniture. He picks up one of my expensive teak lamps and says, "Cool lamp, where did you get it?" I look down at his socks and see that one is worn and black and the other is bobbly and navy. There is a small hole at the right big toe. I ask him if I'd recognize him from anything he'd worked on, but only to make conversation. If I don't distract myself well enough, I might notice that I have started to not feel very well at all. I've been feeling sick all week.

Cristian is going on about two shows that I have never heard of, and with every moment that passes I want to do this less and less. Even his voice is a little too proper, the accent depressingly crisp. I'd like him to drop a few t's, perhaps, or use some slang we both recognize, but he doesn't, and it's ruining the mood. To keep myself from running upstairs and locking myself in the bathroom, I pour us both a dark drink and hang in the corner, watching him take a few small sips. This time it has the opposite effect than it did in the car. In fact, it verges on off-putting. I am terrified that he may say or do something that will force me to change my mind completely, and I can't risk that because we're too close now, too far in the game. To save the moment, I unzip and step out of my dress like Superwoman. The body I am in looks even better naked and there's no time to be modest about that. The look on his face makes me throb where it matters. The look on his face is, frankly, the highlight of the night.

He pulls off his pants at once, backing me along the exposed brick wall. He is heading, perhaps, for a bedroom, but no. I feel the near-blue coming, the edging stress, the clamoring need. With no time to spare, I make him kneel beneath me on the floor, behind the sofa, and after he has done a few seconds of a too-wet offering that I can barely feel, I push him down on my open yoga mat. "Lie there," I tell him, angling myself on top of him, in the way I like the most. Without stopping to see or feel much of anything, I guide him inside me.

In theory, he does not disappoint. The shape and size of him, his smell and pleasing weight. It is the first grounded, inside-of-my-body feeling I have had in weeks. Whispering a script into his ear as a prompt, I have him say what I need him to say to get me to where I need to be. Then I stare hard at the not-blue-nor-grey surf in his eyes again. I need it to carry me somewhere, anywhere. We fuck on the living room floor. There is no real chemistry between us, but there is urgency; somewhat more useful. We gather speed, velocity. He is an excellent backdrop, strong and large, and we are both instruments enough to satisfy ourselves. Together, the nothingness we make is stunning. I get lost in it, let the sensation wash over me. I sail away. I overlay, I dream of a current,

of a fatal storm. All the waves in me are crashing, and my body is saying no no no no but my body is always saying no no no no, or something to that effect. My insides are crying out, but I will not stop, and I get to where I need to get in record time, once, then again, again. I call out when I come, words of a faraway language, words offshore and intangible, dripping with heat and salt. Atop him, the body I am in shudders.

Afterwards, I finish him off. He tastes of seawater with iron inclusions, bitter-sharp.

"You sound different onstage," he says, buttoning up his trousers, and looking even worse, I notice, in the truthful living room light. By now, his skin and eyes seem positively venomous. By now, I am traveling outside my body again, and I want him out of my house right now. Right now. I note him clocking the network of raised hyperpigmented marks on my upper inner thighs and arms. I go to the bathroom and pull on my robe.

Back in the room and the scene, I offer him a nightcap to close the night out in a polite manner. Thankfully, he shakes his head no. I feel sure that he imagined this would be better, but that's on him.

"That was amazing," he says, as though searching my thoughts. He says it like a question.

"Who was the girl you were with at the reading?" I ask, as if I care.

"My girlfriend," he says.

"We're open," he says.

"I mean, with you? I couldn't not," he says, and then he adds, "would you have invited me if you'd known?"

"Yes," I tell him, "it makes no difference to me."

His car comes at eleven eighteen, and I let out a groan of relief, which surprises us both. Well, I don't have the energy to pretend.

"Could this happen again?" he asks in his horrible accent. I say nothing. He stands up and does a sad little wave, which makes me want to kill him, or myself. For some reason I say, "Thank you," and then I don't know what else to say so I add, "Take care of yourself," while handing him his jacket.

At the doorway he turns, places both hands hard on my shoulders. I step back at once, terrified that he'll try to kiss me. He takes an affected pause, looking down on the floor, and back to meet my eyes. A coquett-ish mannerism. Distasteful, even.

"May I ask you a question?" says this Cristian guy.

"Go on," I say.

"In your book," he says, "you talk more about the protagonist's daughters than you ever do about her. And then she disappears? Like, into the ether? What happened to her? Will we ever find out?"

"You read my book?"

He leans his head to one side, in a manner I find grotesque. "'Course. I'm a bit of a superfan."

Behind him, a shadow in the hallway shifts, and for a second, I am worse than afraid.

"Okay," I say, trying to play it off. "That's cool."

A line of orange light dances across Cristian's face. Outside his Uber is blinking a signal, but still he lingers, like a man who has all the time in the world.

"I guess I'm trying to find out if there'll be a sequel," he presses, drawing closer.

And just like that, the terror in my spine dissolves into extreme, familiar irritation; at his hands on my shoulders, this long, intense stare, this embarrassing attempt at seduction. How unnecessary. It is more than time for him to be gone, and he is not picking up on it. I reach past him to pull the door open and the tough night air stings our faces.

"Oh, look," I say. "Your car."

His eyes light up a little, like someone who just remembered a joke.

"One more thing,"

"What is it?" I bark, sharper than intended. Cristian points both fingers at me, gun style.

"Is there anyone you have loved so completely and so fiercely that you thought it could be the end of you, or them?"

Quoting a book to its author.

Only to be expected from an actor.

I put both hands on his chest and push him backwards onto my doorstep. He thanks me for the car, and waves to the Uber.

"Your agent has my number," he calls out behind him. "Please, please use it."

When vehicle and passenger are down the road, safely out of view, I go inside and double bolt the door. Then I go back to the living room and kneel on the floor. I rest there a while in child's pose, nose to rug, my chest filling up with something like hate. I go over my yoga mat with the antibacterial wipes, twice for good measure, following up with a sponge and more antibacterial spray. I imagine all the billions of new bacteria and fungi that must be multiplying inside and outside of me by now as I step into the shower. There, under the hottest stream that my skin can bear, I soap myself up until I'm swathed in suds. After, scraping my teeth and gums with my electric toothbrush, I can't help weeping. My orgasm is still settling at the top of the legs that are carrying me, and I am crying,

because it is almost midnight, because I am a person of *that age*, and cannot shake the feeling that I have been here, alone, long enough for my liking, because I would NOT have fucked the stranger if I'd known he'd read my work, because *that* feels fairly gross. Even for me.

Outside, there is a moving flare, fireworks or sparklers. I rush to the window to meet the peculiar display happening above the lake across the road. These are not fireworks at all, but a somewhat curious mingling of precipitation and thunder, a near-electric storm arching across my field of vision. Billows of cloud, thick and dark. It has begun to rain, too, fast and hard. I tune in to the patter of the water on my windowpane. The head on my shoulders is already pulsing. I need to slow down on the booze. I get into bed and squeeze my eyes shut, feeling that comfortable, reflective hatred. At least I am home. *Home.* Well, at least I am in my house;

or at least I am here in a house that I paid for, and there is a safety to that. My pillow is cold and I am grateful for this small, important lifeline.

How can a person who cannot prove themselves real
produce anything of resonance, anything of note?

My eyes flick open.

"Your child, you ungrateful dick," I hear my mouth saying. "Not everyone gets a child, you know."

But I am speaking to the dark, and everything inside it. Low in my mind, a dream is unfurling, wet, ready to be alive. The clock hums a warning. Tomorrow is now.

CLARA K
IS SEEING THINGS

I wake with dry mouth, in a pool of something more concentrated than sweat. The doorbell is ringing, and I sit up at once, my line of vision askew. The damp that has gathered underneath each of my breasts and the small of my back smells almost metallic. There is a sickly, empty feeling in my stomach, and the sides of my toes feel rubbed raw. When yesterday floods to mind, I hobble to the bathroom, but huddled over the toilet bowl, I can't get anything to come up. All that happens is the ache, the horrible retching, and nothing more. My legs and arms are trembling. There is a small glare in the bottom right of my vision. The person insists on ringing and ringing the doorbell.

"One minute!" I shout down the hall, but they press on the doorbell creating a shrill, drawn-out sound, which grazes my temples, causing me to retch again. When I catch sight of the mirror I smile, if only to see if I can, and there I notice two patches of blood budding along my gumline.

"Coming!" I yell. "Just a minute! Please!"

Downstairs, the courier, put out at having to wait so long, thrusts the silver balloons into my arms. A large three, a larger zero. Mismatched.

"Happy birthday," the courier says, flatly. I watch as he unloads an unreasonable number of pink peonies in tall cylinder boxes. The flowers have been spray-painted fuchsia to match the front of the book. I spot their original softer pink on some of the petals' undersides. The courier speeds off, and I try to replay the thing last night. Someone was in my house, and we messed around for a while. I remember even less than usual: How were his face and hands and body? How young or old might he have been? I divide the flowers among four white ceramic vases and, from my array of good nightwear, take out the white silk pajamas with the pink detailing. I choose a brown goddess braid wig, arranging it into a high ponytail. I look more natural and relatable today—or I will, once I've added the necessary filters. Next, I set up the tripod, warming the ring light hue so that it emits the flattering peach glow that goldens my skin, making sure all the flower vases are visible in the background. I tilt the camera downwards to accentuate the upturn of my eyes. I add a retouch filter for my face. Then I sit half in, half out of my bed and work it until I find a frame I am happy with, some video I can send to the publisher's Instagram. I recite two paragraphs about milestones, hopes, dreams, and never giving up. When I have done all of that, I check my one message. *HAPPY BIRTHDAY U! HERE'S TO ANOTHER BRIL-LIANT YEAR OF U!!!* Emma is using the champagne emoji, the cake emoji, and annoyingly, the dark-skinned black fist emoji.

I Uber Eats order French toast, hash browns, chicken sausage, scrambled eggs with avocado, mushrooms, and baked beans on the side, and orange juice and consider the day ahead. I have a radio meeting at two and an "in conversation" event at six p.m. in Piccadilly Circus with a writer whose book I can't be bothered to open. The food arrives twenty minutes later and I get stuck in. Even when the polystyrene trays are empty, save for a few crumbs and remnants of yolk, I'm nothing close to satisfied. The thing that feels like hunger remains. I deserve a cake today, the largest, most colourful cake I can find. A cake with all the chemicals, all the non-digestible ingredients. But first, I order the breakfast again, and when it arrives, eighteen minutes later, I make a special effort to work on it slowly. I draw it out, concentrating on what I can taste, until finally, I feel my stomach expand. Then I want more, of course. By late morning, I am in the car, heading towards central London.

It is summertime in the city. People are walking around with their skins on display. They are wearing caps, mirrored sunglasses, terrible

T-shirts. I watch the varying shades of exposed bodies, soft and vulnerable, walking on their legs, eating ice cream. They do not know when it will be over for them, but it will be; of course it will be, and what nasty work it is to be aging at an alarming speed, all of the time, with no takebacks, no option to pause, each of us trapped inside a body that will eventually let us down. We wait around for summer. To escape the bad insides of everything, we stand in line for street food and beer and restaurants and nightclubs and department store sales, all the while knowing that there is sickening news afoot. It might not be today but it will be tomorrow. It is coming. It is always coming.

In the store I'm sweating under my coat. I consider the dress bunched in my hands. The dress is woollen, blood red. *Do not be distracted*, I warn myself, placing the thing back on the rack. I try to pass by the warm lights in the Luxury Goods department, but I fold, crossing the threshold toward several impossible, sparkling things. In the corner of my vision, several objects gleam. Following the glimmer, I find myself magpie-drawn to an eye-level row of watches. I have never owned a watch before. It strikes me that in this year I may as well make a friend of time. A heavy gold Rolex is exactly the kind of thrill I'm looking for. I try one on, and the timepiece warms on my wrist. It looks heavy and serious, as though it has always belonged there. There is nothing of the past here, only the me that I deserve to be, the me that I was born to be, slightly out of reach. And why shouldn't I have a thing to remind me of that? My field of vision jolts, and I feel the nausea rising. Why are these shopping malls so fluorescent, so frighteningly lit? I wipe the sweat from my hairline, leaning over the counter, both hands on the glass.

"Big purchase. You wanna be sure," says the sales assistant. "Is it a special day?"

"No," I say, looking somewhere beyond his shoulder. I breathe out, catching the night-old brandy smell in the air around my nose. My stomach lurches again. The undulating lights of the shopping centre meet my eyeline, gathering bright spots of doom. If I don't get some water I might keel over right here. I snap off the watch, laying it down on the counter with some force. The sales assistant retrieves the item quickly and places

it back, out of reach in its glass casing. He gives me a strange look. I feel
a dull itch where the lace on my wig meets my hairline. If I faint or die,
I hope I'm blended.

I hear myself asking him where I can sit down, and a dull recognition enters my body. From deep in my chest there is a whooshing sound,
some bright dam breaking. I cough, suddenly gasping for air.

"Yes, absolutely," the customer behind me is saying to the salesclerk
on the opposite till. "Well, you know how it is, hahahaha."

It is the voice that grabs me; smooth. Inky. Troubling. I spin around
too fast. There I spot the back of the head. The person stands a little
shorter than me and sports a jagged, messy afro with hints of copper. I
shift my weight. There. I study her. She looks up and to the left, to the
awful light. As I edge forward I catch her delicate profile, which almost
resembles a bust one might see in a museum, like she could have been
carved from ancient material. From my peripheral view I take her in for
a few long seconds, and then,

I swear I see her place a shiny thing in her pocket.

I let out a small sound and, hearing me, she freezes, looking up
and around herself. When I see more of her face, it is as though I have
stepped into a bucket of cold water.

The legs that I am on buckle.

More seconds. I go to speak, and nothing. The sounds of the store
around me feel faraway, background. The woman in question is breez-
ing through the front door, her cream coat swishing. I try to move
but am weighted to the spot. Feeling extremely faint, exceedingly Not
There, I follow her, trying to catch my breath, and all the while, the
man in at the counter is barking, "SECURITY!! SECURITY," as I exit
after her.

More seconds. Everything blackens. Here I am and I am here,
being brought roughly to my feet by two large security guards. They
are marching me back through the door, back into the store. I gather

myself up to protest, to threaten everyone's jobs, but as we approach, my sales assistant is screaming at the security man. "It wasn't her!" the man pleads. Everyone crowds around me, looking on, towards the door. The security men release each arm, apologizing. This first guard makes for the door, the other guard in hot pursuit. I grab at the spot where they gripped me hard.

"Right under my nose,"
someone is saying,

and two clerks are approaching me, talking at once. "I'm fine! I SAID I'M FINE," I am saying to the two clerks, but they aren't listening. They are offering me water, a seat, an explanation.

"Racists!" I spit, knowing that will cause panic. A tall man with glasses and a suit and floppy hair has lots of frightened words and there is talk of vouchers and a personal shopping experience and what can they do for me and whatnot and—"I told you I'm fine," I say, getting to my feet, scanning the counter. "I don't want anything from this place. And don't you touch me again. Don'tyoufuckindare."

"We understand, madam," he says. "We'd like to offer you our deepest . . ." As he talks, I threaten to take legal action. I say I have never been treated like this before. I really should milk it and maybe get the red dress for free, but there's the unfinished thing in my gut, happening and happening in waves. Sweat is dripping off my forehead and stinging my eyes. People are stopping to look, and I can't be having that.

Outdoors, everything is terribly luminous. I scan the streets. No sign of the woman. Some part of me feels misplaced. My hands have begun to shake. Catching my breath in the street, I feel the urge to go and lie prone, in the middle of the road—but that would be absurd. These legs go to cross the road anyway. In the middle of the road I pause, looking up ahead at a bus approaching. The bus lets out an unearthly shriek. There she is, at the front of the double-decker bus.

The woman is on the bus. She is my mother. My very own mother. She is my mother and she is on the bus. My mother rides the bus. The number six bus. Let me help you understand, because I need to be understood. Though I might never have known my mother, I know my mother when I see my mother. She died in nineteen ninety-five, they told us (or) she was missing, presumed dead in ninety-five and then they found her remains, (or) what they said were likely her bodily remains—what they said were her remains but can't have been her remains, all washed up on the banks of the River Thames—swollen as two people, slick with green moss. There was no foul play, none at all, they said.

Few things have I been surer of: the woman at the front at the top row on the double decker is my mother. I know my mother when I see my mother. Her hair, hands, and height are the same. I saw the face and I swear to God, I knew. I heard the blue voice, and I *knew* it was her. I know it was her. I have known it was her.

Everything has slowed. The bus is still making its terrible sound. It is grinding to a halt in front of me, and its driver is shouting. The people in the store's glass windows are all watching, open-mouthed. A crowd has gathered in the street. I think I jump out of the way.

The bus grinds and coughs and finally breaks to a stop. The driver has his hands on his chest. The driver is shouting obscenities, and the cars behind are honking their horns. People around me are staring, pointing. I find my way to the bus door, but the door stays locked. I beat on the door, but the driver shakes his head, swearing some more, and starts up the bus again. People on the bus are talking and pointing. I look up to catch my mother's face, but it is hidden by the mean glare of the sun. Pushing through the bystanders, I run into the side street where my car is parked, certain that I could die, right now, before I get my key into the ignition. The body of mine gets into the car. The body of mine takes its trembling hands, backs its car out onto the busy street, turns left onto the main road. The machine is driving the machine and I am stuck somewhere and nowhere, pushing the levers. Everything is hyper-real; larger than life.

We stop at the lights, the bus still visible a few cars ahead. I scan the top window for her disturbing outline and spot the back of her head. All that loud, soft hair. There is a drum beat in the middle of my neck. Her neck looks like my neck (or my neck looks like her neck). My mouth is filling up with saliva. I'm in the car, four vehicles behind the bus with my mother up ahead, a ship's figurehead, all golden, all brass. It takes all the focus I have to dial Dempsey's number.

"Hello?" says my sister, sounding a million miles away.

I cannot make the words come.

"Hello?" says my sister, again. "Clara?" says my sister, now aggravated.

I cannot make the words come.

"You never call on our birthday. What's up?"

"I just saw her, D," is all I can manage.

There is a silence, then, "Who?" says Dempsey.

"Mum."

"*Mum*," I say again. "Our mother."

"What?" she says, and then, "where?"

"In Selfridges," I say. "I think she stole a Rolex."

Then there is a click,
because the bitch hangs up.

I trail the bus until it pulls in by the Elephant and Castle station. My mother gets off and marches for a while before turning the corner into a block of flats. The block sits there, grey and forbidding, and she enters the entryway to the left, slamming the door behind her. There is a sign. DRINKWATER TOWERS. My mouth and throat are now dry as anything. Knees trembling, I climb out of the car, half-blocking someone's driveway. I stumble towards the brick-red entryway in the direction my mother went. I try the door. Locked, of course.

I tread around the back of the block of flats, hoping for a sign, spotting a flutter of movement high in the small dark window around the side of the building; a stairwell, perhaps. Eyes darting, I survey the back side of the block of flats. More movement. Another window, where a light from inside pops on. She appears to have landed on the third floor.

I wait a while, until everything shifts into focus. The scene feels familiar. There is a rust glow about the room, and I wonder if I'm going mad. Through the smeared rectangle, I watch the lithe, dark shape of that same woman take off the cream coat against the rust walls. I watch her place one hand on her hip. My mother walks towards a man with no hair. They are talking. I watch her straddle him. Their framing inside the window is perfect, like a classic wide cinema screen. I watch them kiss, and kiss again. These are filmic, unreal kisses, theatrical in length. She pulls away and looks at him, and then, in the blur of the window, I see her face change.

I would have moved, but it happens too quickly. With a flick of her head, she looks away from him and out the window, down, down, right into my eyes. As my mother smiles at me, I raise a hand to my mouth. Her teeth are not as I expected; a little smaller, sharper perhaps. Does my mother laugh at me? In her mouth I spot a flash of silver, a suggestion of treasure, lost. She moves stealthily away from the man and towards the window, towards me, a black look in her eye. I find my feet and I run. I do; I fucking run.

DEMPSEY'S NOT HAVING ANY OF IT

"You do know," I say, trying not to sound as though I'm reasoning with an insane person, "our mother would be sixty by now. The person you're describing probably just looked like her, and I just think it's triggered you somehow."

I'm making perfect sense. Of course I'm making sense, but she's not about to give me that, because she never gives me anything.

"Triggered," she repeats. "Fuck off with that."

"Can I get you a bottle of water?" I ask, but Clara is still staring at the floor, muttering words. I ask again about the water, but she peers past me, squinting somewhere into the deep beyond.

"For argument's sake," I try again, trying to swallow the heat in my throat, trying to coat the tender, specific rage appearing in my chest. "Suppose that was our mother that you saw. Suppose she just happened to be in Selfridges, stealing watches. Do you really think she would look exactly as she looked thirty years ago?"

Hand across my forehead, I see I'm getting nowhere.

"It was fucked," says Clara. "She *definitely* saw me. I know she did. I know she knew. I know she knew I knew . . . and she knew that . . ."

I hit the table in front of her, lightly. "Clara. I need you to listen, or at least to talk me through this. Because you're really not making sense."

Clara drops back into the room again, looking at me in that way that

she does; the all too familiar superior expression of hers. Why do I hold
all the shame, all of the time? Here I am, humoring her, trying to make
sense of a complete impossibility. I watch my birth twin, who is horribly
backlit against the window. She is beginning to look transparent, like
mist. Another telltale migraine aura. My head-pulse is starting to wane
a little, giving rise to a sharp pain in my right temple. I draw my breath
in slowly to the count of seven, hold for a count of seven, breathe out
for a count of nine and a half. I had a small attack last night, my first
in months. It was mild, as migraines go, more visual disturbances than
anything else, stripes of colour and fog across my eyeline, dividing my
visual scope. A pre-birthday migraine. I wasn't surprised.

"How old was she, Clara, the woman you saw? Roughly?"

"'Bout thirty," my sister says. "Yeah, about our age. Happy birthday,
by the way."

"Happy birthday. Okay. About *thirty. About our age*," I repeat, hoping she hears how this all sounds. But no. Clara must still be in the grips
of whatever she was on last night. She had a show or reading or whatever
you call it, so it's likely that she went out to celebrate. I've read all about
cocaine and everything, and wouldn't put it past her. All the minor
celebrities are on the stuff. I'll never understand doing drugs. I wouldn't
even take an aspirin. I have the utmost respect for my body.

I am trying to keep this conversation logical, but Clara's in no space
for logic. She must at least *think* this is real, because this is not the kind
of thing you joke about.

"Clara," I go to pat her arm. "Today is always going to be a tough . . . I
mean we . . ."

She snatches my hand off hers.

"Show me all her stuff, Dempsey. I need to see it."

"What stuff?"

"Now!"

"Now?"

"For fuck's sake, Dempsey, move!"

I should not enable her. I need to hold her eye contact, but it's
getting difficult.

My sister moves closer until she is just about an inch away from my face.

"Are you listening? Did you hear me?" she presses, enunciating every word, her long arms outstretched. My sister's limbs go on forever. In some lights, she's inhuman.

I cross the room toward the hallway, to the tiny adjoining room that is not quite an attic and not a closet, either. Inside the room are my wig caps, hair wraps, never used Kanekalon braiding hair, miscellaneous Amazon orders that I haven't got around to opening, and the ASICS box Clara is looking for, on which I scrawled in drying black marker, aged sixteen, *ALL ABOUT MUM*. The box is only a third full.

Clara stands close behind me in the Not Closet. I feel her sour breath warming my neck and think about how alike we might have been, if things were different, if things were better.

"Can you back up?" I ask, irritated, and my sister growls—really growls, like a thing in the zoo. She grabs the box out of my hands—because she is that kind of person—and hurries back into the living room. She throws my birth certificate to the floor, and our adoption papers, going right for the WH Smith photo album containing *those* photos, which I know and have known by heart.

In the first picture, a striking, unusual looking woman with a free-form afro leans back on a sofa. Her name is Serene Marie Nkem Droste, and she's none other than our mother. Her hand is cupping her face. Our mother has the most elegant hands. Behind her, the brass edge of a large floor mirror. At her feet sit four shimmering green beer bottles. Around her, the room is rust coloured, beckoning.

Picture two: Serene Marie Nkem Droste feeding the ducks at the park, wearing a coat that looks like Clara's. Long, cream, and mother-soft.

Picture three: The two of us as newborns in a pale blue cot, with Serene Marie Nkem Droste curled up on a couch looking pinched and worn. The picture is haunting, because we know how everything ends. Clara looks like a cherub, a perfect little toy, but there is a black stain where my face should be, which I know is a film camera thing, but also just my luck.

Picture four: A very blurred photo of a man; our father? We'll never know. He has both hands covering his eyes.

Picture five has been destroyed by the light. I don't know why it was left to me, and why I can't seem to give it up.

"Is there anything to drink in this place?"

I don't exactly know what she means by *this place*. I don't rise to it though. I won't, because of my breathing exercises and the recommendations from my life coach. "You know I don't drink," I reply, as evenly as possible, thinking of meadows and green fields. My sister is hunched over the photos like a goblin. "I'm not crazy," she is saying, to me, and the room. "I know what I fucking saw, alright?" It would not be the first time my sister has seen things that are not there. Who does she think she is, barging into my home on a day like this, pulling a stunt like this?

"Want some water," Clara says, still looking at the photos. "Please, Dempsey. I just need some water." The sudden whimper in her voice squeezes a place in my chest. I know that sometimes when people are high, they can collapse from dehydration, and I don't want that. Even though I'm unimpressed with her behavior thus far, I go to the kitchen to sort out a drink, because that's the kind of person I am.

"How was the show? Did you go out afterwards?" I call back into the living room, trying not to sound judgemental. I couldn't go yesterday because I have a problem with crowds. Plus I tried to read *Evidence*, but it was just too difficult. It read like fantasy, and I have no time for that. I prefer murder mysteries, or cookbooks, or books on self-help. I locked my copy in the airing cupboard, where it remains, untouched.

Perhaps I should have stuck with it. The book did well, *is doing* well. If Clara wants to make money from exploiting our trauma, that's up to her. I put away the silent heavier feelings associated with that and get a bottle of filtered alkaline water from the fridge.

When I get back to the lounge, Clara is pawing at the photos and paper documents in a way that makes me want to knock her out. How dare she handle these old artifacts, these original records, some of them yellowing, some of them tarnished, green with an odd mold (there used to be damp in the flat), all of them delicate, like this?

"Careful with those," I hear myself whimper. Of course she ignores me, pulling at those tender and finite reminders with absolutely no reverence or care, tipping them out of their clear folders that I and *only* I took the time to arrange. No one else cared to do so. No one else has ever cared anything about our mother's life. The contents of the ASICS box only came into my possession because Clara's adopted family said she had no need for them. They were a hand-me-down to me, from the twin who didn't care. And if this twin wasn't a whole foot taller than me and erratic right now, I'd knock those photos out of her stupid hands.

"She looks *exactly* the same,"

my sister keeps saying. Were our mother alive she would be greying, growing thicker around the middle. Her hair would not be so full. Her eyes would be hollowing. I could tell Clara all this, smash this claim into the ground. I could make her feel like Absolute Shit, but I only watch as Clara sinks to the floor ashen, wordless.

We drink our cups of water,
and stay close to the floor.

"I don't want any part of this," I say. "You didn't care about Mum before, why now?"

Clara looks at me. Clara looks as though I've just *slapped* her, for god's sake, and then she gets to her feet. I stand up too.

Above us, there's a sudden crash. We both look up at the ceiling and frown.

"You know what, Dempsey?" she says, turning to fix her eyes on the water stain in the wall, just above where I am standing. She bunches her hands into fists.

"What?" I say, fearing for my head, but she has already pivoted, is already in motion.

"If you won't believe me, I can't force you," she says, brushing past me and out the door with the shoebox clutched to her chest. As she heads down the stairs, her cream coat swish swishes. I stand there for a minute. There is always some level of pain when I see her.

••

I sit down at my table, bewildered, ill-hot, and, as my life coach Dr. Rayna Panelli has often suggested, I get a notepad and pen and write down the feelings to get them out of me.

> I LET HER WALK OUT WITH THE PHOTOS.
> THOUGH I PAY ATTENTION TO MY INNER CHILD,
> THOUGH I HOLD HER AND MAKE SPACE FOR HER, I AM
> NOT A CHILD ANYMORE. WE ARE NOT CHILDREN ANYMORE.
> MY SISTER DOES NOT WANT ME TO DIE / MY SISTER DOES
> NOT WANT ME TO HAVE A HEART ATTACK AND DIE. MY
> SISTER MIGHT NOT BE LAUGHING AT ME.
> MY SISTER DOES NOT HATE ME AND IS NOT TRYING TO
> DRIVE ME MAD.
> MY SISTER IS TROUBLED, AND SOMETIMES I AM
> TROUBLED AND THIS IS NORMAL/WORKABLE, AND WE ARE
> ALL DOING OUR VERY BEST TO SURVIVE AND THAT IS ALL.

In the top corner of the page, I write down the word COMPASSION until my breathing slows, gets close to normal. I write the word PERSPECTIVE. It's not like I don't love my sister.

> I DO LOVE MY SISTER I JUST DON'T CARE FOR HER AND
> THAT IS OKAY.
> I DO LOVE MY SISTER BUT RIGHT NOW I DO NOT FUCKING
> LIKE HER AND I DO NOT FUCKING RESPECT HER AND I
> HAVEN'T IN YEARS. THAT IS OKAY.
> I DO LOVE MY SISTER AND I WANT TO KILL HER OR
> MYSELF OR SOMEONE ELSE BUT THIS FEELING TOO WILL PASS.
> THIS FEELING WILL PASS.

DEMPSEY NICHELLE ELIZABETH CAMPBELL

Now that she's gone, I can't breathe properly. I settle down into my chair, and it's like being little all over again. I hate how much taller my sister seems, forever hovering feet and feet and feet above me; above us all. I'm younger by three minutes and three seconds. Younger meaning I'm runt of the litter, and it shows. As a child, my growth was stunted. I had difficulty breathing, though no one could ever work out why. The fact that I am always soothing myself with is that I was longest with our mother, by three minutes and three seconds. This is a small but very relevant matter. Sometimes I wake up in the night cradling my body as if it were a child, soft, with rolls of fat and a toothless mouth. Sometimes I'd like to give birth to a new self, a self I could do right by. I would feed her organic fruit from the market and no sugar, ever. I would read her affirmations before she was old enough to understand them so the affirmation would become a crystalized truth. I would be the kind of mother that children everywhere wish they had. My biological clock is ticking. At least that's what I imagine the feeling is. Sometimes. I can't get over the fact that perhaps all I need to do is go to bed with someone and I might be able to create a whole small person. If I can't find anyone to do it with I might just do the whole thing myself. I'm quite responsible. I know how to carry out tasks to a high standard. I just have a few things that need working through.

For starters, I have it rough on our birthday. It is a bitter reminder, so fraught with alarm and disappointment that announces itself up to ten days before. Migraines, stomachaches, chest tightness, a weird rash around my middle. Dr. Rayna Panelli has prescribed somatic and alternative therapies. She made me read *The Body Keeps the Score*, and teaches me to ground myself with chanting and vetiver oil and guided meditation. Every now and then for thirty-five pounds extra, she'll throw in a sound bath.

It is one thirty in the afternoon. I have some data entry work and other administrative proofreading tasks that I need to make a start on. The company, Medical Foot Health Clinic, aren't the most glamourous, but they pay regularly and on time. Normally, I have strong organizational working skills and a fast enough brain, but today I can't think straight. It isn't only what just happened with Clara, and the fact that it's my birthday. Upstairs Neighbour is banging overhead again. Upstairs Neighbour is clattering and banging overhead again and has been since morning. In fact, I woke up to Upstairs Neighbour dropping some heavy object right above my head. The banging is very loud and so this is not about being a highly sensitive person or "noise sensitive." It makes me sound fussy, and I'm not fussy. Upstairs Neighbour doesn't care about anyone but herself, never mind the fact that I took the time to write a carefully worded note, not blaming anyone as such, simply explaining that when the banging begins at five forty every morning, it steals twenty good minutes from my sleep. These are important minutes. They add up in a person's life. It's all numbers. I know this because I read *Why We Sleep* from cover to cover. I clock my resting hours as fastidiously as my nutrition and sugar intake. The banging happens every single day, for most of the day, and it happens right above my head. I considered starting some kind of petition, but that would involve talking to the neighbours, and they're all strange and unfriendly. Sometimes, when it gets really bad and I'm not sure what to do, I think about dismembering Upstairs Neighbour, calmly, with classical music playing in the background, like a villain in a film, and if this *were* a film, I might hide the bloody remains in the chute where the rubbish goes, because no one can tell what came from what flat. But they might see the letter, and the letter would be incriminating, because in the letter I tell her I might be forced to take action soon, which they could trace as a motive in a court of law.

I put in my AirPods and turn Dr. Rayna Panelli's playlist on. Dr. Rayna Panelli is amazing at making playlists. She sends me instrumentals and sings high-vibrational affirmations. All tuned into 432 hertz, which is the divine frequency of healing, for those who care to know.

There are seven frozen lunches in the freezer and two keto lunches in the fridge. I opt for the fridge pack (a low-fat vegan Senegalese-inspired casserole) before placing it into the oven, biodegradable sleeve and all. I'm a tight ball of tension and fear, and the ball of tension and fear is growing, gathering speed. It is not the dark, obvious fury, but resentment without a name; a thing that builds up on the inside, forcing nice and ordinary people to do the unthinkable.

I'm not sure that I could eat now after all. An old feeling is aroused; I would have to consult Dr. Rayna's "wheel of feelings" to say exactly what the thing is. All I really know is that it is BAD like a sphere or wicked triangle—something mossy with moving holes. Dr. Rayna has me meditate each morning, so I'm only just observing the anger triangle and its harrowing edges. I know the triangle lives in my body, but I also know I don't have to live inside of the triangle, and there is an important distinction there. If I could smash my sister's face in, I would. I would love to make her sorry and ashamed. Just once.

I tear up the block capitals list I made. I go to the area where I sleep, and I haven't cried for a while now, not a long time, but if anything will do it, it's my sister, so I get in bed and cry for all the things we are and all the things we are not and can never be to each other. Afterwards, I search on my bookmarked site for a hard distraction to chase the shakiness out of my body, to bump up the shame, to make good use of it. It takes me ages to find a porn clip that will work for sure and it clears my mind for a few interesting seconds. It takes me to the edge, and then just about tops me over, and after the small underwhelming spasm, I close the page, slamming the laptop shut. I'm about to unfavorite the page, for good this time. I am always empty once I come, but I don't know what you do about that. On the other side of it all, everything is still wrong. Upstairs Neighbour is still banging overhead, and this is very difficult. Quite tough.

CLARA, THE FIRST-CHOICE TWIN

My body is driving me back to Peckham to see what I am made of. I can't stop thinking about Dempsey—the way she looked at me this morning. The way she has always looked at me. She's so passive aggressive, so cowardly and evil. I never trust people who won't say what they are thinking. People who hide.

••

Nobody would adopt us.

We were not, as you can imagine, anyone's top choice, due to our scaly skin and ill demeanors. By the time we were eight, they had tested and tested and tested for autism (they were convinced, especially in Dempsey's case) and sickle cell anemia (for which we have the trait, not the disease). They noted that we might be suffering the effects of partial fetal alcohol syndrome. Dempsey took the brunt of the damage. The feeling was that I was thriving physically but could have a few behavioral/reasoning issues. True enough.

But I always knew I would amount to a lot. I knew it would be powerful. Being the chosen one, I really had no choice in the matter. Claudette and Adolphus Kallis said that I had *appeared* special right from the beginning. There I sat, catching the light, announcing myself with a few qualities they thought they may be able to nurture into success. I was a cute child. My features were in the right places. My IQ was borderline genius, and that is why I was the one they chose. Claudette and Adolphus made no bones about telling me this. They did not say anything about my sister being not so special, but it was implied. Dempsey was wheezing and small and not even saying full words yet and they didn't know what to do with that.

Claudette was a light-skinned Jamaican woman with the crispest English accent you ever heard, and Adolphus was a Greek chef's son who made his fortune in the East End of London selling office equipment and customizable stationary. Having ticked many other things off their list—holiday homes in Kent and Spain, a BMW each (plus a vintage Rolls-Royce for Adolphus), and a detached house in Crystal Palace—Claudette and Adolphus were next looking to acquire a child. They wanted someone to carry on their name, to make them satisfied with themselves. They wanted just one child.

We left Dempsey behind. She was adopted a year later by a man in his late thirties called Kendrick Lewis, a councilor whose wife had recently left. They went to live in Bermondsey, and we would see each other on the last calendar Saturday of each month. Kendrick would bring her around and everyone would sit at the table swapping pleasantries. Dempsey and I didn't have a lot to say to each other, but we would look closely at each other with despair and a little wonderment that we might be opposite halves of a strange truth, both born from a force unknown. Sometimes my sister smelled a little, and when they were gone, Claudette would talk about Dempsey drawing the short straw. I wanted to understand that figure of speech. I had presumed it more literally at the beginning, as though we might have unwittingly taken part in a game of luck and chance and I had been crowned the winner.

"It's nothing you need worry about," Claudette said, smiling but not really smiling, as per. "It's one of those things. Your sister needs a little more time and special needs care than we have to give right now, but still, we want you to *know* each other."

My sister *did* smell unusual. A mixture of mammal and earth, and it was strong, though not unpleasant; a rich, alive scent, as though she might have lived somewhere in the forest. Claudette could hardly hide her distaste. Whenever they left, she would say things like, "Your sister has wild hair, doesn't she, Clara? I'd just love to get my hands on it and neaten it." We'd been working on my hair for years. I wondered about Claudette and her beginnings, whether she might have had hair like me once upon a time, but didn't dare ask. Somehow I understood that a truth bound us, our hair the source of a shared pain. The hair she wore was flat ironed, pinned away from her face. Over the years, this hairstyle never changed. According to Claudette, the best kind of hair was "quiet" and "tamed." She maintained that it must frame the face without drawing attention to itself, enhancing what needed enhancing and doing no more, and certainly no less. African styles could sometimes be elegant enough, she said, in their context, in the continent or whatnot, or even in places like America where they were more expressive and "louder with it," but the artful nature just wouldn't allow you to be taken seriously, not really. Simplicity was needed. A style that "calmed me down" and "allowed my features to do the talking." A bun (good), a ponytail (better), a single plait—two, if I really wanted to express myself. At first, we ironed my natural hair straight, but when a boy at school asked me why my hair never moved, I got upset. I wanted hair that swished; a mane that moved when I did. When I told Claudette what had happened, she started straightening only the front sections of my hair and I wore partial wigs instead. Claudette didn't like the idea of grease (it stained the sheets) or braids (too intricate), and so I graduated into wearing full-head wigs or sewn-in hairpieces, shining and heavy—colour two, which was two shades away from jet black. Claudette got the hair shipped over from Bangladesh and hired her local hair person, Ava Lee, to come twice a month, to weave the hair to my head, adding sensible, realistic-looking extensions. The blends were to be seamless, the closure exact, and if it took all night, it took all night. We had to time it just right. When kids asked if my hair had grown over the summer and winter breaks, I would lie as I had been coached. We agreed on many hair-related things, Claudette and I. We were fooling everyone and loving it. Most of all, I loved the once-over from Claudette when my hair was freshly done. How soothed she seemed by my "improved" appearance.

"This does so much for your face, Clara," she would say, watching Ava Lee out of the corner of her eye.

"Softens you so much. Calms your face down, I might say. You have very pronounced features and you need to flatter them, not play them up. Ava Lee, you're really good. Very talented."

Ava Lee would nod her head benevolently, a world behind her eyes, and as soon as she was gone, Claudette would make disparaging remarks about the electric green and blue in Ava Lee's fluffy textured twists. "Oh, you can't buy class, I suppose. If I had those skills, the places I would go! She's talented—I'll give her that—but she walks around looking *anyhow*. Always elevate yourself, Clara. We, more than the rest, must remember that." These were the only times she would use the word "we," in a grim, conspiratorial manner, as though we might be nearly the same thing. I loved this, but pretended not to notice, for fear that she might stop.

"Honestly," Claudette would say, looking wistfully into the distance. "You never know. We don't know that your dad was *actually Black*. He could have *actually* been any exotic gentleman. I mean, just look at your nose. We just don't know. That's the thing. We don't *actually* know."

"Come off it, Claudette," Adolphus would put in if he ever overheard this talk.

"We have to admit," Claudette went on, unable to be stopped. "Clara has something of the model about her. I really think she might be mixed. I really, really do."

"Was *your* dad an exotic gentleman?" I asked Claudette once, while we were making a boiled chicken salad in the kitchen.

"Perhaps. No idea," she replied. "My parents adopted me too. You and me. The chosen ones." She gave the not-quite smile that she used so often it seemed part of her face.

Dempsey's appearance plain irritated Claudette, to the extent that her unkind words post visit began to intensify. One day, she decided to take action.

"Do you think we might like to wash it?" She looked to me, as if willing me to agree. Dempsey's hair looked like my hair before the cream and the wigs and the hot irons. It wasn't ugly seeming to me, but it hardly seemed acceptable, either.

"It would behoove you to take notice, Clara," Claudette said. "She's *your* sister after all. Out in the world, she represents you."

"You know, it's not really our business, love," Adolphus said, lightly. "She isn't our daughter. You saw to that. Now can we drop it?"

But Claudette would not let it lie. And now, increasingly on Dempsey's visits, she would stare and stare at her, eyes narrowed. It had become almost compulsive—the disapproval, the assessing. One day Kendrick put down his knife and fork.

"What's the matter?" he asked Claudette.

"I'm pleased to see Dempsey enjoying her food," came the curt response. "Though she might want to save room for some organic fruit." Kendrick bristled; glared at us all.

• •

One Sunday afternoon in August, Dempsey and I got out my dolls. I was aging out of that a little, but often made concessions for Dempsey, who has always felt a little younger. But Dempsey was boring to play with because she never knew how to act normal, how to make the dolls kiss and fool around. So when Claudette interrupted our play to do Dempsey's hair, I was probably relieved. Kendrick showed up to collect Dempsey a little earlier than usual. He knocked on the door and waited a while, but Adolphus was mowing the lawn in the back and apparently hadn't heard him knock. The door to the kitchen was ajar, so he stepped in and waved to Adolphus, who was framed in the kitchen window. Their eyes met and Adolphus would later admit to having had a jump scare, unnerved by the Black intruder. On seeing that it was only Kendrick, he turned off the mower and came inside.

"I could already tell he was on the warpath," Adolphus recalled. "He must have been having a bad day. I could see it in the man's eyes, soon as he walked himself into our house."

They caught up casually, keeping it civil, Adolphus recalled, until the two of them heard crying coming from our bathroom. Adolphus, know-ing the mood was about to turn sour, assured Kendrick we'd all be down soon. But Kendrick was agitated and brusquely enquired as to what was going on upstairs. Adolphus tried to engage him about football scores, but Kendrick, being a man of snooker and cricket only, was not having any of it. He kept saying, "We should be getting back; traffic gets bad on football days." Then, Dempsey let out an almighty scream, and Kendrick came tearing up the stairs. He flung the bathroom door open and there was Dempsey, sitting on our toilet lid. Claudette stood over her, looking a little caught out. I don't remember where I was or what exactly I was doing at the time. Hanging around, nowhere and everywhere, between the landing and the deep black sea. Kendrick's mouth did a hanging-open thing. He stomped over, waving his giant hands around.

"What IS that? It stinks!"

"It's *medicated*," said Claudette. "It's just a softener. For her hair, you know. It'll be lovely."

Even Adolphus, who hadn't truly understood what was going on besides some kind of girly makeover, seemed genuinely surprised at his wife's actions.

"Does it feel okay on your head, love?" he ventured to ask, and Clau-dette actually hissed.

"I can smell the shit from here!" Kendrick ripped the box of chemi-cals from Claudette's manicured hands.

"This better not be what I think it is."

"Hair relaxer," said Claudette, slowly, trying not to sound panicked, but also managing to sound as though Kendrick was the most stupid man she'd ever met. But she was. Panicked. We all were. Even Adolphus.

"What the hell is hair relaxer?" Adolphus laughed, nervously, not helping anything. "He does have a point though, love, smells a bit toxic!!"

"Anti-frizz," snapped Claudette, eyes fixed on Kendrick. "Don't fuss, Adolphus."

Kendrick dropped the box. "IT IS FUCKING TOXIC," he bellowed, gesticulating wildly at Claudette, then Adolphus, then Claudette again. "We don't do this to our hair. Do you hear?" I felt my skull tighten.

Dempsey was clutching the side of her head. I took her hand and led her out of the bathroom, past the adults.

"If you weren't a woman, I'd punch you up and down the fuckin' stairs," Kendrick was saying.

"You'd better leave, mate," said Adolphus now in a new voice, stepping forward, chest puffed up, and then they all started shouting. Kendrick dragged his daughter, who was by now sobbing loudly, back into the bathroom and over the sink and proceeded to wash the cream out of her hair. Her pitiful sobs went through me. All the little curls were gone, and the soapy locks were hanging dead and limp on her head. It didn't look lovely at all. Kendrick was shouting about pressing charges and then he called Claudette an "interfering white bitch" (interesting) before thundering away with Dempsey down the stairs. And that was it. They were gone. I went to my room and closed the door.

"I've a good mind to call social services," Claudette could be heard saying. "That child is not safe with that man."

But she never called because she got busy and forgot. I didn't see Dempsey after that for three whole years. In three years, things fall apart. Then they stay apart.

••

Night has fallen by the time I get back to Drinkwater Towers, set just across from the newsagent's, which could be from another time, if you squint in the right light.

I park my car far up the road. I take a breath, take several breaths, get out of the car, moving towards the house. All around, it is quiet. The streets are empty but for a man sleeping in a dull red car opposite. Before I have time to doublethink, I press the doorbell. Twice. Three times, then, after waiting a while, I call every single doorbell. Twelve doorbells. There is a high-pitched buzzing sound, and the front door gives.

I cross the dark, concrete foyer and climb two flights of stairs. I follow the brown carpeted path to the farthest door on the left. I knock loud and fast, before I have time to talk myself out of it. Nobody answers, which is just as well.

There is a damp-looking balcony outside the third-floor exit door running along the left of the flat. It is narrow, and silent, and it leads me into the adjoining balcony at the other side. Now I am facing the room I was peering into earlier. Separating us is a window of cloudy glass. Through the glass I notice the burnt amber walls of the photo. A room I have seen before. A deterrent. A warning, perhaps, but when I try the window, it moves outwards a little at the bottom.

I snake my hand in and unlock the latch, and the window gives from the bottom, a weak lock. In a swift movement, I thrust the window towards myself and climb inside. I place my foot onto her soft carpet, gingerly at first, as though it might be a hologram, as if it could disappear from under me at any point. When I am sure that the room is really a room and its floor is really a floor, I look up and around me, and it is almost as though I have fallen inside one of our photos.

The collection of objects that surrounds me renders a scene that is not a replica of the photo, but close; as though they might be sisters. The furniture is sparse but for a TV console and speakers. There is an empty rectangular patch in place of the large brass mirror in the picture. But the colour scheme, the *feeling* of the room, are all present, all correct. And I've been here before. I understand that I have lived or at least dreamed this, the knowing hue of the place, the honey wood of the floor. Even the sound of the floorboards feels tragic and familiar. On one wall, I see a glamour picture of Serene—her tall, slender frame adorned in orange and peach feathers. There are green beer cans and odd boxes of tools and electrical wires. There is so much orange and red and blue, and a collection of small mirrors on every shelf. In the dark, I catch myself reflected three, four, five, six times. The mirrors betray my lips, flaking and white. My heartbeat now quickens; I smell the beast in myself.

I take my phone from my pocket to obtain some proof. *Dempsey will die when she knows about this.* Dempsey will have a heart attack. Dempsey will *have* to believe me now. I snap the point where the wallpaper meets the floor. Immortal. I snap the woodchip on the wall and the too-old-to-be-from-this-decade curtains. Unquestionable.

I snap the photos of her. The space where the large mirror should be. And then I hear the door close behind me.

Sometimes, if it is nighttime and I have had a drink or two, I might see shadows that remind me of mice, or moving things from the underworld.

It is a head trick; anxiety, I tell myself. But no. Someone is with me in this room. Before I have time to make a decision, I feel a cold thing between my back ribs.

"Turn around," says the ink voice. "Or I'll beat the shit out of you."

Bargain.

"I asked you to turn around." says the voice.

Run. Or play dead.

But I can't move. My mother's sound; a spell.

Quickly losing patience, she spins me around. For a second, there is just the two of us in the dark, eyeballs shining.

I take a chance. I move.

She moves swiftly and does a trick with her legs that has me on my back. I lie there, trying to take everything in. She climbs on me, her face over mine, using the weight of her head and body to pin me down. With her elbow underneath my chin, she forces my head over to one side.

"I'm going to kill you now," says my mother, in as deliberate a tone as I have ever heard.

In the stillness of my body, I feel calm. I study the deep brown nape of her neck, at once exhilarated by how familiar she smells. Earth. Smoke. The Woods, the Trees. As though wild things might be growing inside her. I close my eyes and wait for it. I hold my breath and I almost hope it hurts.

CLARA AND SERENE
IN THE LIVING ROOM

In a dim room of burnt orange with teal accents, two grown women are panting. The window is smudged with condensation or hair grease or petroleum jelly. Through the fogged window, the outside lights are twinkling. Foreign electronica plays from somewhere else in the back. Strings begin. The room has a dream-tint. My mother, awake and tall. My mother, circling me like a wild, wild cat. There's this glint in her eye, as frightening as home. We look like each other, like dashing opponents. We look like each other the way only people who share DNA can resemble each other. We look more alive, more aglow than most, and the whole scene is outrageous. Outside, the orange streetlamps are blushing, warming up the dark. Who will win the fight? Not me. Surely not me.

The music of the room is falling on top of us. The notes are in our hair, getting lost in the coils. Around us, the earnest orchestra continues. We move around the room in slow tandem, a choreography of impending threat.

My mother is bravest, first to leap. My mother jumps on top of me, and all I can do is sink to the floor, ready to die.

And the brass continues. Strings fall in. I hear the piano adding its two pence. Then the timpani, marking my heartbeat. Is this bad jazz, or a lullaby? Here we are, moving inside and alongside the thick, robust notes. There is blood on my face, I think. The ambers, golds, brasses in the room pop. It is a gorgeous sight, a carousel.

"I'm going to kill you now," says the other woman, again. *"I swear I'm going to kill you."*

She looks into the black of my eyes. The woman looks right into the black and softens a little—or do I imagine it? The woman looks into my eyes, and puts away the . . . the knife? No, it's only her knuckles pressed hard against my ribs.

"What you doing in my house?" she asks.

"I can explain," I say, gasping for air. But I really can't. How do you even begin? "I saw you in the shop this morning."

"I saw *you* in the shop this morning," says the woman. "But I'm not creeping around your house."

"You like my house?" she asks me.

It's the complete opposite of my pristine, monochrome dwelling. I wonder if that's a psychological thing, we stray from our mothers to save our own lives. To stop our mothers from eating us up.

"Stop lying. Why are you here, taking pictures?" barks my mother. "I know you're not the police."

I am not sure if an answer is required, so I stay quiet. My mother prods me hard in the neck.

"Well?"

I feel like I might faint, so the woman lets up. Perhaps she senses, quite rightly, that I'm no match for her.

"I swear, if you don't answer me . . ."

"I was led here," I tell her.

"You followed me, you mean," says the woman, "and don't think I didn't see you spying on us earlier. You into that?"

By now I am shaking. I am trying to mask this. She takes in my distress.

"If you are, just say," she finally sighs. "It'd be better for you if you just admitted it."

"I'm Clara," I tell her, feeling as though I should at least offer that. She frowns at me.

I am mopping blood from my eye and cannot think what else to say. She gets herself a drink, comes back, sits down on the floor beside me.

"I'm Serene," she says. Well, I could have told her that.

"Come on," she says, swirling the ice in her glass. "This is getting stupid. Get yourself up, now. Sit there."

So I do. I sit on the terra-cotta couch as she stares me down. The terra-cotta couch is a thing you sink into, a thing you could get lost in if you were not careful. If this was not your mother, and you were not trying to make a good impression.

"Your lips look crazy," she frowns, looking almost disgusted. "They're all chapped." She stands and reaches into her jeans pocket, throws me some tangerine-flavored lip balm.

Embarrassing.

I accept the balm, even though it looks well used and there's lint stuck to it. She hooks a small bar cart with her foot, bringing it close. Then she pours more brown liquor into another glass, handing it to me.

"Drink."

We drink. It is arch and bitter with woody notes. Serene gathers papers and tobacco from the table and proceeds to roll a cigarette, licking the rolling paper with her pink (forked?) tongue. She lights it at her lips, pulls, offers it to me. I want to say no, but this feels impolite. When she smiles, she has two teeth missing in the middle left.

"Trying to get yourself killed?"

It hadn't occurred to me before, but yes, maybe.

"Didn't you nearly get knocked down by the bus earlier?"

"That wasn't me," I say, and she throws back her head and chortles.

"You jumped in front of a bus," she almost sings. I make no reply.

"It's a good name, Clara. A *rich* name. You rich, Clara?"

"I do alright," I say, my voice somewhere behind me.

"I'm giving you time to explain yourself, babe," says Serene, taking another large pull. "Did you come for the watch?

I shake my head.

"I *saw* you see me."

"Yeah, but I don't care about the watch."

"Not trying to rob me?"

"No."

Serene narrows her eyes at me; lays the roll up on an orange saucer.

"You're pretty."

"I know." It's the only thing that will come out.

Her face clouds. She leans towards me.

"I won't ask you again, you know. Why you here?"

How to phrase this?

I think you are my mother,

or I *know* you are my mother,

or Do you know . . . you are my mother?

or

You, my friend, are my mother.

This is the moment, if there has ever been a moment, so it can't go wrong. I just can't work out how to phrase it. There is too much there. It is all behind my teeth. It is a whole ocean, and the ocean is a badland. There are all sorts of unsayables reaching across my mouth, trying to claw my tongue, showing their blue hands.

"It's complicated," I tell her. "That's why I'm here . . ."

"Well, you need to explain," my mother says. "You need to use those nice words of yours, or I'm gonna fuck you up."

I look around, as if for help. My mother, growing bored with this, springs up. She really does. My mother stands over me with all her height. My mother is spectacular. She raises a fist to the sky.

But the door makes a sound. The door opens, and who should be there but the guy with the meaty head from earlier and two men who are staring at the floor.

"Who's that?" he says, motioning to me. "She needs to be gone, now."

"Yeah, you should go," says Serene, suddenly seeming quite tired.

I don't move. I mean, I can't, and the men look at me. Serene puts her feet up in the chair and breathes out of her mouth. The air around us is static, unpredictable thunderstorm air, for sure. I turn to my mother. I want to say, "Can I see you again," but that sounds wet, this doesn't look like the forum for that, and yet there it is, as Serene drags me up, sees me out. There it is, out of my mouth and onto the floor. Serene looks at me, a blue note of pity, perhaps disgust. "If I see you first, worry."

I am in the hallway, the door closed behind me. The tops of my arms sting where she gripped me up. With unsteady legs, I find myself walking down the two flights of concrete steps. In the alleyway, past the pungent street, there is only the pale moon and the orange streetlights, two figures linking arms up ahead crossing the road. The man in the car is still sleeping, head on the dashboard, and apart from all this, nothing has changed except everything. I touch my eye socket and walk without stopping, without turning back. I can feel my mother's eyes, two lasers through the window in the sky.

At the car, I pat my pocket, and notice my phone is gone. My phone is lost in the house of dreams, but there's nothing I can do about that now.

CHAPTER TEN

As far as anyone could tell, or care to note, Serene Marie Nkem Droste left the hospital sore and smiling with twin baby girls on June 26, 1995, one full day after they were born. One full day after her own birthday, too. The twins were not quite identical, a fact for which Serene experienced more disappointment than she thought possible, but still, she consoled herself, one for her, and one for him. And oh, the ease of it, as though they were *destined*, gifts directly from the gods. Serene pushed them out without effort, slippery and eager to get here as they were. They were warm, glistening, blue-black as the galaxy. Their limbs were wrapped, almost entangled, in the tightest embrace. They had striking little grown-up faces, more defined and lovely than any babies she had ever seen in her life. It was a strange likeness that they bore to her, one that couldn't be seen in the eyes, nose, or lips, more the way their small chests rose and fell in sync with her own, the way they stared calmly back at her from the crook of the nurse's arms. They probably looked more like their father. Then again, maybe they didn't. They had to belong to her, right? She readied herself, smiled, and stretched out her arms towards the beautiful breathing new things.

Yes, it was nineteen ninety-five. The sun was lemon-gold and beginning. The flowers on the trees were pale pink, perhaps white. Gardenia bushes brought forth an explosion of fragrance, glowing ivy dancing in the light. Serene arrived home by taxi. There was a bioluminescence to the entire night, the night after that, and the several nights following. Everything felt rich, oversized, extremely possible.

The thing she had known for sure was that she was finally about to have some order and stability. It was not as though she would have much choice in the matter. Babies required a routine, and so might she. She could finally finish her novel and do all the things that she had promised herself, and nothing was going to get in her way anymore. Heartbreaks happened all the time, she decided, and no one died. Anyhow, when Abbé saw the girls things might change. His family might accept her. They might move to the tropics and raise the girls there. Everything that had happened up until now wouldn't matter.

But Abbé was a shapeshifter—one foot in this world and the other in the next—and he had shown her this from the very beginning. She had always known he was a wild card. She'd gone into it with eyes open. But once home, amidst the emerging colour of the moment, things took a new turn. Against her louder judgement, she called him. Abbé was home, and so picked up the phone, and it was in that moment that she told him.

"They're here," she said. "Our babies are here."

The man made a noise of surprise, a gurgle. Serene said, "Well, Ab, you can't deny it now. You *are* here, even if only sometimes, and so am I. You belong on this planet now. You belong to two girls."

She listened to his breathing for a while. Eventually, she put down the phone. Well, this would be interesting and new, and Serene had never been one to shy away from a challenge. Here were two brand new challenges, mismatched and mewling and dissonant.

But then,

things are rarely as we hoped, are they?

There was much about the extreme loneliness of it, once she had the babies home. It was blooming even truer, spreading like an ink drop in water, and there was so, so much that was cruel and unceremonious about the work of it, the day in day out responsibility that lulled Serene into numbness. She would put on the television and there would be her numbing procedural dramas on the TV. Actors saying the kind of things they always said and behaving in the same predictable ways, and everything about it would make her feel as though she was in fact not *real*, and how could someone who was not real do anything of worth, anything of note?

She read anything she could get her hands on pertaining to new motherhood. She felt sure there must be some hidden code—some recipe for success. And then the babies were crying, and then they needed to latch and feed, which hurt—it *fucking hurt*—and then they needed to be changed; and it was every moment, or that's how it seemed. It was a circular situation, but this, she felt, might anchor her in the world somehow, even if the father could not be *got*, would never be anchored.

If there was no love for the taking, there were always words. Words were always there for her. She made a vow to tell the girls everything, in case anything was to happen to her, in case things got too much. She had taught herself to read in the seventies, when she was a young one. It was the only thing that could decimate the brutal realities of everything going on outside, replacing what was rough and unsettling with what could be imagined, dreamed up. Before the girls, she would go to write, and worlds fell from her fingertips. Before the babies were born, when she was filled up to the brink with them—ready to drop, any day—she dreamed up large ways in which they would coexist. How she could teach them. How they would make her Good. She thought she might have two clear friends for life.

But things are rarely as we hoped,
are they?

When the twins arrived, the worlds dried up on the page. The picture was hidden out of reach. It would never be friendship, would it? She was the caregiver. She was the garden; the babies cruel, demanding interlopers. No, no, this wouldn't do. It would never work. She was frightened for her daughters and frightened of herself. She would love them so fiercely, so *truthfully*. They might not survive it.

And then came the numbers. She was not prepared for the hidden numerology in this new phase of life. Numbers everywhere, on walls, on floors, on bus stops, or outside in the sky, from the living room window. Everything came together, tallied up in the world that she constructed. This is how it was for the first few weeks, when the truth was topsy-turvy and there was no sleep to be had. All these screaming numbers, questioning, unaccounted for. She would see numbers everywhere, even in place of letters that made up the words in books. The only thing that would stop the constant multiplications and fractions, the twisting algebra of it all, was writing it down, writing about what she supposed it all meant. They were difficult to decipher at first. It was words that she had the natural facility for, words with which she flexed all her muscles. But suddenly, there were the numbers, bellowing truth and reason.

All through the loud oppressiveness of July, mean, muggy August, and the neon-electric pain of September, whatever had been wrong before was magnified. There were several things that allowed her to understand that she was not of this world. Sometimes the house would be flipped. The hallway would run in the other direction. Sometimes the stairs would be to the back of the estate instead of the front of it. Perhaps she was becoming mythical. Yes, perhaps she was becoming celestial. If this was so, then what was happening seemed perfectly legitimate. She had always felt *chosen*, *other*, and there are things that you accept about being a chosen one, things that you must make peace with. Several glitches run in the parallel realms, things that make no sense. Sometimes you see two of the same one thing. Yes, sometimes ordinary objects in the house will go on and twin themselves. Sometimes you cannot get out of bed for fear that the objects will start a mutiny. Sometimes you die of boredom and sleeplessness. Sometimes you cry about your nipple sores. And sometimes you time travel. Serene had always felt that she was unusually set up, the way she thought and felt and made swift, life-changing, terrible decisions. How had she thought that she would fail less with children? How had she expected to pin down a not-yet-grown man? Had she thought his cool safety in the world would be transferrable, would become hers? There were days, and many of them, when everything felt like too much. Days when moving on to the next thing felt too difficult. She'd have every intention in the world to go and do a thing, but by the time she had gotten herself together in the morning and looked after the babies, it was afternoon, and by the time she felt ready to brave whatever was outside, the day had tumbled over as if on its side, emptied, the contents strewn across the floor. Sometimes, blue thoughts would stream late into the night and before she knew it, she would be into the small hours again, wondering where everything had gone. Oh, the blues themselves were nothing new. This was, after all, how she'd met Abbé, not too long ago. He was there, and so was she, that was all they needed to have in common. Funnily enough, they met on a bus, when Serene plopped down on the seat and suddenly got the very peculiar feeling that she was never going to move from the spot, not now, not ever. Together they rode into the treacherous, beckoning sunset, until the bus stopped at Peckham Multiplex. Abbé had been on a mission, too, slumped, almost comatose, trying to get to the edge of somewhere. She had had to help him home that night, safely back to his place. He was not of this world, had substances to aid him. He moved like the rough body of water he was. He had a rugged face, a down-turned smile. Sometimes he was there in the room with you, and mostly he was not; in a way, he was an apparition. After all, she had no real proof that he had ever existed, nothing much to attach herself to. Not until his futures were growing inside her. The way she felt about him did not make sense. She knew from the start that he was a weighty, broken thing and that he would slow down anyone who was willing to stop. Serene had places to go, things to become. They were not meant to be together. He wasn't strong, or brilliant. But the chemicals won out. The need, her emptiness. Their biology started to mesh and it was as if it was written. If he had offered his heart,

if he *had* a heart, she could have swallowed the thing whole. People who are loved at arm's length rarely learn how to *do* love.

One day, when it was the usual too much, she woke up and decided what was at play. She sat up on the sofa. She stared at the painted orange

walls and knew that she could not come back. It was all about the carpet. The way the curtain fell. This room had become a place she would
not return to, just like that. So on the first of October, when the trees
were reddening, bursting into flame, Serene Marie Nkem Droste walked
out to meet Abbé at a party in a housing estate on the Old Kent Road
and never came back. The twins were home with a babysitter, some girl
from upstairs with a lip piercing and a ring of pimples round her mouth.
Serene said she would be back by around one, and that was that. Her
clean, unwrinkled clothes were said to have been found three mornings
after her disappearance, as though she had just stepped out of them. They
were lying on the banks of the River Thames and everyone knows that
whatever goes in there either does not come back or comes back dead.

The babies with the grown-up faces knew, she had thought. As she
darkened the doorway to kiss them goodnight or goodbye or goodnight,
she felt there might be a world where they found her out, and—who
knew—this world could even be happening right now. But the thought
could not deter her, and she slipped out the door, already smelling of the
riverbed, of cruel things that grow. Her daughters would live and thrive,
she told herself, and they might forgive her one day. They would understand how hard it was to do everything, to stick around. She did not wish
the blue world on her babies, but if she did not leave that very minute,
they were certainly doomed. *Everyone* in the story would be doomed,

and so on, and so forth.

DEMPSEY
REMEMBERS IT DIFFERENTLY

"Let's fix this mop on your head," Claudette said. "You're really quite pretty, you know?"

I shook my head at once, recognizing this as a lie. Manipulation, if you want to put a name to it, and I must.

"Well, at least you *could* be. You could be with some nurturing," said Claudette. "That's all you need, a little hair love, a girls' club. That's what we're here for, my love."

She tugged at my afro puff without care, shuddering at the touch. She sniffed and said, "This situation, my love, is salvageable."

Claudette's smile was kind of terrifying, and the way she kept saying *my love*, was bad, bad, bad. I knew the truth. I disgusted her. I knew that she thought I smelled wrong. The last thing I could ever be was her *love*, because I was nowhere near good enough. Throughout this exchange, Clara nodded her perfect little head and her shiny hair moved, framing her face like the brown dolls from the expensive shops. I didn't have a very good feeling about any of it, but Clara kept on, saying, "You'll look like me if you do it, Dempsey," and of course I wanted to look like her, who wouldn't? We should have been exactly alike from the beginning. I had been waiting what seemed like forever for my shiny hair to get here and my skin to be warm-toned and smooth or when I would stop having to blow my nose all the time and my skin would stop flaking off onto my sleeves, collars, and socks. I still had chest problems—my breathing was completely up the spout. On top of that I had chronic sinus infections and always had to breathe through my mouth, especially during the winter.

Anyway, on that day, I was sure I didn't trust Claudette much, or at all, but I knew for sure that I needed to be transformed—and quickly. Happy to do whatever it took, I took off my cardigan and socks as instructed, and got into the bath.

"Wild, *tough* hair," Claudette kept saying. "Just sticks up everywhere and everywhere, doesn't it? We'll help you manage it a little better. And look at this skin, oh lord, what's he feeding you? Don't you eat fish at your house? Fish is great for the skin and hair. Eat fish."

Clara helped Claudette spread the cold, pink cream onto my hair. They were a complete double act, those two. And then there was some time while they were chatting about things I didn't understand, gossiping about people I hadn't met before. I was a little worried even then, but I didn't say a thing. And then I felt the pain. Tiny wasps were stinging my scalp, invisible red wasps, and then Adolphus came upstairs and asked Claudette what she was doing. Over my head, they made faces and talked a lot with their hands, but I couldn't figure it out because the wasps were entering my brain and trying so hard to kill me.

"It's very cool what all of your hair does," said Adolphus after a while, though he clearly wasn't sure to whom he should address this, and I wasn't sure whether he meant all of *my* hair or all of *our* hair.

"Very cool!" he was saying. "Well, I wish I had hair like that."

Adolphus patted his bald spot; forced out a laugh.

"Mmmm," Claudette went, just like that. "Mmmm."

Of course, Adolphus could not be useful here, so he went back down to watch the football and Claudette stood over me to make sure I did not move. Even though there were even more wasps now and everything was getting quite a bit worse, I was trying to be grown up about it. I didn't want my sister to think I couldn't be pretty. I tried to ignore the pain by concentrating on Clara, to remind myself of all that I might become. She was kind of looking through me by now, and it was a little scary and the wasps were multiplying, so tears were coming and would not stop. Sobs were escaping my body. I put my hands to my temples and wailed. With her gloved fingers, Claudette slapped my hands away.

And then Kendrick was there.

"Get that off her head!" screamed Kendrick. "Now!"

"Anti-frizz. Don't fuss, it's fine," said Claudette, not even looking at him.

But then someone was washing stuff out of my hair and Kendrick, well, Kendrick was really upset. He called her an interfering bitch and grabbed me up and we left.

"She needs fish in her diet." I think I remember Claudette saying that as he pulled me down the stairs. All the way home on the bus he was talking about "these people" and using a lot of f-words that were just too much. He turned his head away from me and looked out of the window, because looking at me would start the f-words up again.

••

An hour or so later, in the quiet of my yellow room, I turned some Christmas music on in my CD player, even though it wasn't anywhere near Christmas, and wrapped my scraggly hair up in a blanket. A squelching sound came out of my mouth again and again when I did the sucking on my bottom teeth thing. I liked the way it felt. So I did it again and again and again. I kept on doing it and it kept feeling good and when I had done it and done it for a while, the horror in my head had given way.

Outside my window, everything now seemed brighter. The sun had come out of the clouds and I could see Kendrick down in the greenhouse, watering the young tomatoes. I couldn't help thinking that my sister must hate me, must have somehow orchestrated such a terrible day. I closed my eyes for a while, and had some daydream about my sister and me holding hands and floating, floating. I did the thing with my mouth some more and still found it pleasing.

That evening, Kendrick made tomato soup and buttered bread and apple pie with Neapolitan ice cream from the corner shop. All the curls were gone from my hair. We tried rubbing cocoa butter through it to remove the smell. Whatever we did, we could not be rid of it. Every time I shook my head, the burned parts of my scalp would flutter to the floor.

••

It is dark now in the flat. I have barely moved. Upstairs Neighbour is running back and forth like some kind of bat out of hell; which feels impossible—the woman is in her eighties—but this is not even the worst thing in my life right now, because the worst thing is Clara. I scroll through some of her "talks" on YouTube, speaking in a voice that is not hers. Everywhere, all over the world, people are seeing the girl and missing the monster. I watch *Vogue* tour the inside of Clara's home. There she is, pretending to be natural. Pretending not to be beastly, in long silky trousers and some strange wraparound top that is far too flimsy for anyone wanting to be taken seriously. There she is, showing them around this large, empty-looking show home.

I prefer to live amongst a bit of colour, myself, a bit more life. Serene Marie Nkem Droste knew how to work with colour and I'm sure I must get it from her. Kendrick always said it must have been tough dealing with her condition, and when I asked him what he meant he would just sigh and say, "We'll talk further one day."

Well.

Kendrick and I don't talk anymore. We just don't. He tries to make contact. He's been trying to call since I turned eighteen. That's more than a decade. You have to admire his dedication. He still attempts with the birthday cards, which I always put straight in the bin, even when I can feel that there is money inside. Even when I'm broke. Today's envelope is a perfect blue square.

Upstairs Neighbour's noise is building and building on top of itself; is slowly crescendo-ing towards the downright unbearable. Upstairs Neighbour is bang-banging into the wall. It sounds as though she is dragging heavy furniture to and fro, just for the sake of it. She sounds possessed. I stare at the card in the bin. There is a new itchy rash along my jawline. I have a tiny bit of blood inside my mouth because the squelching feels so good. Just then, Upstairs Neighbour drops a heavy object and the clattering makes the whole kitchen reverberate.

I turn around and walk away from the kitchen and out the door and into the cool stairwell. Then, for some reason, I do a Kendrick. That is to say, I tear up the stairs and land there in a lather, beating hard on the neighbor's door. Enough now, no more of this.

DEMPSEY AT THE TOP OF THE STAIRS, WITH THE NEIGHBOUR

The first thing I do is gasp. The first thing that he does is smile, until, of course, he sees my hands, balled tightly into fists. But wait, what is this? Upstairs Neighbour has taken another form, is tall and black and dashing. "Can I help you?" the stranger asks, sounding unsure.

"Can I help you?" he asks again, taking a step towards me. I have never seen this man before. He is in Upstairs Neighbour's flat but he is *not* Upstairs Neighbour. He is dark with a beautiful smile. He is wearing a T-shirt that kind of hangs off his lean frame and his locs are tied back from his face with a piece of golden string. I place my fists behind my back, though it's too late now, isn't it? He knows I'm not alright in the head now, doesn't he?

"Where is Upstairs Neighbour?" I demand, sounding daft. The man laughs at me. He scans my person, eyes lingering on the fists that are creeping back in front of me. I force them away.

"I think that's me, isn't it? I'm your upstairs neighbour." He holds out a hand. "Hello, I'm new."

"You've been very loud all morning," I accuse, watching his bottom row of small, perfectly formed teeth outlined in gold. He has perfect black gums. I used to be bullied in one of my foster homes for my black gums. Clara's gums are pink. 'Course they are.

"I'm Marcus," he says, extending his hand. "Marc if you like."

"Marcus is better. What's that accent? Can't place it." It's coming out in a weird accusatory tone, and if I could hit myself in the face, I would. I would slap myself ten times. The man smiles, nods his head. His smile is unreal.

"Trinidad. Where are your people from?"

I don't say anything. Marcus looks at me.

"I just moved in," he says. "Sorry for the racket. I was trying to get the piano in place. I'm a musician."

"Fantastic," I say, raising my eyes to the ceiling. "Just what I need."

"Don't worry, I'm going to soundproof everything," says Marcus. "And it's mostly electronic. I do everything through headphones these days."

"You want any help?" I ask him, though I hate helping anyone do anything. But the new neighbor smiles with all his mouth. He doesn't look like the kind of man you say no to, if you know what I mean. He is interesting, with that mouth of black and gold; attractive in a very intimidating way, but also seems like kind of a nice person, so there's all of that to be confused about.

"Hey, listen," says Marc. "I'm all good here. I heard the last neighbour was a bit of a nightmare."

"A total effin nightmare," I snort, and then I have a bad thought. "Um, do you know what happened to her?"

"Old persons' home, I think," he says, shaking his head. "Sad, innit? When you don't have no family?"

We have a moment of silence then, for Upstairs Neighbour who is no more. I look up at Marcus, and Marcus looks down at me, and I want to grab his hand.

"Might do a little housewarming thing this weekend," he says. "Nothing too crazy or loud. You should come. I'll be doing a cookout. You can even bring a dish, but no pressure. There'll be 'nuff food here."

I start nodding stupidly. Usually, I would say, "I don't cook," but it doesn't feel as though someone like Marcus would understand this. He seems like the kind of person who "throws it together" and comes out with a banquet for ten. He probably doesn't even use measurements or recipes or the oven timer. I tell him I'll come if I'm free.

"Soon, then," says Marcus, looking at me in a way that makes my body feel peculiar.

"I'd better go downstairs," I say. "Got some food on the go."

A BOLD-FACED LIE.

"Really," he goes, eyes twinkling. "What ya havin' tonight?"

"Chicken," I say. "Don't want to burn it."

ANOTHER BOLD-FACED LIE.

"And chips," I say. "Homemade," I say.

BOLD-FACED LIES. Dr. Rayna Panelli would go nuts with her analysis.

••

When I am back in my flat, I go online and watch pretty people make decadent meals with their large kitchens and colourful ingredients and matching cookware, particularly Chrissie Wang, a Chinese South African influencer with bleach-blonde hair who makes her own nut milks and matcha, and Jack Spratt, her boyfriend, a model and MMA fighter who makes decadent sugar-free desserts. Ah, but there's really nothing to this. If they can do it, I can. All I really need to do is to memorize the steps.

First, I order some cookware, just the basic stuff. Saucepans, pots, a frying pan, the same sage green as Chrissie's, because it almost matches the kitchenette wall. Then I order a cake tin, two whisks, greaseproof paper, and three different types of sugar because Jack Spratt made vegan carrot cake and it was a huge hit with his friends. For the party I will do a vegan quiche and a carrot cake with an actual carrot on it and Marcus will be impressed.

Later, I click all the tabs shut, resting on the final open page—my sister's *Vogue* clip. I watch Clara show them round her house again and again. This time I turn off the sound. There are no pictures on Clara's walls. Everything is shiny and new looking, fresh out the catalogue. Her surfaces are all marbled and white. Her ornaments are what some people call neutral. She doesn't even clean her own house, I bet. The thing about living the way she lives is that you can't keep it up forever. I actually feel great pity for her.

EVIDENCE,
CHAPTER FOUR

I t wasn't that Serene hadn't written a good enough book. It was daring and inventive enough, or so she thought. It was part memoir, part dark fairy tale, part speculative fiction. It collapsed timelines and talked frankly about women, men, and sex. The problem was that she couldn't get anyone who mattered to look at it. They dismissed her at the first look. She wasn't the type of girl to write; she was the type to get knocked up and live off benefits. She hadn't been to this school or that school; she didn't know this person or that person. Eventually, this white man from a creative writing course at the city college offered to help her find a home for this oddball book. He had an in with a publisher and wouldn't stop going on about all his contacts there, how much weight he carried with all the editors. But in the end, he only wanted to sell her his fiction writing course, and maybe exchange favors if she was up for it. Serene was angry. She bought his stupid course and agreed to go for drinks, and for what?

"*I'm* all about Female Pleasure," Gene Harris said as they chain-smoked outside. "I'm like, really about it. I'm all about turning *you* on, you see. You really have to *want* it for me to get excited." As if trying to convince himself, he continued. "No, no, I'm not one to take advantage. I'm not one of those men that you must be used to. I want to go down on you first for an hour and a half, minimum," said Gene. "We're both adults here," he said, staring at her bump. But when she declined the offer to go back to his house to "eat soup" one afternoon, he said she might have an issue getting her work published. "But where are your credentials?" he kept saying, with his oily voice.

Life, dickhead, Serene nearly said. As if reading her mind, he went, "Look, I know you say you've lived it, and who am I to argue, but the audience requires you to have some level of experience in the thing you are talking about before you can sell it to other people. That's just the way it is. It's all about having a piece of paper to say you know what you know, or even some letters after your name. And is it a memoir? Is the lead character *you*? You're using allegory to illustrate what is essentially a memoir, right? A book about what is real and what is psychosis, and maybe you *do* know, but *how* do you know? Where are your credentials?" he said again, for good measure.

"That's exactly what it's about," Serene said.

But Professor Eugene Harris looked at her and said, "Well why not a full fiction book, a less complicated story. I mean personally, I love it. You can *write*. But my problem is the subject matter. Who's buying this kind of story? You have to think about packaging. You have to consider commercial appeal. *Who* is your audience? To whom would you compare your writing? And can't you make it less esoteric?"

"What are you saying?" Serene asked.

"I'm asking," said Gene, in patronizing effect, "do you really think Black people will read this?"

In the silence that followed, Serene considered stubbing her cigarette on his face.

She didn't. There would have been witnesses.

"Why not write about Black womanhood—that's a topical one—or oooh, romance; I bet you have a few tales about romance, ha-ha. Or, might I strongly suggest that you write about the earlier part of motherhood—as in the part you're experiencing now? Women's lib and everything means those books are flying out now."

"I'm not a mother yet," she snapped, and Gene Harris looked at her and said, "I find pregnant woman extremely erotic; you'll forgive me for . . ."

Gene *had* loved the name of the book, though, since he *simply adored* one-word titles.

"*Evidence*. Mmmmm. It's kind of like a B-movie feel, mmmm, love it, love it. Take my advice and write a story that is more universal. Love without all the anguish. Why do we need all the confusing imagery? How about pithy affirmations—that's the next wave, you know. An easy sell."

Serene drew in her breath. "Look, I don't mean to be unkind," Gene went on. "But the book reminds me of a bad acid trip. Believe me, I'm all for psychedelics—I'm taking a tiny bit of LSD as we speak. Just a sub perceptual dose, don't worry haha. But who are these twins?" He nodded to her belly. "Wait, *are* you having twins?"

Serene said nothing. Gene put a red hand on her knee and Serene said nothing to that, either.

Later, when they were back in the café, and he had gone to use the bathroom, she lifted a crisp fifty-pound note from his blazer pocket for her trouble, and a hundred from his briefcase. It served him right. Who carried briefcases anymore?

It was a book before its time, she decided. It was about getting it into the right hands. Around two years ago, she had started her book as a way of exploring what it was to be dark and female and hunted, what it felt like to be born with a womb full of all the possibilities you would ever have. And then an interesting new being appeared who came round whenever he felt like it, dug his feet into her. The womb of possibility became activated, became full of life, and all because of a man who wasn't really there.

The first time she watched Abbé shoot up, it was as curious as anything. There was a kind of reverence and practice to it, needles, pipe, belt, followed by moaning, and a blissful silence. She gave him her arm, but he shook his head and made a warning noise, motioning to the golden-brown treasure in the glass she had poured. She took her liquor in one hand, held his jerking head with the other. As he fell away, one ear pressed on her thigh, she examined his hands, his face, his hair. Here was someone lost like her. That day they met on the bus, he was trying to ask for help, all the while crossing and uncrossing his legs, clearing his throat, and blinking before each sentence. It was a unique assortment of tics, she remembered thinking.

They were together-apart for all the best parts of a year. Abbé had displayed excitement when he first learned she was pregnant—or had she imagined it? The closer the twins got to being born, the more he fell through her hands. He hadn't told his parents, who surely would have helped them. He hadn't got any help for her, or himself. It was exactly as though he hadn't expected any *real* children to materialize. As she grew larger, and the truth became more and more, well, *evident,*

he became less and less real to her, until he was only a theory, a walking habit.

ALL FINE,
NOTHING TO WORRY ABOUT

Six women are on the video call. Six women want to know what happened at the interview last week, each aggressively amicable, with measured, inquiring tones. There were, Emma relayed carefully, A Few Little Concerns about my behavior on BBC's Angie Resnick culture show. The gentle feedback from the publisher is that I didn't seem as *positive and coherent* as usual. In other words, I hadn't spoken enough about the book.

"It's just important," said someone with a colour-coded bookcase in their background, "that we make the most out of every media opportunity."

"You looked amazing, though," Emma assures me, and the others nod.

"Absolutely stunning," says someone with frizzy hair.

"As always, as always," says this woman with a statement necklace, who always wears the same statement necklace. "If you don't mind us asking, what happened to your eye?"

A shadow framing my eye socket has bloomed since the scuffle in my mother's house. During the interview, the host, Angie Resnick, hadn't been able to stop looking at it. I have to say that I love it; I think I look formidable. I wouldn't let the makeup artist near it. Mid-interview I paused, wondering if Serene Marie Nkem Droste might be sitting on the terra-cotta couch, watching my face in real time.

"I love how bravely you wrote about your father's addiction," Angie had said. "Was it difficult to revisit, or was it cathartic?"

I lost the thread for a moment,
tried to catch up.
"Revisit?" I repeated,
"Revisit?" I repeated,
and then, understanding . . .
"Oh no, no no no . . . the character in the book, she isn't me."
Angie R looked confused. "It isn't autobiographical?"

"It isn't," I said, smiling wickedly. "It's fiction with a twist. It's a terrible tale about my mother, as though she told it to me herself."

I think I rubbed my hands together. At this Angie leaned back a little, appraising me.

"So it *isn't* your life?"

"Fictitious," I said, "Fiction, I mean."

"Totally," I said. "Totally Fiction." I think I started laughing, though nothing about this was funny.

"Wow," she said, "wow, okay, lemmegetmyheadaroundthis. You just shifted genres, right in front of my eyes." She wanted to talk more and more about the pink book.

"Let me tell you again," I interrupted, slowing my voice down. "It's just fiction. It's my fantasy."

The colour in her cheeks deepened. I felt a little guilty. I'd had a couple of glasses of red in the greenroom—could she tell? I thought it best to stop right there. I nodded to myself, hands already unfastening the microphone.

"Going somewhere?" said the host, laughing nervously. A moment of grief, Emma tells the six concerned women on the screen, and they nod their heads and try to look less,

well,
concerned.

But the viewers liked it. The newspaper did a feature on me, on how raw and interesting the interview was. A think piece emerged in the *Guardian Online*.

IS BESTSELLING AUTHOR CLARA KALLIS
THE BAD GIRL OF LITERATURE?

People were talking about it on X, all from one small interview, where I had had just maybe one too many drinks.

Such an interesting interview, said @thedreambunny
She felt alive tonight. Extremely *human*, said @billthewhiteguysorry.
Crazy black bitch, said @youfkingwish, from a private account.
Mean af but always really kind of funny, said @adeloanotforyou. It's nice to see people who aren't afraid to appear flawed. Here for it.

"Now we have some downtime," Emma assures the publishers. "Clara's going to get some well-deserved rest—you're such a trouper Clara!—and we'll be on track."

My U.S. publisher is on the phone, and we have some important updates that we can't wait to talk about. I stretch my lips into a tight, upturning line. Then I remember my teeth and their winning effect, so I bare them a little, which seems to do the trick. "I'm very excited for the next leg of this tour," I say, for what seems like the twentieth time in this conversation. It's exactly what they need to hear, though. The women fizzle and melt, looking less perturbed by the minute. When Emma has prostrated long enough on my behalf, we do a drawn-out goodbye, and then we are cut off by whoever was hosting the chat.

I sit at my desk a while, holding my head. I realise I might not have been breathing. I imagine Serene, sitting on the floor, surrounded by green bottles, watching her chosen daughter.

Smiling glossy with her orange-rind mouth.

CLAUDETTE &
KWESI AMANKWAH

I park outside the house on Grove Park and sit a while, preparing myself for what surely comes next. Squinting at the lacquered white door, I remind myself of the mission. This is a research trip and must be treated as such. I will not lose my nerve. I will not allow them to get under my skin. I must be collected, impenetrable. With a straight back, I switch off the engine and strut towards the house.

Kwesi pulls open the door of the house they share and comes in for a dominant, smother hug. As he pulls away, grinning, I see Claudette standing behind him, that thin, knotty vein pulsating under the skin of her pale narrow neck.

"Good afternoon, how *are* you both?" I enquire, cooly.

Claudette looks me up and down, in the way she always does.

"What happened to your eye?" she wants to know. "We saw it on the show, but good God, it looks even worse in person."

I go in. I arrange myself on the blue leather sofa.

• •

When I was ten, I called Claudette "Mother." I tried it out for three entire weeks and every time it felt more wrong. I sensed that it was unpleasant for her, too, so I stopped trying to force it. Somewhere in my teens, she did a kind of pivot. A rebrand. The first shift happened in January 2010, when Adolphus died suddenly of a heart attack, and we moved from our comfortable home in Dulwich to a three-bedroomed semidetached home in Camberwell. Less than six months after I saw Adolphus for the very last time, propped up in a hospital bed attached to tubes and wire, we were in a new space with tiles, and neutral rugs; so much beige, unrelenting space. Once Adolphus was buried, so then was any talk of him—after twenty-seven years of marriage. I found this psychotic. Claudette did not like to dwell on, as she put it, "upsetting, unhelpful topics." We all had to move on, said she, to meet the days with determination and vigour. Looking backwards did nothing for anyone.

To this day, Claudette believes in buckling down and getting on with it and having good hair and a proportional waist. Claudette says that no one has a good enough reason for getting fat, or anywhere mildly close. Claudette says that depression is an excuse, a state of mind.

As far as any enquiry into Serene Droste—I tried no fewer than three times over the course of my childhood to bring her up. There was no point, unless I wanted to hear someone berate my birth mother for the next half hour. Claudette didn't believe in women who shirked their responsibilities, and as far as she was concerned, that was exactly what Serene Droste had done. She had quite spectacularly failed at life, at the task in question: motherhood. After all, she had left us there all alone in that house on that day, with no explanation, no note. I changed this fact in the novel, because this one truth was too ugly. There we were, bawling for comfort and milk until the girl from round the way walked through an open door and called the police. And there it was. There we were. We could have been anyone's. We might have been dead.

On our new lush, tree-lined street in Camberwell lived Kwesi Amankwah, whose house directly faced ours. Kwesi Amankwah had darker skin than anyone I had ever seen before. He was always sitting on his front lawn in a wrought-iron chair, reading the *Telegraph* and drinking steaming hot liquid from a flask. We found him curious. He would only answer Claudette's brisk "Good morning" with a nod. This had an interesting effect on Claudette, who had by then resurrected her double-barreled family name, Marshall-Whyte.

I would never call Claudette a flirt, or obvious, even someone who was particularly looking for attention, at least not in the usual manner. But Claudette was not at all used to being ignored. People noticed her. She was no more attractive than anyone else, but she was proud and stately and knew how to put herself together. Often I would find her washing the dishes staring out of the kitchen window with peculiar interest.

"Look at him, Clara," she said, once or twice. "Even in the rain." Sure enough, Kwesi would be sitting underneath a gazebo-type contraption, smiling into a newspaper. Claudette waved, and Kwesi held her eye, before doing his tiny nod thing. One time he waved. Claudette flushed. I went upstairs to sulk.

Claudette's personal metamorphosis began in 2011 with a generic piece of wax print sourced from the African market. Soon after, versions of the same orange print began to appear everywhere, on coasters and the undersides of tea towels. I was sixteen then.

"An injection of colour," Claudette said, in a voice that had deepened somewhat. "I've never noticed their charm until now."

Next, Claudette was reading books on Pan-Africanism. If I had disliked Claudette before, I hated her now. At least I had known what she was before. Now I knew nothing at all. Alarming, when a stuck thing attempts to change on you.

Kwesi came around for dinner one day.
They were married within the year.

•••

In the deep-blue living room, Kwesi begins to blather about the elections in Benin. Claudette smiles her not-smile as he continues, on and on and on and on and on. When Kwesi has paused for a sip of tea, I take the opportunity to state my intention.

"I was wondering," I begin, "if I might look at some of my old records."

"Those tatty CDs? You have to know that I threw them out years ago. We've discussed this. I don't like clutter, Clara."

"No," I say. "I was thinking about my birth stuff. As in the hospital stuff."

Claudette looks at Kwesi, now, for some reason, until Kwesi nods his head.

"Well, what in particular were you after?"

"Anything about the adoption, really," I tell her. "Or rather, anything to do with Serene Droste."

At the very mention of her name, Claudette raises her eyebrows.

"Interesting. You want that *now*? As in today?"

"It would be useful. If you can."

"Well, there's a first time for everything," she says, her back already to me. "Good to know everything, isn't it?" she goes, already out of the room.

When she comes back downstairs, she hands me some notes about Dempsey and me, which are nothing new at all. Adoption papers, hospital reports, and a report I've read a million times about a supposed personality disorder.

"Is that all?"

"Meaning?" she asks, but I know her all too well.

"Anything in the way of more photos, or any other details surrounding . . ."

"We don't have any press cuttings of the suicide. You know that I don't hold on to things like that. Heavy negative energy."

Kwesi is nodding his stupid head. "Couldn't agree more, Mama. This is a house of positivity." He taps his silver rings on the table, in some strange drum patter, as if warding off a bad spirit. Claudette stretches her lips at him and turns back to me.

"And we gave your sister the personal photos," Claudette is saying. She shrugs, so I know she is lying. Claudette is not a person who shrugs. Ever ever.

"I'm going to make another cup of tea," says Kwesi, loudly, but he gives Claudette a pointed look as he leaves. There is silence. I watch her, strained and upright, skin clear as glass. She's still wearing her hair slicked back. She's definitely started botox. She makes a slight face as if she just remembered something.

"Oh, there's one more item," says Claudette. "I put it to one side because . . . well, I thought it might be upsetting."

"What. What is it?"

Claudette gets up and crosses the room. She goes to a cabinet over her Royal Doulton ornaments, right on the top rack, and pulls out a thick yellow A4 envelope that has been folded in half. She hesitates a beat before handing it over.

"She was a fantasist," she says, watching my face. "These are letters. To you and Dempsey."

There is a pause, then, "She rather fancied herself a writer. I suppose that's where you got it, only you're much more succinct."

"*Much* more succinct!" booms a voice from the other room. "I found it impossible to follow, myself," says Kwesi, coming in with three steaming cups.

"That's all?" I ask, hoping Claudette isn't holding anything else back. "That's definitely everything?"

"That's all," says Claudette. "That's all she wrote."

Kwesi bellows with laughter. Claudette does another grin-thing. I want to scream, or knock the hot drinks into Kwesi's lap, but I push it down. I don't say

why have I never seen this before
why is it set apart from the medical records
why did you never tell me this before?
I don't even say, *why has Kwesi read this before me?*

I feel what I always feel when I am there. The tremendous, over-whelming urge to get the hell out. "I'm sorry," I say, pushing the letter into my bag. "I have to go now. I hope you'll understand. Are you okay for me to take this home with me?"

"You should keep it," says Kwesi, as if I need his permission.

"You won't stay for a bite?" asks Claudette, though it's not as though she wants me here another second. To keep up the pretense, we drink the weak tea and talk politely about *Evidence*, Kwesi interjecting every now and then to tell me what I could have done to "enhance the reader's experience," and Claudette nodding sagely. When an acceptable twelve minutes have passed, I jump up and out of my chair, mumbling about having to be home, and can't get out of the house soon enough. Once in the car, I let out a low, singular howl, the thing that has been building for days. I open the envelope, take out the letter.

Four pages.

For The Girls.
Monday, Sep 4th, 1995
 I always knew I was different. Not in a self-important way, but yes why not, my Self is very important. My differences were clear from the beginning. You know at first the obviously physical things you know, growing up in Nottingham in foster care. Imagine this—there's no one else who's Black in the whole little town and you have to run all the way home from school because some people literally want you dead, and their families want you dead and you have to want to be alive more than anyone wants you dead, you get me? (Don't feel bad for me either. Made me tough.) The other notable difference is how I look. I never met a man who didn't want me. Imagine the confusion of a man wanting you, and wanting you dead, because the two are not mutually exclusive. Dangerous water.
 If anything happens, know that it's for the best. The most successful people come from the worst origins. I often wonder if it's part of the story. My mother was gone too, away most of the days of my life and I don't even blame her. Thank God I hear her voice. Honestly. She was tortured alright, God knows what it must have been like back then if it is this bad now. Some of us can't help but leave. We know that if we stay around, it will become too much for everyone involved. What I'm saying is some of the boldest, greatest

people were motherless. Leaving you might just be my gift to you, and if you are reading this, you got the gift didn't you? Try not to be upset about things. I have gone away with purpose. In a desperate attempt to stay here and be—normal I suppose you'd call it.

I fell in love with a projection, or rather a project, an inverted reflection of myself. I think this is true of most loves. Often, when we find out the truth, we're too far gone. We have committed to too much, agreed to too many things we didn't want. The love has become a contract, and no one walks away before they're spent. I'm not doing this out of heartbreak or anything. Your father is selfish, but so am I.

I'm going to win.

I keep getting called towards bodies of water, because water holds all the truth in the world. Call it a baptism of sorts. I might need to be cleansed. Dreams keep telling me I have other places to be. I have some streaks inside me, girls, mishandled energy. Sometimes existing feels painful, sometimes hollow, mostly a façade, but I can deal with the pain of the thing. Pain means that you are alive, doesn't it? But what I cannot bear, not now, not ever, is how meaningless everything can seem. It's every day, and I can't escape it for the death of me. Sometimes it feels like life is a book and the pages are curling up on me, and you know that shrinking feeling, when you take a flame to a piece of paper? Everything gets smaller, dark round the edges. I would like to be free of this. I have a memory of this somewhere underneath ~~but I seem to have lost sight of my guides~~. I'll be back around. I know I'll get to meet you again, time and time when you are old enough to have conversations with me. Motherhood is a scam, girls, I won't lie to you, the SCAM being the idea that it can save you. These days, I find myself no more real than I ever was. I am disappearing and have been every day since I was a girl. A thing happens to girls who aren't visible. They go to unnecessary lengths to prove themselves real. Some of these methods are fatal.

There is more; I skim to the end, letting my eyes trip down the page.

It's obviously some kind of joke, but how evil. I think back to a few minutes ago, when Claudette said that she hadn't mentioned or showed me the letter before this very day, because she was afraid of upsetting me. But Claudette has never cared whether I might be upset.

••

Claudette opens the front door again, eyeing me suspiciously. I slow clap, giving her what I hope is an icy stare.

"For heaven's sake, what is it now?"

"Not funny, Claudette," I say. "You missed the mark with that one."

"Keep your voice down," she warns, stepping backwards into the house. "We have neighbors, you know. What's gotten into you?"

I thrust the paper into her hand. "What *is* this?"

Claudette looks at me squarely, sets her mouth into a neat line. "You need to get a handle on your aggression," she says. "You've always been aggressive, and it's ugly."

I charge past Claudette and look back inside, all the way to the kitchen. There stands Kwesi, who is staring at me as though I might have run in there naked. I flick my eyes down at my body, which is still well dressed.

"You both read my book," I say, coming back to myself. "You read it, so you would know! You would know!" I tell them, steadying myself on the kitchen counter.

"What on earth are you talking about?"

"Oh don't be cute, Claudette," I snap. "This so-called letter from our mother? This is the exact letter that the mother writes in my book! Word for word!" I shout, clapping my hands together. "Word for damn word."

"Calm down," says Kwesi. "Good vibes only."

"Chapter Seven!" I shout, cutting him off. "What's the point of this? Don't you think it's cruel?"

Kwesi looks at Claudette. Claudette looks at Kwesi. I have both elbows on the counter, shaking against the weight of everything.

"Oh, I haven't read your book, dear," says Claudette. "I wouldn't know what's in it and what isn't."

The corner of her mouth turns up a little, as though she's proud of herself. I turn away, so she does not see the wounding.

"Kwesi," I say, looking to him. "You read both. You didn't catch it?"

"Well," says Kwesi, with a look I've never seen before—is he embarrassed? "I didn't say I read the whole thing. I'm more of a speed reader myself. Saves time. I have *so* much nonfiction material to get through, you know. I speed read the beginning and speed read the end. I got the gist, though."

"He wanted to support you," goes Claudette. "But it's not really his thing, either."

"Not really," says Kwesi. "Not really my thing." Then he leaves the room, the fraud.

"I'm sorry, but you reek of wine,"
says Claudette, from somewhere beside me.

I leave the house as quickly as I entered, Claudette staring after me. I sit in my car, holding the head that is on my body. I try to imagine Claudette and Kwesi laughing at me. Pranking me. Playing an evil, evil joke. But it doesn't ring true, for either of them. What rings true is this: the person who wrote this letter is my mother. She is the one who came to me in dreams and the like, got into my head. She is the person who stole a watch, who led me to the flat in the photo. Perhaps I brought her here. Perhaps I summoned the dead woman from the water? Perhaps there's a spell, a blue trick that happens somewhere between wishing for a thing with everything you've got, and the dream coming to life, as the clock strikes twelve. All the parts of the fantasy make cold, rude sense.

Before I start the car, I snap photos of the letter, postmark, address and all, and send them on to Dempsey.

I title the email *EVIDENCE, bitch.*

DEMPSEY'S UPSTAIRS NEIGHBOUR: REMASTERED

The first cake comes out sunken and the second one is overbaked. I end up buying one from the Polish bakery on the corner. I'm not a party person, but I'm going to push on through. Chrissie Wang did a whole vlog sponsored by Samsung about your dreams being at the other side of your fears. Everybody hearted and commented. It was very inspirational.

At eight p.m. I push open the door to Marcus's flat, where I am greeted by a short, bald man whom I recognize a little from the downstairs block. He is wearing a red Hawaiian shirt and sweating. "Come in, come in," he is saying, "party's through here." Well, obviously.

The music is not what you would expect. There is muffled techno coming from the main room, which is full of random, vaguely familiar bodies. Marcus appears to have invited the whole bloody building. All at once, I am troubled by the overwhelming fear that tonight could be a lot more difficult than I thought. I spot Marcus standing at the end of the hall, but he just kind of waves in my direction, before turning his attention towards some swampy-looking woman. When I go to try and greet him, I am intercepted by two people who decide to embrace midway between us. By the time they have pulled away from each other, Marcus has slipped into the back room, closing the door behind him. Rude. I carry the cake into the kitchen. There are lots of white women and men in varying shades of brown chatting energetically into one another's faces. I consider where to stand. There are two large Dutch Pots on the counter filled with meats, and foil containers filled with yellow rice, cooked vegetables, peppers, fish and okra, and some other dishes that look considerably less enjoyable. There is a sad looking quiche and a large, withered salad. There are countless bottles of wine, beer, and vodka and a pitcher of Sangria. Most of the people here are people who I pass often in the stairway and the communal garden. One of the browner men is smiling at me from across the room. God.

He starts to make his way over. God.

"Food's good," he says.

"Looks it," I say. I'm trying to smile back, but the thing won't happen on my face.

"I think you live below me," he says, snapping open a bottle of beer.

"No," I say. "I'm definitely under Marcus."

"Well, not directly below," says the man. "But . . . almost. I live next door to Marcus."

I nod again, wondering when Marcus will come out of the room and actually be a host.

"I'm Raoul. Good to meet you," the man says, sticking out his hand.

"Good to meet you, Raoul," I say, looking at the hand. Raoul has his hair in a bun. He is olive-skinned and green-eyed—good-looking in a way that is difficult to trust.

"You Spanish or something?" I ask him. He lets the hand fall to his side. He blinks and his smile dips. Another one replaces it, right away. If I weren't so good at spotting things, I might have missed the slip.

"Or something," Raoul says.

"Right. Okay. Where *is* Marcus?" I ask him. He shrugs, but I don't trust it. I just don't.

"So how do *you* know Marcus?" Raoul goes on, intent on forcing this.

"I'm his downstairs neighbour," I say, not meaning to be funny or anything but Raoul laughs, slapping his thigh, and says, "yes, I feel we established that."

We stand there a while, looking down at the cake.

"Looks incredible," he says, rubbing his hands together in an unbecoming way.

"It's lemon drizzle," I say, setting it farther away on the counter and then Raoul moves towards it, so I have no choice but to get between him and the cake. I tell him I'll cut it when Marcus comes out.

"Got it," he says, and gives me a wink, the smile falling somewhere else again. We stand there for some seconds longer and then Raoul taps me on the arm and says, "Well, good to meet you."

The party is getting irritating; people keep trying to squeeze past me and make for the cake. I have to keep obstructing them and telling them that the cake is for later. So much for this being a good time. So much for Marcus.

My breath halts as his shape passes the doorway. He is on his way again, to the small room at the end of the hallway. This room is towards the back of the flat, away from the living room and kitchen, its door slightly ajar.

I sip a small glass of tonic by the kitchen counter, wondering if I should go there, too, watching the bodies who have collected to dance, if that's really what they're calling it. I never usually drink from strange cups in new houses, but I need to do an action with my hands. Very quickly, the liquid in the glass is finished. I wander into the hallway, eyeing the room he went into.

I go into the bathroom and stare in the mirror for a while. I bought a wig for tonight; it's synthetic hair but on the website, the girls said that it fools everyone. It was twenty quid, which was not a lot, but more than I had to spare. Now, in the yellow bathroom light, I'm not sure what I was thinking. It almost looks plastic. The curl pattern is unnatural—a poodle perm, which I think makes me look older. I'm even wearing lipstick, for God's sake. It is coral, kind of orangey—wrong for my outfit and crumbling off my lips.

I sit in the closet room at the front with an exercise bike and a covered drum kit. There are coats draped all over it. Every so often someone comes and, startled at seeing me perched there, promptly leaves.

Count to ten, Dempsey.
Keep counting to ten.

My mouth is doing the tic. All I wanted was a little acknowledgement, a little *hello*, at least . . .

"Don't know," I hear someone saying, just outside of the door,

". . . from downstairs . . . just sitting in the coat room on her own."

"The funny one?" says someone else. "Oh my God."

"Oh my God . . . did she stop you from touching the cake?" says the other voice.

The next thing they say is inaudible and it makes them both cackle. A sudden flush of anger makes its way up my spine. "I CAN HEAR YOU," I shout to the voices,

instantly regretting it,
and the voices stop and then move farther away.

After twenty-three minutes of scrolling through my phone, I feel like it's now or never. The flat has a similar layout as mine, but Marcus has the two-bedroom unit, while I have the studio version. Each room seems farther apart, a difference somewhat enhanced by the mirrors everywhere. Even the hallway feels trickier, longer. At the second bedroom door, I knock, and to my surprise, Hawaiian Shirt opens it. Beyond him inside the room is Marcus, sitting on a beanbag, a glassy look in his eye, smoking and sipping on a beer. The room is dull and smokey. There are controls and technical dials everywhere you look.

"Heya," mumbles Marcus, waving his hand lazily. "Just showing him some music."

There is a sound travelling through the air for sure, but it doesn't feel much like music.

"It's experimental," says Marcus, as though apologizing.

"Er, I think I'm getting off now," I say.

"So early?" he says, almost scrambling to his feet, looking larger and smaller at once. I suddenly wonder if he's having a not-so-great time too.

"Yes," I say, too afraid to look at him now. "I have somewhere else to be."

Back to lying, then.

"One min, I'll walk out with you . . . one sec."

Marcus struggles to stand up straight for a second. Hawaiian Shirt has a pipe at his lips, looking at nothing in particular.

Marcus walks me to the door, breathing all weird and jagged. My heart is suddenly beating fast. I don't want to leave anymore, but it's too late now, isn't it? Made a show of leaving now, haven't I? We walk back through the main room, and as people are dancing up to him, saying hello and dancing and smiling, I watch him playing a part, looking mostly at the ground. He picks up the pace. I can feel a strange anxiety on him, a need to escape. When we are in the doorway, I get up the courage to look into his eyes. They are large and dark and he is talking with a different part of his voice, a booming, dreadful, "happy" voice, and showing all his teeth. His smile is as beautiful as I remember.

"Stop by again soon!" he is saying.

"Thanks so much for coming!" he is saying, sounding very London and not at all Trinidadian like the other day.

Hmmmm, I think. *Hmmmm*, and then I feel the sudden need to get into my safe flat where there is no one else and speak with Clara and ask her if she's okay, because at this exact moment, I feel as though no one in the world is, in fact, okay. Like everyone might just be pretending.

I have dissolved on my couch into safety, where there are the videos and there are the feed posts and other people's faces and hair and families and food. I fall into a fresh, saturated portal, where things match, and if they don't match, it's all curated, all for a reason. Everything on screen is louder and shinier, and I climb dutifully inside, where I know what's what. I fall into the buy-me land of voices, opinions, and fashion and beauty and intricate recipes, the MMA boy and the ex-model, their young, impossibly beautiful nineteen- and twenty-year-old friends and all their closely knit, loving relatives. I click through and buy a few things, even though I have no money, just a credit card. And now I'm feeling calmer. but there, burrowed amongst everything, is Clara's email.

First, she calls me a bitch,
which is rich.

There is a picture attached to the email, which will not load. My laptop has needed replacing for years. I squint at the rainbow wheel of doom, watching and waiting until the yellow paper comes clearly into view. By now I have a bit of a headache from the stupid party and the music and Marcus's bewildering energy, which all but seeped into my skin. Feeling overstimulated, I get my blue-light glasses and a cup of water and study the thing a little closer.

I don't get what I'm meant to be looking at. I look again, thinking that she can't be possibly saying what I think she's saying. On her live interview, she looked a complete mess. I don't quite know what is happening to my sister, but it isn't good. Clara has never, ever been *good*. I hear feet stamping above, and then my phone is ringing. There is no number shown, just Clara's email address. I connect the call.

"Clara?

"Clara? Are you there?"

"Hullo?" says the slurred voice. "Ss'that you?"

"It's me. Are you calling me from your computer?"

"Mmmp, Dempsey."

"Clara what's this all about? The email?"

"Letter," says the voice. "Claudette has been hiding this all thizz-time, can you believe it?"

I could believe anything of Claudette, but that's beside the point. I try to focus on what Clara is going on about. She is talking in riddles, like she was on that interview, which has garnered a lot of negative comments on YouTube, by the way. Jabbering about the letter being what she wrote in the book, which she's assuming I read. I'm not going to tell her any different.

"So you expect me to believe," I say, once she has paused to take a breath, "that you and our mother had the exact same idea? Only she wrote hers thirty years ago, in a letter to us?"

Clara coughs.

"Uh huh."

"And you've never seen this letter before?"

"Thass whaddI'mfuckin saying," says the voice. "Try to keep up, Dempsey."

She pauses. I hear her gulp.

"Clara, are you drinking right now?"

"Can you just listen?" bellows my sister.

I set the phone down on its side while I try to count to seven again. For a while, we are both silent. After a minute of Deliberate Breathing, I put the phone back to my ear.

"Clara," I say. "Go back to sleep, alright? I'll call you back first thing tomorrow—that okay?"

"Do what you want," says the mean, hard voice. "If you're not interested, do whatchu fuckin want."

Now she is video calling. The woozy feeling from earlier is returning. There is a blaze of heat in my throat and I can't hold it down. I accept the video call. My sister is on her bed, in the dark, face harshly lit by the computer glare. She is twisting her hair. She looks tormented.

"I want you to remember, Clara," I tell her, my voice closing in on itself. "I want you to know that all these years, I have been the only one who has ever been interested in discussing or learning about our mother and the events surrounding her ... dissa ... her death. Her death, Clara. Her death! And out of the blue you see her in Selfridges, and she's somehow a writer in her thirties, like *you* ... just like *you*? And you've published this entire book that she somehow wrote all those years ago?" I am shouting now. "Is that it? Is that not a little self-centred, Clara?"

Clara's head lolls back and forth. "Went to her house, Dempsey."

"What are you saying now?"

"Went to her house."

"What?"

"We had a fight."

"Is that how you got the black eye?"

Clara makes a noise in her throat that sounds like a laugh. She comes right up to the screen, so I can only see the blackened eye in question.

"Her name is *Serene.*"

"Clara," I go, trying to be careful about it. "Did you do any drugs tonight?"

"People do drugs, Dempsey," she replies. "Sometimes People Do Drugs."

"Clara, I have to go."

I feel quite scared to do so, but I disconnect the line, because the thing that broke is falling everywhere and the damage is spreading.

I wish they would have called the police. I would have known that they cared.

In February 2001, before the incident with the hair relaxer and the wasps and the police threats, we are playing with Clara's pink dolls up in her pink room. Everything is the colour of Pepto Bismol and strawberry Hubba Bubba. Clara says sweetly, and out of nowhere, "I met Mummy, you know," and I believe her, I really do, right away, because Kendrick only ever says she is missing and will never say she is dead.

"Where?" I ask her, shivering a little. "She was with me on Friday, in the sandpit . . ." says my sister, "and she looks like us but prettier. Because she's an adult. But you can't tell anyone, okay?"

"Is she nice?" I want to know.

My sister's large eyes narrow a little. "Not really," she tells me.

"Oh."

"I still like her anyway," says Clara.

"Okay," I say. "That's good."

And then we go on playing with Barbie. In our game, Ken gets on top of Barbie and starts making weird noises. It is confusing and a little thrilling. It feels like needing to pee but in an unfolding, delicious way. The other Barbies are sitting next to them, happily watching the scene unfold.

"It's sex," says Clara, when I ask her what we're doing with the dolls, why they are hurting each other, and why they sound like wild things. "It's easy," sniffs my sister. "I can tell you how to do it if you want." I say I don't want to learn it right now.

"Suit yourself," she says, going back to Barbie, Ken, and the rest, and I wonder why the good things always happen to her.

EVIDENCE,

CHAPTER SEVEN
or
THE OTHER HALF OF THE LETTER

Monday 12th September, 1995

Well, I'm not going to sugar coat it; Abbé overdosed again and there was no one to take him to the hospital. One of his so-called friends called me first, then called the ambulance, and left him all alone. That's how they are, his friends. They had taken the drugs away with them for "safe keeping," can you believe it? By the time he gets out they'll have blown the whole lot. Anyway, he's stable and he's come round and everything, now he just wants to go home. They want to put him in a rehab centre but I don't think he'll go.

If you were old enough to understand, we would have the conversation. I would tell that your father exists and will not exist. It's a trying situation.

"What do you mean," you would both ask, and I would steel myself to tell you.

"What I mean to say," I might begin, "is that there are whole-wide worlds in which people like us thrive. But this is not that world." You would stare at me, not getting it yet, and I would continue,

"Think of your winter coats, their woollen linings. If where we are is the outer core, your father is just inside. All happening at the same time but different materials, different rules."

"So, he's happening underneath us?" you might ask. But not quite. Who's to say inside is underneath? Think about it. There's the wool of the lining, of the coat, then there's the wax cover, the air trapped in between the cloth and the thread. He's trapped air. Inconsequential.

In other news, I keep on seeing numbers. I'm not making them up. They're always the same ones.

7, 19, 5, 8, 24, 16, 30, 24

I'm not a numbers person. That's why I am so perturbed to have them (the numbers) following me around like this! (And they're not even chronological, which bugs me no end!) When I'm all alone, they catch up with me. Sometimes they sit on my body, pin me down, keep me in dark rooms. Sometimes they steal all my language. These days, I am learning to work with them.

7, 19, 5, 8, 24, 16, 30, 24

I think I'm going to get into numerology next year! The numbers are telling me things that I did not know before; large facts, and I can't list them all here. Who knows who might read this letter before you—or worse, steal it?! But girls, listen to this and tell me it isn't fate.

In your dad's corner in the hospital, I go to sit down on the only chair available. Someone has left a dog-eared Elle Magazine and I hardly give a shit about Elle Magazine but it's there—anyway I read while he sleeps. Anyway, why does it fall open on **QUESTIONS YOU NEED TO ANSWER RIGHT NOW TO HEAL YOUR HEART PRONTO!!!** And girls, why do the very sequence of numbers from my waking dream 7, 19, 5, 8, 24, 16, 30, 24 correspond with the very questions that I need answers to! Coincidence?! No way!

CLARA,
AT THE READING

I have Emma sneak me a whisky. Or two whiskys. She gives me the look that says, *are you sure?* I tell her to hurry it up, I'm on in fifteen.

Back to audience questions.

"Why do you write?" asks a tall person with copper-coloured braids hanging to their waist.

"Because I don't know any other way to make sense of things. Writing articulates what is real to me. I set it down on the page, and there it is, a little more concrete. It separates thoughts from actuality."

"Speaking of separation," says another. "How would you best describe the thing that separates those who do and those who only dream of doing? How to get rid of the fear?"

"I have the sense," I tell them, "that I'm running out of time. It is either a fear or a great relief, depending on the day. There is this growing awareness that I have less to lose with every single day."

The person smiles at me. "You're quoting the book."

I hadn't realised. Also, I've forgotten the question, but I carry on bluffing. "I don't worry about getting it wrong, because when you are writing your truth, you can never really get it wrong. Truth is a shifting thing. We are all writers, in a sense."

I'm not sure how I get away with this rubbish.

At the signing line, my mouth feels sour. I pose for a lot of selfies in my red woollen dress, smiling and smiling as though my life depends on it. Mostly, I float out of body. I hold hands with people who are happy to see me because they do not and will never know how not me I am, and I tell them all that writing is easier than they think. While looking down at the woman-thing in the red dress who is spouting platitudes, I have the feeling that I would not care if I died right now, suddenly, by some freak explosion. I imagine being blown apart from the inside, guts shattering like hot glass. The fantasy sits in my mind a while, heavy and seductive.

Just when I feel as though I might pass out, a shadow approaches the desk.

I feel her before I understand what I am feeling, because the shadow around my eye begins to pulse.

"You left your phone," says the voice, sounding irritated, and the ice is all over my body again. Standing over me, dressed in orange, is my mother. She places the phone and a gin and tonic in front of me and steps back, tilting her head a little, eyes on my face.

"Thank you," I manage, hands already gripping the iced glass.

Serene holds a copy of *Evidence*. I feel euphoric. Awakened.

Everything around my mother fades out of focus as I watch her fingers curl around my book.

"Thank you for coming to find me," I whisper, becoming a puddle on the floor.

"I haven't read a book in a while," she tells me. "But this. This is special. Mate, you didn't say you were famous."

From the corner of my eye, I spot Emma watching us. Serene follows my eyeline. Emma, being Emma, stares and stares. No manners.

"Wanna get a drink after?" Serene asks, unbothered by this.

"Yeah, sure . . . Yeah."

"I'll wait for you over there," she says and turns and walks over to the bar where they are serving premixed cocktails and prosecco.

By now I can't cope any more with what I am doing, because the only place I want to be is with her. I stare out at the long line of people waiting to talk to me while I plan my getaway. There is no way I'm getting through all these people tonight.

Suddenly, Emma is at my side. Emma the spy. Emma the controller.

"Y'okay?"

"Mmmm."

"Sure?"

"Just a headache," I say, glassily, leaning my head against the table. "A really terrible one, if I'm honest with you. Emma, I might need to leave soon."

At this, Emma looks worried.

"Are you okay? Think you can hold out? Still a good few people to go. And the *Elle* photographer wants to shoot you at the signing line for their socials."

"I'll do my best," I tell her. "But I'm really not feeling well, Emma. I wouldn't say it if it wasn't . . ." I scan the crowd for my mother. *There she is.* "If it wasn't serious." I hold the side of my head for good measure.

"No, no, got it, got it . . . I'll let the organizers know," Emma says, trying not to look too flustered. "Leave it to me. Is that a friend?"

Emma is looking over at Serene again, who has a glass of something green at her lips.

I sigh, pointedly, because I can't be bothered with her right now. Emma is meeker than usual tonight, a little bloated and unsure.

"Why, Emma?" My voice is full of bite.

"She looks out of this world. That's a fabulous coat she's wearing." And it is. Floor length. The colour of a thing burning. And she is. Out of this world.

"She's family," I tell Emma. "I haven't seen her in like, forever. I'm sure she can take me home."

• •

An hour and half later, Serene and I are in a pub garden in Waterloo. There is a blue warmth creeping up my neck and stinging my ears.

Friends huddle in groups sharing chips for the table and pitchers of cider. Men are wearing football shirts and shorts and other unimaginative accessories. Serene turns to me, the moon on her hairline.

"Explain yourself," she says. "You were up there, telling my story. Explain yourself."

I cough. "Your story?"

"More or less," she says, spreading her hands on the table and looking at them.

"It got me thinking. Stories like ours mean something, you know?"

Has my mother come to get me? Is that what this is?

"Yeah." She searches my face. "But we don't come across them. You know what I mean. I *know* you know what I mean." I steady myself and let her continue. "I'd love to write someday. To tell my story myself, *my* way."

I don't know what she's trying to tell me. Of course she knows who she is. She was the one who visited at night and would not leave. The one who made a home in me, who gave me all these new words. I can't say all that right now, so I decide to play the long game.

"I *was* good at writing at school, you know," she goes on. "Before the problems set in."

"I could help with that," I tell her, trying to weigh up the situation. "Everyone has a story. I can help you get it published."

Her face becomes childlike for a moment, an expression close to shy. "Maybe."

I order a double whisky to calm myself down. Serene orders a sea breeze.

"Who was the white girl staring at me?" she says, screwing up her face.

"My agent," I tell her. "She manages the tour, talks to the publishers."

"Okay," says my mother. "I didn't like her energy."

"Oh, she's awful," I say, drawing in closer and lowering my voice. "I do most of it myself anyway. She just kind of sets things up and fields calls, that kind of thing."

"Like a PA?"

Wildly inaccurate—quite diminishing, but I look into my mother's black eyes and nod.

"I used to be in that line of work," says Serene.

"Publicity?"

"Yep," says my mother. "Let's call it publicity. Why not?"

"At what company?"

She ignores the question. "I'm very good at it, but it gets hard, doing work you don't believe in. For things you don't believe in. For people who don't pull their weight."

"I don't think she likes me too well," I say, surprising myself with the admission. "I think she tolerates me. And I tolerate her."

"Fire her, then," says my mother, just like that. She gets a notification on her phone and picks it up, then places it back upside down.

We talk a little further and I learn that Serene grew up in Brixton. She's about to tell me more of the particulars, but has a new thought.

"Wanna come to a party in Hackney?"

I say yes.

• •

At the party, the whisky helps a lot. We sit side by side on an oversized leather couch. Serene, still in her warm coat, kicks off her shoes and pulls her feet into the chair underneath her. I am at once overwhelmed with the sudden need to lay my head on her lap. Someone hands us two shots, and as we drink, I try to think up what to say next to seem more interesting.

Serene goes off to talk to someone for a few minutes and sits back down beside me, carrying a thick line of yellow-tinged coke balanced on a coaster. She places the coaster on her knee and begins to separate the line into two. She takes the first line, neatly, then turns in towards me.

"Go on," she says, her eyes alight. "Ask me. Do."

"Ask you what?"

"About the thing in the store with the watch? I know you want to."

I take the coaster and follow her lead.

"I used to do it to survive," my mother is saying, "and now I just *do* it. It's . . ."

"My God!" drawls a man with dirty long Jesus hair and the suggestion of a beard. "You two are gorgeous!" He flops down onto a beanbag beside us, his eyes wide as saucers.

He pushes his face in just a little too far to my mother, who meets his gaze, cool enough. He breaks the stare, reddening.

"You really are," he says, now looking down at the joint he is building with his hands. "Are you like, sisters?"

My mother rolls her eyes, turning to me. The coke has reached a place in me, warming the creases. I suddenly want to kiss or scream lovingly at someone.

Her cold hand rests on my face.

"Wanna go and dance?"

I feel the warmth taking over, a bright armour of indestructibility. We move away from Jesus and into the middle of the party, where everyone is dancing to "You Don't Love Me (No, No, No)" by Dawn Penn. My mother takes my sweaty hands in hers, spins me around. The atmosphere is fizzing, melting on my tongue. We hold hands and move together, as if she could be me and I could be her, as if all of the above could be true. When we go to sit back down, we do another line and my mouth is running faster than I can control it.

"I think you're spectacular," I spit, rubbing hard at the material on my dress.

"You're not so bad yourself," says Serene. "You were on fire tonight. You're on fire now, bitch."

My body is vibrating. My toes are still dancing. I want to say a whole lot of things. Still, important not to lose it. "What was it about the reading?" I ask her, still rubbing my dress, still doing a thing with my teeth. "Why do you love it, er, why *did* you love it?"

"Well..." she says. "The woman in the book. She sounded just like me."

I feel like screaming, but I hold it down as my mother corrects herself.

"I mean, it just felt like me ... it was very loud. Very loud."

"Oh?"

"But everyone must tell you that, right?" She's shouting over the music now.

"Not quite," I shout back. "So, the woman's you? Is that what you're saying?"

"Think so," says my mother. "Think she's all of us."

The party feels like a dreamscape. Serene is beside me and I am invincible. I am talking to strangers and not quite knowing where to put my hands. My mouth, too, is everywhere. I don't know how to hold it. Suddenly I am in the middle of the crowd making jokes and jokes and more jokes, her hand resting on my shoulder.

"How did you get your black eye?" someone wants to know. "Not gonna lie, it looks kind of cool."

"Doesn't it? I did it," says Serene, and everyone laughs, like it's the funniest thing they ever heard. Serene laughs. I laugh, too. The night passes in a blaze of colour. I barely notice the party thinning out. Suddenly I turn and glimpse the window, and to my dismay, I see the frightening orange sun. Suddenly it's beginning to get light, and the dread in my body is threatening, threatening.

"I might make tracks," my mother yawns, when the dance floor has cleared and the hosts are touching each other up on the sofa.

I start to get the gnawing, empty feeling, so I grab up my coat and hers.

"Wanna have a nightcap at mine?"

"A nightcap?" she laughs. "It's five a.m."

"Come on!" I say. "Let's end tonight properly." We take a cab to my house, laughing and joking about the people at the party. I don't know what I'm saying for sure, but Serene laughs and laughs and laughs.

I watch for the look on her face when our car pulls up at the driveway. She falls silent, nodding in approval, taking everything in. I try to stop myself from beaming with pride.

"Beautiful house," she says, catching my self-satisfied grin. "Done alright for yourself, haven't you? Well done."

My insides turn to water. "All this from one book?" she asks, doing the math in her head.

I nod, not minding. Once inside, she starts walking around and picking things up and putting things down, then arranges herself on the sofa. I put on the radio. My mother puts up her feet.

"Ooof," she goes, her voice decidedly soft. "Think I'm tired now. Mind if I stay here tonight?"

"You're tired?" I say, getting worried. "So no nightcap?"

I hear gurgling upstairs, like water running through the pipes. My house comes alive at night, I swear it.

"Can I sleep here?" she sighs. "I'm not sure I could get up again. I can be right here on the couch and be gone before you wake."

"Lightweight," I accuse, my throat tightening, because if I had it my way, time would be paused forever, and no one would get to go to sleep ever again.

"Don't be silly. I have a guest bedroom."

"Couch is fine," she says. "I like to be close to the ground."

"You live on the third floor," I laugh, passing her a soft chenille blanket from the airing cupboard. For some reason, I'm afraid to ask but I do. "Was that your boyfriend I saw . . . at the flat?"

"One of them."

"You have more than one?"

She raises her eyes to the ceiling. I can sense the exhaustion, but I can't have the night end yet, I just can't.

"It was a joke."

"I don't understand men," I say. "I mean, I like them well enough, but I'm not sure what to *do* with them. What about you? Do you have family?" This is artless, messy. I hear all my words running into each other.

"I'm knackered," she says, giving me a sideways glance.

"I don't have family, either," I continue breathlessly. "I don't have anyone, really. But you learn how to do it, don't you? You learn how to survive."

"Whoa," she says, flicking up her hand. "That's a lot for this time of the morning."

A wall rises inside me. I might cry if I weren't so high. I hang there, not quite knowing what to do. And then I say the thing I shouldn't.

"What?" she goes, shaking her head.

"Don't you want children?" I repeat, a little desperately.

A darkness comes over her face as she sits up even more on the couch, regarding me for a moment or two.

"I'd *hate* that," she says, looking me dead in the eye. "That isn't for me at all."

I am using all my might to not say the thing in my head, but the coke and God knows what else has hold of me, in a way I can't avoid.

"How do you know?" I demand. "You can't know," I say, approaching her.

Her face closes over.

"Let's save that for another day, babe."

I nod my head. Or shake it. I'm not sure.

"I'm sorry. I'm sorry. I'm high. I'm just talking. I don't mean to be a downer.""

Serene takes me in, as if working out a sum.

"You might just be coming down. Yeah, I think you're crashing, babe. Should I go home?"

"No!" I tell her, more forcefully than I mean to. "It's totally okay to sleep here. Look, I'm going to bed, I promise. Stay here." She nods and I set about finding a pillow for her, and some flannel pajamas to sleep in. When I hand them to her, she regards them, wordlessly.

"Goodnight," I say.

"Night," says she, after a few delicate seconds.

Leaving my door a little ajar, I strip my clothes off and climb into bed. There I lie awake, feeling worse than a person has ever felt. In fact I have never felt so alone. I can feel my insides drumming on my ribs. From the living room I can make out a distant mumbling, as though she might be on the phone. Then, after a while, silence. I sleep, or, I close my eyes and go somewhere or other and it is fitful. Incomplete.

• •

A couple of hours later, it is bright, too bright. I wake to the sound of her moving about in the bathroom. It feels so very right—*my mother in my house.* I stay there for a while, enjoying how this strange thing feels. When the movements stop, I pad into the living room. She's dressed and ready to leave. She has stuffed one of my towels in her bag, her hair piled on top of her head, that crazy orange coat burning my sofa. She is wearing my favorite lipstick, the one that lives in the bathroom.

I feel the fog catching up. I feel the nearly blue.

"I'm sorry if I said anything weird earlier," I tell her, looking at the space between her cupid's bow and the curve of the full lower lip.

"God," she says, shrugging it off. "Coke makes everyone talk shit, really, don't worry about it."

"Still, I'm sorry I talked so much."

"I wouldn't know if you did. I black out a lot when I drink," she says, raking her fingers though her head of hair. "You could have told me I was anywhere and there's a chance I'd believe you. You could have said we went across the sea to France."

Though I know exactly what she means, it sounds dangerous coming from another body. I want to ask her why she would overdo it, but then she might ask the same of me and who knows the answer to that?

It is seven fifty-four. I call her a car. If I were not so disturbed, I might almost be excited. My real-life mother came to stay. My real-life mother's skin touched the place I am touching right now. My real-life mother came into my house. The blanket I gave her is folded on the couch. I hold it to my face. Still warm.

DEMPSEY DOESN'T LIKE
THE SOUND OF THIS

"I don't think the tea is working," I say to Dr. Rayna Panelli, who I can tell is only half listening. The doctor is positioned directly opposite me, staring in concentration at something that isn't me. Her phone is balanced inside of the book that she is holding; I can spot it in the reflection in the window.

"I'm pretty sure it isn't working. I'm not calm at all. In fact, I might even be more anxious than usual."

"That can't be," coos the doctor. "Stick with it. And double the dosage. Maybe you're mixing it a little light. Make sure you let it strain for at least two hours. Are you following along with the breathwork files?"

I am not. There's a problem with the files. Once they hit my computer, I can't get them to load.

"Most days," I lie.

"I can tell, Dempsey, I can tell," she says in her lilting accent. "Good work. Are you keeping up with the tinctures?"

Things are getting quite out of hand with the tinctures in my cupboard. There are now thirteen glass bottles stuck to the bottom of my overhead shelf in the closet, a brown ooze forming underneath them. And I can't remember which plant I'm supposed to be taking for which ailment. I don't even like opening the cupboard door anymore.

"Yes," I nod. "I'm alternating. It's just . . . well, there are so many of them."

"All essential," says the doctor. "We need to heal your nervous system and your insomnia." The difficult thing is that I don't have insomnia. It's more like the opposite. I think she is mixing me up with someone else. Still, I'd rather not contradict her.

Dr. Rayna's office is tonal but nothing at all like Clara's. She is a glowing example of how you do minimalism right. Her décor is beige and golden, a little like Dr. Rayna Panelli herself. She is just about as tall as Clara with huge almond eyes and subtly placed gold jewelry resting against her collarbone and the fleshy olive lobes of her ears.

"Also," she says, "I think you need my book, right?"

I panic. "I thought I had all of them."

"That's right, you do, that's right. But I don't think you have them on audio. It sometimes helps to hear the affirmations in my voice. Look, I'll give you a discount. There's a bonus hypnotherapy section and some ambient sounds. They'll help with the PTSD."

"PTSD?"

She purses her knowing lips and nods a little, and I hand over the forty pounds.

"I don't think I have a CD player," I whisper, knowing full well I don't.

"Where there's a will there's a way," she replies, still looking at her phone.

I'm too embarrassed to argue. I have way less money than anyone should at my age, and I'm trying not to draw attention to that.

"And what of your sister?" says the doctor. "How is she?"

"Doctor Rayna." I shake my head, raising my hands to the sky. "She's keeping on with this fantasy. She's convinced! Last Saturday she sent me this insane section from her book, but it was all written out in handwriting that she says is our mother's . . ." I stop to catch my breath. "And then she called me a bitch, and it was just awful. I think she's fully gone crazy. I really do."

The doctor looks at me, and I realise I've used a wrong term.

"Not *crazy*, you know . . . I didn't mean to use the word *crazy*, but you know what I mean."

Dr. Rayna Panelli nods at me again, the expression on her face enigmatic. She leans forward, puts the phone away. The tops of her breasts, bronze orbs.

"Your sister is experiencing some emotional distress. Confusion, you say?"

"Confusion for sure, yeah."

Dr. Rayna stares at the window behind me and sighs.

"Have you thought any more about the retreat, Dempsey? Places are filling up quickly and I'm holding a space for you because I think that, given our explorations, it'll be so, so valuable to you. We have healing circles, space to share and be seen and held. I've done it each year for the past three. It's a very safe and loving place to be."

There's no way I'll ever have the five hundred pounds for her retreat.

"I still have that work conflict," I tell her.

"Let's talk more about it next week," says the doctor.

• •

On the way back from her office, I stop into a cookware shop and stare longingly at the juicers. Jack Spratt says the right smoothie maker will change your life. I find the model he was talking about, which is more or less the same price as the doctor's retreat. Both distant dreams for now. By the time I get back into the flat, Dr. Rayna Panelli has already emailed me a twenty-five-percent-off discount code and reiterated that it won't be the same without me.

Just then, someone knocks on the door.

No one ever knocks on the door but the Amazon people.

I open the door to see Marcus standing there, holding two silver triangular things.

"Come in?" my mouth says, before I can stop it. He thinks about it for a second, then decides against it.

"Just wanted to say thanks for the cake. We all loved it. God, you make good cake."

"You're welcome," I say, my face burning up.

"You left in a rush," he says. One of his eyes has begun to run. He places a hand over his eyes. "Sorry. Allergies," he says.

"Were you okay?" I ask without thinking. "Were you okay at the party?"

He makes a face like he isn't sure what I am talking about. Someone passes us on the steps, and he draws a little closer, towards me, inside of the doorway. We are almost touching now, and I feel a current of recognition enter my body.

"It was a lot of fun in the end," he says. "Everyone round here is really lovely."

I feel like telling him they aren't at all, but he'll find out for himself soon enough.

"Anyway," he says, still not crossing the threshold. "Saved you two slices." He passes over the foil-wrapped triangles.

"That's sweet," I tell him. "Thank you. That's sweet."

"What's on the agenda for today?" he says, peering beyond me into my home.

"I have a lot on," I sigh, trying to sound like a busy person with too much to do.

"Yeah?" he asks. "What *is* it that you do?"

"I'm a writer," I say in a voice that is not mine.

"Wow. What kind of writer?"

"This and that. Articles mostly. About various things."

He shifts his weight on his left foot.

"What kind of things?"

"Wellness."

"Ah, a health nut," he says. "Well, it shows. It shows."

That's a reach. He turns to go and thinks.

"I might have a gig on Sunday night. You want to come? Bring friends. I need people to come."

"Can I think about that one?" I ask him, as per Dr. Rayna Panelli's instructions for situations where someone asks you a thing that you don't know, a thing that causes discomfort.

"I'd love to see you there," says Marcus, looking at me as though I'm a very curious object.

"Perhaps," I say. "I'd like to come. Thanks for thinking of me."

The questions are doubling and multiplying as he turns and ascends the concrete stairs. Can I show up alone, like I did to the party? Things never work out for me where other people are concerned.

The only person I might call is Clara, who is in what you could call a crisis and even if she was not in what you could call a crisis, Marcus might be all taken with her.

Even though she isn't as pretty as usual, with that terrible punched eye. This is what Dr. Rayna Panelli would call Future Tripping, but it is a very real possibility.

• •

It is now more than an hour after Marcus left, and I can't stop thinking about Clara. I need to go and visit her; and no matter how much I fight myself, the instinct won't leave me alone. So much is wrong with her—and the problem with being a twin is that the pain is always shared. Some things are just too acute to ignore, too loud to pave over with errands and Instagram and podcasts. I try to get rid of the thought by cleaning the house, but it will not let me be. Somewhere between vacuuming the corners of the living room and spraying dust repellent onto the worn skirting boards, I give in.

Clara's house is thirty-five minutes away by bus. I read Pema Chödrön's *When Things Fall Apart* the entire journey, because everything's a mess and Pema knows just what I'm talking about.

• •

It is one forty-six.

"Were you burning something?" I ask my sister, once inside her house, with my shoes off. There's a scent I cannot name—steamy, almost damp. I pray it isn't my feet.

"No," snaps my sister. "Want a tea?" We are sitting on her sofa in the near dark. The TV is playing a sitcom with the sound too low to make out.

"Only if you're having one."

"I'm not," says Clara, and doesn't get up. She is puffy under both eyes and her face looks drawn.

"I'm more than a bit worried about you," I tell her.

She studies the awful socks I am wearing and sighs. "Dempsey . . . I know it sounds . . ."

"Wait," I say, suddenly sensing someone else. "Is someone here?"

My sister smiles a secret smile, looking in the direction of her bedroom, and I suddenly feel quite foolish. What was I thinking, showing up here unannounced? "Why didn't you say?" I whisper, sliding my feet out of view. "I'm sorry. I wouldn't have come if I knew you have company."

"Calm down. It's just you and me," says my sister.

"Oh." I look around. This smell of the outside is getting in my throat. "Do you want to open a curtain or a window?"

"No," she says.

A horrible thought occurs. I want to ask, but I'm afraid of the answer.

"Was *she* here? This . . ." I can barely get the name out. "This *Serene* person?"

Clara smiles, a detached look settling on her. Her eyes go kind of unfocused and I'm not going to lie, it freaks me out.

"Maybe. And next time, call first, yeah? What if I hadn't been in? I mean, it's impolite. What if I *was* indisposed, Dempsey?"

My sister turns her face away from the light, still looking right through me. A bleak feeling comes over me and I have to say it. I do.

"Clara," I begin, feeling the dread in my bones. "Remember what happened to you when we were younger?"

She sniffs the air. Coughs a bit. "Clara, I'm scared the same thing might be happening again."

No answer. She turns her head all the way to the left, away from me, so I am facing the back of her head. The movement is unexpected, a little unsettling, as though the head could spin the whole way round.

"Can you be more specific?" says the back of the head.

But I know what I'm saying. I won't be put off. "That time in the sandpit?"

The owl snaps around to look at me now, her eyes filled with a memory.

"Yeah, but I barely remember that now."

"But you remember what you saw?"

"'Course I remember."

"You sure?"

"Yes," says my sister. "I could have sworn I saw our mother."

"Exactly," I say. "And she was seven, same as we were at the time, right?"

"Yes," says my sister. "Oh, Dempsey, I was seven. Who knows what I saw if anything? It was so long ago."

"You've just said that you remember." She chews on a grown-out gel nail.

"Look, do *you* accurately remember everything that happened when you were seven, Dempsey?" Clara is a master deflector, but I won't be put off.

"How did it feel?" I want to know.

"The same," my sister says.

"Right," I say, trying to make my voice soft. "And, Clara . . . it wasn't her, was it? It couldn't have been, could it?"

She is playing with the blanket on her sofa. Finally, she looks up at me, exasperated, and hits the sofa pillow with force.

"I don't know, Dempsey," she snaps. "Then was then and now is now. You have no business telling me what I saw and didn't see!"

"It was you who said you felt the same. What I'm asking is *what* same?"

"I don't know, Dempsey! Alive?" Clara shouts. "Believe what you want to, okay? You didn't see her. You've never seen her. Maybe that's the reason she's never appeared to you? You're not open! You're so full of fear about everything!"

She's right about that one.

I want to tell her that I do not feel good about this. I want to tell her that this person feels wrong wrong wrong. Instead, I look at her, feeling I have lost all hope of something, most likely forever.

"Sometimes, Clara, sometimes I just . . . I wish we were *sisters*. I wish I knew you at all."

I am expecting her to scoff, or at least to shoot me a look of derision, but she shrugs and says, "Well, I wish the same thing, you know, Dempsey." There is a some hollow quality in her voice—in the vowels. I want to reach out and hold her hand, but I don't, because *we* don't.

"Anyway how are you? Have you been well?" she asks me, out of nowhere, which is a very weird thing to say, given the conversation of the last fifteen minutes. It is the kind of thing you say to a person you don't know, not at all. I decide to tell her.

"I'm seeing someone."

"A man?" she says, straightening up as though she can't believe it, which irks me plenty. "You're seeing a man?"

"A counselor."

Clara relaxes back in her chair because this is more believable, apparently. I tell her about Dr. Rayna Panelli and her studio of gold and her beautiful hair and commanding voice and strong eyebrows. I'm supposed to go on some kind of retreat, I tell her, but I don't feel like going, and anyway it costs a fortune. I don't know why I tell her all this, maybe in the hope that if she isn't already seeing a therapist, she might consider. But Clara's body language has already changed. She is looking at me as though I am the one who deserves pity.

"You fancy your therapist," she says, bursting into horrible laughter. She throws her head back. There is a mark on her neck. A bite?

"Only you, Dempsey! That's classic *transference*, you know. It isn't very original."

"No!" I almost scream it. "Clara, that's not it at all! She's really helping . . ."

Clara sings at me, pointing at my skirt area, "Yooooou want to fuck your therapist."

"Clara!" I want to cry, "I'm not gay."

"More fool you," says my sister. "*Gay* would be interesting. Gay would make you make sense."

"Are *you* gay?" I ask her.

"Sometimes. How much is the retreat?" she asks, sounding more like herself again, and when I don't reply she says, "Go on, how much d'you need?"

"I'm really not trying to go," I say, feeling defensive. "That's not what I came all the way here for, Clara."

"Uh huh," she says, looking me up and down. "What else am I supposed to think? You never visit."

Shame floods my body. I try to shake it off, to get us back on track.

"Clara, the . . . the woman who hit you . . ."

"Her name is Serene, Dempsey. Serene. Think you can remember that?"

You need so much patience to deal with my sister. You need so much. Too much.

"Yes, her," I continue, being the bigger person. "I just wanted to tell you, it's textbook, what you're going through. Our mother was troubled. It sounds like whoever you're in touch with is troubled too. I'm worried, Clara." I feel like telling her it Isn't Very Original, but I wouldn't dare. I take another deep breath because the next thing will be hard to say.

"Clara, I really think that you should see someone."

As if hearing me from faraway,
as if slowly understanding,
my sister stands up.

"What," she says, "is there to be worried about?"

"She gave you that black eye."

"It was a misunderstanding. Honestly, Dempsey, you're ten steps behind. Always have been."

I have a thing about being called an idiot, so I don't say anything. I want to ask about the drugs, and why her eyes look so dull. I want to ask about the candles she is burning because the room smells musty. I want to ask about the lipstick she is wearing, because she looks too made up to be staying in, and also, she looks a mess, but my sister stands up, her frame towering over me.

"I have somewhere to be. If you'd only called first, I could have saved you the journey."

"Of course," I say, feeling ashamed again, and struggling to my feet. "Yeah, of course. Sorry."

"Have fun with your therapist," she mutters as I pass her in the doorway, and as our eyes meet, hers gleam. I feel the terrible urge to karate chop her twice, in the throat. Not that I would know how to do that.

By the time I get home, there's a voice note via email welcoming me to the retreat. In her silken tones, Dr. Rayna Panelli thanks me for settling the balance and tells me she's thrilled to be hosting me at the weekend. "It's a place where people make friendships for life," the doctor purrs. "Also, your sister is a dream!"

Sometimes, I think, opening my fridge door, *I could happily decapitate my sister.*

I select an oven-made vegetarian taco from my fridge and go to warm it up, then decide against it, because I no longer have an appetite. I don't feel like porn or junk food or even buying anything online. Everything feels like too much effort.

It is just past five. There is Marcus. Marcus exists. I could thank him for the cake, let his stare warm me a little. I climb the stairs, palms already wet, pulse beating in my ears. I stand at his door, breathing in a familiar scent. There is a Wailers sticker on his door, a red, gold, and green welcome mat on the floor. I knock, but no one comes. Inside, I hear snoring.

DEMPSEY'S RETREAT

On Thursday afternoon, I make it to the train station with seventeen and a half minutes to spare. I timed it like this so there would be time to get one banana, one vanilla chai, one bottle of water, and two packets of vegetable crisps. My tummy is bloated for no good reason and I'm trying to be okay with it because self-love is really the only love you can depend on. I find the best-looking front-facing seat and pull on my headphones, trying hard not to look like the kind of person people want to sit next to. It always works unless the train is full.

"*Slow down*," Rayna Panelli murmurs, into both ears, and her tone resounds, caught in the place between my belly and groin. Marcus fixed the files and now they are loading just fine and I can hear exactly what the doctor is saying to me.

"Everything is perception."
"Life shifts according to what you believe."

Yesterday, Marcus seemed pleased to see me. I knew he was up and about because I heard his footsteps overhead. I had pulled on a new pink shirt and the only pair of jeans that will fit these days and decided to try him again. At the door, he looked a little dubious, eyes downcast. "I'd invite you in," he said. "But last night got a little out of hand, so the flat's a complete mess." I stared at his stubble rash. "No problem," I said, feeling my own face get hot. "I have to get back anyway, in the middle of troubleshooting."

"Troubleshooting what?"

"Ah," I said, waving it away. "Nothing important. Stupid computer stuff."

"I'm fairly good at stupid computer stuff," said Marcus. "I built my entire studio." Then his mouth was moving. I watched his irises bloom like moons.

"I have a weird little brain," he was saying. "It's going to kill me one day. I have terrible headaches. I can't remember what I go upstairs for, and I can't really spell, but I'm very good at troubleshooting. Cars. Telephones. Video games. Computers. Want me to take a look?"

I nodded my head.

Well, I wasn't going to say no, was I?

In my kitchen, we had mint tea sweetened with orange blossom honey, right from Jack Spratt's mother's orchid. She has a site on Etsy with pickled things, homemade condiments, and sugar-free cookies. All of which I've purchased at some time or other. I want a mother like that. It isn't fair. Marcus bent over my computer, brows knitted in concentration. One of his locs kept touching my elbow. Usually, unexpected sensations like this freak me out, but I stayed exactly where I was, enjoying the scratchiness every now and then.

"Okay," he said, finally, breathing out through his lips. "Your default opener was all wrong. And you needed some updates. That's all it was."

He sat up straighter. The loc left my skin and I wanted it back. Then came Dr. Rayna Panelli's voice, all-knowing.

"Everything is a multitude of things. A lifetime of things."

Marcus looked at me.

I looked at him.

"I have to be getting back to clean this flat," he said. "It's a nightmare."

Can I help you? I nearly asked. In any way, can I help you?

But no, Marcus got up

and then I got up.

When we said goodbye at the door, the moment felt full of meaning. I thanked him and, for some reason, threw my arms around his body, though I never hug anyone. Though he seemed a little hesitant, he hugged me back, and I felt his tight body sag against me. Then he pulled away, winked, and left. I wanted to smash my own face in. How desperate, how pathetic.

In thirty-five full minutes we'll be at the destination. A knot has been forming in my stomach ever since Clara paid off the balance, because now I will have to go to this damn place and *get to know people*, which is my least favorite activity. I know I will have to act NORMAL, meaning FAKE. Outside the train window, the patchwork of green and yellow fields unfolds, spreading endlessly alongside the tracks. I decide that I will need to play at being someone else, someone open and generous and relaxed in their skin. Someone who will walk tall and smile as widely as Marcus does and make other people feel comfortable. I make a list of things to say in case my mind goes blank, which always happens.

"Hi, ladies!" I'll say, "I'm Dempsey!" Then I will give them all firm but not crushing handshakes, because that is the mark of a confident woman, the kind of woman you can count on and the kind of woman who will definitely not resort to cruelty.

"Hi, ladies," I will say, beaming. "What are all your names?" When they give me their names, I will not show that I am terrified. I will laugh in a very self-deprecating fashion, hand on my forehead, and say, "God, I might have to write this all down, I'm hopeless with names, I tell you!" and then I will actually go and write them down so I can use their names every time I am addressing them and each of them will know that not only am I the kind of woman you can count on, but also a person who listens. I will be animated, an active listener, making sure that I am mirroring, and ENGAGING, because people really like that. Now that I have a plan, I eat the last of my vegetable crisps, folding the packet into a neat square. I practice my Marcus smile on an old woman who is stealing glances at me from across the aisle. She doesn't smile back, but it doesn't matter what other people do. I can't control that.

ACCEPTANCE.

The buffer of time runs out. The billowing quilt of fields gives way to
a thicker forest with gnarled trees and flowering bushes of scarlet rho-
dodendron and marigold buttercups below. As advised in Rayna's email,
I alight the train at a town called Lost Embers and, lugging my over-
packed extra-large suitcase, walk the twelve minutes to a collection of
cabins set back from the main road. Someone has written,

THIS WAY TO THE WOMEN'S LODGE

in black marker on a lilac sheet of paper,
and someone else has crossed it out to say,

THIS WAY TO THE WOMB-MEN'S LODGE

and drawn a row of smiley faces. I hope the women aren't too raucous
because I close up around big personalities. I follow the arrows marked
under the sign, which lead directly to a large wooden suite. The door is
open wide and in there sits Dr. Rayna, dressed in loose cream-coloured
loungewear. She is writing on dainty blue place cards. On seeing me,
she smiles but doesn't get up, stretching to hand me a bottle of spring
water from her desk drawer. Her arms are toned, covered in dark blonde
peach fuzz.

"Dempsey," she coos, "I can't tell you how pleased I am to see you."

"Me too," I tell her, trying hard to seem light and carefree, like
the kind of black girl who goes on retreats in the countryside all the
bloody time.

"I've coordinated you a room with Sunny, Jen, and Sally," she tells
me. "I think you'll love them."

The knot in my belly becomes a rock.

"Dempsey," she says, touching me on the elbow. "You'll be fine."

"No, that's great, I'm excited," I say, avoiding her eye. Rayna goes in
her pocket and fishes out a blue keycard with a tree on it.

"For your room. Feel free to get settled, meet your roommates, take a walk around. The welcome dinner is at six thirty. Until then, the time is your own. See you soon, Dempsey."

I must be just standing there staring, because the doctor holds her pen over her workbook, smile fixed on.

"Everything okay?"

"Oh," I croak. "Yeah. Bye. See you soon."

As I trudge to the room, pulling the suitcase on its four wheels behind me, I try my best to rehearse the lines I wrote on the train, but the sentences are already jumbling up in my head. I stop before the door and take a moment.

Thank God! The women in the room are not as pretty as I feared. Well, two of them aren't. There is another Black woman in the corner, and she looks like a model or something. She nods her head at me and stares at my trainers, which I must admit are not great.

"Hi," says a small, ruddy-cheeked brunette, making her way over. "I'm Sally."

Sally is smiley and energetic, hair hanging over each of her shoulders in two thick plaits. Streaks of grey in her hair catch the light.

"Love the hair," I blurt out. "It's very . . . it's youthful."

Sally's eyes widen at this, then she smiles again, which is kind of her. "Want a chocolate bar?"

"Thank you," I say, accepting the Crunchie, though I won't be eating it. Sally nods and goes back over to her bed.

"I'm Jennifer," says a woman with an expensive-looking blowout, who is replacing the pillowcases on her bed with pink silk covers from her bag. I nod. I should have thought of that.

"I'm Sunny," says the Black woman. "What's your name?"

I turn to look at her. "Your name is Sunny?" I say.

"Yes," she says. "That's my name."

I smile, but it isn't returned.

Sunny is dressed head to toe in mustard and is wearing some kind of fedora and matching scarf. Not the kind of thing you'd expect at a retreat, but what do I know about anything? I take my sweater off my waist. Sunny assesses it and me and gives the other two women a look. If they understand, they pretend not to.

"Dempsey," I tell them, "my name is Dempsey Nichelle. But you can call me Dempsey of course. Or D! Ha. Pleased to meet you! God I'm hopeless with names but I'll do my best to remember them. I'll definitely remember yours Sunny, it's so unusual!"

No one says anything. The three women are laying clothes out on their beds, so I park my luggage by the remaining free bed and follow suit. I still feel Sunny's eyes on me, but I could be imagining things.

"How long have you all been working with RP?" says Sally, clearly the friendliest of the group. "Bloody amazing, isn't she?"

"'Bout three years now," says the woman called Jennifer. "You?"

"'Bout three months!" Sally laughs, and raises her hands, palms outstretched. "But I tell you, I'm all in."

"Same," I tell them, trying to laugh like Sally.

We look to Sunny, but she is back and forth, unloading her toiletries in the bathroom.

"Tell me about it," says Jennifer. "She's the best alternative life coach I've ever had. Fuck waiting a year and a half for clinical nonsense, am I right?"

"And unhelpful diagnoses," Sally puts in. "Really the NHS is in a terrible mess."

Sally and Jennifer start talking about finding themselves again and again in The Process and about The Process being nonlinear and I don't know what to say about this or how to say it, so I use this as my opportunity to fill up my sports water bottle, excuse myself and explore the grounds. Trying hard not to freak out about all the conversations I'm going to have to have with these women, I start off on a path winding through bushes of scarlet and large oak trees. Every now and then I'll touch the patch of skin that Marcus's hair grazed. I feel that the area is raised, a little angry.

•••

At dinner, we meet the three women bedding in the other room. Indigo and Jessica from Enfield and Toyah from Jamaica by way of Birmingham.

Dinner is butternut squash soup for starters and this weird black bread thing followed by a so-called botanical curry with quinoa that is so soft it's nearly stew-like. It's not great, but all the women who are not Black keep talking about how tasty and nourishing it is. It's hard to know whether they're just being polite. The doctor has us state our intentions for the retreat, everything we want for this trip.

"Intention is so important," says the doctor, and the women coo and look at each other and nod. The evening is muggy and we are flanked by two gardens, which accounts for the warm honeysuckle air surrounding us. There are all these flies buzzing around. I *hate* flying insects and forgot to pack any repellent. I zone out somewhere in between Jessica speaking about deep wellness, deep in the spirit, and Toyah talking about being mentally overextended with the children and the fourth child aka her husband *ha-ha*, because all I can think about is whether the flies will buzz around my head and make me look like someone from a cartoon who smells bad and whether my face looks normal enough, or if I am laughing in the right places and why the floor is uneven below me. I wonder what is wrong with me. Why am I sitting at this table, fearing the worst? Toyah must be feeling the same way, because she ever so gently enquires as to whether there might be wine available, to which Rayna smiles and shakes her head.

"I might have mentioned that this is an elevated mission," says Rayna, in a tone that you could almost misinterpret as mean. "I always find intoxication to be an escape. This trip in *itself* is an escape, don't you think, Toyah?"

"Right," says Toyah, looking a bit confused. "Right, yeah. Sorry . . . does that mean there's nothing else to drink here?"

Silly Toyah.

"That's what it means" says Rayna curtly.

"Right," says Toyah.

A fly lands on Rayna's water glass.
I watch the fly. Rayna watches the fly.

"And you, Dempsey?"

"Me?"

"Do you have anything to add?"

"Me?" I say again. "What, me?"

"What would you say has been coming up lately?" says Rayna, finally crushing the fly with her spoon. "What are some common themes?"

I look at the circle of women staring back at me and realise I can't say anything about anything because I don't know anything about anything.

"Can you come back around to me? Is that alright?"

"Dempsey," says Rayna, scolding me with her soft brown eyes. She knows far too much about everything, like the porn, and Kendrick, and being terrified of Clara Kallis and all the dark mess following us everywhere.

"Well, let me ask you a different question, then."

"Okayyyyy," I go, feeling like this might somehow get worse.

"How are you feeling right now? Right now, without any filters? There is no wrong answer. Be honest, Dempsey."

"Umm . . ."

The doctor sighs, and there is nothing more for it. She isn't messing about and I don't want her to get angry, plus I really need this to be over.

"Well," I say, "I kind of feel. . . . like, I feel . . . like, *ashamed*?"

The women shift in their seats.

"Okay," says Rayna. "I understand that you're experiencing shame."

"Yeah," I say. "Often, yeah."

"And right now?"

"Yes," I say, and feeling my truth opening inside me, I go on. "I'm ashamed of everything about myself. I'm always making it worse, I think."

"Now we're getting somewhere. Define *worse*," says the doctor, leaning forward. "If you can."

"Sometimes I feel ashamed," I say. "For being what I am, if that makes sense."

"What are you?"

Sunny yawns loudly, but the rest of the women are silent, invested.

"Oh, nothing," I say, wishing everyone else would disappear, so there would be only myself and Rayna. "Nothing at all. That's just it, I think. Sometimes I just . . . I think I'm nothing."

Rayna allows for more dramatic silence. She narrows her eyes. She leans into the middle of the table. Offers her hands for me to take them.

I indulge her. Her hands are hotter and harder than one would think.

"And do you see how untrue that is?" says Rayna, her voice syrupy, not letting go. She turns to the group.

At once, I imagine myself unclothed and on my knees before her. The image presses against me and will not leave.

"Dempsey is anything but nothing, isn't she?" the doctor is saying to the group. There is a hum of assent. Most of the women are smiling kindly at me. I daren't look at Sunny.

"You see, I'm not discounting your experience. I want you to know that. I'm simply reflecting back a story you are telling yourself." Beside me, I see Sally and Jennifer nodding in rapt agreement. Dr. Rayna talks some more about new and old stories and transformations. I try to move the other thing from my mind. In the distance, I see the fireflies blinking.

"And of course, thank you for sharing, Dempsey," Dr. Rayna is saying. "We'll touch some more on that."

"Okay," I say, wondering if it's possible to feel any more stupid. Sally starts talking about her husband, and how he doesn't know anything about her even after twenty-four years! He buys her random, "useful" things for her birthday, like garden shears and bifocals, when all she'd really like is a weekend away, or a pendant. He just doesn't have a clue. Sunny tells us that everything is going well in her life, like things are really on the up and up and that really, she is only on this retreat to connect with other like-minded souls, because it's hard to meet people for real in this digital age, you know? No one believes her, least of all the doctor, who only nods, staring ahead into the roses.

At night, you can hear everyone breathing, shifting in their beds. I watch Sunny's pink sleep bonnet shifting on the pillow.

• •

In the morning, we take a walk in the dark up through the gentle hills. We chatter, declaring that we are going to come together often, and we

will be friends and take on the shared nickname Womb-Men, and whoever messes with one of us, will have to deal with all of us. Even Sunny
agrees. Doctor Rayna seems pleased with this, with us. Hiking along
the worn dirt paths, seven sets of legs before me, I feel close to peaceful.
Hello, new life, I think as the dawn breaks. I look down, panting, holding my shins, because one thing I am *not* is in shape. After the morning hike, Indigo takes everyone's details and before I know it, I've been
added to the Womb-Men's Google group!

The trouble begins at lunch, when Rayna lets slip that the celebrated
author Clara Kallis is my sister.

"Oh, but *Evidence* is an absolute dream of a book," she explains,
banging her hands down on the table. "It's bizarre, but a book I'd like to
study. Tell me, does she often speak of timeline jumping? I'm deeply into
the concept, and others besides. You two must talk late into the night
about metaphysics and the like?"

This causes me to wonder if the doctor has actually heard anything
I've told her in our sessions about my sister. Still, I don't want to disappoint her, so I make my head nod.

"From time to time," I lie, trying to keep the conversation to a murmur. But it's too late. Sally has heard and whispered to the other two
roommates. In my peripheral vision, I clock them making the link.

Back at the lodge, they get it out of me.

"Clara Kallis saved my life," goes Jennifer, green eyes wide. "I mean
really, really, *really* saved it. Her first book was magical. I mean it's not
for *me*, per say, but I refer to it all the time to my POC clients when I'm
doing my life-coaching. I read it to my yoga students, too!"

"But this one," says Sally, "this current one. It's a novel, right? Based
on a true story?"

I nod my head, all the while trying not to wince. Jennifer wants to
know if there'll be a sequel. "More than likely," I tell them, trying to
sound like somebody who knows.

"I can't get into her books," says Sunny out of nowhere.

I look to the other women for support. There is a vaguely concerned
look on Sally's face. Jennifer stares at her shoes.

"Each to their own," says Sally, in a high voice. "Look, shall we all head to the lake?"

Sunny goes on as though she hasn't heard. "Yeah. I mean, isn't personal. I just didn't understand it at all. No offense . . . what I mean is I didn't know what it was trying to be."

"None taken," I say. "*I* didn't write it."

The other two sort of laugh politely, so I try to laugh it off too, but Sunny just stares at me, determined to make it awkward. Sally pretends to be looking in her bags for something.

"Yes," says Jennifer. "I think the lake."

"Was it time travel? I kept getting lost," Sunny goes on, not satisfied with having insulted us once. "Like, what she was dreaming or what? Was the boyfriend a figment of her imagination?"

"That doesn't make any sense," I say, wanting to punch her. "Could a figment of imagination get you pregnant?"

"But she doesn't have children, your sister, right? So how would she be qualified to talk about those things? Like, how would she know what post-natal depression is? Like, I'm a mother. *I* know what it is."

I've had enough now. "If you were reading correctly," I say, feeling my face get hot, "you would know that it isn't a memoir. It's fiction. I don't find it hard to decipher at all."

"Well, you'd be biased wouldn't you?"

Time for me to stand my ground. "Not at all. If it wasn't a masterpiece I'd say so. But it is."

"I'm just saying," says Sunny. "I suppose I couldn't follow it because, well, there are things that only mothers know. In a way I could tell that she was writing in another voice. It didn't ring true to me."

"Tell that . . . tell it to the *Sunday Times* bestseller list," I say,
                                             which is cheap,
                      but does the trick. Sunny shuts right up.

Sally shakes her head and gives me a she's-not-worth-it look. Later, everyone leaves for lunch, and when they do, I steal Sunny's toothbrush from her washbag and I think about cleaning the toilet with it or similar, but I'm not that kind of person, so I hide it away in my tote.

••

In the evening, around the campfire, we split off into two groups to do a team building exercise. It is a feelings association game in which we each have to act out everyday tricky communication scenarios and the thoughts that come up in the action. Like we have to explain to a friend who is always belittling us, that we want to end the friendship while only using I statements and never resorting to blame, or we have to tell our partner of ten years that we're not satisfied in the bedroom anymore without turning it into a catastrophe. I love games like this. I get to team up with Sally, Toyah, and Jennifer against Sunny, Indigo, and Jessica, which feels just about right. We win the task, although Rayna says it's less about winning and more about intergroup bonding than anything else. But we do win. Sally gets a bonus prize for tact and diplomacy, because she is able to make you feel good about anything, even if it's negative.

••

In the morning, Jennifer and I are the first to rise. We eat poached eggs (slightly too cold and runny) with rye bread and vegan butter and we giggle over the fact that Sunny says "me personally" before almost every other statement. I'm not great with words, but even I know you don't actually have to say "me" if you're saying "personally" because it is obvious that it's personal if you're the one saying it.

"Why would you diss a bestseller in front of the author's sister?" Jennifer laughs, rubbing sun cream onto her freckled arms. "Want some?"

"I know," I say, shaking my head. "No thanks."

"Black skin needs it too," says Jennifer, looking quite concerned. "I'm always telling my girls that."

"Oh, I know all about that," I tell her. "I have sensitive skin, that's all. I'm allergic to most lotions."

"What a rude bully Sunny is turning out to be," Jennifer suddenly says, pointedly.

I feel like asking her why she didn't stick up for me in the moment but then Jennifer clutches at my hands, looking aghast.

"Were you okay last night? I wanted to speak up, but she has a strong personality and I'm afraid I chickened about a bit. Dempsey, I'm sorry about that. I want to stay accountable."

"It's okay," I tell her, though I'm having trouble deciding whether it is or not.

Jennifer dips the tiniest bit of bread in her yolk and looks at it. "Are you close to your sister, then?" she asks, carefully.

"Close enough," I lie again. "You know we're twins?"

As soon as I say it, I wish I hadn't. New and improved Dempsey has a lot to learn. The look on Jennifer's face says it all.

"Twins!" she says, before she can help it. "No fuckin way!" Then, looking at me hard and trying to correct herself, "Wait! I see it now! But your energies are so different!"

I nod, and we both go quiet.

"What I mean is," says Jennifer. "What I mean is that you seem a little younger."

"I am," I say. "By three minutes and three seconds."

"Well, there you go," says Jennifer, wiping her mouth with the napkin.

• •

News travels quickly. I am accosted again at lunch, which is even more irritating than all the bug bites I seem to be accumulating on my wrists and ankles.

"Is your sister into this stuff?"

"Are you two fraternal, then?"

"Wait, what kind of twins are you if you are both women, yet not identical? Does such a thing exist?"

I field everyone's questions to the best of my ability. I am getting the worst-ever vibes from Sunny, who I feel sure hates me, for reasons unknown.

• •

For a closing ceremony, on Saturday night, the doctor leads us to a lilac-coloured gazebo inside the encampment. There are mats and cushions set out for us, and a blanket each.

"We're on our final evening," the doctor says, holding both hands up to the night sky. "And beloveds, I wondered if I might offer a little reflection."

We stay quiet, waiting for the doctor to bestow her unending knowledge. She takes her time about it, drinking the moment in. We can barely breathe for the anticipation. What will Rayna say? What conclusions has she come upon, given the time spent with all of us? What solutions might she offer?

"I believe," she begins, thoughtfully, "that a lot of us experience daily panic and fear due to early experience, due to misinformation about our desires. Oh, but we are goddesses. Goddesses of this land, and the lands beyond. Goddesses! I want you to really take this on board, take it to heart. We have powers beyond measure."

She pours us each a tiny cup of what she is calling a heart-opener tea, made from rose petals, chamomile, tulsi, and lavender. We sip it, and each nibble a dark, sharp bite of cacao.

"Sex magic is a real thing," says the doctor, "and did you know you could use it to manifest?"

I look around at the other women seated on the ground. Everyone is watching Rayna, who smiles at every one of us in turn. "I had planned to talk tonight about the stories we tell ourselves about truths that are constructed and mutable, but an *inspired action* has come up for me and I feel compelled to walk through this with you. I recognize that this is a little out of left field, but I feel sure that you might feel inclined to engage in a sensual meditation. Whatever that means for you."

The women look bemused as Dr. Rayna passes around tiny glass jars of what looks like an essential oil, smelling of geranium and patchouli. Everyone seems a little mystified. The expression on Sunny's face, however, appears to have soured. The doctor sits in the middle of us on a woven mat, cross-legged, smiling serenely. She thanks us for being here and trusting her and reads a passage about self-love and the sovereignty of our bodies from her newest book, *If You Wanna Be Your Lover*, the scented room lulling us into a deep sense of comfort, her voice hypnotic.

"Lie down, face to the stars, hand on heart," says the doctor.

We lie back on the hard wood floor, a rattan mat underneath our prone bodies.

"I invite you to journey inside," says the doctor.

I squint, looking around, feeling quite sure that the doctor isn't saying what I think she's saying. On instruction, we warm the oil in our hands. We massage our hairline and necks. We touch our chests and bellies. At first, the room feels tense and unsure. But then there is a change. Her voice begins to carry me away, to somewhere not here. Dr. Rayna starts on a part of the text that I know almost inside out. It is called

"A LETTER TO MY BODY, TO THE ANIMAL,"
BY RAYNA LAKSHMI PANELLI

"My darling body, I love you. I WANT you,"
begins Rayna,
with no sense of irony.
"How I marvel at the seat of your desire.
Your inner beauty and wisdom. How I buckle under the weight
    of your grandeur."

Toyah stifles a giggle, but Dr. Rayna is unperturbed. "It's alright to be nervous about this, sisters," she tells us. She loses me a little at the word "sisters." All I think about is Clara, and I suddenly realise that Sunny has Clara energy, which is why I hate her or why she hates me. Thankfully, she is on the other side of the gazebo, face covered with her fedora.

"My darling body," Rayna goes on. *"Goddess empress, child of*
    war . . ."
a bit much?
"lost child. Abandoned ship. My deep child, my chest of longing."
The next words that the doctor utters, I do not hear. I

experience them. This is the chorus I know, that we all
know . . .

> *"My beloved;*
> *my sanctity of divination,*
> *I call on you. I evoke my divine feminine*
> *my divine feminine.*

After the next seven, eight, nine, or ten divinations, we begin to
    relent,
and the air in the room cools. Next, we touch our chests, the
    insides of our thighs,
slowly, *deliberately*, without a sense of urgency or movement to
    the next place. Dr. Rayna gives us more oil than we know
    what to do with, but the oil is less of an oil and more like a
    slippery viscous substance that gives me all the slip I need.
    Underneath the blanket, I shudder underneath hands that
    I have felt a million times before, but never like this. I have
    never, ever touched myself with such,
well,
Love.
"Bring to mind a thing you desire," Rayna is saying.
"Bring to mind anything you desire and bring it close. Hold it
    before you."

Well I can't help it. First there is Jack Spratt, naked but for his baking
apron. He is beautiful and interesting to look at. I try to stop the other
thought from coming up. I try to focus on Jack Spratt, but nothing is
happening. Jack Spratt bending over. Jack Spratt touching my soft parts.
Jack Spratt tasting the place where I get wet, but nothing.

    I imagine the other women gone from the room. I imagine myself,
naked, lying flat, while Dr. Rayna Panelli watches me closely and tells me
I am nothing. Nobody. Nothing.

A world begins to build inside me; a small, delicious pressure, starting in my lower middle.

I see Dr. Rayna's firm hands working away at me under the blanket. They linger a while, and I feel that place in me, the pit, the core.

It hangs there for a while, beating against itself. Under the blanket thing, Dr. Rayna is still touching me, and has pulled my underwear aside, and will not stop. I feel my back begin to arch, as my body attempts to fight the thing.

not here, Dempsey. *NOT here,*
but

I am the first. The very first. I go louder and harder than I would like. The thing comes up through my toes and damn near knocks my head off. My orgasm has taken full hold, trembling and insistent, and I hear my own voice as if from a different universe entirely.

I am about to die, but then next to me, I hear Sally following suit, which is shocking and downright hilarious, and then Toyah, who emits a high-pitched squeak. Someone gets up and leaves. In the light window, I make out Sunny's glossy dark mane as she marches away and through the courtyard at high speed.

I lie there awhile, listening to the silence and waiting for the usual shame, but nothing. And then, after a few minutes, more sounds from the others. I turn onto my side and quietly survey the scene. Some of us perfectly still, some writhing, some settled in deep satisfaction. In the middle, on a cushion, Dr. Rayna, who has not moved from where she was, looks on benevolently.

What power.

After all that, we drink hot cocoa with honey and oat milk, careful not to meet one another's eyes. Dr. Rayna bids us goodnight and we trudge back to our respective cabins in silence, a thick balm settling over us.

"Well, that was interesting," says Sally at the door, and we all burst into embarrassed laughter. Her hands are shaking so much she can barely line the key up with the lock. Once inside, we notice Sunny's things are gone from the room and I smile.

"Something we said?"

I quip, and we all laugh.

••

Sunday is a long, decadent morning and afternoon, as mornings and afternoons go. Sally and Jennifer and I share a canoe after breakfast, and we row out into the middle of the still lake, looking back at the shore.

"You know," says Sally. "All jokes aside, I actually think last night might have moved so much that was blocking me. Several things. Frankly I didn't know I had it in me."

"Same," I put in. "It was so, so beautiful."

We nod. Above us, the birds make a V line in the sky.

"Can I share my truth with you, Dempsey?" asks Sally in a gentle voice. Usually when people soften their voice like that and get serious, I worry, because I know they're going to hurt me.

"I think you're incredible, Dempsey," says Sally.

"No," I tell her. "I'm really not . . . but it's so, so kind of you to say."

"You *are*," says Jennifer, who has been quiet and reflective until now. "Like, you have all this quietly wonderful stuff deep inside you."

"Yeah," says Sally. "Wish you knew it."

"I know you've gone through it," says Jennifer. "Not that I know what is true and what is fiction in the book, but it can't have been easy for either of you."

They have made me a little uncomfortable and they can tell, so we start talking about Sunny and we wonder how far she even could have got in the middle of the night, dressed like she was. I picture her next to the road, head to toe in mustard, hat and all, thumbing down a lift, and

I describe this in detail to Jennifer and Sally. The two of them howl, and I feel a little mean, but also very much part of the group.

Going back on the train that night, things feel easier, as though some of the heaviness has been lifted from inside me. I replay moments: how, this afternoon, I was more grounded and freer; I spoke a little about the pain of having a gorgeous sister who's always in the lime-light; I made some jokes here and there about it all; I even had Dr. Rayna laughing. Jennifer, Sally, and I have made plans to stay in touch outside of the Womb-Men's Group and check in with each other fort-nightly from now on, come what may. Even if we get really busy with work or there's a death in the family, we swore to each other, even then.

I arrive at my door ready to be New Dempsey. I will ask Marcus out this week, on a *date*, because it's bloody 2025 and I will go to his gig-thing tonight and be the kind of person who arrives on her own, has a great time, and leaves with the band members, throwing her head back and laughing at all the banter.

• •

Some hours later, Marcus phones down to let me know the gig is can-celled because his bandmate went into rehab. He asks if he can bring down some beers and wants to know if I smoke.

"No," I say. "It's awful for you."

"Not even weed?"

"I don't do drugs," I say. "Ever, under any circumstances." Marcus laughs.

When he gets to my flat door later, he laughs some more about it, and holds his hands up like I'm the police. He has left the weed behind but brings down some beers for himself. We watch a game show about peo-ple who have high-powered jobs but have forgotten how to connect with the Great Outdoors. One of the men can't even tie a knot! Pah! Marcus has large fingers. I bet he knows how to tie a knot or two.

We watch for almost two hours. Next to me, I notice his eyes rolling up in his head a little, his head bobbing. He has completely nodded off and has kind of leant his shoulder against my arm. I don't want to move, so I stay right there. I allow my eyelids to flutter a little too. Everything feels so very real, so very present,

until it doesn't. I wake up with a stiff neck, and the sudden understanding of loss. Marcus has gone back upstairs it seems. I wash the plates we used and climb into bed.

Things will only change when we do,
says the doctor.
Things will only change when we do.
I start to count all the ways I can be different . . .
a curvy Black woman who everyone likes because she is always
    jolly
a curvy Black woman who everyone likes because she doesn't
    take herself too seriously and is always, always smiling
    through it all
a curvy Black woman with a super-hot boyfriend; tall, so he
    doesn't make her feel fat,
not at all
a curvy Black woman who loves her family NO MATTER
    WHAT (will move mountains for them).

My sister comes into my dreams tonight and tells me I'm disgusting. She says I am so disgusting that she can't bear to be around me a moment longer. She packs all her stuff up and leaves the retreat and then later in the dream, I learn that I never had a sister. She was only ever a figment of my wicked imagination.

You have always been my only child, says Serene Marie Nkem Droste, back from the dead and smiling, smiling widely at me. Smiling wide, like heaven. *I never died,* she says. *What are you talking about and who the hell is this Clara person? You were always my Only, my most beautiful.*

OUT OF THE BOOK-VERSE
SHE COMES, SHE COMES

The heaviness inside abates on Wednesday, when I am driving home from the supermarket and see Serene's name flash up on my screen. It has been a week of radio interviews, unnecessary texts from Emma, and podcasts about change and wellness, grief and addiction, et cetera. I pull over at once, almost sick with anticipation.

"Fuck me," she says, as though we'd been talking as recently as five minutes ago. "Girl, I've been half dead for days. Talk about a hangover. Not twenty-nine anymore, I suppose."

I bark out an odd laugh, new life flooding into me.

"Thank you for letting me crash," she goes on. "God, we were totally fucked up the other night."

"We were," I say, letting the breath escape my mouth. "Totally."

The motorist behind me speeds by, giving me the finger. I place the call on mute and scream, "You're a fucking prick!"

"I was thinking," my mother's voice begins.

I feel it touch the backs of my legs, the sides of my ribs, all across my collarbone.

I pull over onto a residential street, sticking my head out of the window. Beads of sweat form on my hairline. Above me, the clouds are lined and iridescent. She lets everything go quiet.

"Tell me. What were you thinking?"

The sky is blooming blues, almost too much. Almost neon. For a moment there are only the birds, the bad blue and the sound of our breath.

"Well," continues my mother, "about you, your book and all the things that you talk about. I'm just gonna come right out and say it, Clara."

I wonder if she's going to talk about the numbered list, about the thing I saw in the letter. I wonder about the penalty for plagiarism. Might she sue me for such a thing? Might she blacken the remaining eye? A plane is flying low overhead.

"Please do," I say, trying to still my voice. "What's wrong?"

A plane is flying low overhead.

"Well, do you feel in line with that stuff that you are doing?" my mother says. "Like, do you feel you're making the most of things?"

"Making the most of things how?"

"You'll tell me to shut up if you want?"

"Yeah," I say, though I never could. Never ever.

"You're visible now. Very. Right?"

"Right," I say.

"People know who you are, right?"

"They do."

"People recognize you in the street."

"Only sometimes," I say, not quite knowing where this is going. "If I'm in the city."

"Right. Isn't there more you'd want to do? People you want to work with, clothes you want to wear? Don't you want to go on a better tour, given how popular you are right now? Because I'm not gonna lie, from where I'm sitting, your dates look weak, and the venues are not saying anything much. Don't you have someone working on this?"

I nod my head, even though she can't see me. It is everything that I have been thinking, but no one has ever asked about it before, and the fact that my mother the stranger is asking me about this is love indeed.

"I suppose," I say. "Instead of doing small venues in bookshops, I might like to do a few bigger things. Like the things I see other authors doing."

"Okay, like what?"

"Maybe some bigger places, outlets and stuff. Maybe . . ."

"One thing I learned," says Serene, "is that people close to death always wish they had taken more risks." The plane is so loud I can't be sure I just heard what I heard. "What?"

"I just mean think bigger," she shouts. "Think bigger, Clara."

"Tate House? Royal Albert Hall in London?" Then, for some reason, I laugh.

"What's funny about that?" snaps my mother. "I told you, you need to think bigger. Anyway, what's Tate House? This here in London? Never heard of it."

"It's a venue a lot of writers go to. It's fairly prestigious. But they book far in advance, and . . ."

"I'm looking it up now."

"Okay," I say, imagining the plane flying low enough to take me out. Clipping off my head.

"What are you doing this afternoon?" the voice on the other end of the line is saying.

"I have a fitting later this evening, but now I'm on my way home."

"I'll come over."

"Yes please," comes out before I have time to stop it.

• •

An hour later, Serene is tapping away on my laptop. I watch from the sofa as she types a number into her phone. Shortly after, she leaves the room. When she returns, she looks smug, more than a little cruel.

"What *is* this publicity team of yours doing? Tate House is interested. They have a space in ten days. They'd love for you to fill it."

"What do you mean? That's impossible. There's a whole process to it. You have to book so far in advance for a booking like that."

"That," says my mother, "is a very limiting belief, Clara. As I said, you have a date in a little over a week. I can work on finding you an interview partner, but that's gonna be easy."

I shake my head at her, trying to let this one sit.

"I don't have a pessimist mentality like your PR, agent, whatever she is. They *know* who you are," says Serene, for good measure. "They know your reach. Anyway, I gave them her details to get things moving. They're gonna call her."

"I don't understand," I say.

"You don't need to," says my mother. "Worry about what you're gonna wear."

We go back on forth on this for a while, Serene being fixed on the opinion that my wardrobe needs "life support." Then my phone rings.

"Hiya," Emma is shouting, her voice nearly drowned by the London traffic. "I'm calling because . . . well, I just had a strange call from *Tate House.* They want to be added to the tour list as soon as next week . . . which is . . . crazy and . . . but . . . yeah, I don't remember speaking to them. Do you know anything about this?"

Serene motions for me to put her on speakerphone, which I do without thinking.

"Hello, Emma," drawls my mother, in a phone voice that sets me on edge. "I don't think we've met, Emma."

"Erm . . . I don't think we have," says Emma's voice. "Sorry, who is . . . who am I talking to?"

"I'm an associate of your client, Clara . . ."

"Kallis," I whisper.

"Kalise," says Serene, making a face. "I had a lead, so I followed up. I hope I didn't tread on any toes."

"Hmmm," says Emma. "Okay. It's just not how we do things—due to the fact that I have other venues to keep happy."

"Hmmm," goes Serene. "A conundrum, I'd say."

"Yes," goes Emma.

"But a great opportunity," says Serene.

"Typically . . ." Emma says, and then fumbles a little. "Typically, our in-house PR would deal with things at this level to avoid cross . . ."

"Emma, it's just that this venue is huge, and while the book is on the charts, I didn't want us to miss a trick."

"Well, it's great to have more forward motion," Emma finally admits. "If we can get the bums on seats."

"Oh, there's no *if*," says my mother. "And what a strange phrase."

"It's in ten days," says Emma, quietly.

"I only have to post about it once or twice," I call out. "And it'll be as good as done."

Emma falls silent. When she speaks next, her voice is a mask. "Then that's fabulous! I'm all for it."

"Oh, well that's useful," says Serene.

I feel a little guilty about all of it. Serene motions to me to speak.

"It's brilliant," I say, warmly. "A golden opportunity."

Emma must go, she says, to attend an appointment, and when Serene finishes the call, she makes a face at the phone and says "*bums on seats*" in a very Emma accent and we laugh.

"God. You might need to replace her eventually. Anyway, it's done."

"You sure we'll fill it?"

"Of course you will," says Serene. "You're you. You shouldn't question things so much. You were just on that late-night show, acting all weird. People love that. They lap it up."

I watch the shadows the trees are making on the pale wood floor, thinking how good it feels to finally have someone advocate for me.

"I needed that," I say to her, or to myself.

• •

Later, I have to go to a fitting on Bond Street, so Serene tags along and helps me go through the items that the brand will lend for my three-day publicity stint in Ireland. She nods her head or shakes her head and each nod feels wonderful, as though I have suddenly acquired a mother-friend and everything will turn out okay.

"No!" she says to the jersey dress. "Too blah."

"No!" she says to the oversized blazer and skirt combo. "Stop hiding in the box. It's *boxy*!"

"Not very modern, is it?" she says, of the white, flowing number.

"You might as well be wearing a head wrap and long earrings and teaching art history in some backwater town." For the Tate House reading, we decide on a green dress that makes me look dangerous and angular, like a cartoon villainess.

"This elevates you," my mother says, finally satisfied.

"I don't know," I say to the mirror. The dress looks theatrical in all of its structure. The top is a corset, the bottom a kind of fishtail thing.

"It'd look better on you," I tell her. "I'm losing too much weight." She considers this, saying nothing. I shudder a little as she watches me in the dress. The shop assistant nods her head furiously.

"She's right, girl," she says, nodding. "If you've got it, flaunt it. What's the occasion?"

"She's a famous author, soon to be famouser," says my mother, "and she needs to step it up."

"You go girl," says the shop assistant, not knowing what else to say.

When we have taken more clothes than I can possibly wear in such a short time away, I take us out to dinner to talk things over.

"Do you still want to write?" I ask her. "We could work on your story together if you like. Call it a thank-you."

Serene shakes her head. "I learn best by observation," she says. "Words don't really teach, you know."

The server brings us prawn crackers, white wine for me and a mojito for Serene.

"You were asking about my boyfriend," says my mother, taking a rather large gulp of her moss-coloured cocktail "The other night. I was too high to talk, but I think I remember."

"Oh yeah?" I've been trying to forget it.

"Well, he's into some sketchy stuff."

"Oh?" I say, biting my cracker, though this is no surprise.

"White-collar stuff."

I wonder if I could imagine anything remotely "white collar" about the meathead and his friends.

"Naturally," she says. "I'm not going to stay with him. He was a stopgap."

The spring rolls arrive at the table. I add two to my plate at once, wondering why she's telling me all this.

"Okay," I nod. "Good." There suddenly occurs a thought so dreadful, I can barely keep it in.

"He hasn't ever hurt you?" I said, "Simeon? He hasn't ever . . ."

For a moment, her eyebrows dart up, then she lowers them, leaving a slight crease in her forehead.

"Did I tell you his name?"

She adds a spring roll to her plate. Her face relaxes and I see a flash of Dempsey for a brief but significant second. Then I see flashes of myself, only somehow more daring, and energized. She turns, outlined in the peach and gold of the restaurant lighting. When she gets up to use the bathroom, it is almost as though she floats.

While my mother is gone from the table, I try to think of how to play this. I must get a stronger grip on what is happening. I must know if she knows what I know. I wonder if she feels anything of this exquisite, romantic pull. I can't risk it. I'll play it stoic. I'll listen to all she has to say. I'll become a confidante. I need to know more and more and more. I won't ask ridiculous questions about boyfriends and families and having babies. I'll be cooler than cool.

But my body is not in the mood to listen.

"Tell me," I blurt as she approaches the table. "I want to know why you are helping me like this."

She stares at me. A dead stare. A stare that makes me wonder if there is carpet underneath me, or whether I'm balanced on uncertain ground. She takes her time sitting down. Picks up a water glass. Takes a long sip. Places it back on the wet ring. Under the table, my legs start to do an involuntary jumping thing. I press my knees down with both hands.

"When you broke into my house," says my mother, "I think I liked it."

"What do you mean?" I ask, leaning in, nearly breathless.

"Well, I knew I had to know you. I had to follow the feeling. I think you're talented. Gifted. It's as simple as that."

I wonder if it really is as simple as all that. Does she know more? Is she trying to throw me off the scent? I decide that it's of no consequence. I wanted my mother, badly. Now I have my mother.

"Work with me," I say, watching the frosting on the glass. "In any capacity. Events, if that's what you're into. You're absolutely right, we should capitalize on this moment. I still can't believe you got me into Tate House." She regards me for a few silent seconds, considering this. "What I mean is, I want to help. And if you're in a situation . . ."

I almost touch her hand, but I don't. She looks at my fingers, catching this.

"What you mean is," says my mother, her voice even, "*I'd* be helping *you*. Don't wanna be rude, but you seem lost."

"A little lost is right." I admit. "To be honest, I need help, and have for a long time."

"I'll work with you if that's a true offer."

"Cross my heart," I tell her.

"Good," says Serene. "Can't just be the white girl, know what I mean?"

By the time we finish dinner, Serene has outlined a lot of the things she thinks I need and has listed them on a shared note between us on her phone.

"If you're going to be in this generation," says my mother, rapping her black nails on the table. "Really be in it. Really do it. You could be involved with so much more. Engage with your audience. Use everything for content. Record things, let us know what you are doing, wearing, eating, seeing. Optimize everything. I've got work to do if we're going to utilize every opportunity."

My mother the . . . PR person? I try to put it together with the woman in the dream house who promised to fuck me up. She tosses her head in a very *me* way and then, unflinching, "Shall we talk about a salary, then? I'm sorry, I'm direct."

"Of course," I say, my mouth full of prawn.

"You'll get used to it," she says, chomping loudly. She writes a number on a paper napkin and passes it to me over the table. I look at it, have to adjust, and we agree on a price that I guess she's worth.

"One more thing," she says. "I'll need a laptop. I've never had a Mac computer before."

A Mac computer. Strange way to say it. I nod, still squinting at the figure on the napkin.

Before we get up from the table, we have a photographer, videographer, clothing rental company, and social media person in mind to make things easier for me, which Emma has never thought to do. When I drop her off at Drinkwater Towers that night, I linger with my headlights off, a little out of sight, wondering where the night is taking her, wondering about the gravitational pull that wants to drag me up those stairs behind her to a place I might belong.

ON THE ROAD,
MOTHER AND ME

At the end of the week, Serene accompanies me to a small reading in Bristol. It is a polite and welcoming event, part of their summer literary festival. But this is no longer the kind of thing my mother or I have in mind. We've moved on. Serene rolls her eyes as we pull up to the venue. In the backroom, sitting amongst first editions and packaged books waiting to be shipped out to customers, Emma is balanced uncomfortably on a tall stool.

"Hiiiii," she sings, trying to smile as best she can, eyes on my mother. "Are you Serene? We spoke on the phone."

"I remember," says my mother, staring at Emma's shock of neon pink hair, and again at her patent green clogs. In the low light, Serene's face reminds me a tiny bit of Claudette.

"That's some outfit," says Emma, nodding her head at me, "It's . . ."

"Fabulous?" offers Serene.

Emma's eyes widen and she nods more, one hand on her plump stomach. "It is."

Outnumbered, she looks from Serene to me and back to Serene again. "Only, didn't we say we were going with the Lucy Ford outfit tonight?"

"I felt like tonight called for a different look," I say, turning my back to her. "I'll post Lucy's dress over the weekend when I'm out."

"I just need to text Lucy," says Emma. "I think she was expecting the posts tonight. It was an agreement, I think."

I suppress a flash of rage, since Lucy Ford never pays me to wear her stuff, so ought not to be making demands.

"You do that," I tell Emma.

••

"Amazing look," says someone in the audience. "I love the green on you."

"Thank you," I say, looking for Emma in the back row.

"You're welcome. I want to know about the shapeshifting in the novel. Sometimes it is as though you flew into bodies, bodies that were not your own?"

"Isn't every woman a hundred different women?"

The audience bursts into applause. I can't believe I get paid for this shit, honestly.

After the show and before the signing, we are in the back room to catch a breath, my mother nose-deep in her phone. Emma bounds up to us excitedly.

"Tate House is already sold out, Clara. I can't believe it!"

"As her agent," says my mother, "why can't you believe it?"

Emma's cheeks glow red.

Serene stands up and moves towards Emma, who steps back towards the sofa I am sitting on.

"I just think that's a strange thing to say, when you consider how many books have been sold already."

"I didn't mean *I can't* believe it," says Emma.

Serene takes her place beside me, shakes her head. "You didn't mean what you just said?"

I've never really felt much for Emma before, but she looks like she's about to cry, and I can't be having that.

"I think Emma was saying that we've never had anything sell out so fast," I put in, turning to Serene, who goes back to whatever she was doing on her phone, a shadow crossing her face. My stomach plummets. I'm beginning to feel the not-so-real feeling again, the feeling that everything might be singed around the edges, and I may need to stomp them out.

Once the signing is done, we're ready to get out of there. We say goodbye to Emma and walk over to the car. Serene's face is still clouded over. The thing in my stomach gains weight.

"Is everything okay?" I ask once we get in the car.

"If this is going to work," she says coolly, looking out of the window at the black trees ahead, "I need you with me. Never against me."

"Of course," I say. "I'm sorry."

"I can't work like that."

"I'm not against you," I say, putting on my seatbelt, but my voice has taken on a thinner, reedy quality. I don't sound like myself. I sound a little like my sister. Serene falls silent, and I beside her. But when we make it all the way to my house and she says, "I think I'll stay," I am relieved. I don't argue.

In the house, we drink a little bourbon, eyeing each other with suspicion. I can't stop getting up and walking around, tapping my nails on my palm. From the sofa, Serene says something under her breath and, rather than asking her to repeat it, I lower myself onto the ground and soon find myself sitting below her on a floor pillow.

"I want to thank you again," I tell her, not quite daring to look at her face. "For the way you took charge like that."

"It's what you deserve," says Serene. "Don't ever forget that."

We order a pizza and watch an episode of some Baltimore cop drama that Serene is really into. The floor is making my bottom go numb, but I don't want to move. As the TV casts light on her face, and she begins to doze, spreading her legs across the sofa, I watch my mother intently. She is the most beautiful person I have ever seen, though not in any manner that I can interpret. Close to me, her face becomes eerily familiar. I know then that I want to be where she is. Wherever that will take me. Her skin is slick, stretched, perfect.

"Mum," I mouth lightly, looking at her.

"Mother," I mumble.

"Mummy," I whisper, willing her to open her eyes, to wake and suddenly know me.

..

In the morning, Serene and I go to the home and garden centre because she says that my place has a dead energy that she finds difficult to work in. We buy succulents for my windowsills, which are otherwise bare. Next, we pick up four fragrant white orchids with petals ringed in violet. The man at the shop only looks at her, even though I'm the one handing over money. It is almost as though I am not there, which is a feeling I am unaccustomed to. I could be four again. Five, six again with my tall, commanding mother in a store, fading while she handles everything. It feels sublime to be *handled*. I give over my credit card and we buy dahlias in the deepest purple. I didn't even know they came in that colour. We buy plenty of wildflowers, too, to "add more dimension."

"Too much negative space in there," says Serene, blowing air out of her mouth.

We set the flowers into two large bags and I want to drive her all the way home, but it's rush hour, quicker for her to take the train. We walk together by the canal on the Kingsland Road. The next train isn't coming for twelve and a half minutes, so we sit on a bench by the station.

Outside, three teenagers are giving an old man the finger and shouting insults. The old man calls them "three little shits" and threatens to beat them up. The teenagers collapse into laughter and run away.

"How do you feel?" I say, out of nowhere. "About working with me?"

The old man is cursing now, at no one in particular.

"It's a job. I need a job," she says, looking somewhere in the middle of me. "What? Too honest?"

"No."

I try to look away, but her eyes have taken on the quality of two dark holes. I cannot shirk the gaze.

"What diagnosis did they give you?" she asks, finally.

"Diagnosis?"

"Yeah."

"What do you mean *diagnosis*?"

"At the children's home."

"I didn't go into a children's home," I tell her, too quickly. "I got adopted."

"Clara," says my mother, sounding impatient. She pulls out a dead balled-up leaf from my bunch and points it at me. "You talked about it the other night onstage. At length."

"No," I tell her. "I don't think I did. Did I?"

She nods her head yes.

"You said that you defeated the odds despite a personality disorder. You didn't say what it was."

"That doesn't sound like anything I'd talk about," I say. "Ever, ever."

"You need to watch yourself," says Serene. "Maybe less of the booze before heading onstage?"

I must look embarrassed, because Serene playfully pinches me. Hard.

"I don't believe in labels, C, but I'd like to hear what they said about my girl."

Her girl.

"You can tell me."

Keep it to yourself, Claudette had always warned. *You're a woman. You're a dark, just that little bit too tall Black woman. That's enough. Clara, it's enough.*

I clear my throat. Serene waits for me to speak.

"It's erm . . . borderline personality disorder. Apparently. Well, that's what they said."

Serene freezes a moment, both fingers pointed at me, peony bud and all.

"Say that again."

"Borderline personality disorder," I whisper. She throws the bud at me and laughs, and I want to die, right there. I do.

"I'm so sorry," says my mother, gulping for air, "but I could have told you that."

"Really?" I ask, feeling like all kinds of shit.

"Yeah! Following a stranger home. Breaking and entering.

Fighting ... and I have to tell you, you're a bit of a fiend. You can out-drink me ten to one."

"Sounds like a mess," I say. "Sounds ugly."

Serene stops laughing and shrugs. "So what?" she says. "It's you. It's real."

A tear drips down my chin, falls onto my chest. Serene looks at it.

"Aww. You're so sensitive, Clara. You're a long time dead, you know. Means enjoy everything while you still can."

It feels like a warning. I open my mouth to ask more, but then I think better of it. Serene leans forward, kisses my forehead.

"Babe," she says, standing up. "It could be worse. You could be *boring*."

"Are you leaving right now?"

"I am."

"Where are you going?"

"Simeon needs me to finish a little project," she says, "and you have to know, I'm tying up some very loose ends there. One last bit of ongoing work with him, then I'm gone."

She fishes in her pocket for her train pass and heads across the road, then down, down to the dark underground.

A TRIANGLE
AND ITS HARROWING EDGES

I text Sally and Jennifer to see if one of them will come to Clara's event at Tate House with me. I went out on a limb and ordered three extra tickets. It's a new Dempsey, one who isn't afraid to Disarm the Triggers, as Dr. Rayna puts it. I plan out the texts so they sound unbothered and light, not too eager or like I'm begging for their friendship, but warm nonetheless.

TWO SPARE TICKETS FOR MY SISTER'S SOLD-OUT TALK AT TATE HOUSE, I say. *ANY TAKERS???*

Sally says sorry, she has the children that weekend and Jennifer says she'd really love to be there but she's off doing a shamans' retreat in Surrey. I extend to the Womb-Men's group chat but no one else responds. In the end I resell the tickets on the site, as it looks like I'm going alone.

On Thursday night, I sit at the mirror, pep talking myself, determined to see this thing out. I am trying to be a better person, a kinder, more supportive sister. Chrissie Wang is best friends with a Style Kween called Marie Antoinette Palmer and Marie Antoinette Palmer the Style Kween is doing a (no-makeup) tutorial for darker-skinned sistas. She uses a lot of makeup, actually . . . foundation and pressed powder and even more concealer on top and then some kind of setting powder, which is also makeup, but who am I to argue with the experts? Last week I ordered all the brands she used in the video, including her very own lipstick and eyebrow duo. Tonight, I follow her closely, doing the no-makeup makeup look step by step. When I have finished, I look a lot less like me and a lot more like Marie Antoinette, which is great from where I'm sitting. I dust my wig with talcum powder just the way Marie did. It works. The shine is gone, and I love how natural I appear. I sit back, flawless and new, intrigued by how much more I *like* myself. I look a little like Clara; the contouring saw to that. I'm nearly beautiful.

I feel like knocking on the door and inviting Marcus out with me, but now maybe isn't the right time. I'm not sure I want him meeting or even knowing about Clara, especially after all that stuff I told him about being a writer. No, it'll only mess everything up. I put on *Kiss* by Prince and move my hips a little in my underwear, mouthing to the beat. Marie Antionette Palmer actively loves her curves and does affirmations in front of the mirror, thanking her belly, arms, and thighs for supporting her through it all. The video got nearly a million plays. When I see her doing that, I think I could maybe learn to love my body, too.

There is a wraparound viscose cardigan thing of hers that I bought from her Depop three months ago. It is bright green and has been hanging at the back of my wardrobe. Inspired by the green outfit that Marie wore in her Halfway 2 Christmas video, I decide that if there ever was a time to wear it, the time is now. I put it on over a purple shirt dress, tying it firmly around my waist. Amazed at how positively glowing I appear, I do two full pirouettes before the mirror. (I always *was* quite good at dancing. Don't know why I never pursued it.)

On the way to the venue, the bus driver lets me on for free! I sit on the top back of the bus like I'm driving, heading into City Centre, smiling hard at all the lights.

Once inside Tate House, I keep on acting normal. There is a great mix of people here, fashionistas and more men than you would imagine (but I put that down to Clara's latest stints on breakfast TV wearing next to nothing). Say what you like about my sister, she can pull in a crowd alright. She has this way of talking to herself and everyone, and when she answers a question, she knows how to make it resonate with every person in the room. She could sell your own soul back to you, and you'd go for it.

I take my seat in the middle left.

Eager, but not too eager.

Ha! My sister walks out wearing a shirt-style dress like me! Elegant, hair pulled back into a tight ponytail. She doesn't need the makeup she's wearing. The makeup has overpronounced her features and she looks hard and unreal. I watch, feeling a little nervous for her and for me as she takes the stage. I have now read the first twenty-five pages of the book four and a half times, and daren't read ahead. The hidden parts of the thing surprise me, the thoroughness of it. Clara wrote a richly imagined life of a person she is calling our mother, the things that she saw. It makes me wonder how someone so numb to the feelings of others can be at once so perceptive, so empathetic. It aches, it does; but it's awe inspiring, seeing her onstage. The moderator for the event is a girl from a bad Channel Four reality documentary about family dynamics. She stands up and gushes about how Clara is saving the whole world with her prose, which I think is a little much. Clara gets up onstage and talks about her book . . . which casts our mother as some witch-like siren from a bad part of town who cons everyone with her looks and ends up causing disaster. She alludes to what the disaster might be—it is something to do with water—but she won't tell us, because she doesn't want to "ruin the ending."

The interval comes, and I'm still doing okay, I think. I took my tinctures and vitamin D and iron, am not even short of breath, and I don't even mind that much that people keep bumping up against me—well, not that much. I am high on ashwagandha and L-theanine and life! The atmosphere is bustling and I, Dempsey Nichelle Elizabeth Campbell, am part of it!

When I go to the toilet, I see that my makeup is creasing in my frown lines along my forehead and under my eyes. The brown that I felt sure blended with my skin tone looks chalky and too light. It is less my hue and more the hue of Marie Antoinette the Style Kween, who is a whole three or four foundation shades lighter than I, only I hadn't factored that in back at the flat. The wig has a grey cast to it where I went overboard with the talcum powder. I drew my eyebrows on too thick, too dark. Oh no. Everything about this new face is caked on. I watch the other women around me, how effortlessly they walk around on their legs, talk to each other. Without any apparent fear.

I look hideous.

I want to be swallowed up by the ground. A woman compliments me on the cardigan I'm wearing, but in the fluorescent bathroom light her face has a mean, sarcastic expression. Another woman smiles at me as she dries her hands under the hand dryer and it all feels like a cruel school-trick. I squelch my lips against my teeth and walk away as fast as my legs can carry me. When I find my seat again, my pulse is thudding in my ears. Who did I think I was to even be here? Clara isn't even going to notice. I wish I could be home. If I keep fixating on my breath, I might forget how to breathe at all. Sweat has begun to form under my left armpit. I sit at the chair, twitching, desperate. I feel like the woman who smiled at me and the one who complimented my cardigan are in the back of the room somewhere looking at the wig and making a dreadful evaluation about me. Should I leave? I wonder if I can slip away.

But now everyone is returning, and quieting down. The Channel Four girl tells the audience it's our chance to "interact." I can never understand this kind of thing. Even if it were not my sister up there, I am not the type to draw attention to myself by asking stupid, navel-gazing questions. The first person gets up. They ask her about the research it takes to write a book like that. Has she studied psychology? I watch Clara crossing and uncrossing her legs. It seems obvious to me that she has had a drink or two over the break. She paws at the air in front of her.

"Noooo," says my sister. "Nooo, never. Sometimes there is a force acting through you and you must be the vessel. You just have to be open, you know?"

What a load of rubbish. There are these telltale changes to her voice, nicks and tears in it, the way she is articulating things. Things that only a sister would notice, but the crowd laps it up, of course. Clara swipes something just in front of her face again. I scan the crowd, but no one reacts.

Just then, in one of the rows ahead of me, someone else stands, and the change in my sister's face unsettles me. It's an expression that doesn't go well with the rest of her. Trancelike, almost beatific. When the person begins to speak, there is a stabbing pain in the corner of my right eye. Though I feel my throat tighten, I follow Clara's eye into the audience.

"Could there be a sequel to your book, then?"
the person is saying. "For example, how do you think her life
would have changed, having gained access to the thing she
wanted the most?"
My sister nods her head, as if mesmerized. Her mouth parts
slightly. Her face breaks into a smile.
"I . . . I think . . ." says my sister, suddenly giggling, "that things
are about to change. And perhaps there will be a sequel, you
know. Why not?"
"There should be," says the woman, whose voice is doing
strange things to my chest.

In the instant, I know that this is her. The imposter. The one who Clara is all messed up over. And as I listen to the voice, I can almost understand it. From behind, as far as I can see, the body type is similar to our mother's—a tall, slender frame like Clara's. A burned-red afro, just like our mother's. But not her. I mean, impossible. *All the same*, I will the woman, *don't turn around. Don't you dare turn around. If I can't see you, it won't be true. If you don't see me, it won't be true.*

She is not going to fool me.
No, I won't be made a fool of.
The woman turns around.

"You heard it here first," she says, flashing our mother's eyes. The audience laughs. The woman has our mother's pink, wide lips. Her overbite, her too-full mouth. Everyone laughs out loud and as the woman scans the crowd, I know that the last thing I want is for her to see me, whoever she is. I do not need to lock eyes with that woman. If it happens, I could be held in place, maybe forever. I pull hard against my chair, which is sunk halfway into the floor somehow. I fight up and against the damning gravity, darting out of the chair and onto my feet in one go. Clara watches me from the stage, her head to one side at a frightening angle. "I'm glad you asked the question," she is saying to the woman, and to me. "Things are about to change. And I'm ready for my main character's comeback. I've been ready all my life."

"All your life, you've been ready?" the woman goads.

"I AM ready," goes my sister, three sheets to the wind,
arms outstretched.

The audience looks on, wondering whether to laugh or applaud. What kind of a flirt is this? In front of everyone, too. Clara may as well jump into this woman's lap. Clara looks at the imposter, the imposter looks at Clara, and all at once, I just *know* I'm going to be sick. Not about to vomit in front of everyone, I turn, scanning for the nearest exit. I make a run for it. People are looking, and it's awful. As I leave the auditorium, my sister's eyes follow me, and she flashes her ugly, wicked smile.

In the street, I catch my breath as the nausea recedes a little. It is a sticky horror of an evening, and the South Bank is full of tourists, drinking, swearing, telling lies, queuing up for the London Eye.

I walk and walk and walk. If I didn't look so horrendous, I'd text Marcus and tell him to come out for a while. I might even drink alcohol again. But no, Marcus is probably out somewhere having fun. Probably eating a meal with some white girl with short hair and a dirty laugh. I follow my eyes to the darkening sky brooding atop the Thames. By now, I have made my way down to the Thames Beach.

If there is a sign, I will the air, *let it come. Let it be now. Let it be quick.*

To the left of me, a woman rests on the rocks like a mermaid, staring right out onto the water. She is holding a shawl-like thing, and when I look even closer, I see that it's a baby. I stand there a while, watching her from the corner of my eye. She motions her head towards me and her mouth is moving. Though I can tell that she's speaking to me, I can't make it out. Specks of rain appear on my face and shoulders.

"Sorry," I call, still keeping my distance. "Didn't catch that."

The woman beckons me over. Still, I don't move.

"I'm Veronicohhhh," she calls.

"Sorry?"

"Stop apologizing," she says. "I'm Veronicohhhh."

"Oh, Veronica?"

"That works," says she, "or Vee. Actually, just call me Vee, yeah?"

"Okay."

"You alright, luv?" shouts this Vee person, full Manchester accent on show.

"Not really."

"Well, what's your name? Let's start there."

"Why?"

"It's not a trick," says the woman. "Come closer," she says, "I'm not gonna eat you or nothing." I take a few tentative steps towards her, my mini heels sliding on the wet pebbles.

"You look like you saw a ghost," she laughs, balancing the baby on one arm, adjusting her shawl with the other.

"Oh yeah," I say, finally getting close so we are no longer shouting. Then I think *what the hell* and sit on a damp flat rock next to her.

"I did. And I didn't."

"It's raining," says Veronica,
as though I hadn't felt it.

"My name is Dempsey. She's not a ghost. She just looks like one."

Veronica takes out one of her boobs and guides the nipple into the baby's mouth with all the ease of someone who has been doing this kind of thing forever.

"Don't you mind doing that?" I say, a little flustered.

"Mind doing what?"

"I'm a feminist and everything," I assure her. "It's just that every-one can see."

Veronica shrugs her bare shoulders. "When he's hungry, he's hun-gry." It has begun to rain properly now, but Vee shows no sign of getting up. I don't move either.

We watch the rain fall to the river.

"When you say you've seen a ghost," murmurs Vee, after some time, "say more."

"She's not quite a ghost. I mean, she can't be can she? Ghosts don't exist."

"'Course they do," says Vee, holding her chin out to the rain. "Come on, Dempsey. They *do*."

I pull some dry skin off my lips. Vee coughs and produces the cheap-est looking business card I have ever seen, on stark white cardboard.

VERONICA THE SANGOMA

08768 888 9088

"Are you serious?" I laugh, and then, "what the hell's a sangoma?"

"I'm a high priestess," says Vee, with the straightest face imaginable for such a claim. "I'm a mistress of light."

I can never tell when people are joking, so I wait a bit, but Vee is star-ing at me expectantly.

"Okay," I go. "Okay. What's that mean?"

"Someone who knows what they're doing when it comes to Ghosts Who Don't Exist. If you need me, let me know."

"Like, for what?"

Vee frowns a little at my confusion, sniffs the bluing, salty air. She puts the baby on one shoulder and starts to burp him. "Let me know if you have any more problems with this ghost woman, okay?"

"This ghost woman," I say, "has my sister in some kind of meltdown."

"Your twin, right?" says Vee. At this, I gasp.

"If you can't beat them, join them," says Vee, shaking her head and covering the baby's face with the shawl. "Hold him a second."

She bends down to untuck her dress from her Dr. Martens. The baby feels hot and fragile in my arms, a tiny living doll. I peer down at the black lace obscuring his face.

"Can he breathe?"

Vee ignores that. "He likes you."

"I like him, I think."

"You'd have been a great mother," says Vee, taking him back.

"Well, I've still got a few years yet," I say, but it gets carried in the air somehow.

Veronica places the baby in the pram, and we say goodbye. When I walk away, I can barely feel my legs. It is as though some other entity is carrying me.

"She isn't a ghost, she's a con woman," I say to no one in particular, because Vee is long gone. While waiting for the bus, I can't feel anything. Not even the rain.

WE ARE FAMILY,
I GOT ALL MY SISTAS WITH ME

"So, wait," Serene is saying, putting it together in her head, I suppose. "Let me get this straight. That was your *sister*? I thought she looked familiar."

I don't want to talk about this. Anything, just not this. Sometimes, I could happily strangle Dempsey. Not only does she have no sense of style (she wore a lime-green bargain bin cardigan to my show), but the way she got up and ran out the door was ridiculous. In front of our new mother. In front of everyone.

"I don't think we look alike at all," I say, feeling petulant. We are back at home by now, listening to some jungle track from the nineties that Serene says she's really into at the moment, and when she suddenly disappears upstairs without excusing herself, I assume she's using the bathroom. Although she is no longer what I would call a guest in my house, I am surprised only few minutes later, to hear water being drawn in the bathtub. The vetiver-and-smoke scent of my favorite bath oil wafts down the stairs. I sit to attention on the sofa, listening to the small movements and splashes overhead, a small curiosity awakening in the lower part of my mind.

I flick on the TV, trying to keep myself from being too pleased about anything.

"Clara," I hear her calling. "Clara, can you come here please?"

I climb the stairs and reach the top. The bathroom door is wide open. From the tub, my mother looks at me.

"Is everything okay?" I whisper, not daring to move any closer.

"Come in," she says. "Shut the door. Keep me company."

It's creepy. Of course it is.

Still, following her orders, my legs walk me into the steamed-up room, and I take a perch on the toilet seat, feeling more than awkward. Once sitting, I try to meet her eyeline, not her dark nipples bobbing on the water,

not her black eyes resting on me,
not her hair hanging around her square, angular shoulders,
not any of that. She smiles at me.

The oil smell is not as strong as it was from the bottom of the stairs. Some other fragrant note is competing from underneath, one or more hints of musty river water. I shake it out of my mind at once, the threat and disease in it.

"It's fine," I tell her. "Do your thing. I'll just go downstairs . . . and."

"Pass the soap, then," she says, rubbing her toes together.

I grab the soap from the far end of the tub and, as she reaches out her right arm, I spot a familiar pattern of pale shiny lines in the inner elbow. At once I know for sure that they are on her thighs too, but I daren't look. I touch my own inner elbow, tracing the pattern I know by heart.

"Snap," I murmur, lightly, under my breath.

"So," she says, settling back in the water. "Here we are."

If I weren't awake I'd think I was dreaming. If I weren't sober I'd swear I was still drunk.

"Yes, here we are."

"Tonight went well. Despite . . ."

"Yeah. Despite . . ."

"I have a question," says Serene. "You talk to this sister?"

"Yeah . . . but it's dysfunctional."

"How?"

"We didn't grow up together."

"Okay," says Serene. "I think I understand."

I wonder if it's safe to ask a question. If I don't try I'll never know.

"What about you? Did *you* grow up here?"

"Here as in where?" says Serene.

"London? England? Where are your parents from?"

"I don't know any family. Grew up in the system."

Bingo.

"Whereabouts?"

"Here and there," says Serene, eyes fluttering up to the ceiling. "In the midlands, too. Like in your book."

"Where in the midlands?"

She says nothing, just plays in the suds some more with her toes.

"Look," she goes, finally returning my stare. "It isn't a good story. Can you get us some wine?"

My phone vibrates in my pocket. It is Emma, who has been forwarding the itinerary for Ireland in dribs and drabs all day. So inefficient. I deep sigh.

"Work?" says my mother, leaning her head back, foam around her neck.

"Yeah," I say. "Don't suppose you want to come with me tomorrow, do you? Emma's sitting this one out. She's getting so unreliable."

Serene sits up and the water drips down her front. "When's she due?"

"What?" I go, and then it all makes sense. How could I have missed this? Furthermore, why didn't Emma say anything?

"Um ... she has a way to go I think," I say, avoiding Serene's questioning stare.

"You *did* notice she was pregnant?" she asks me, after a moment.

"Obviously."

Serene runs the hot water tap for a few seconds, watching the jet of water disappear into the tub.

"I've never been on a plane," she says. "But you're going to be away, and I wonder if I might stay here. If it's not too much."

"Yes, of course," I say, still wracking my brain about Emma and a possible baby. There is an unexpected rage appearing, though I can't place its origin. I find my mouth to say again, "Of course you can stay." She settles in the water with her eyes back, retreating away from the conversation, into her head. I take that as my cue to get up. "I'm going to let you enjoy that," I tell her, getting to my feet.

"Good tub," murmurs my mother, eyes closed.

••

Later, Serene pulls out clothes for my trip, giving a commentary on every item. It's jarring and comforting, if a thing can be both.

"The white, not the black. You wear too much black."

"Don't go without this one, what are you thinking?"

"No! Never wear that one again. It does nothing for you. Nothing at all."

We carry on like this for so long that I don't notice time is escaping us. I don't know when I fall asleep, my suitcases wide open in front of me, or when Serene slips out of the room, leaving me drooling on my sheets.

At just after two a.m. I am roused by a shrill, incessant sound—the ringtone that I assigned to Dempsey, which is mean, I know. I consider letting it ring out, but my hands won't let me.

"What I don't understand," says my sister's voice, "is what the hell is going on!"

I'm not in the mood for this. "I have to be up in four hours to catch a plane. Why are you calling me in the middle of the night? Also Dempsey, running out of the place like that was the most attention-seeking thing I've ever seen you do."

"You're the most cynical person I know," my sister shouts. "I've been lying awake wondering how could you even think this possible? You were crazy tonight! You want locking up!"

"Everything matches," I tell her, trying to be calm, so that going back to sleep won't be too difficult. "She doesn't know her family or anything. She grew up in the midlands! The midlands, Dem!"

"It sounds like the same story," says my sister. "In a public book that you just published about our mother, right?"

"So, you agree?" I press. "You agree that it's her?"

Dempsey falls silent and I feel something of a win.

"Clara," she finally says. "What I'm saying is this . . . she'll have read your book. The clues are in the book! Don't you see?"

There is suddenly an overwhelmingly bitter taste in my mouth. Fear for now, for the immediate future.

"Dempsey," I warn, my voice catching. "Don't spoil this. Please don't."

Silence, then, "Okay," my sister says in the smallest voice. "You do you."

I hang up.

A shadow passing by my doorway has stopped to linger. I stare at the ceiling, feeling faraway things, experiences that have never made sense clicking squarely into place.

••

One day, when I was six and a half, I was playing in the park across the road. Claudette was keeping an eye on me from the living room window. When I walked over to play in the little sandpit, my mother appeared. She was six too, with the blackest, most mournful eyes. She told me to throw a stone at some pale boy in a wheelchair and, when I knew Claudette was not looking, I did it. Of course I did it. His mother was right there, which made me want to do it even more. Not everyone gets a chance to have a mother, and life isn't fair. You lose parts of your insides when you lose a mother. Cells, or veins, or blood. You grow colder, by three degrees or more. Soon as I threw the thing, the boy started to whine and I ran away home as fast I could. The mother knocked on our door some minutes later. Of course she did; it's what mothers do.

Claudette and Adolphus said that there was no way I would have done that. Ever ever ever. Once the woman had left, frustrated and unsatisfied, Claudette looked me up and down, as though I was the lowest thing on earth.

"Don't embarrass me again like that, Clara Kallis," she hissed. "Oh, I know you did it. I can see it in you. I won't have it. You'd better learn to curb those behaviors, or you'll go nowhere fast. You'll go right back to · where you came. You'll end up . . . well you know where you'll end up."

Another time, when I was just shy of sixteen, a feeling came around that was more powerful than me. It was a sudden, righteous hunger that would not leave. Serene Droste came to me in a daydream and told me to surprise the boy who was always passing me lewd, coded notes in English class by taking him at his word.

The boy happened to be Andrew Milner, my best friend's blond boyfriend. That little fact made no real difference to me. I needed the recognition of it, the conquest, the very real feeling that I, too, was a person, somebody worth wanting. Someone deserving of attention. The spaces in me were ready and empty. We finished our mock English exam early—I because it was too easy, he because he wasn't the kind of person who cared about anything enough to apply himself. After we had excused ourselves, we messed around in the boys' bathroom while everyone else wrote about what Dickens meant when he wrote, "It was the best of times, it was the worst of times."

—How else might he have explored such a sentiment?

The sex was really nothing to speak of—was it even sex? I think I flew up and away somehow. I think he was nothing but a clean backdrop, a way to see myself. Later, he would swear that it had been The Full Thing and that we had to be quiet about it. I took his word for it. We were still very inexperienced, but the moment was everything. I felt vindicated and important, like a weapon in disguise. Afterwards, he was horrified and kept calling me to worry about it. *You won't tell her, right?*

Of fucking course not. I told him. *I've forgotten it myself. So should you.*

I don't think anyone ever found out, but I didn't much care. I was no longer a fairy tale, having learned how to make myself real. The next year we all fell out of touch. I think they're married now.

• •

My alarm goes at six and when I wash and dress and look in the mirror, I notice small patches of light travelling through my body. There is a pale, unearthly finish on my skin, as though I may be disappearing a little. My teeth clatter involuntarily and I study my hands, which in some lights might appear translucent. Serene doesn't seem to notice. She is sitting downstairs on the couch, still and bright and well rested, like she slept for about a week. I make strong coffees for us while she showers, and when the taxi pulls up at seven fifteen, she walks me out, smiling. I am trying my best to smile, too. Serene looks like a picture, like something you'd like to keep.

"Bye, Clara," she says in my dressing gown, wet curls clinging to her furry swan neck. "Travel safe."

The goldenrod T-shirt clings to her, casting a gorgeous glow on her chestnut brown skin.

She looks at me, and as the taxi starts to pull away, I am starting to tremble all over now, and I don't know why.

"Don't ever leave," I mouth to her in the car, from behind my hand. It is a wish-command, a hope-filled spell-thing.

CHAPTER FIVE

Serene's father, name unknown, had been nonverbal. He was described in the adoption notes as being A Simple Man, Of Afro Caribbean Descent. Her mother, Diana Bradnock, according to the notes, was vicious and difficult to understand. She barely used her words either. They met in the secure care unit in Nottingham in spring of 1964. By that time, Diana had abandoned English altogether. She was, she surmised, beyond words, and if no one could understand her, that was their problem. She spoke nothing recognizable most of the time, like lyrical pidgin. They conceived Serene in the secure unit, and were declared unfit parents right away on account of Diana's violent outbursts and shady endeavors and the father's extreme reticence. By the time Serene was four, the two of them were dead and gone. Old beyond her years, Serene knew all about what it was to cling to a new thing for dear life, lest it try to shake you off. It happened with foster family after foster family. Then a children's home. Then a secure unit. Then out in the world. This thing had already begun, this belief that her needs were more valid than the rest's, that her being very, very special meant the world was hers to take. After the first children's home, she learned how to move. When you're a tall, sharp-talking dark girl and you look like you have nothing much to lose, people have a way of handing stuff over first, complaining about it later.

Once she became a teenager and grew into her looks, other people started to act differently. Before, they had only feared her, but when desire came into play, there appeared a new set of colours with which to paint. It was a curious mix of power, people coming to her, expecting to be hurt, and being drawn to her anyway. Sometimes, she supposed, they wanted to be hurt, and she would gladly indulge them. She was always someone's secret liaison, someone's obsession all to themselves, and this was so painful and so very useful. Oh, she was still quite violent (a lucky heirloom from her mother), but in a new way. Diana hadn't had those powerful looks. It seemed to Serene that some people just plain wanted to be taken advantage of, came to her open, lust drunk, with their contents proudly on show. She was only giving them what they expected. When you have grown up without much of anything, not knowing how to keep anything, least of all yourself, it does not matter if people think you are beautiful. It does not matter if you score higher on the IQ test than the other kids. You cannot apply yourself if you do not know *what* and *why* you are. If the people you came from did not know what and who *they* were. You always find yourself wanting. Here and not here.

It hadn't changed much in her twenties. The book Serene was writing was different, was confounding to her. Not the work itself, but what to do with the work? It seemed not to be a thing you could force or talk your way into. Not common for Serene, who had been liberating items all her life. The man she was with before she met Abbé was all muscle no brain, no real clue how to apply himself. Simeon had an edge but wasn't smart with it, stayed frustratingly small time: minor burglaries, car break-ins—nothing impressive. He came up rough like she did. The two of them were opportunists. He liked her company. He put up glamour pictures of her all around the place. He helped her pay for hers. She knew how to play him. That summer, she had turned twenty-nine. She'd felt like she'd been around forever and was fresh out of steam. All her life, she had manipulated other people, told them what to do and how best to do it. Exhausting, is what it was. She began an Introduction to the Humanities Open University course by day, added pages to the novel by afternoon, and by night she would be out with Simeon, who was better company than not having any at all, but not enough, never enough. Furthermore, he did not understand the creeping, pervasive need to escape.

That last year, before the numerology and the girls, the chasm widened and she found herself falling beyond the floor. Nothing was satisfying anymore, not even if they lifted seven and a half grand from a house one day, damn near two grand from the next. Nothing was cutting it. It was all very well and good to go to a boutique and walk out with some new shoes (even a TV once, can you imagine?), but she was destined for more than this, she knew. She'd put her heart and soul into this book, and some dumb fuck professor who had never experienced anything was asking her about *credentials*.

Professor Gene Harris seemed to twig about the hundred and fifty that went missing from his briefcase and pocket and, waving his fleshy arm, said words along the lines of, "If you needed the money, or anything like that, you could just have asked. You can always *just ask*, Serene. We're friends, right?" No. Where Serene was from, you didn't ask for things. And she didn't have *friends*. She understood that overall, people were weak, and you had to take what you wanted before they noticed, or got up the nerve to refuse.

"I don't know what you're getting at, Gene," she told him sweetly. "If you have something to say to me, just say it. You honestly think I stole from you? That's what you're saying?"

Gene, who had been trying to ascertain what he thought he knew, shifted under her cool, unremitting gaze and began to doubt himself. She could tell, and it pleased her no end.

"Alright, let's drop it," he said, raising his hands in a dramatic sign of surrender. He gave her another onceover before adding, "Made any changes to that sci fi manuscript? If so, I'd love to take a look."

"It isn't sci fi."

Gene laughed then, in a way that was not kind. "Your fantasy book then."

That had done it. She shook her head, resolute.

"It's finished. I'm not going to take any more notes on it, Gene. If I can't get it published right now, fine. Perhaps it's here before its time."

••

They say that when there's a nine in your age, you lose the plot. You start taking financial risks or risks in your marriage and personal relationships. You enter a time of near crisis. You sleep with people you aren't meant to. This was working out to be true for Serene. When she met Abbé on the bus, she had been so uncomfortable in her life that she wanted to die. Abbé himself was going nowhere fast. The two of them drew into each other like a pair of the very same thing. There was no sense to it, but it had all seemed very destined, so very precise, as though his was the temperament that would work best with hers. All of his interest lay in his silence, his withholding. He did not offer much, but he didn't ask for anything, either. When he was around, everything was dead and quiet, and it was a relief. Abbé was from a wealthy Caribbean family and hadn't wanted much of her. He lacked direction, having vague intentions of being some kind of multidisciplinary artist. She could direct him, perhaps. It couldn't hurt to be part of a wealthy Caribbean family. It was surely better than anything Serene had going on. On-off girlfriend to a small-time criminal or minder to a good-looking kid with a burgeoning addiction and the right family connections? Seduced by the promise of a new project, a fixer-upper, family resources, even—Serene, ever the strategist, told Simeon that they were going down two different paths, to which he had snorted and said, "Good luck." Simeon tried to do the things that tough men do, laugh it off. They both knew the truth: with Serene, he had always been somewhat out of his depth.

"You're like an older brother," Serene had told him, for maximum sting. "It just doesn't work the way it should anymore."

Simeon moved towards her, and, though it had never happened before, Serene braced herself for a slap. But the man reset himself at once.

"You won't survive without me," he said. "You think you're smart, but you're following a trajectory."

"Do you even know what the word trajectory means?" she had shot back, meaning to wound him, but Simeon looked at her squarely and simply said, "You'll be your mother."

A low blow.

It had already begun. The trajectory. Diana used to speak in tongues, and Serene had, for a while, found herself receiving odd messages in cereal boxes, perfume scents, the miserable drone of the earth when the day was drawn out and violent. Huge, unrelenting messages. A crushing three p.m. boredom; the sensation of feeling trapped by air or water, a bold, existential hunger. The feeling that something needed to change right now—yesterday, even. It started with the faint understanding that something (some*things*) travelled alongside her, a clear split self. She didn't know what it meant, of course. She called them the spirits. Suddenly, she would be out at a store or in a bank or the park or on a street and hear her mother's pidgin calling to her, as though from far away. It was Diana, in fact, who told her to be on that bus that day, driving into sunset. Diana who directed her to love her life as if she didn't have much of it left. In Abbé, Serene spotted a person of interest. A black cloak of a man drenched in silent longing, and when she touched on that, when he gave her access, she took whatever she could. He only needed to look at her, to moan into her mouth, to flail in the bed, and she was thrilled to the point of danger. It's always like that in the beginning, before you know them. Before you get close enough to see all the mess. The thing about a thrill is that in the end you learn that you made it all up. The thrill came from you. Whatever you needed, you saw. Whatever you saw, you likely imagined. It was all pretty hopeless in the end, a last-minute attempt at hanging on. Sometimes your story is written, and that's just it. Abbé was not as quiet or as interesting as he appeared. You could have called him a drifter—absent, even. He was broken, fairly spoiled. Diana's loud advice was bad advice, as it happened. She got pregnant right after they met, such was the doomed magic. In a matter of days the spell was done, done, done. Getting pregnant was not the plan, but it was not, not the plan. Dirty, scheming Diana!

CLARA, NINETY-SIX HOURS LATER

The day is simmering into dusk as my car pulls up. My house, some four days later, feels different from the outside. The weeping willows hang down obscuring the roof, like a picture in a children's book. There is a deep secrecy to the scene, as though, somehow, while I was away, it rearranged itself. A mild orange glow reflected in my floor-to-ceiling windows, a telling reflection of the retreating sun. Around the huddled trees, the birds are cawing. I tell myself I'm imagining things; that there is nothing menacing about the way my house looks today against the gloomy backdrop. My heart skips as I go to fit my key into the lock. So much so that I have to concentrate to line my key up in the door.

The key will not turn.

"Hello?"

I press my ear to the door.

"Serene!" I call, banging.

From inside, I hear thumping, as though something is retreating from the door, then nothing. I am just about to call her name again when she opens the door. She is wearing my expensive linen pajama bottoms.

"Welcome back," she says. "But why you shouting, fam?" She sounds like she's reading from a script.

"Oh!" I say, feeling silly. "I couldn't get inside."

"Oh," she says, mimicking me, in a slightly cruel manner. "Keys were in the door."

She stands there for a second, then moves from the doorway. I feel something amiss as I step over the threshold. I spin around, noticing a large brass mirror along my normally minimal wall. It is the mirror from the photograph from Dempsey's house. I touch it, suspiciously, noting my worried expression. My eyebrow is doing a twitching thing. "Surprise!" her voice is saying. "Adds even more light and space, don't you think?"

There's a layer of dust on the mirror's surface. I touch my eyebrow, where I am sweating.

"Well? Like it?" my mother smiles, her voice oddly placed, oddly chipper.

I don't.

I don't at all. The mirror is brass, arch shaped. I know it too well. It doesn't fit the house. "I . . . I'm not sure," I stammer. "Where did you get it?" But Serene only smiles, clasping those hands of hers together.

"I *love* it, so I'll take it if you won't. It's no big deal. Just saw it and thought of you."

I say nothing again, so she asks me if I'm okay. I have an awful hangover, but don't feel like telling her this. In the corner of my eye, a dark shape scuttles from left to right.

"Need some water, I think."

I sit down on the sofa and my hands are trembling. Serene throws me a bottle of water from the kitchen counter.

"These bottles are bad for the environment," she tells me. "They clog the rivers and seas. It's bad down there."

"Ireland was fun," I interrupt, cracking the lid and taking a long sip. "I mean, full on, but good."

"And the plastic in your body. Very toxic. I read today that it adds up in your body like a ticking clock and makes cancer."

"We're all ticking clocks," I say. A bird caws outside. My mother says, "Galway, right?"

"You know my schedule better than Emma does."

"I don't think that's difficult. Anyway, she probably has baby brain. It starts before the baby, you know."

"You know a lot about babies," I say, almost accusingly. I'm not sure why there's an edge to our tones. My head has begun to hurt more. "I'm sorry. I'm just really tired," I say, laying my head on the sofa. I draw my knees up into the soft seat and lie prone, closing my eyes.

"So what about Galway?" she is saying, but the sound trails off somewhere. I start to talk about the rows of coloured houses and all the music, but my voice gets carried away too. After a few seconds, I feel her weight on the sofa next to me. Perhaps I fall asleep for a few delicious seconds. Gently, my mother takes hold of my head, drawing it closer. Before I know it, she has her hand in my hair, stroking my scalp. It feels

out of this world.

Moments later, there is a smell of a sweet meal coming from the kitchen. Then somewhere behind me, Serene is plating meat onto a dish.

"Not one of these vegans, are you?" she is saying. "No one does oxtail like I do oxtail."

"No way!" I hear myself say, in a child's voice. "Not vegan. Yuck!"

Then I am at the table, looking at chunks of meat and white rice. I bite into the side of the softest, most fragrant meat I have ever tasted. Then the butter beans. I wipe my mouth, going back for more. Her eyes do not leave mine as I chew and chew. She passes me a glass of white wine with ice cubes, and I knock it back in one swallow. When I go to cut the meat again, my hands have turned to rubber.

"Come," she says. "Let me help you."

I try to tell her I can feed myself, but she has already positioned herself behind me.

"Shhh. You're overstressed, I think. Let me help you, Clara."

My mother wrestles the cutlery from my too large fingers.

"Let. Me. Help. You."

Hands over mine, she cuts up the dark tender meat into small, bite-sized triangles. My hands feel like jelly again, so she takes a seat across from me, spooning the red rice, green peppers, yellow peppers into my wide, open mouth.

NO, NO,
NOT *THAT*

I open my eyes.

I open my eyes, having drooled all on the sofa. The kitchen is empty. There is no pot on the stove. No fragrant meat. Serene is nowhere to be seen. My left leg has gone to sleep. I shift, trying to regain some feeling, attempting to sort what is real from what is not, could never be.

Pull yourself together, I warn the girl in me. *Pull yourself together or I might have to hurt you.* Above my head, someone is pacing.

I get to my feet and pad towards the stairs, pulling my dead leg behind me. Why didn't I take off my shoes? I would never not take off my shoes! Gingerly, I climb the stairs, which appear to go on forever, my left leg still not doing what left legs should. When I reach the top, I notice that the door to my bedroom has been pulled almost shut. In the thin rectangle, the space between, I see her stalking around the room. I clear my throat. In the two-inch window, I see my mother stop and turn, one eye fixed on me, the other somewhere unknown.

"Hi," I say, pushing the door. "Sorry."

The gap in the door widens, and the woman who is my mother changes her face.

"Good. You're up. You were snoring the place down."

"I do that."

Serene yawns, turning away from me. "Got to get home."

"Stay for dinner?" I say quickly, still in the doorway, because the thought of eating alone is suddenly unbearable.

We settle on Thai food, because the restaurant is only a half mile up the road and we're too hungry to wait for anything else. Twenty minutes later, the doorbell goes. Food's here, thank God. I rush to open the door, peering through the glass. To my absolute dismay, there, standing on the steps, is my twin's depressing shadow. I am suddenly overcome with the urge to retreat, to hide, to pretend no one's home. But it's too late. Dempsey has already stepped inside, is shaking her head at me.

"We need to talk."

I bristle.

"Why do you keep turning up unannounced like this?"

"She's here, isn't she?" says my sister, trying to peer around me. She looks sweatier and ashier than usual.

"Keep it down!" I hiss, but it's too late. Serene has appeared behind me, eyeing my sister keenly.

"Well, hello," she says, all the way down in her throat, a flash of amber in her eyes.

"Hi," says Dempsey, breathless, feeling the orange light.

"We just ordered food," I say. "Dempsey, this is quite inconvenient, actually. We're working together and . . ."

"Don't be awful," says my sister, quietly. "Please not right now, okay."

Serene bursts into her frightening laughter. Dempsey looks as though she wants to disappear. I wish she would. For her sake. I wish she would just go and get terribly, terribly lost.

"We ordered so much," Serene is saying. "Come on, there'll be enough. Dempsey, is it?"

From behind me, Serene holds out her long hand. Dempsey and I regard the pointed dark nails.

"Yeah," says Dempsey, taking the hand, as though spellbound.

"Come in, girl," our mother the siren says. My sister looks at me, still hanging on the doorway like a lost soul. She's looking at me for confirmation, and I will myself to allow her in.

"Cool name," our mother is telling her, the long hand still gripping my sister's.

Dempsey takes a chair at my dining table. We wait for the takeaway, silence settling over us. Serene is watching some show called *Columbo* and is not at all perturbed by the silence. Once the food has been delivered, we arrange ourselves around the table. Serene takes the chair next to Dempsey, at the head. I sit far away at the other end. Dempsey is staring and staring at Serene—she just can't help herself. Serene is busy texting someone. I am desperate to ask her anything, but I don't know what the thing should be.

Pad see ew, egg fried rice, mango salad, and roast duck and pancakes. Dempsey favors the salad. My mother and I mix everything else on our plates. We eat hungrily and at speed, Serene pausing only to appraise me as I pour myself my second drink in between arranging strips of the duck meat on the white pancake. I start to feel extremely faint. All I can do is swallow and swallow, as fast as I can.

"You drink every day?" Serene asks, eyeing the glass of rosé.

"Yep," goes my sister, not missing a beat. "She never stops."

"How would you know?" I spit. "Shut up, Dempsey."

Dempsey does not reply, is still staring at Serene, who seems amused by this exchange. She crosses and uncrosses her legs, looking from me to my sister, finally setting her plastic utensils on the table.

"I'd never have said you were twins."

A twitch happens on Dempsey's face, and I want to laugh. I want to scream, GO THE FUCK HOME, BITCH, YOU ARE NOT GOING TO WIN THIS. GO HOME GO HOME GO HOME!!! Understanding what Dempsey must be feeling, I decide to plunge in the knife.

"I agree. There's nothing alike about us."

Dempsey looks at the floor.

"Oh, I wouldn't say that," our mother says. "Same fears."

"Same fears!!?" I almost shout.

"Same *ears*," Serene is saying. "Same hairline. Same teeth. Kind of."

I put my forehead on the table. Dempsey starts to do the weird thing with her mouth. I think I am whimpering but I cannot tell, because there is an airplane outside and it's too loud. I cover my ears. "Anyone hear that noise?" I am saying, but Serene is asking Dempsey about something else and I'm losing track.

"It's too much!" I tell whoever is listening. "I don't like loud noises. At all."

But no one is taking any notice. Dempsey is going on about cakes and wigs and someone called Jack. I might lose it

"I can make it look better, I think," Serene is telling my sister. "You just need to pick it out with the wide-tooth comb and then you blend it. Use gel at the front. It's all about the blend, Dem."

Dem

doesn't say anything and then Serene is up, is making her way round the table to Dempsey. Before I know it, she has Dempsey's cheap wig half off and is touching her nasty, flaky scalp, assessing it. My sister lets her head fall back, eyes closed, mouth open like a fish, and I feel white hot rage starting in my gut, my ribs,

rising,
bile, rising.

NO WAY NO WAY NO WAY, I am saying, and before I can think what to do, I am up and out of the room, tears rolling down my face.

I stomp upstairs.

Minutes later, Serene is at my open door. I lay face down on the bed, crying.

"Clara Marina Kallis," she says, hands on hips. "You gonna come downstairs or what? All your food's getting cold."

"Why don't you give it all to Dempsey?" I cry out. Serene pushes the door open, walks right into the room.

"What's going on? What's all this about?"

I say nothing, my sobs muffled. If I push my face far enough into the coolness of the pillow, everything might soon be over.

"Dempsey's wigs are awful," I say into the silk. "They're fucking *plastic*, can't you tell?!"

"I know, I know," I hear my mother say. "I'm going to help her with that."

"But she's ruining the environment!"

"Okay," says Serene, a new hint of tiredness in her voice. "Okay, my love."

The image of her behind Dempsey, her hands touching Dempsey's mess of a scalp, is all I can see. I lurch towards the bathroom. My mother follows.

"Okay," comes her voice. "So, we've established that Dempsey has bad wigs. What else? What now?"

In the mirror, my eyes are red rimmed.

"What is wrong with you?" presses Serene, moving towards me. In the mirror, I watch her face watching mine. The fruity wine's acidity tickles my mouth.

"Yoooou," I tell her reflection. "You are wrong with me."

She looks more like *me* than Dempsey. At least there's that.

"I know," says Serene, holding me by the shoulders, turning me around to face her. Her strength is unexpected. She purses her lips together. "Want to talk about it yet, or what, Clara?"

I can't pretend anymore.

"I knew all along," I tell her. "I knew you were you. But it's weird and impossible and I'm scared. I don't know what to do with it."

"Try." Serene is still holding my shoulders, looking dead-straight into my eyes.

"Try what?"

"Try," says my mother. "To do something with it."

"I'm scared."

"You said that."

". . . and I don't want to frighten you."

"You, frighten *me*?" says my mother, who now looks like someone I don't know. She looms over me, tall, tall, tall. Something about her face gains ten years, and then more

and then she's our age again.

"Impossible," she says, "I'm a grown, grown woman."

"How old are you?" I ask, already knowing the answer.

"How old did you want to make me?"

In a second, she has pushed her face right up to my nose. Her smell is acrid, offensive, and I am almost swallowed by the black as she presses her hard body against mine. When I realise what might be happening, our lips are already touching. It is the smallest and most terrible of deaths. All the lights in my head flicker shut. Suddenly I am drowning. Rousing all the force I have inside of me, I push myself up and away from the damage, from the dank, dank universe closing all around me. I reject the deathly current, and with all my might, shove her away. She falls backwards. The shower door splinters into a thousand tiny pieces. All I see is Serene, passing through the screen like a fucking ghost, and then sitting amongst the shards on the tiles, surrounded by glass, glass, too much glass.

At the door, my twin has appeared. Serene stands up, as if in slow motion, shaking the glass from her arms and clothes.

My mother stands up without a single fucking scratch.

She waits a second.

She narrows her eyes.

Around us in an arc on the floor; shards of glass are pointed in all directions.

"What the fuck is your problem?" Serene growls, coming towards me. Her teeth are yellowed, smaller than I remember. Underneath her feet, the glass goes

crunch.

"Not that!" I am saying, backing into my bedroom
where Dempsey is standing, looking on, mouth opening and
closing like a fish.

Serene makes for me, but my sister blocks her. "It's okay," says Dempsey. "Everyone, calm down!"

"Are you fucking crazy?" goes my mother.

"I don't want that!" I am shouting.

"You're her," Dempsey lumbers towards Serene,
trying to touch her face. "You really are."

Serene slaps Dempsey's hand away, I feel a surge of anger. Suddenly, my sister is backing away, hands protecting her face, saying,

"it's okay it's okay it's okay it's okay it's okay"

and Serene is heading out the door and down the stairs, calling us awful, awful things.

Dempsey and I run to the landing before making down the stairs after her and out the open front door. Barefoot, I follow Dempsey outside into the wild lane, but there is no sign of Serene.

A rough wind moves over the trees. I watch my sister, who is bent over, hands on her shins.

"What did you do?" she whispers, trying to get her breath back.

"I don't know, I . . ."

"Did you hit her?" Dempsey bellows in a voice I've never heard before. "No."

Dempsey is breathing out of her mouth. She has this wild look. She has the same face as the woman who departed the stairs. She has our mother's cruel mouth.

"I love her," I hear myself saying. "But not like that. Not that. Not that! I didn't mean to, D. I promise I didn't."

"Liar!" Dempsey screams. Before I can say anything else, my sister has leapt on me, is kicking and punching me. God, she has some fists on her, no one would guess it. I grit my teeth as the fists pummel me. I let her get on with it. I know that if I hit her back, she's finished. Plus her weight and the pain feel a little like relief. I'm the sky, I'm the air, I'm in the trees staring down, as my sister straddles me, panting. I try to get the last scene out of my head, try to make sense of the pieces of glass that could not cut my mother—how she had remained there, somehow unhurt. Unmarked. Undead. Did she levitate? Were there strings playing in the background? A cello in the corner of the room? Did she really *try to kiss me*? "You're a disgusting drunk!" Dempsey is shouting. "Not everyone wants to have sex with you, you know! You're an embarrassment." I come swiftly back into my body. My sister, it seems, is forgetting herself, so now I am out for blood. "You're the embarrassment," I tell her, keeping my tone low and measured. "Have you seen the fucking state of yourself, Dempsey? Have you honestly seen what you look like, you foul bitch?"

Dempsey stares at me, letting this sit. I watch, somewhat satisfied, as her small eyes begin to flood. She throws herself down and does a whole kicking and screaming and punching the ground thing. She's making a scene and I've never had problems with the neighbours before, so I'm going to need her to shut the fuck up. But also, I get it. I should be on the ground crying, too, but I have way more control than that.

There is nothing to do but wait it out, since I have little skill when it comes to dealing with a hysterical person. I flop down next to my twin and hold her shoulders tightly. She's shaking, so I take off my sweater and cover her exposed, flaky neck.

After the theatrics, we go back into the house. Dempsey makes herself a cup of cocoa and cries a lot and loudly. In the end, I give up on her and go upstairs. There is glass everywhere, a spectrum of colour and no blood or anything like it, just a faint dank smell, like something that expired a long time ago. The shattered glass is casting rainbows all the way through the bathroom. It looks like heaven in there. One triangular shard had landed on the toilet lid and is balancing there, half on half off, gleaming brilliantly. I resist the urge to take the shard to bed, to press it into my thighs and belly,

but perhaps I am a coward.

Serene would tell me to do it, would egg me on from the sidelines. My mother would say that you only live once, but that would be just like her, wouldn't it, to say one thing and do the opposite. Here she is, back from history.

It takes everything I have to dim the head-noise. I close the door on the rainbow room. I climb into my bed, stretching the covers over my head. I cover my ears to drown out Dempsey.

IN THE MORNING,
EVERYTHING HURTS

I wake up with my face pressed deep into Clara's very uncomfortable cord sofa and decide to get gone before she has time to wake up and try to blame any of this mess on me. My phone says six twenty-three and my head is woolly, as if I were the one drinking like a fish. Clara's two empty bottles of wine sit on the table behind me. She was not in her right mind yesterday. Her behavior last night was disgusting. The names, the drunkenness, the awful attack. I need to leave immediately.

The thing about matters of the mind is that they are sticky, and I am suddenly feeling a lot of my sister's wrongness as if it is part of me. I don't want any of it. I've done far too much work on myself. I take too many remedies, trace minerals, chaga, and cordyceps to be undone by this, by her. Imagine thinking that this stranger, who looks the very same age as us, could ever be our mother. Imagine being entranced by her.

At the reading, I had known with all of myself, hadn't I, that the woman was a fraud? At the reading, the woman was only an approximation of our mother, a doppelgänger at best. I hadn't cared for her nasty, entitled energy. But at the house, she had put on a different face. And when she touched my hand at the table, something rich dripped into me. I understand now that it was a weird kind of spell, likely something to do with being too close to Clara and her latest obsession. They say stress seeps into you, is transmittable through the skin. I was listening to a whole podcast on it yesterday. They said you have to be very careful about not only who you talk to, but who you sit next to, who you are calling your family.

Shifting on the couch, I feel something wet and familiar, and when I move my body I notice, to my horror, a tiny patch on the sofa where my blood has leaked. A round copper stain. It's a whole five days early, too. I remove as much as I can with cold water and one of Clara's kitchen tea towels and decide to get out of there. I put on my coat and I pull the door closed behind me without saying goodbye. While walking down the road and out to the street, I text Dr. Rayna to ask if she can see me urgently. As fast as I can, I hike it to the nearest bus stop. The day is new, and I'm free to be outside of the delusion, outside of the house of horror. I shudder at the things that woman called us. They almost made me feel bad for my sister, who probably hasn't ever had anyone square up to her like that before. No one but *that person* would dare.

I'm not going to let myself be dragged into this anymore; there was something so cold and dead about that Serene girl, now that I'm think-ing of it. The hand that Serene touched feels colder than the other, or maybe I'm just imagining things. Psychosomatic, Dr. Rayna might say, or perhaps she'd simply tell me to listen to my soul. I'm going to tell her everything. I'm going to tell her that my sister needs psychiatric help and that I love her but absolutely cannot be part of her life anymore, which I'm sure Dr. Rayna will agree is fair enough. Sometimes we've come as far as we can with family, Dr. Rayna always says. Sometimes the kindest thing we can do, she says, is to leave them behind with the bones of our former selves.

I wait eighteen windy minutes for the bus. The driver stops and I board, and when the feeling is back in my fingers, I try calling Dr. Rayna. The call goes directly to voicemail and I garble something about needing to see her sooner rather than later if she doesn't mind. Then I try to focus on my breathing as the bus makes its way into real, proper, living London, where no mothers are coming back to haunt us and no sisters are around to turn you mad and ruin your life.

I have two hundred and fifty pounds in my account from some online proofreading I did for an academic journal on podiatry, so I stop at the flower shop and treat myself to some peonies in Peckham. Then I buy things I wouldn't usually stretch to like macadamia nut milk and golden turmeric latte mix. If I'm going to Love myself, if I'm really going to Love myself, I cannot deprive myself of Things anymore. I dial Rayna again for good measure just in case the message didn't send. I leave her a calmer message this time, about how it would actually be really amazing if she replied because I'm worried that my sister might do something to herself.

Camberwell is not so far away, really only around the corner, so when I find myself outside Dr. Rayna's office, it feels less like I went out of my way and more like I was just passing because I was in the area. I knock loudly though I know this is what you might call an imposition and probably not what you do when you have a professional working client relationship. I stare at the red brick of her building and knock and knock and knock, but no one comes out.

It's just as well.
I go home.

I expect to feel even worse in a short while, so I make a batch of guacamole and chips and preemptively line up a roster of YouTube videos and Change Your Life podcasts to keep me calm.

I keep thinking about my sister's choice of words. Piss-stained. Foul. Piss-stained. Foul—expecting them to bore a hole in me, but the result is surprisingly benign. All that escapes me is a wash of pity, far from the usual shame. The thing that has lingered, though, is the thought of Serene. How she held my head in her cold hands. It was a moment of real looking, as though she might have understood me. Then my sister had to go all Real Housewives and attack her. In another life, I think, Serene could be the friend I never had. We could be good for each other. She the assertive, rough-around-the-edges one, me the calming influence.

I'm not sure why I'm thinking like this. The Serene person was quite cruel to us both, but my sister can inspire that in anyone.

I start a hot, hot shower running, and as the bathroom begins to steam up, I peer in front of the mirror and peel the wig from my head. There is a line of clear glue on the perimeter of my hairline. I carefully wipe away the excess with a steaming towel. Serene was right. I have really pretty hair underneath, and it's nice that someone has noticed it for once. I untie my Bantu knots, climb into the shower, and soap my hair until the curls zip up, small. I notice how uniform and full they are becoming. I've never really studied the pattern before. Even Clara doesn't have a head of hair like that; she's straightened hers far too much. I inspect the curls springing down my nape and alongside my temples. I'm not beautiful, but in some lights I think I could be called an attractive person, why not? I have a nice nose and honest eyes. I can see in some lights how the girl Serene might look like me, how in some other lights I might even look like her. Let's take the mother thing out of it. Obviously, because my sister is a lunatic.

Out of the shower, I spray my body, face, and hair with some rose spritz that Marie Antoinette the Style Kween was always raving about before she had beef with the brand for not taking a stand on police brutality on Black people in the United States. She moved on to a different product entirely, but by then I'd already bought three bottles. I put on my almost satin robe and sit for a while when a text message comes in from Jen.

The Womb-Men have scheduled an emergency Zoom, and would I like to be part of it? Obviously. The so-called emergency Zoom is scheduled for three p.m. GMT. I wonder what could be so serious that we're having a last-minute meeting. I tell her yes, of course I'm coming. Must stay social. Must stay connected. I listen to the podcast of a CEO who made a fortune by selling vending machines to schools and I keep it playing in the background but I also put the television on where they are playing *Baywatch* reruns just to calm me down. I wonder what Clara's going to do now. I wonder if they've made up already. Why does Clara get to create a whole plot, a whole fantasy mother? I get changed into a sanitary towel nappy and, shifting around on the couch for a bit, I log into Instagram and type in our mother's name.

@SereneDroste01

is an Instagram page of an older Nordic-looking woman with mousy hair who does very average watercolours and

@SereneDrosteMinister

is another Instagram of a preacher of the same name who lives in Jacksonville, Florida. I do a deep dive on the preacher woman and then her son, Raheem, who is damn gorgeous and calls himself Christian GRFJ (gangster rapper for Jesus). I didn't know such a thing existed, so I do some snooping and see that there is a specific type of gang who consider themselves Christian. A lot of them were in prison and have turned their lives around. A lot of them are Born Again. That said, when something has to be done or someone gets disrespected, they have to do what they have to do.

I type in our mother's entire name. *SERENE MARIE NKEM DROSTE* Suddenly I see her. There she is. Our girl from last night. The girl who screamed at my sister and me. The one who I don't like and wouldn't mind being friends with.

There are only three photos—a single row. She has 333 people following her, but there is something a little off about the photos: they look colour-corrected or at least filtered over with some kind of vintage effect. Even though I am the kind of person who never has pictures of myself up on IG (mine's a kitten avatar with hearts), I am the queen of spotting filters, even slight ones. Chrissie Wang uses them to death—although who knows why because she's twenty-one and stunning. Jack Spratt uses them on his abs. I mean it, I can recognize any filter anywhere.

Picture one
Serene Marie Nkem Droste in an orangish room against the window. This orange is bothering me. I've seen it before. In fact, I know the room. It's the room from the photo that Clara stole.

Picture two
Serene Marie Nkem Droste in front of an unmade bed. I don't
recognize the room. Her arms are over her head.

Picture three
Most curious. Taken from outside, looking through a window
into the room with the terra-cotta walls. She is sitting on a
man's lap. The caption reads CATCH ME OUTSIDE and is followed by a laughing emoji.

The scene looks doctored, or maybe it's candid. It has two likes.
Two! The first thing I should do is call my sister to make her aware
of my findings. I try her number but when I call, there's a sustained
tone. Did she block me? I call a few more times and come to the con-
clusion that yes, she did. I take a justified stand and block her number
right back.

Picture four
Serene looking right at the camera, face pixelated around the
edges. Serene doing a bad not-real smile thing. I zoom in on
the pores. People's little imperfections always make me feel
better about life. I see right into the skin, which is pitted and
uneven. There is something recognizable, something I can't
quite reach. The someone looks to be the same woman I met
yesterday who is going about calling herself Serene. The someone could be our mother in some lights, but that's impossible.
Our mother has not been living for thirty whole years! I feel
my pulse start to race a bit because surely this is impossible.
Two people, same name, that happen to look alike. Could it be?
Odder things have happened. I think about my sister's sickness, her malaise, her frightening alcoholism wrapping around
my neck like seaweed, pulling me down, down, down with her.
Enough!

I NEED TO STAY AWAY FROM MY SISTER
I NEED TO KEEP AWAY FROM MY SISTER
I NEED TO BE AWAY FROM MY SISTER

Just then my notification goes and it is a YouTube account, some random girl speculating about the fact that Jack Spratt has definitely split up with his girlfriend Chrissie Wang. Oh no. Of course then I stop everything to go and investigate further. I watch the video, the host of which has correctly pointed out that Jack Spratt is still showing pictures of him and her from Valentine's Day, so the plot thickens. But when I go on Chrissie Wang's page I'm shocked to see all her content about him has been taken down. I start to get worried. I look at her stories to find white writing on a blacked-out page. She is grateful for everyone respecting her privacy at this time. I put my blue-light-blocking glasses on because my head is hurting a bit at the news. I click on Chrissie Wang's mother's page. She posts every Sunday when they come around for dumplings and dim sum and does this cute segment thing on TikTok where she and Chrissie and Jack make food; but Chrissie Wang's mother hasn't posted anything in two weeks. Well, now I'm invested.

It feels a bit hot in my flat, so I open up some windows.

Above me, someone is singing and I hear a light giggle. It is a woman's voice. For a second, I'm not sure what to do; it's vaguely troubling.

Baywatch is still harping on in the background. Mitch the lifeguard is dating an older woman, but the woman looks around Mitch's age so I'm not sure why I think of her as older. It's the patriarchy. I might be a misogynist. Anyway Mitch has a son in this who looks to be eleven or twelve, which is not in line with the last episode in which Mitch didn't have a son because they're not showing the episodes in order. Mitch is imparting wisdom to his son and patting him gamely on the head, which makes me a bit upset.

When I refresh the page on my phone, absentmindedly, a brand new picture has appeared in Serene's feed. With my heart in my mouth I click on the box. This is a picture of her, afro turned away from the camera.

I don't understand how the new picture could have materialized in the space of a minute. Is this a joke?

I click back on Chrissie Wang's story slide two and she is talking about taking a trip to Lake Como to "heal" with all her girlfriends. Everyone is going to Italy this summer. Chrissie Wang is doing something in association with a drinks sponsor. She's dyed her hair to its original black. She has posted twice about girlfriends being the only people you can trust. I think about that for a while, because I've never, ever met anyone I can trust, and that includes Marcus, who is above my head making a girl laugh in a very annoying, singsongy way. I'm in a loop. I'm spinning bloody out. If Jack Spratt has hurt Chrissie Wang I don't know what I'll do.

Shit! I look at the clock and it's 3:05 p.m. I log on to Zoom, damp hair and all. Curls popping and all. Every single Womb-Men from the group except Sunny is on there. Sally explains that Sunny has been on X, Instagram, and even her own YouTube page spilling about what went down at the retreat, and she is calling it sexual coercion; and what's more, she went and got someone to hack Dr. Rayna Panelli's TikTok account, which is so not fair! Now all these social justice warriors are calling Dr. Rayna out and saying she's not a licensed professional and saying that what she did was inappropriate and goes against a code of ethics when dealing with people in her care, so to speak.

"So this is the thing," Toyah is saying, "we had to tell the truth."

I can barely grasp what's being said.

"We had to," Jessica is saying.

"Who said what?" I ask, in a small voice. "And to whom?"

"After all," Toyah goes on, "Sunny didn't lie. Did she?"

"We all had to support Sunny, Dempsey," someone says, but I don't even know who because my head is in my hands and I'm squelching my gums.

"What are you saying, Toyah?" I demand, which is out of character for me, but I just can't believe these turncoats.

"A few of us have shown our support for Sunny on socials. Corroborated her story. We sent you the link so you can do it too if you want."

I go to check my email. Sure enough, there are several Google notifications from each of the Womb-Men spanning from last night. I guess my notifications were switched off.

"It had to be done," said Toyah, and much to my surprise, Sally is also nodding! Wow, I think to myself, women really are terrible, terrible people! I would never ever have imagined this from happy, friendly Sally. It just goes to show. I'd have been better off never meeting them. Even Jen looks like she's on their side.

"But what about Rayna?" I ask them. "What about her job?"

"Thing is," Jen says, "I've a career in yoga to think about. I don't want to cosign what happened, you know?" Sally nods sagely, and so does Jessica.

"But didn't we find it healing?" I almost squawk.

Everyone falls silent, looking off into different parts of the atmosphere.

I try again, a little louder. "Didn't it help some of us?"

"I think," says Sally, "that might be beside the point."

"I think we might have been led," says Toyah, who I feel like never forgave Dr. Rayna for not having wine at the retreat. "We were hungry and there was all that weird incense, you know? I definitely felt affected by something. Light-headed."

"Oh come on!" I'm getting loud now. "She hardly drugged us! Are we really doing this? Are we?"

Sally speaks for the group. "I'm afraid so," she says. "I'm afraid it's done. Dempsey, we adore *you*. You know that. We're just going to have to agree to disagree on this, since it's so polarising."

"SOOO polarising," echoes Jen, who I am starting to feel never has an original thought about anything. As everyone nods, I swallow back my rage. How come everyone is suddenly sticking up for Sunny? Since I'm the kind of woman who sticks up for people, I can no longer be part of this, and I go to tell them as much but by now they are all talking about what funny things their kids did, and by the time we're ready to hang up there's nothing to say anyway. I thought it would be different this time, that I'd have a bunch of friends I could rely on, but if they'd turn round and stab Dr. Rayna in the back like this, there's nothing they wouldn't do to me. In a panic I text Rayna. *HAVING A ZOOM WITH THE WOMB-MEN ABOUT U.*

"Oh my God," says Sally all of a sudden. "Saw your sister on the news. She's such an amazing speaker."

The others nod, smiling. I try to figure out whether they are being genuine, since my sister appears to be all but falling apart and it seems frighteningly, frighteningly obvious. But of course they'll never acknowledge it, they'll just fawn and fawn and tell the truth behind my back. Some women love to see other women flailing. They just do, only they'll never even be honest about it. Dr. Rayna is calling now, so I tell the Womb-Men I have to go and log off. I do my box breaths and, hands shaking, accept the call.

"What do I need to know?" asks the doctor, right away. Her voice is tight.

"I need to see you," I tell her. "I called round earlier. I desperately need to see you."

"I'd like that," says Dr. Rayna, quietly. "I'd like that very much. But come to the house."

A real invitation? To her *house*? I put down the phone, considering the exchange, which now I'm thinking about it, could be read as selfish. I think I need Dr. Rayna but maybe Dr. Rayna needs me. Right now it feels important to be needed.

WHEN YOU WAKE UP IN THE MORNING AND IT'S STILL UNBELIEVABLY TRUE

The clock says 6:23 a.m. All I can think about is damage control. Dempsey needs to leave. Immediately. She almost ruined everything between our mother and me. I reach for my phone. Serene knows I like a drink; perhaps I can blame it on alcohol and antidepressants—say it was a new combination that didn't work out. Not that I take anything for my brain. I prefer to handle the elements alone. I like to know what's what. When I call the number there is a dead tone.

"This number cannot be connected," says the disembodied voice on the other side.

Oh, my sister's her absolute best at looking like she needs help; it's one of the things I hate the most about her. Poor fragile little Dempsey, always needing to be pitied. People look at a person like me and presume I've had it easy, that everything I want comes to me just because I know how to dress and prioritize my looks. Just because I know how to pull it together and present myself and don't expect the world to feel sorry for me.

After trying Serene's number unsuccessfully for the next ten minutes I figure that the only way to not look like a crazy person is to give up. Once I get downstairs, Dempsey is gone, having left a brown stain on my sofa. If that isn't the perfect analogy.

Sometimes, in my softer and more pensive moments, I feel bad about the distance between us, but at times like now I know that there is no way in this world that we could have lived alongside each other. Something about her brings the pain in me up to a seething, palpable level ten, and I cannot risk it. I need to stay complete.

Something stirs inside, and I wonder if I should reach out to Emma for Cristian's number. There is something in me that demands to be released, and I need a person to lie beneath, someone to pour into me. I scour my site, but all the men on there want to have long conversations for a while before meeting up. Everyone seems to be very anti ONS (one-night stand) these days, which I never understand. It's getting harder to get what I want, since I don't like to have my face on my profile for anyone to see. I use an old picture, where I'm wearing a chocolate-brown weave.

I take a look on Craigslist, but there's nothing on there that'll happen fast enough. It takes me twenty mins to set up a dating profile on AdultFriendFinder and set it to incognito mode. It takes me four minutes to take a photo in bed and edit it in Facetune so my face is turned upwards and my lips look full and wet. It takes thirty more seconds to make my tits rounder and delete the under-eye bags. And then I'm live.

In five minutes I've garnered fourteen likes. Hands trembling with anticipation, like some kind of crazed person I scroll past seven people. The eighth is actually two people, an Indian couple who look like they have a bit of money. I send the first message and ask them if they'd like to meet today. The man is called Pritesh, and he says that they'd like to see if there's rapport first.

FINE, I write, feeling annoyed. **WANNA DO A CALL NOW OR WHAT?** But Pritesh says that Ramu, his wife, is at work and they usually talk about these things and they do every part of it together and that maybe we can talk tonight, but by now I'm scrolling through, past, and beyond, until I'm on number fourteen. The last like.

Number fourteen is someone with a lot of face tattoos, which I think can work. Pritesh is sending me a question mark. I block him at once and ask Tattoo Face how close to central London he is, and can he get to the Nobu Shoreditch Hotel within the hour? When he says that it's possible, I make the appointment and get into the car. While driving I feel farther and farther from death or disaster.

In the Nobu Hotel, the lights are dim. Here, one can see all the way up into the truth of anything. The man with tattoos orders jasmine tea to the room, and I nurse a premixed Negroni or two from the bar. He hands me a glass of water, takes my face in his hands (also tattooed; nice!) and tries to kiss me. No thank you, I tell him. Get over there, on the floor.

Later, when he has left, I order crispy black cod, macarons, and some sort of orange polenta cake and shove it all down from a horizonal position. I drink the other premixed cocktails and wish I remembered more of what happened. Tattoo Face said some sweet things that hardly seemed important at the time. When I'm in the shower, I try to squeeze one of them out from memory, but it won't come forth. I try to remember the tattooed hands, but they are already gone. Back in the room, I notice that before slipping away, he had scrawled a note on the hotel notepad.

Clara,

You. You. You.

You are a beautiful person with so much passion. I don't want to come on too strong, but I wanted to let you know that I'm six months sober, and it's by far the best thing I ever did. If you ever wanted to join me at a meeting, here's my number, and if it's not like that and I'm overstepping / missed the mark, just ignore that part and call me for another good time. I want to worship your body some more. You deserve everything. I want to give it to you.

With love, and the utmost respect,
Elias.

Also I love your work! Your writings have helped me so much in the past year. Peace & Respect!!!!

The blue-grey water in my throat threatens, so I order a real mojito to the room and scroll a while, to numb myself out . . . Instagram, Rightmove, YouTube, more AdultFriendFinder.

Could I go again, get rid of the feeling of being exposed, the feeling of yet another person knowing me, knowing my life? I scroll some more, adjusting my usual settings. I am a WOMAN looking for MEN. WOMEN. COUPLE. TRANS. I tick every box available, then move my search from 25–40 to 21–65. I adjust the map to "within 5 miles," because I don't have time to waste. I scroll again, and see something that stops me.

I sit up in bed.

Kendrick Lewis. Screen name BADMAYOR.

Kendrick Fucking Lewis.

Kendrick Lewis, using a picture that looks as though it's from the eighties.

Kendrick Lewis, shirt off, in some kind of nondescript gym.

Kendrick Lewis. Looking for WOMEN.

Looking for ages 18–24.

Looking for CASUAL HOOKUP.

Looking for ROLEPLAY, NSA FWB, ONS, DDLG.

This is too good. Too good. I have to. Have to.

I make a new profile, just for Kendrick. Just for him.

IT'S NICE TO BE NICE
BUT IT'S KINDER TO BE KIND

On Sunday afternoon, Dr. Rayna is waiting in the open door, looking more sumptuous than ever, if a little pale. She is wearing a rose-coloured silk shirt and matching expensive-looking wide pants. She watches me as I walk up the garden path and it's a long path, so it starts to freak me out. The garden is set with rhododendrons and manicured bushes at either side of the pathway. "I love the hair," she says, as I get closer. "New hair, new start."

"Thank you," I say, hands reaching for my curls, already feeling as though I'm in some kind of big trouble. I want to say sorry for the circumstances, but Rayna has already turned on her heels, into the house, is already marching off down the hall. I close the door carefully behind me. Inside, the faint smell of lavender. The house, ever her style, is cream and gold, full of textures, earth tones, the softest whites.

"I have some blueberry hibiscus tea brewing," she calls from down the hall. "Why don't you sit?"

I sit in the open-plan dining room, taking in her camel butter-leather furniture and shelves of large amethyst and rose quartz spheres. There is a diffuser on a burl-wood credenza emitting a pale lilac fog.

After a few minutes, Rayna comes in without the tea. She sits opposite me and closes her eyes, for at least twenty seconds. It gets a little awkward, to tell the truth. Just me on one side, trying not to stare, and on the other side, Rayna rolling her head around clockwise, then counter-clockwise, placing her hand on her neck.

"My shoulders are sore," she tells me. She rubs some oil from a small bottle and spreads it on her collarbone. A thin line of drool escapes the corner of my mouth. I wipe it away quickly. Rayna has her eyes closed again. There is nothing to do but watch her.

"Lavender," she says, finally opening her eyes and fixing me with a long stare. "You want?"

But this is all a bit too much for me.

"I want you to know I'm not with them," I blurt out. Rayna freezes.

"I suppose you've heard, then? All the nasty little details?"

"Yeah," I say, recalling Jen's text from just this morning.

FOR FULL TRANSPARENCY, DEMPSEY, WE ALL DID TIKTOK AND INSTAGRAM VIDEOS TO BACK UP THE CLAIM BECAUSE WE REFUSE TO GASLIGHT A BLACK WOMAN. YOU'RE WELCOME TO JOIN TOO, IF YOUR HEART FEELS RIGHT ABOUT IT AND WOULD OBVIOUSLY LOVE FOR YOU TO BE ON THE RIGHT SIDE OF THIS, BUT NO PRESSURE.

"I can't. I think they're awful," I say.

Dr. Rayna leans back. "They?" Then in a quieter voice, "Oh. The other women too. Right. They're about to back up Sunny's ridiculous claims then?"

I fidget a little, watching a sparrow landing on the hedgerow on the other side of the glass doors. "I mean, I don't know. They were talking about it. I mean—I think they already did."

Rayna looks wounded.

"Wow," she says, getting to her feet. "Well, you learn who your people are, don't you? Let me get this tea."

Rayna stalks out of the room, leaving me alone again. I watch the sparrow hopping around for a few minutes.

A shadow breezes past. We hear the front door brush open, then slam shut. A tall, energetic, thin-lipped man with lots of designer stubble walks in and right up to where I'm sitting. He sticks a hand out and I reach for it.

"Hello. Hello. I'm Raymond. Rayna's better half haha."

The man, who has intense blue eyes and a grip that is slightly on the tighter side, introduces himself again as Raymond Rayna's Husband and puts his helmet on the coffee table with some force. Then he announces we're all having cocktails.

"I don't drink," I tell him, but he has already gone into the kitchen where Rayna is bustling around.

"Babyyyyyy," I hear him saying. "Let's have a drink."

He clacks back into the room in his bike shoes and rather rudely, I think, switches on the radio unit surround sound. James Blake starts singing away at us. Dr. Rayna comes in without the tea. Again.

"I'm making old-fashioneds," says Raymond, who I've decided I don't like. Rayna nods and looks at me.

"That fine?"

I nod, because what else can I do? I'm shocked that Rayna even drinks, is the truth. Rayna comes back to sit on the armchair opposite me. Her husband hunches over the bar cart, limes in hand.

"So the others . . . what were they saying?" Her voice has become hurried, desperate.

The husband turns off the radio, then resumes his position at the bar. "We talking about Sunita?"

His wife nods gravely. They're both looking at me now, he while viciously attacking a piece of ginger. He has a very intense stare. I tell them about the call, because I can't not, and the two of them do a whole lot of looking at me and even more at each other.

Rayna's husband finishes making the drinks and hands them to us. Then he clears his throat and promptly leaves the room.

"Just a minute, Dempsey," Rayna says.

She follows him into some back room or other. I can hear them speaking to each other at the other end of the house in low, urgent tones.

"That isn't the way I'd like to approach it," I can hear Rayna saying. "Raymond. Just. Listen."

Raymond and Rayna? I think, settling a little onto the soft, soft couch, being careful not to spill. I try to drink the drink quickly, because it is HORRIBLE.

Raymond comes out, cheeks on fire.

"Can I make you another drink?" he asks, a little gruffly.

I don't know how to say no. Before I know it I'm nursing another one while the two of them are watching me again.

"I can rely on you, can't I Dempsey?" Rayna says, breaking the silence. She is next to me on the couch now, stroking the length of my arm.

"Of course," I say. "You can count on me. Always."

"How have you been?" she asks. But how to even begin to fill her in on everything? Where would I start? The woman who isn't my mother is awful, but I can't stop thinking about her? My sister assaulted her? My sister insulted me? My sister thinks the woman who isn't our mother tried to kiss her? What?

"I've been okay," I lie. "I wanted to see how *you* were." Also a lie, I realise.

Rayna smiles, but it does not reach all the way up the eyes.

Her husband does a light but significant tap on the table.

"Debbie . . ."

"Dempsey," Dr. Rayna corrects him.

"Pardon me. Dem-sey, we're going to need you to help us."

"Whatever you need," I say, and really mean it.

"We need to refute what this bitch is saying," says the husband.

I spin around to Dr. Rayna, expecting her to correct his language, but she does not.

"How many women were on the call? Was it everyone?" Her eyes bore into me.

I study the creamy Berber rug on the floor.

"Dempsey. Was it everyone?"

"Pretty much," I admit. "They're cowards," I say, for good measure.

The two of them swirl the ice in their drinks.

"My wife has some . . . um . . . unorthodox methods," begins Raymond. Rayna shoots him a look. "We want to know," says Raymond, "what you think we should offer the others for their discretion."

I'm not sure I understand. "You want to pay them for . . . ?"

"It would be taken out of context, you see," says Rayna, hurriedly. "Most people don't fully understand my practices the way you do."

"What we mean is," says Raymond. "Well, to put it bluntly we have a bit of money and we'd be willing to pay. We know you're struggling and I'm sure a couple of the others might be too. I'm just saying we need to make it go away."

Rayna gazes into the rug.

They ask me to stay for dinner, which is bad quinoa and worse vegan chili. I eat all of mine and Rayna just eats a third of hers while Raymond eats a half. When it's done, Raymond makes us drink another cocktail, which he brags is mostly only bitters and vermouth. He and Rayna are still exchanging looks. Then, all of a sudden, Raymond has stood up and is making his way over to me. He places his hand on my shoulder. There's some force to it.

"Desiree," says Raymond. "Do you understand? This is my wife's career we're talking about. Her entire livelihood."

My senses and head feel warm, as though there might be a chance at happiness. My belly feels woozy. I nod my head yes. Not only do I want to be available, I want to seem useful.

"She's built it up over many years," he says.

"Just tell me what you want me to do," I say.

They settle a little, and Raymond gives me the strict instruction to call another emergency meeting among the Womb-Men, and to report back afterwards to let them both know how it goes. There's a sense of unease then, as though they're suddenly tired of having me over, so I make some excuse about needing to be back at home and I get to my feet. While waiting for the bus I try to understand why anyone would want to hurt Rayna, or Chrissie Wang. Or even my sister. The world is full of evil people.

••

Once home, I try to make it happen right away but Sally can't really talk right now, and Jennifer just doesn't think it would be a good idea; and when I check, I've been deleted from the group WhatsApp, and I never took the time to save the other girls' numbers. This is *not* good for the plan. To relax a little I get even more wrapped in the latest TikTok drama: Jack Spratt has now challenged someone to an MMA fight and the someone is the brother of the new person that Chrissie Wang is dating. Allegedly everyone is calling her names for moving on so quickly. It's a mess. Everyone's follower count is way up except for Chrissie's. Chrissie Wang is not commenting on that or anything else, because she is at New York Fashion Week.

An hour later I get a text from Rayna thanking me for coming round and telling me to text her when it's done, which is so stressful that my stomach starts to feel as though I've swallowed an entire box of sharp tacks. Marcus texts, finally, with the details for the rescheduled show and a cross-and-bones emoji and in a way it sort of trumps everything.

WOULDN'T MISS IT!

I type back, and then wonder if I should have texted back so quickly. With the stress of everything. I leave my phone in the tincture cupboard, not to be touched until morning.

• •

Sometimes I think of myself as a person who does not know how to do the right things. I blame myself for the break between Clara and me. I overreacted during the hair-relaxing fiasco, which, when I think about it, couldn't have hurt that much; everyone had hair relaxer in those days. I don't know how I repeatedly manage to mess things up. Anyway, I blame myself for the three-year split during those important bonding years.

Clara and I fell back into touch in late summer of 2008. I had seen my sister in snatches, of course—when Kendrick was sworn in as Lambeth city councilor, and at two tense but polite lunches thrown by Claudette, a kind of peace offering. My sister had grown taller and upsettingly, fiercely beautiful, and everyone was always in awe of her for no other reason than this. God knows, it wasn't her personality. She always had nude lip gloss in those days, and it never came apart on her lips. Her hair was hot-combed into a half up–half down position. She often wore this thick, well-attached ponytail. We were fourteen, and Clara was to take me shopping. Much to her dismay, Adolphus had contacted Kendrick and proposed this. I'd spent two whole days before I was due to meet her deciding what to wear. She was taking me *into town* with her, meaning Oxford Street. Who knew it would end the way it did?

As I got off the bus to meet my sister, I noticed her sitting on a bench across the road from the bus station with four moody-looking girls. No one seemed particularly happy to be there. They were the kind of girls that looked like they should be in soaps. They were wearing a lot of gold jewelry and everyone's makeup was excessive and perfect.

"Hi," I whispered as I approached them, trying hard not to do the funny mouth thing. My sister was the only one not to look up. The pretty girls all squinted at me and turned toward Clara.

"Who's this then?" said a brown girl with green, green eyes.

"My cousin," said Clara, and I felt the bottom drop out of me. I nodded vigorously, to keep up the pretense for her and also to stop myself from crying.

"Ah right," said Green Eyes. "Cool. Cool."

No one said anything. A girl who looked plump and happy walked past us holding her mother's hand. The group I was standing in thought this was the most hilarious thing ever. They stared at the girl, who could not have been more than twelve years old, until she averted her eyes and then they all burst into laughter. Green Eyes gave her the finger. Unnecessarily.

"So where are you from, Clara's long-lost cousin?" said a girl with a blonde bob and freckles.

A dark look fell upon my sister. "Don't worry about it."

The girls and I stood around, glaring at passersby.

"Wanna do a run or what?" said Clara, suddenly sounding common as muck.

"Obviously," said Green Eyes, then, peering suspiciously at me, "Is she gonna be alright, or . . . ."

The girls assessed me in a way that made me want to hide.

"Dem," said Clara, "maybe wait outside."

"She'll get us followed," said Blonde Bob, and the others snickered.

All except Clara, who fixed her with a look. Under her glare, Blonde Bob reddened.

All the girls stared at me again, and then, when it was more than I could take, they turned their attention to the job at hand. We all walked across together to Boots.

"You first," said my sister, to Blonde Bob.

So first, in went Blonde Bob, and then went Ponytail and then Green Eyes and then the angriest-looking girl—with a purple streak in her hair—and then went my sister. "See you later," said Clara at the door, not looking at me. "Maybe wait in the alleyway."

I waited in the alleyway. It began to rain.

I walked into the store. There was my sister, helping herself to red and blond boxes of hair dye, helping herself to anything. Bizarre. I stood and stared. She didn't see me. I walked back outside.

The rain stopped. I needed to pee. I'd had a can of Coke on the long bus journey. When I could wait no longer, I pulled down my pants and let it go right there. Clara appeared in the alleyway midway through the relief, her face the very picture of disappointment.

"Come on," she said. "Let's go. Now! The police just took Jackie. Idiot. I told her not to take anything electronic."

We walked to Debenhams in silence, because Clara was, as she put it, *starving*. In Debenhams, I watched her put away two scones with jam and cream, a cup of tea, and a baked potato with cheese and beans. She had all this stolen stuff in her book bag.

"Gonna finish that?" she asked, motioning to the bag of crisps I was holding.

"Go for it," I said. My sister snatched it from me and proceeded to gobble up the crisps without even breathing.

On the way back to the bus station she vomited in an alleyway. I rushed to move her ponytail out of the way, and ended up vomiting hard in sympathy. My sister held her belly and groaned.

"You should go home," she said, not bothering to look at me. I turned to go, and she grabbed my hand. "Wait," said she, "got you these."

She threw me a handful of tiny concealer bottles, three mascaras, some pressed powder foundation, and a box of brown hair dye. "You need to try a bit harder," she said, wiping the sick from her chin. "With your looks."

Then she waved me away with a manicured hand, eyes still on the ground. "You know your way back to the bus, I think."

As I walked away, my sister stood up, arch straight, shaking and shaking her head at me.

CLARA
REMEMBERS IT DIFFERENTLY

She turned up with trousers at half mast, peeling lips, sleep nestling in the corners of her eyes. It's like Kendrick did nothing to help her out, you could tell that from a mile off. She looked uncared for and feral. We were already fourteen, for God's sake. Worse still, I knew the girls would be taking it all in. At that age we assessed everything about other girl-people, split ends, good skin or not, good hair or not. So when the cruel attention was inevitably turned to her, it didn't make sense to admit she was my sister. Too many sticky questions would have arisen from this. All my friends needed to know was that I was pretty and mysterious. Might be adopted. Had some money, that was it. And high school was hard enough. The act was hard enough. Imagine forcing these girls to like you. The only way to sell was to lead with a detached sense of cool; to beat them at their game. Everyone knew you began that with your looks. You had to be a little mean, too, or they'd take you for a mug. I suppose in that way, I was lucky to have Claudette, who would not have had me out on the street with anything less than perfect hair. I even had my nails done every three Fridays. Pretty hands were so important, said Claudette. Hands are always a dead giveaway as to your class. Claudette favored French-tipped or natural pink. Oval, never square. A light shine.

Anyway, Dempsey met up with us that day, and the girls appraised her like hungry dogs. She was terrified; I could feel her stress in my body, and I didn't like it. I know she was hurt when I called her my cousin, I saw her shoulders droop, and I felt like the devil herself, but then another feeling came over me. I looked at Dempsey and her perceived helplessness, her easy, manipulative lessening of herself. If I could have taken her apart that day, I would have done. Not only did Dempsey look disheveled and awful, but she was doing this ticky eye-blinking thing, which made me want to smash her in the face and comfort her and cry and scream at the same time. I prayed to God that the other girls weren't noticing this, that this was an insight afforded by the kind of deep looking that only a sibling could give to another.

"What's your name?" Tracey was saying, in a somewhat combative manner. I knew, how I knew what was coming next.

I left Dempsey outside the shop and there I felt the discomfort subside. I got some stuff for her, which for some reason I decided to pay for like a real person, a person who deserved to be alive, and acted like it.

I walked by the alleyway next to the store and hid for a while, watching my sister release a steady line of piss. Her mouth was open; she was squinting, concentrating. As her eyes came up to meet mine, we regarded each other, and I felt my rage evaporate into love. Pure love— and deep pity. Then I felt a telltale feeling in my body. The not quite blue. The smothering thing.

"Come on," I felt myself snarl, "I'm really fucking hungry."

Dempsey pulled her knickers up.

"I said can you hurry up!" I bellowed, and the alleyway crooned in response.

We sat in Marks and Spencer's and I got a sandwich, and Dempsey picked at some crisps, and we shared another packet between us. I wanted to talk, then, but Dempsey only stared at the table and I suddenly felt exhausted, so very tired. So very like I wouldn't have cared if this was my last day on earth. After about forty minutes of sitting there, staring into what felt like space, we decided to call it a day.

I walked Dempsey back to her bus stop and waited a while, until she was safely on the bus. I stayed to wave, but she turned her head away.

I walked home past the travelling fair, where a boy with dirty hands called me over and said I was pretty for a Black. We went into the control rooms and messed around. He smelled of petrol and rust.

When I got home just shy of an hour later, Kendrick was on the phone with Claudette. Had Dempsey told on me? Would Claudette find out and finally send me away?

But no, nothing like that. Claudette handed me the phone and got back to cutting up cubes of sweet potato, placing them carefully on the roasting tin.

"Thanks so much for today," he said. "Dempsey would kill me for telling you this, but she came back much happier. I think we need more of these little outings. I do."

"Yeah," I said, masking my surprise. "Yeah, definitely. Well bye, Kendrick."

Feeling even more miserable now, I tried to pass the phone back to Claudette, who waved it away with irritation. I carefully placed it back on the receiver.

• •

It is Tuesday and I am slapped over the front page of the *Daily Mail*. The dress Serene talked me into appears a size too small, and despite wearing more makeup than I ever have before, I look puffy. To me the pictures are awful, the fashion dated. Plus you can see where I've been sweating. I try to call Emma to demand her opinion but it's going to voicemail. Here is the rub: to warrant the lending of the dress, I have to post it to my profile. When I go to upload, I see that I'm tagged in lots of versions of the same video. Again and again and again. The odd thing is that people are hearting the videos and images. Brands are trying to get in touch with me. My follower count is up. I've been tagged on a lot of audience photos. When I look at the photos again, they have shifted before my eyes. Perhaps I look great? Was my mother right? Did my mother know best? Everyone seems to be loving it. By the time Emma calls back, I've settled in my body a little.

"Oh, it was nothing," I say, almost cheerful. "I was just checking on *you*."

"Oh," says Emma. The line goes quiet.

"Yes," I say, nodding my head to no one. "Yes." And then I say, "How's everything going with the baby . . . and everything?"

I hadn't meant to sound so clumsy, but feigning interest when there is none has never been easy for me. Emma seems to baulk at the question and in a voice I haven't heard before says, "The baby and everything are well, thanks for asking, Clara."

There's some curtness to her voice, as though she might just have forgotten that I'm her newest superstar client. Not knowing what to do with that, I garble something insincere about it being a Really Special Time and that everyone who does this kind of thing is like . . . almost superhuman to me. "I couldn't imagine it," I say out loud. Emma's tone changes from clipped to informative. Something about the last trimester.

"Of course," she tells me, "Willow is so, so excited, they're bursting at the seams."

Willow. Willow. Oh, Willow is the partner. It occurs to me that I have never thought to ask Emma anything much about her private life. I rarely think of Emma as little more than a vehicle, some link in the chain—a facilitator of my career. Someone I got in lieu of Janine Arterton. All I really know about Emma is that she lives in Queens Park and is, well, having a baby. Any day now.

Emma has stopped talking so I say, "Oh my God that's amazing," to I'm not sure what.

"How's your friend?" Emma wants to know. "Your . . . your relative. She's pretty dynamic."

I think about the way Serene has been speaking to her, cutting her down at every opportunity. Serene and I still haven't spoken. I feel something hard forming in my throat.

"She's well," I reply, with some caution. "We're planning some shoots."

"Mmmm," says Emma. "I'm so grateful to her for handling the fashion side of things. You deserve those connections. You're the *perfect* specimen. She's the *perfect* person to do that. She has the *perfect* personality."

Emma, it seems, is playing the game. There is a silence, and I tell some flat lie about someone being at the door.

I'm back on AFF. My new profile is Davina Doll. I am twenty-four and a half and I look like a Black model who looks a lot like me, but curvier. (I found her picture on Pinterest.) I have been speaking very clearly to Kendrick Lewis about needing a Friend with Benefits and an "older mentor, to work on some *very* specific fantasies." This morning, Kendrick appears to have taken the bait.

HI, NT INTO GAMES, he has written. *IF WE MAKE CONTACT. WNT TO MEET. OR FACETIME TO MAKE SURE YR RL.*

I'M RL, I write back

PROVE IT BY CALLING, he replies.

When I refresh my bookings@clarakallis email I see that I have two beauty campaign offers, fashion lending from another brand, an invite to a director's house for a sit-down dinner with other "key women in literature." I try texting my mother again.

I'M SORRY. BIG OPPORTUNITY. TV MAYBE. NEED YOU. CAN WE PUT IT BEHIND US. PLEASE????

And then, emboldened by the new developments, I transfer two thousand pounds to her account.

THERE'S MORE WHERE THAT CAME FRM, I text, like some gangster in a film.

YOU'LL NEVER EVER MAKE THE INNER CIRCLE

There is a picture of my sister on her feed looking pretty dazzling in a dress that is the colour of blood. She smiles, and her new teeth, which are perfect but a little too white to look real or anything, gleam. Something about the picture sends an awful chill up my spine. Her follower count is up by a cool eight thousand; it has been jumping up a lot in the last week.

On YouTube, comments such as

Is it drugs?
Def drugs and
Cocaine, anyone? What a mess.
litter the comments.

Needing to put my mind elsewhere, I log into the Medical Foot Health Clinic portal and begin updating the most recent spreadsheets. That's the thing about this work: it's reliable. Plus, numbers are facts. They won't lie to you. There's a voicemail on my phone from an anonymous number. I can't help wondering if it's Dr. Rayna's husband. What an absolute creep. The most significant thing I remember about that Sunday is how much Raymond's presence appeared to flatten Dr. Rayna, to quiet her down. I hadn't liked that at all. I press play on the message, and a low sound escapes the speaker into the room.

"Dempsey, it was so good meeting you," says the red voice. "I'm so sorry Clara and I got into it, I was looking forward to getting to know you."

There is a sound of splashing on the line, as though the caller is in the bath or something.

"Not my finest hour," the voice goes on. "Dempsey. I take complete and absolute responsibility for the mix-up. I do. We had a terrible argument, Dempsey. Please do call me back. I'd like to make it up to you."

I dial the number back out of pure compulsion. If the phone rings, I don't hear it. There's an immediate click, as though the person was waiting.

"Hello," says the voice that sounds like it's from Nowhere.

"Hello," I say, not being sure what comes next.

"Dempsey," says the voice. "Will you meet me somewhere? I'm worried about Clara."

"Me too," I tell the voice, and then, "I don't want to pry, Serene, but what happened to make her go off like that? Did something happen upstairs?"

"Dempsey, I don't even know," says Serene's voice. "I went up to see how she was doing when she ran up the stairs, and she was in the bathroom staring into the mirror. Just staring into it, in a trance or something. When I tried to approach, she came at me. I've never seen her act like that before."

"Yeah," I say. "Well, the thing is, Clara's got a temper. It's horrible. I'm telling you."

"Not in my experience," says this someone. "She's a bit passive if anything."

"Passive?" I say. "Not ever in my . . ."

"The thing is," says the voice, "I'm not sure how to help her. We're doing well. We're in the middle of the tour, things are happening Dempsey but I don't know . . . the drinking, and the other stuff."

"Other stuff?"

"This is huge for her," says Serene. "She's Black. She's a woman. You can't fumble an opportunity like this! You just can't, Dem."

I suddenly feel quite protective of my sister. Who is this person? What's any of this to her? Why should it matter if Clara is missing her chance or not? But the voice sounds stern. This voice is attached to a temper, too, a volatile *you never know what*. I saw it up close last week.

"I don't know. I think the fame is getting to her head."

"It isn't that simple. That's your sister," snaps Serene. "You have to be good to your sister. Who will if you won't?"

And in comes the flooding guilt, the telltale absence of the things I ought to feel; things I ought to do. This person is right. This person is looking at me, catching me out. Who am I to dismiss my sister in that way? Even if she's horrible? Even if she did call me a foul, ugly, piss-stained bitch, which is about the worst thing anyone has ever said to me, and that's saying something?

"You'll never guess what she said to me," I find myself saying. "It was awful. It was really mean!"

"What did she say to you?" says this person, already sounding bored and even more faraway. But I don't care. I'm in telling-on-my-sister mode.

"Clara called me a foul, ugly, piss-stained bitch."

To my shock, there is the sound of muffled laughter, but perhaps I imagine it, because surely no one would laugh at that. Dr. Rayna is always trying to tell me that I have a tendency to imagine the worst of people.

Serene finishes coughing. Regains herself.

"That's really awful," she finally says. "You shouldn't let her talk to you like that, Dem."

I say nothing.

"Can we all meet for a cup of tea? No alcohol for her. Nowhere she can get a drink, understand? We'll walk in Burgess Park or something."

I watch a money spider climbing up my windowsill on a thin translucent line.

"Why are you doing this?" I want to know. "If she attacked you, why are you forgiving her?"

"Look," says Serene, "I think your sister's going through something. I've been there. I want to be of help. And frankly, Dempsey—can I be frank with you, Dempsey?"

"You can," I tell the voice.

"Well, I need the work. She's my main source of income, hun."

Fair enough.

"I'm so so sorry if I added to the fight," I say. "I think it was just the awkwardness of the moment."

"It's all okay," she says. "Everyone was a little off last night—I mean week."

When I hang up the phone, my head hurts and my mouth is ticking like crazy. I can't call Dr. Rayna because I didn't do the task at hand and the Womb-Men are still freezing me out, it seems. I sit for the whole morning thinking about the voice, and the hands attached to the voice. I'm still angry and disgusted by my sister, and the awful things she said, but I try to write something positive, something edifying. It comes out like this:

CLARA NEEDS HEALING.
CLARA NEEDS TO DO THE WORK.
IT LIKELY ISN'T HER FAULT,
BUT WE ALL MUST TAKE RESPONSIBILITY,
SOMEHOW, AT SOME POINT.

••

At eight fifty-four p.m., I push open the door to the Grime Cavern, which is almost punched in. I tried to be fashionably late to Marcus's gig in case there were lots of people there, so I wouldn't have to mingle. The bar has the feel of an old theatre, and Marcus is crooning sweet nothings into some kind of effects machine. There's barely anyone here for viewing or support. In the very front row a lone girl in a sundress is watching him and swaying to the beat, almost lovingly. To my alarm, there is a face I think I recognize. I can't quite put my finger on it, and then . . .

"Hi Dempsey!" he says, making his way over, "it's so good to see you!"

I must look confused, because then he adds, "It's Raoul. From the party?"

I see no reason why Raoul should be happy to see me at all, and am surprised he even remembers my name. I give him the look you give to people when you're trying to be polite but you also know they're trying to trick you.

"Well," I force a laugh, "I got the text flyer."

It's a sore point, to be honest. Marcus has been pretty absent in the worst way. I barely even hear him moving around upstairs anymore. It must be something to do with the girl, who could be fresh out of a Scandinavian fashion ad. I wonder if she's the one who was laughing over my head that night. But this girl doesn't look like she has it in her. The Scandinavian model looks too wispy and self-conscious to emit such a sound. I need something to do with myself, so, mustering all of my social strength, I ask Raoul how he's been doing, and he launches into something boring about social media. I try to keep up and nod a lot. Must appear normal. Like someone who goes to bars and is sometimes friendly.

"You're getting a bit low," I say, as though I say this kind of thing all the time. I nod to his drink. "Can I get you a top-up?"

"I'll get *you* one," says Raoul, draining his beer. "What you having?"

What do people drink? Can I ask for sugar-free ginger beer? I decide against this.

"Whisky please?"

"Neat? What kind?"

"Um no, a margarita please," I say, hoping it was convincing, but I don't think it is, because Raoul giggles.

"A skinny one?" goes Raoul. If this is a joke, it isn't funny. Still, I nod my head yes.

"Coming right up," sings Raoul.

"Are you TikTok famous?" I ask him when he comes back with the drinks. He's pretty enough.

"Not quite," says Raoul. "But I'm addicted." He shows me his profile, which is all talking heads about people in the music industry and who they are dating and who they violated. The margarita is gorgeous and fake-sweet, so I drain it. Before I know it, Raoul is off again refreshing our drinks. Must go easy. I'm not Clara, after all.

Raoul has left me with his phone. When I notice Jack Spratt on his feed history, I almost shriek in excitement.

Raoul dances back over, amused.

"I follow him on Instagram!" I almost bellow.

"No way," says Raoul.

We listen to Marcus's set—which really could be described as a long, connected wail—and then I ask Raoul for his take on everything Chrissie and Jack related.

"I think that they haven't been together for a while," he says, excitedly. "But Jack Spratt just kept up the pretense, and Chrissie Wang's met someone new that she likes and wants to be public with. So, they had to stage a breakup."

I consider this, slurping my drink.

"You know what?" I say. "Raoul, you might have something there."

Ahead of us, Marcus is still wailing into the air, singing some terrible tune.

"But then why make it so dramatic?" I say.

Raoul shrugs.

Scandinavian Model comes to the bar to order fizzy water and sort of smiles at Raoul but barely looks at me. I pull up Instagram now, to Serene Droste's page. I decide to quiz Raoul about Serene and the doctored images. He looks like a man who knows his way around a face filter.

"Look at this profile. Weird, right?"

Raoul puts down his beer and inspects my phone.

"How odd," he says. "It's almost as though the person taking these is crouched down in the corner, like a pet or something. The face is so, so filtered."

"Bingo!" I say, slapping down my glass.

"Is it AI? See here. The pictures appear as if flipped."

I like the way Raoul says "as if flipped" and I notice his eyelashes are very very dark, like mine. I must be looking hard at them because he laughs.

"You okay Dempsey?"

"Yeah," I say. "I mean I don't know what I think of this music. Is that a bad thing?"

"Well, Marcus has his own sound," says Raoul, staring longingly at the drum machine. "I'm very into it."

I can see that he's being kind and I'm being mean, and, not really wanting to engage any further about Marcus's "sound," I start to talk about something else. I decide to do one more drink if Raoul offers, but nothing else. Raoul says we need to end with a shot because we're out and here and alive, so we might as well. Good logic.

"How long have you been doing celebrity gossip?" I ask him, but then, from the stage Marcus launches into a slow and melancholic chorus, a love-moan. We listen, at once taken over by his raspy, mournful tone. To the left of me, I'm shocked to see Raoul is sobbing lightly. The next thing I do completely surprises me, because I have never ever touched a man, not on purpose, not since Kendrick. I slide my hand into Raoul's. For a second he stiffens, isn't sure how to take it. Then I feel his hand relax a little.

"It's okay," I am purring, in my sister's voice, my own face wet with tears.

"I just miss him," Raoul is saying into the void and I don't know who he is talking about but also, who cares?

Later, Marcus doesn't want to walk home with us. He mumbles something about having to stay "around" and goes out the back way to avoid bumping into the girl with the floral dress, we think, the only other audience member. Before they part, Raoul nods his head and strokes Marcus meaningfully on the back.

Raoul and I begin walking back to the apartment in the dark.

"Marcus is really something isn't he?" says Raoul, as we pass below three oak trees that are growing into each other's arms. "He's so enigmatic." Raoul's eyes gleam silver.

"You have a crush on him!" I accuse, a little horrified. "Oh God, you totally do."

"Well, don't you?" says Raoul, turning to me, incredulous. "Doesn't everyone?"

"It isn't that," I say, softly. "I just . . . I think I just like him a lot."

Raoul giggles again; a jarring little idiosyncrasy. Now that we're out in the cold I realise that my initial instinct is correct, that for some reason Raoul is not at all the kind of person I would elect to spend any more time with than necessary. He just isn't my kind of person; but then who is?

"Anyway," says Raoul. "I'm not about to steal your man. I'm in love with someone else. He just can't be with me right now."

I nod, as Raoul begins to tear up again. Unsure what to do, but feeling a surge of something bright inside me, I do some pirouettes in the dark. This is one of those real-life moments that other people probably have all the time, one of the rich, brilliant moments where if life stopped now, it would be okay, and you could actually say you've lived, whether good or bad. You were here. You existed. After all, you are alive now, aren't you? Aren't you?

"Do you want to go to bed and cuddle?' Raoul slurs, from somewhere in my periphery.

"No funny business. I just don't know where Marcus's head is at and I just really need a friend right now." I spin around to my not-friend.

"Me?" I ask, giggling.

"*You*," he says.

We have reached our building. Somehow, Marcus beat us home. We both look off to the corner of the building, out on the patchy yellow lawn, where he is swaying and speaking to the air,

to a tree,
to the air.

"No thank you, Raoul," I say, smiling into the dark.
"Come on. Let's help this one inside."

• •

I wake on Wednesday morning drenched in sweat, starfished halfway down my bed, legs hanging off at the sides. My wig is still on, and totally flattened. My joints ache for some reason; *was I dancing last night, running— what?* The edges of the items in my room appear to glimmer. Underneath it all, that familiar migraine might be happening, along with the faintest sense of foreboding. Before I know it, I'm up and out of bed. I'm eating dry gluten-free toast with dairy-free butter. I'm calling the woman I met on the rocks. The self-proclaimed personal witch!

"She isn't a ghost," I say hurriedly into the receiver, once it's clear that someone has picked up. "She's a con woman."

Vee doesn't answer. She draws in her breath. Then a Tears for Fears song intro comes on.

"*You have reached the Centre for Divine Timing.*

I can help with lovers, chakra alignment, akashic records, family constellations and warding evil, evil spirits," says Veronica's recorded Manchester voice. There is something about the warding evil spirits thing that catches the hairs on my neck. "*The centre's hours are between five and nine p.m. Walk-ins available. Please leave a voicemail stating your name and reason for calling.*" There's a long beep.

"She isn't a ghost!" I tell Not Veronica. "She's a con woman. Veronica, I need to see you. I need to know what I'm doing. Veronica. . . ." I take a breath to control my speed, "I'm sorry to bother you—only you say you're an expert on Ghosts Who Are Not ghosts. As such, I need to come and see—" But the line cuts off. I stare at my phone, feeling like an utter lunatic.

Suddenly, the phone lights up.

I REMEMBER YOU!!!!! HOW TOMORROW? 3:30?

155 HOLLINDALE AVENUE STOCKWELL

BRING SOMETHING SWEET AND DARK

COLOURED FLOWERS OK. 50 POUNDS PLUS TIP IF U WANT

• •

I'm hardly in a position to say this, but Veronica's house isn't up to much. It's a dated one-bedroom in Waterloo, right by the tube on top of a KFC. In the crib in the corner of the room, the baby I recognize from that day on the rocks, and a white baby in the same cot. The babies are playing together, cooing and gurgling. I didn't quite know what "bring something sweet and dark" meant, so earlier I rushed to the petrol station at the top of my road and bought Veronica one of those Ferrero Rocher pyramid things on my credit card. I get the pyramid out of my carrier bag and pass it to Veronica, who regards it with glee. Veronica's furniture is dark, the woods mismatched. She seems to have a penchant for Asian-style chests and apothecary tables—they're everywhere. In the centre of the universe, there is a round table that's meant to look like marble. It's the colour of deep water.

Veronica motions for me to sit at the table. I pull out a soft wicker chair, taking a seat.

"Want a hot bev?" she goes, and without waiting for me to answer, she turns to the stove, pours a black pungent something in a cup, and places the warm mug into my hand. I put it to my mouth to be polite but don't dare sip.

We settle at the kitchen table, where Veronica has her tarot cards and crystal spheres set up.

"How's the ghost?" says Veronica, placing both elbows on the table and balancing her chin in both hands. Her eyes won't leave mine. It's almost sisterly—or confrontational.

"She's a con woman," I say, with slightly less conviction than was there yesterday. In the space between then and now, something warped a little. Veronica continues her deep looking, seconds lost between us.

"You know," she says, finally. "I'll be able to tell you from a picture."

Sometimes I don't know if people are serious. I laugh at all the wrong times. I laugh now and realise it's a wrong time, because Veronica just frowns at me.

"Honestly. It's easy if you know what you're looking for."

I open my phone to Serene's Instagram profile and pass it to Veronica. Her nails are matte black with green and silver embellishments, each one filed to a sharp point. I wonder how she looks after her babies wearing these.

"Ah, you get used to it," she says, reading my thought. "I can do anything with these nails by now." She raps them on the table, then pulls into the display on my screen, zooming in as close as possible. After a while she leans back in satisfaction and places the phone in between us.

"If you look," she says, "really zoom in the pictures; they seem old, lower resolution."

"What do you mean?"

I squint at the pictures. There's a sepia vintage effect on them. Obvious.

"Maybe she just likes using filters," I say. "People love that film effect. It gets used to death."

"To death," Veronica repeats, but her voice trails off somewhere.

"Whoever she is, she isn't real," Veronica says, in a new, restored voice.

"What do you mean she isn't real? Is she a ghost or not?"

"Could be a ghost," says Vee. "Could be a con woman. I need concrete, ordinary proof. A maternity check, if you will."

"How do we get that? Like a lock of her hair? A swab of her cheek?"

"I need," Veronica says, "some birth records. Like, a passport will do."

I try to hide my disappointment. A fucking birth certificate. For fuck's sake Vee. Anyone can tell who someone is from a bloody birth certificate. Where's the magic in that? Just when I'm thinking a PI or truly anyone might have been more helpful than someone who was sitting on a rock by the water, boobs out, surrounded by bird poop, Vee has a new thought.

"Do you mind if I print these out in high res?"

"Go ahead."

Veronica screenshots the page and sends the image to her printer, which whirs a lot before emitting a satisfying selection of beeps. When the page is printed she stares at it, for a very long time. I shift in my seat and watch her. Eventually, she parts her lips, smirking.

"Come, Dempsey, you have to see this."

She passes the page over to me. I stare hard at the pixelated images of the woman—three squares. Side by side. Vee's computer is running out of ink. The image is lined, tough to decipher. As I look at it longer, following the stressed lines of ink, a dull truth starts to emerge in front of me. In the first, I make out a familiar face and, blown up like this, I see that it is my sister's. Then in the picture beside it, I make out my own unsmiling face. The third looks like a peculiar mix of both.

"This is weird," I say, pointing to the first image. "This first one looks like a doctored image of Clara. But that one," I say, pointing to the next picture in line, "looks like a doctored picture of me."

Vee nods.

"But why?" I say. "Why would someone do this? Is this a camera trick?"

"It could be a trick, couldn't it?" says Veronica. "And conversely . . ."

Vee stops herself.

"Conversely?" I urge.

"If she's your mother, such a resemblance would make sense, wouldn't it?"

One of the babies in the cots sneezes. Veronica makes no move.

"I'm not sure," I tell her. "There's a made-up look to these pictures."

"You mean you think they're fake?"

"I don't know," I tell her. "The last one looks like the person I remember, but also looks like both of us. Like if you were to meld us both into an AI app." I stare down at the almost black sludge in my cup. It's beginning to smell more and more like aniseed, which I *hate*.

"What is this?" I say. "Smells nice."

"You have to meet up with her," says Veronica. "You have to at least figure out what she wants. And in the meantime, for me, you want to be getting hold of an official ID for her. Your sister hired her, you say?"

I nod.

"Then this will be easy."

The whole thing feels like an optical illusion. In the picture of Clara, one of her arms looks to be facing the wrong way. Maybe. Perhaps. But the third person does resemble someone. A certain Serene Marie Nkem Droste who died in 1995, and the real live third person who is calling herself Serene *does* look like a computer image of both of us, and it *is* more uncanny than I realised.

"Did you get a look at her hands?" Vee wants to know. "They're cut off in the photo."

"Yeah," I say, although I'm not sure what Vee is getting at here. "In real life, they're beautiful." At this, Vee looks troubled.

"Not the most encouraging news. You see, ghosts have very beautiful hands, and that's a fact." Suddenly Vee claps her hands together. "I have to feed the kids. Go meet up with her. See what she is all about. I'll do some digging. Try and get me the passport, okay?"

I nod.

"You haven't drunk your tea. Do that. It'll calm you down."

I do as she says. By the time I've drained the cup, I feel a little less like screaming.

"A light sedative," says Vee. "Don't drop the cup now."

Thirty or so minutes later, I am ambling home, a little out of it. Time to do whatever it takes to get to the bottom of this. I text Serene when I get back to the flat.

WANT TO MEET TOMORROW AT BURGESS PARK?

PERFECT she texts back.

The sedative is doing its work on me. In my limbs I feel the slightest of tremors, like when you're coming down with the flu. I get into bed to touch myself, to soothe myself, but there I fall into a bizarre dream, where someone called Serene is in my house, and the house has become a body of water, and the body of water is deep and also she is not my mother, not at all. Just an ugly green siren at the bottom of the dark, pulling us into truths we dare not imagine.

I wake when it is still dark, inside the bittergreen memory of a thing that happened once.

Kendrick and I got by quietly, on unwritten rules. He didn't like to hug or kiss me goodnight. Though his sullenness was rarely aimed at me, it seeped into anything we did. He was always out somewhere, always off doing other things, always off at this meeting or that. Sometimes he would leave the house all weekend and come back smelling of women or cigars. I'd catch him in the shed, lifting his weights, humming away to himself, smiling a little. Those were the only times I remember a peace surrounding him. Sometimes, when he came and went and came back all relieved like that, I would feel this bubbling, unspeakable urge to make him suffer. I'd mirror his treacherous act by refusing to speak with him for days until he got the message. *Don't do it again*, was the message. *Don't leave me alone, all by myself, just to get happy.*

One night, when I had just turned eighteen, Kendrick came into my doorway, belt unbuckled at his waist, and just kind of stood there. Neither of us said anything, and Kendrick did not explain himself. The inference hung in the air between us, as loud as the black night. When it was clear that he was not going to move towards me, and I was sure as hell not getting out of bed, Kendrick only told me not to worry, that it was no big deal.

"Well look," said Kendrick. "I'm not sure what you want. I have no interest in little girls. But you're . . . I mean you're not anymore, I suppose."

There was another silence.

"What I mean is, I know what you're getting at," he coughed, then added, "I'm just saying, make a decision. Otherwise, we can go on like before, and we don't need to mention it."

The next night, after weighing up my options, I went into his room and hung my nightdress at the door, because I loved him and no one else loved him, as far as I knew. And he loved me, and no one else loved me. And I didn't want him to kick me out.

"You can get in if you want," he said, face turned away from me. I couldn't see his eyes.

And that was it. The thing went on for longer than I imagined and was a struggle for us both. We got through it, and I couldn't look at him again after that, so I moved out. We fell out of touch a month after the thing, quickly, with purpose.

BY THE DUCKS AND
THE TREES THAT GROW

The woman who is calling herself Serene is positively glowing when we meet. Her hair is pinned to her head in finger waves. She is carrying a lot of bags around on a trolly-type thing and wearing a shirt dress with an artist's impression of tall woodland trees. As I approach, she turns and smiles, showing all of her teeth, which are not perfect, nowhere near, but charming, and on the sharper side, like my own. It is a frightening image in the light. My head begins to throb a little. Up close, her hair is slicked, wavy, a tiny bit dusty. She looks chic enough, like the fashion models, if a little misplaced among her surroundings.

Marcus falls into step beside me. I haven't been able to shake him since he saw me leaving the flats this morning and insisted on walking with me all the way to the park. He "wasn't really vibing" with the feeling of his apartment today, he said. He felt trapped. Had to clear his head. Had to talk to the air. Marcus went on and on, chattering to himself. He's an artist. He's like that.

Serene stands there, smile fixed like in a photo, still looking as though she might have stepped out of another time, another place. I feel the exact moment Marcus stops breathing, arms hanging limply by his sides. His mouth has fallen open. I regret not putting my foot down with him and telling him he couldn't walk with me, but it's all done now.

"It's so good to see you," Serene says almost formally, kissing me on both cheeks. She looks at Marcus expectantly; takes a step back.

"And you," she says. "Who are you?"

I say, "This is Marcus . . ."
at the same time as Marcus goes
"I'm well thanks, how are you?"
and then I realise that Serene said "*how* are you," not "*who* are
    you." Here I am, as always, lost.
"Oh, we've already met," says Marcus, to me.

"You met?" I say, at the same time as Serene says,
                                    "On that bus."

"You helped me," says Marcus, looking decidedly sad. "Thank
God for you."
"Wait, wait." I feel a touch alarmed. "You know each other?"
"Vaguely," says Serene. "Almost."
Marcus remains silent, watching her closely. There's a hint of a story
to it, I can tell.
"I think we both had a bad day that day," Serene says. "It was the day
after the other night—that whole Clara misunderstanding," she adds,
nodding at me.
"Still," says Marcus. "Lucky you were there." He looks at me, as
though somehow willing me to understand. "It was a bad, bad trip."
He shakes his head, eyes trained on her face, the dusty sheen on her
head. Serene stands there for a long time, drawing him in. She's a magi-
cian. She's unhinged.
A bad trip?
But Marcus has fallen into the tide of her eyes, and a look passes
between them, a tangible static energy. I watch, mesmerized by the
exchange, if exchange is the right word. It's more like watching someone
be caught, whole.
A bad trip?
As Serene backs up towards where I am standing, I notice that I can

smell her. It isn't an offensive smell, but it is sharp. *Specific.* To the left of me, Marcus is treading water.

"Yeah, I'm in music," he mumbles.

"You already told me," says Serene. "I looked you up the same day we met. I enjoy you."

Marcus laps this up. It feels like something that shouldn't be happening is, in fact, happening.

"How do you do that?" coos Serene, like a person in a movie, playing a part. "You were telling my story . . ."

"Marcus . . . we have to go," I find myself saying, placing a hand lightly on his arm. "Serene and I have to talk about my sister and it's really, like, serious. Will you be okay?"

Marcus nods, understanding. "It was good seeing you again," he says. Serene nods brusquely, having already become involved with the task of laying several carrier bags out on the ground before her. "I don't like to sit on the grass," she says, looking up at no one specific. "There's all kind of you know what underneath."

Marcus laughs, and it's kind of strained. I join Serene on a Tesco bag and Marcus sort of salutes to us both and walks quickly away, in the opposite direction.

"He *is* beautiful," the person who might be our mother says, watching him leave. "Fucked up though." I feel the immediate need to stick up for Marcus, who isn't here to defend himself.

"He's just tired. I think he's depressed."

"Dempsey," says Serene, folding her hands in her lap and delivering a very don't-mess-with-me stare. "The man's high as a kite. He was on his way to overdosing when we met, you know."

Underneath her, the Tesco bags rustle, and my stomach turns over. All that with Marcus just now . . .

"I'm concerned about Clara," I tell her, changing the subject. "She's out of control."

"Is it heroin?" Serene wants to know. "I thought it might be."

"I don't know much about drugs," I confide, a little shocked. I've never done drugs. I wouldn't put it past her, though. "But the booze I know about. The booze is way out of hand."

"I'm talking about Marcus," snaps Serene. "Is it heroin?"

I shrug. "I have a very worrying detail to tell you."

The woman who is in the park opposite me,
the woman who looks like our mother,

is rapt, poised, ready for information. A tiny piece of her afro is jutting out towards the sun. Above her head, a circle of flies. Serene opens her eyes wide and leans closely in towards me. Her smell is deeper now, more intricate. Layered, yet familiar. I think this is what it means to have someone in the palm of your hand. A delicious power runs through the base of my spine and I wonder if I'm about to betray Clara. But I take the chance. Well, I have to. It's for her own good.

"She thinks you're our mother," I say, just as a leaf blower disappears my sentence into the atmosphere.

"I didn't hear you," says Serene.

Less sure of myself by this time, I drop the bomb again. "She thinks you're our mother, come back from the dead."

There. I said it. I wait for the low, conspiratorial laughter to happen between us.

"That," Serene says, a peculiar glint in her eye, "is interesting. Thanks for telling me."

We lie there a while, looking at the white spaces where the sun peeps through the trees. The two of us close our eyes. Serene takes out a bottle of white Zinfandel and some Jammie Dodgers, which she doesn't offer to me, and it's fine—I don't consume things that are bad for me. I talk to her openly, like I haven't talked in a while. We both grew up in the system. Serene tells me about Nottingham and the girls in the secure care unit. As she talks, I can see the yellow undersides of her fingernails. She talks a little like the girls I came up with—a touch too fast and dotted with expletives. I realise I am quite, quite at ease with her. I rarely feel this way, not even with Dr. Rayna Panelli in her office. I watch Serene drain the bottle, but it's only a little one. It's still late morning. There is a familiar darkening above us. The sky is threatening rain. Serene looks up as though strategising. I watch two creases appear across her forehead.

"Do you have plans later?" I ask.

"No," says Serene. "You?"

I can't help telling her the truth.

"I have some data entry work to do. Besides that, I was planning to warm up leftovers and watch reality TV all day."

Serene smiles, tells me that that sounds like the perfect afternoon, and offers to join.

We trudge back to my house an hour later. It never did rain. Maybe, I think to myself, making friends is just this easy. I've just been meeting the wrong people. I have been worrying about Dr. Rayna Panelli and the task at hand. I'm worried that the doctor thinks I've abandoned her in her time of need. But the women have frozen me out. Even Sally won't pick up the phone. As we approach my block of flats, I start making the funny sound with my mouth.

"Sorry," I say to Serene, who is watching this with interest. "It's just a thing I do when I'm . . . I don't know . . . just thinking too much."

"It's to be expected of us water signs," says Serene.

At the flat, Serene finishes her steaming noodles before I've had time to set mine down, so I scoop my portion into her bowl and go back to warm up some more.

"So, so good," she tells me between bites. "Dempsey, you could be a chef, you know!"

No one has ever said anything like that to me before. I smile, and make her a third bowl, and grate some leftover cheese to give it an extra kick. This only leaves half a bowl for me, but she seems hungry and I could spare the calories, to be honest. We watch some reruns of *Baywatch* and then we turn the TV on to this cops-and-robbers type show that Serene can't get enough of. I make sure she drinks a lot of alkaline water. Serene seems impressed, her thirst unquenchable. It feels good to be needed.

Upstairs, I can make out the dull sounds of Marcus crooning.

I know he likes to smoke but it couldn't be heroin. Could it? Heroin is *heroin*. It's serious. Marcus doesn't seem like the type. I set my work in front of me and begin tapping away at my laptop. Some old American detective show is on the TV.

Serene wants to watch one film, and then another. Soon, I notice it's damn near eight thirty, which is when I usually start winding down. I yawn, looking at the clock, then get to my feet.

"It was so nice meeting up with you today."

I am about to say, "Let's do this again soon," or whatever it is that people say when they're closing out a visit, but Serene stretches herself on the couch, supposedly asleep, and doesn't answer. I stand there for a few seconds, not knowing what to do. Silence.

"You can sleep here," I say, "I suppose. I mean, if it's easier." Serene only yawns and turns her head.

I turn off the lights. And the TV. Serene begins to snore, something like mucus rattling in her throat. The room is a little funkier than usual so I get out my brand new humidifiers because I want her to have clear air, and I place a fleece pullover by her head, just in case she wakes up and feels cold.

I slip into my bed in the corner of the room. I'm tired, but the flat feels colder, a little alien. From where I lie, I can see the top of Serene's snoring head. I tug my duvet up to my chin, and as I try to get myself into position, I wonder if I betrayed my sister's confidence today. And for some reason I can't stop thinking about the night all those years ago with Kendrick, when the unthinkable found its way into me—and then I carried out the unsayable.

I couldn't *not*.

I close my eyes and shudder, a wave of nausea fast upon me, and when I do dream, it is an indecipherable green, all frothy and deep. I am awoken, at some time during the night, by the sound of the latch going in my front door. I'm not sure whether or not I'm dreaming.

I was not. By early morning, Serene is gone and has scrawled a note on my desk calendar saying

thanks for the noodles and the fresh water. Talk soon.
Plz call your sis, she needs you.

What about what I need?
Still, I take the advice.
I take my sister's number off the block list.
The next day, Clara leaves me some bullshit message about being sorry. I am the only person in the world, it seems, who doesn't believe her lies, but two can play that game. I write;
Sry I called you a drunk. I don't really think that.
It's fine, Dem. she texts back, hours later. She invites me to dinner the same night. I agree, only to keep the peace.

RIGHT BACK TO BUSINESS

When I find Serene in the lobby of the hotel, she's wearing a painted vintage Fugees jacket and her hair is slicked back and bobby-pinned close to her head. She looks like someone that you might find singing the blues. She locks eyes with me but makes no expression, no hint of a frown or a smile. As I approach, she turns away from to me to laugh with the girl at reception. There is a printed graphic on the back of her shirt. Lauryn Hill circa 1995 stares at me as if prophesying. I clear my throat, and after regarding each other wordlessly for a few moments, my mother nods, motioning to the seating area, where she slots herself into an emerald-coloured booth. *Time to explain*, I think, settling in across from her and looking down at the extensive cocktail menu. *Be offhand. Be sincere, but don't make a thing of it.*

"I've been taking this crazy mix," I say. "I shouldn't really drink on Fluoxetine."

My mother just looks at me.

"Congratulations on the TV deal," she says. "That's huge."

She smiles at me then, and I don't feel bad about making that part up. TV deals come and go all the time. All the time.

"I'm sorry," I say. "Really, Serene, I feel awful about the other night. And thank you. For meeting me."

"It doesn't seem like the best combination," she says, motioning to the waiter.

"What?"

The waiter comes up and asks what we are feeling like today.

"Antidepressants and booze," says my mother. The waiter laughs. "Gin and tonic please," she says to him.

"Lemonade," I say, though I haven't drunk it since I was a kid.

"She means she'll have a gin and tonic," says my mother, firmly, which is a mind read if ever I saw one. "And please, no ice."

It's before one p.m., which is usually my only drinking rule. I'll let it go. We might be celebrating.

"This is a great suggestion," I say, looking around us. "I didn't know this place existed."

"I used to work here years ago," says Serene. "Of course, no one would remember me now. It's all new staff."

My head reels a little. It is another similarity, another strong piece of Evidence. Serene in the story works at a wine bar that matches this description if you squint a little. But I'm not going to let it distract me from the job at hand. We can't have a rerun of any unhinged behavior. That, we cannot afford.

"Maybe we should talk about things," I begin, desperate to maintain control. "Serene, I feel . . . I don't know what happened . . ."

"The *thing* is," says my mother, waving her perfect hand in the air, "you're lucky I didn't punch you in the throat."

"I am," I nod, feeling contrite. "I'm working through things."

The music blares. My hairpiece begins to tighten, pinching a little. I watch my mother, who is wearing a hard expression, almost looking through me. The waiter brings the gin and tonics. They sit on the table untouched, sparkling.

"Everyone's working through a thing," my mother finally says, leaning over to expel the chunk of lime from her glass. "I didn't ask for this." She throws the wet piece on the table in front of us and sighs. "I've got to tell you . . . that I'm not who you want me to be. I'm not the woman in your book."

A balding man walking by us is staring so hard at my mother that he trips, almost landing right on top of us in the booth.

"I'm so sorry," says the man, huffing and puffing and holding on to the table. "You look like . . . are you *Selena*? I haven't seen you for years!"

My mother completely ignores him. He hangs on for a second, eyes imploring.

"Even so," she goes on, unruffled, "I think things happen for a reason. Let's just put it there and leave it there, okay?"

The man slinks away, picking his briefcase up off the floor.

Though I heard what she said, I am not sure whether to believe it or not. It seems hardly likely that she could just forgive me, just like that. What happened in my house, in my room, by the shower, with all the glass.

"I got your money," her voice says, as if reading my thoughts. "The two thousand. I'm considering coming back to work for you, but you have to be sure that's what you want?"

"Yes. I'm sure."

"How much?"

The man who fell into us is talking to the girl at reception, who is now looking at us too.

"Your salary?"

"I mean: how much do you want it?" she asks. "How sure are you?"

"I think it would be fantastic . . . I—"

"You're not getting it."

My mother covers her eyes with her hands. Then she nods into her lap, and the realisation hits. She places her hands back on the table. In the afternoon light, there's a blue cast on her face.

"I need you," says my mother, "to kneel on the floor, right now, and ask me to work for you."

I look around at the people milling about the lobby. The people at brunch in their loungewear. The tourists. The people who might know who I am. The balding man and the girl at reception—and I think yes, this is fitting, why not?

The room buzzes.

The room hums as I take my rightful place on the floor in front of her. I am wearing expensive cream trousers, and I only remember this on the way down. The thought sparks a curious electricity in my joints, the backs of my knees, my lower neck. I clasp my hands together. I look up at her.

"Oh God, I'm joking," says my mother, once I've made contact with the floor. "Get up, get up, Clara."

As I climb to my feet I notice that the knees on my trousers are sullied. The floor is dirtier than it appears. We both regard the evidence. The waitstaff behind the counter are watching us, and whispering amongst themselves. My mind is a flurry as I slide back into the booth; my act of contrition a strong hard fact. My mother not-quite smiling as my cheeks burn.

"I suppose this means I have to come back now," she says to someone not quite me, someone way in the distance.

"I think it does," I hear myself say, trying not to smile or appear too keen as the drinks appear.

"Thank God that's over," says Serene. "Because I have a whole lot of things I've been setting up, and falling out with you would have gotten in the way. Oh, also, did you get my invoice?"

"Yes," I tell her. "I paid you more this morning."

"Good."

I take a small sip of the drink. It might be the best thing I've ever tasted.

Serene takes out a new iPad from a box and a switchblade from her jersey pocket, cuts off the security pad in a single action.

"I want to ask you a question. A thing I know you're sensitive about."

"Go on."

"I want to talk about your sister. I don't know, I just feel pulled to help her in some way. Do you think we could all meet again, get things out in the open?"

I bite my tongue, wondering if Dempsey is up to the task. I can't have her embarrassing herself again the way she did, bringing me all the way down with her.

"The other night was my fault," I say. "I think Dempsey knows that."

"Still," says Serene, not letting up, "shouldn't we invite her back around to dinner?"

"I don't know. I'll have to ask her. She's been really busy with work."

"Work? What does she do?"

"She's in admin," I lie, although I don't know what she does anymore, if she even does anything.

"That's good. We could use that? Have you ever drafted her in to help you?"

"That would be a disaster," I say flatly. "Anyway, I'm not sure she has any real skills, you know?"

"Not so," says my mother. "Let's keep it in the family. Honestly, between you and me, she looks like she needs it. Likely you need it too."

Keep it in the family,
Keep it in the family.

The words warm their way through my blood. I smile, nod, take a huge gulp of the G&T. I love my sister, but she doesn't know how to act. She'd be a complete liability. I promise to reach out, and decide to let Dempsey hang herself. When my mother has spent longer with us, she'll understand a little more why connecting Dempsey with my public image wouldn't work, how she'd be an unspeakable burden.

We drain our early afternoon drinks. Serene leaves the room to make a phone call. I decide to get the thing with Dempsey over and done with. I text my sister and tell her that I'm sorry about my behavior, and that I can't remember what I said to her, but I take full responsibility, accountability, the works. Dempsey reads it and messages almost immediately.

Sry I called you a drunk.

Serene comes back to the table and we sit there in silence as she goes about setting up the new iPad. She arranges a photoshoot at the Mandarin for next week. She answers three enquiries about speaking engagements overseas. She won't travel with me, but she'll send a PA. Maybe. If we can swing it. She wants to know whether she can sit in on the interim meetings for *Evidence*, the TV show. At some point I'll need to tell her the opportunity fell away. But not yet.

IT'S FINE
I text my sister.

CAN WE MEET? I WANT TO TALK WITH YOU

she writes

SERENE WANTS US ALL TO MEET AGAIN
I reply back.
Dempsey is typing, but nothing comes up.
Finally,
NEED TO TALK TO YOU ABOUT SERENE. ASAP
OK, I write back. *DINNER?*
When Serene comes back, I don't breathe a word of it,
for some reason or the other.

• •

You'd think Dempsey had never been to a proper Italian restaurant before.
She takes forever perusing each item on the menu and screwing up her face.

"I have a lot to say," I begin, once Dempsey has finished grilling the
poor waiter about each ingredient in everything. Apparently she isn't
doing dairy at the moment.

"Gives me IBS," my sister tells him, her face the very picture of mar-
tyrdom. The waiter does his best to seem interested.

"If I'd known I wouldn't have brought you here," I offer, already distressed by her unending limitations.

"It's fine," says my sister, looking suitably chastised. "I'll have a salad.
It's okay. No dressing."

The waiter nods slowly. I order a steak and fries, to make up for
her nonsense.

"I have a lot to say too," she says, once he has taken away our menus.

"I hope it's not about our mother not being our mother," I blurt out,
"because I don't have time."

"Serene and I went to the park," says Dempsey.

My phone starts to buzz. Emma is calling. I silence the call.

"To the park?"

I say,

"Why?"

I say,

"and Clara it was so weird, she ended up staying the night at
my flat."

Emma again. I silence the call. Dempsey takes a massive gulp of
her sparkling water. I try to put on a game face, but it's failing. I hate
my sister; sometimes I really hate her. How could she? I'm slipping
out of control. To keep myself from floating away, I stare hard at her
puffy face.

"Stayed at your flat?"

"All night."

Dempsey is saying something else, but the din in the restaurant is
making it difficult to hear her, let alone take anything in. Perhaps our
mother prefers Dempsey. Perhaps she took one look at Dempsey and
saw her daughter. My hands begin to tremble with the sheer injustice of
it. I imagine wrestling Dempsey to the floor, pinning her down with the
weight of me. I imagine blocking—not crushing, not quite—her delicate
little windpipe.

"Your house is so dirty," is what I hear myself say. "Serene likes
everything around her to be very clean. She's like a cat."

But my sister isn't listening,

"She wouldn't leave," she goes on. "It was weird, and then in the *dead*
of the night, she just kind of disappeared! I think she's a con woman."

"I think *you're* a con woman," I say.

"What's that supposed to mean?

Then Dempsey is talking some more, but making very little sense.
Something like looking hard at a picture of Serene that looked like us.
Well, obviously.

"And then she met Marcus."

"Who the hell is Marcus?"

The waiter is lingering again, like an annoying fly. I am just about to order a G&T before I hit someone, when Dempsey utters the words, "My neighbor. She met him on a bus."

"Wait. Wait," I say, the words finally landing. "What do you mean, she met him on a bus?"

"That's what she said. They'd met before . . ."

I slam down my fork. I am halfway through a honeydew melon starter, only I don't remember ordering it.

"Which bus? Did she say which bus?"

"Out of everything I said," my sister goes, "you're asking about a bus number?"

A half smirk happens across Dempsey's face. Her demeanor is maddening. I grab hold of her wrist. She yelps, a pained expression appearing across her face.

"Listen to what I'm asking you, will you? Dempsey! Who is this neighbor?"

"Marcus. He's a musician. Clara! You're hurting me!"

I squint a little trying to make sense of the room, where everything suddenly feels larger than it should be, and too stark. Too bright.

"Clara! Let go!" my sister cries out.

I let go of her.

"Clara, what the hell!" says Dempsey, holding her wrist and wincing.

"I think he's our father," I whisper, holding the side of my head. "Oh, my God."

"What are you talking about? Marcus is . . ."

"I'm going mad. I swear . . . Listen, Dem. Does he have another name?"

"Another name?"

"Another name? Like?"

"Like Abbé? Abbé."

"No, no," she says. "He's Marcus. Marcus from Trinidad."

"Trinidad?!" I almost scream.

"I'll come back," says the waiter.

"It figures," I tell Dempsey, pressing my forearms into the table.

"Some names have been changed to conceal identity. That's what I say at the beginning of the book! It figures. The man—he's our father, Dempsey. He's our father."

Dempsey falls silent, looking at me as though I've completely lost it. For some reason the fucking waiter is drifting away. I call him back over so I can pay the bill and I make everything to-go because I need to be away from the loud bright restaurant and alone with my thoughts and my mother. I watch my sister watching me, working me out, her mouth downcast like a blobfish. So insulting, when someone not at your level has the audacity to make it seem like *she* wants to help *you*. Like *she's* concerned about you. Imagine. There's a ring of white in the corner of her lips. She starts doing the thing with her mouth, which is awful, a lot like someone crushing a wet bug between their fingers. Or someone chewing gristle. She isn't going to be any help at all.

Once the waiter has returned with our to-go meals, I rush us out of the restaurant and into the car park. In my pocket my phone is buzzing. Emma is calling. Again.

When I turn on the car, I mistakenly accept the call, which ends up coming through on the speakerphone.

"Clara, we need to talk," says Emma.

"Emma, sorry—not now, I can't talk now," I say, breathlessly. "I'm with my sister. You haven't met her. Anyway, we're having a family emergency."

"I think you'll want to hear this. It's about your family member. Clara, I really wouldn't insist if this didn't seem urgent."

"Go on then," I say, holding my breath. "Make it quick, Emma."

Next to me Dempsey is fiddling with the passenger seatbelt, making a real meal of it. It isn't hard to put the seatbelt on. A child could do it. I snap her seatbelt in with some force.

"I've been contacted," goes Emma's voice, "by someone who goes by the name of Simeon."

It takes a moment for it to make sense.

"Simeon? From my book Simeon?"

"Well," says Emma, "I didn't make the connection, but . . . I suppose. What a co—"

Next to me, Dempsey is perfectly still. Listening.

"I'm sorry to be the bearer of bad news," Emma continues. "He says to tell you Serene is dangerous. He wants you to know that. I think he is her partner. Was her partner. I'm sorry, I'm not really sure what's going on."

I say nothing, still gripping the takeout box in my hand. Everything in my body believes her, was waiting for this. My sister places her head in her hands, in a very dramatic fashion.

"I don't want to say I told you so, Clara," Emma begins. "But . . . I think . . . I just think."

"Emma, I have to go," I say, and cancel the call. I turn to my sister. "Dempsey. Please don't say anything."

My sister juts her bottom lip out and in and out again in a strange repetitive motion, making this very wet, disgusting sound. I raise my eyes to the sky.

INTERVIEW WITH
THE VILLAIN

"This is how I know you don't love me," my sister says, her voice a harsh whisper as she whips the car into reverse and out of the lot. "You didn't read my book at all, did you?"

It was a bad idea to ask—but really, who the hell is Simeon?

I shake my head. "It's just that your book . . ." I search for the answer that would get me out of this. "It was too much for me, that's all. It triggers so many . . ."

"Save it," says Clara flatly. We drive the rest of the way home in silence. When we pull outside of my building, a figure that looks like Marcus is swaying in the garden, a lone grey outline.

Clara watches the billowing silhouette for a while, sniffs, and turns to me. "I've decided that I'm in this alone. You don't believe me. You don't trust me. You don't even respect me. Get out."

She leans over me to open the passenger door. "I mean it, Dempsey. Get out!"

"I'm not getting out," I say with all the courage I can gather. "Clara. I . . ."

"GET OUT!"

"You can't make me. I'm invested too! I'm not getting out, I swear."

"You'll get out," says my sister, "Or I'll get out the other side and pull you out. Want to test me?"

I get out. Of course I do. She speeds away. In the garden, Marcus might still be swaying.

..

The next evening, Simeon arranges himself on one of the hard stools of the Ritzy in Brixton. We remain standing, watching him.

He is a large man with a beard and a shiny, squarish head. Standing across from him, Clara looks thin but lovely in a lemon-yellow matching set. For some reason she has doused herself in some very citrusy perfume. Simeon looks her up and down and coughs, then takes a long look at the very pregnant Emma, who we also brought along, since she was the one he contacted. Clara said the only reason she allowed us both to be here is because she needs Witnesses and Safety.

"Listen," says the Perceived Threat. "I haven't got long, let's get to it."

"We're here to talk about Serene," I say.

"Serene," he says.

"Yes Serene," Clara snaps at him. "*You* contacted us!"

"Is that even her name?" I demand.

"Depends who's asking. What are you offering?" says Simeon, turning his evil eye on me.

"I've got money," says Clara, in the smallest voice I've ever heard from her.

"I know. We already discussed that," says Simeon, looking pointedly at Clara. Clara holds his gaze. Simeon folds his hands in front of him.

"So go on, who *is* she?" says Clara, moving her face closer to Simeon's. He drinks her in, enjoying the closeness perhaps.

"You smell good."

His eyes have a red tinge to them, I notice. Under each eye, too, a semicircle of darker flesh.

"Who is Serene?" Clara asks again.

"I'll give you a clue," he says, his face growing mean to match hers. "Probably not your mother."

Clara looks deep into his eyes like someone deranged. Simeon breaks eye contact with her, at once.

"Whatever you guys are smoking, put me on. Please."

If Simeon didn't look both young and old, like a person who has lived a very hard life, I might seriously dislike him.

"I need to know what she's told you," Clara says, evenly.

"She's dead to me," says Simeon. "Been dead. Is dead. First things first: where's the rest of the money?"

"What do you mean? It's here."

"I think I want twenty k."

Emma, Clara, and I exchange quick glances.

"We agreed to ten," says Emma. "That's what we've allotted for you."

Simeon crosses his large arms across his chest. Around us, a football game is starting. The pub erupts into cheers.

"We'll give you fifteen thousand," Clara puts in, "and that's final. All you need to do is tell us where she is."

"What about the guilt?" he says. "Since I'm not a whaddya call it . . . snitch, I need to be rewarded for whaddya call it, emotional damage. I've gotta look myself in the mirror after this, know what I mean?"

Clara opens the envelope, counts out several fifties, and hands them to Simeon, who pockets them as quickly as they touch. Simeon begins talking immediately.

"She told me you've got this kinky obsession with her. Listen, nothing to do with me. I live and let live. Can you be a bit discreet? Can you not throw money at me in my local?"

Clara gets a look on her face that I've never seen before on her. Shame, or something close.

"None of my business, like," Simeon goes on. "Seen it all, believe me."

"How long have you been together?" I ask him.

"*Together*," Simeon mimics, and laughs. The guy is a kid.

"There was no together," he says. "She needed somewhere to stay. I have a few places. It worked until it didn't . . ." He trails off, folds his arms again. "Look, what have you got me here for?"

"We need to know who she really is," I say, as though I haven't been plotting this ever since I knew we were coming to meet him. "So that would mean a passport, driver's license, anything you've got, really." My voice comes out different, thicker. Clara shoots a surprised look in my direction.

"Er, yes," she says. "ID would be perfect. Then we'd know who and what we're dealing with."

Simeon weighs up the situation, blowing out of his mouth.

"Give me the money, I can get you her passport," he says, finally. "That's light work."

"We need more," I say. "Like where's she from? Where did you meet?"

"I changed the locks. She doesn't have anything with her. And for twenty, that's all you're getting. British passports go for a lot of money you know."

"We said fifteen," I say, but Clara waves me off.

"Can you get anything else?"

"I don't know her people," says the man, "she don't have too many of those."

Emma breathes out, lowers herself onto the pub's threadbare couch.

"Fifteen k then. You'll get the money on receipt of these documents," I say, trying to sound official and threatening.

"Nah," goes Simeon. "That's not how it works, girls."

"How does it work?" says Emma, pressing a hand to the top of her belly.

"Two thirds upfront," says Simeon. "Need to know I can trust you."

Emma looks at my sister. My sister looks at Emma.

"Are you the writer," says Simeon, ". . . or are you the self-help coach? Or wait . . . are you the cosmetics mogul? No, *she* ran off to Jamaica."

"There are others?" says my sister, aghast.

"Luv," says Simeon, who almost seems a little sorry for us now. "This is what she does. Gains your trust and uses you."

"We need to know if we can trust *you*?" I say—bravely, I feel. I've never spoken to an actual gangster before. The actual gangster sniffs.

"You probably can't," says Simeon. "Not gonna lie to you though.

She owes me too. She's been doing what she's been doing for a very long time. She'll do stuff even I wouldn't do. Karma, you know. I don't mess with that."

I look to my sister and then to Emma.

"Look," says my sister. "It's more than a third but less than two thirds. I'm good for it. I promise." She hands Simeon a large brown packet, which he accepts and does not count.

"Do me a favour, girls," he snarls. "Tell her I'm looking for her. She'll like that."

I wonder if that's another joke, but Simeon looks like he means business and means mean business.

"How long have you known her?" I want to know.

"We go back," says Simeon, the smallest suggestion of hurt spreading across his big face. He fixes his expression right away, as if catching himself. "You've not brought me here to talk about *me*."

Just then, I hear water hit the floor. I think perhaps I've spilled my drink, but when I look over, I see Emma looking stunned, a pool of water forming underneath her. Simeon averts his eyes.

"I'm out. Give me your address and I'll get you what you asked for."

Clara shakes his hand. Then we load Emma into the backseat of Clara's car, while Simeon walks off in the opposite direction. I find myself wondering what would happen if Clara didn't have a car. Would Simeon have been forced to help? Would he have stuck around?

"Just breathe, or . . . or whatever," Clara stammers at Emma, who is staring straight ahead, as if counting.

"It's okay," I say, twisting from the passenger seat, placing a hand on Emma's leg. "It's okay, we're here with you. Can I call your husband?" I ask her.

"You can call my *wife*," Emma says sharply.

"I'm so, so sorry," I say. "That's amazing!" I say, in a weird high pitch. "Nothing wrong with it."

"We're taking you to King's College Hosp—" my sister is saying.

"No way," Emma grunts. "Take me home! Right away. My doula and midwife are just a text away."

"So all I need to do is drop you off?" Clara is spinning the steering wheel, unblinking.

"All you need to do is drop me off, that's right," says Emma, curtly. "Please, pass me my phone, Dempsey."

I pass Emma her handbag and watch, useless, as she fumbles around for her slim iPhone. She taps away at it, breathing hard like an animal in distress.

"River, it's happening. Call Winter and let her know?"

River and Winter? I look at Clara, who rolls her eyes.

"Call Mum too," says Emma. Clara revs the car hard and Emma groans.

"It's okay, it's okay," I keep purring, in a way that I can tell is angering everyone.

"I'm fine," says Emma, as if convincing herself. "Everything is going to be well. Everything is fine."

"Everything's going to be more than fine!" I say, brightly.

Our driver, on the other hand, is sullen and speeding. It's hard to know what she's thinking.

Finally, we drive off the A5 and take the turn sharply.

"Which way from here?" Clara barks.

"Take the third exit on the left. Go as fast as you can."

Minutes later, we stop in a row full of gorgeous terraced houses.

"Just a little farther up the road," says Emma.

Emma's house is lined with hedges of brilliant red roses. We gasp when we see the dozens and dozens of them. A tall woman with long auburn hair is waiting nervously as we approach. Spotting us, she runs up to the car.

"Thank God," she says, sticking her head through my open window. "Winter should be here in the next ten minutes."

River and I help Emma out of the car and guide her across the manicured lawn. At the door, she breathes out in relief and grabs both of my hands. I realise I'm shaking.

"I'm fine," says Emma. "Go home." She gives me a waxy smile. "Get some rest. It was really lovely meeting you."

"Good luck," I say. They leave me standing on the porch. I lumber back to the car, eyes shining. Clara is still in the driver's seat, nodding, hands clenched on the wheel.

"Isn't new life so special," I say, when I hop into my seat, "but wait, did I look like I assumed heterosexuality back then?"

"I think," says my twin, quietly, "Emma might have been distracted. With . . . you know . . . dealing with a whole baby who's about to come out of her vagina."

"Right, right!" I say, chewing on my lips.

A GENUINE PIECE OF ID

True to his word, Simeon drops off the passport at the Brixton bar on Friday. It is burgundy, looks old, with the front almost ripped all the way off. But the dates match up. She's thirty. Her birthday—the same day it always was. The exact same day as ours. The picture looks like the Serene we know and nearly knew. But looking at the dates, they could be doctored . . . right? It could be a fake.

"You're not gonna wanna hear this," says Dempsey, who has taken to riding shotgun. "I think we should call the police."

"And tell them what?" I ask, miserably.

"This is fraud," Dempsey says, fingering the passport.

"She hasn't *said* she's our mother," I tell her. "Technically she hasn't committed a crime. And can you imagine going to the police with this? They'd probably arrest me for stupidity." Dempsey picks my phone up off the high table and I knock it out of her hand.

"Not stupidity," I say. "Absolute and utter madness."

"I don't think its PC," says Dempsey, "to call yourself crazy."

"I think it's okay if you yourself have a mental condition," I tell her. I want so much to go home and be miserable all alone today, but Dempsey says she wants to stay.

"I'm not going anywhere," she says, her face grim and resolute.

"Where did you get these sudden balls?" I want to know.

"Not Politically. Correct," says Dempsey, her mouth full of purple grapes. I can't help but laugh.

We go back to my house and watch Love Island, where people are pretending to be in love with each other's actual personalities. I make myself a good two martinis with the salt and the lemons and the olive just so. After three, I'm almost where I need to be. I smile in the bath room mirror, observing my collarbones. How they make me look like some kind of goddess of the deep, the almost blue. No one can know that I was this weak. No one can know that I turned over and let this happen. When I look in the mirror I see me, and I see Dempsey, and we deserve more. We always deserved more. Suddenly there is an instinct that floods me. So dark. So absolute.

I go back downstairs and call the number of our wayward terrible mother, who answers as soon as I pick up.

"What's your name?" I shout, when the person picks up the phone.

Dempsey looks up from *Love Island*, alarmed.

"What?" goes our mother, daring me.

"The jig is well up. What's your name?"

There is a silence. Then the sly woman lets out a loud groan.

"Are you drinking on your meds again?" she asks. "'Cause I don't have time . . ."

"I DON'T TAKE FUCKING MEDS!" I shout. "WHAT'S YOUR NAME?"

"As you know," she says, calmly, "My name is Serene. Serene Marine Nkem Droste."

"Don't you mean Marie?"

"That's what I said," says our mother-woman, sounding perhaps a little unsure.

My sister bounds over, clocks the phone on loudspeaker. There we sit, breathing through our open mouths, arm in arm.

"You have some real fucking nerve," goes Dempsey, in what is probably her most threatening voice. "Targeting us like that. Gaslighting my sister! What kind of person does that? We spoke to Simeon. He told us everything."

Serene Whatever doesn't argue.

"You've taken my passport. I want my passport. I need my things," says Serene.

"I'm *real*," she adds, as if that'll do it.

"You're not real!" I tell her. "I'm going to throw your passport and your stupid things in the River Thames. I fucking swear it. I'm going to drop it all where you'll never find it."

"Relax. I'll be round before midnight," says Serene. "No need to drop off my things. I'll explain everything when I see you. Let's not get dramatic, girls," she says, and hangs up.

And so we wait. We wait at the house until just before midnight and two hours after. We call back the number, which sounds like we're reaching some kind of foreign land. I can't take it anymore. I scream into the open line, "Stop doing this to us! Stop doing this to me! Where are you?" From somewhere, Serene garbles a response but it's inaudible.

"What the fuck are you playing at?" I say. "You sound like you're under water."

"I'm not going to make it," says our mother.

I lie in bed and wail and wail. Dempsey holds my head until I have emptied out my lungs onto her wet shoulder. We lie on my bed and we do not move until, at some point in the morning, I hear her pad out onto the landing and creak down the stairs. When she gets back in bed, she's holding the pink, pink book.

"I love you," says my sister, back to her reedy, nasal voice. "I love you, Clara. Go back to sleep. I love you and I'm reading. I'm reading your book. I'm not going to move from here until I've read it all. Go back to sleep."

One day, Serene tried to go to the place that Abbé was sweet on. Well, why not? He was always disappearing and it wasn't fair. Plus, he looked so lonely. He was sitting back a little, falling underneath a mix he had put together. Abbé had the knack of mixing weed with opiates to get the desired effect. It carried you off on a sticky grey cloud, if you were lucky.

"Since you insist," said Abbé. "Sit back and sit still. Think about breath, or nothing at all."

"How does a person think about breath? What is there to *think* about breath?"

"Shhh," ordered Abbé, a finger on his lips. "Let the medicine do its work. If all else fails . . . I don't know . . . imagine yourself on holiday."

"I've never been on holiday," she wanted to say, but didn't.

"Do you think it will harm them?" she said, holding her lower stomach, but Abbé was not the one to ask about such things and anyway, he was already holding the back of the chair, fast fading. After a few drifting minutes, he mumbled, "My mother was a traveler. It never harmed me."

Serene begged to differ. His mother was rich enough to travel alone and never really be lost, could go away all day and be back in time for dinner with her diplomat parents, sweating a little, parts of her left in the world out there. As for Abbé, he was probably beyond repair; his demeanor was sad, so sad that she often wished for his sake that he were back in the other world, back in the coat lining, somewhere between the imitation silk and the soft certainty of a pocket. Still she matched his breathing, let it pull her under.

She landed, at long last. She reached her hand behind her head and felt sand, sand all around her. So, there it was. Quicker than she expected, too. But wait. There was no ocean, and the sky above her was unspeakably dull. It was not blue, nor grey, but colourless. And was there drizzle in the air? It wasn't even warm, for God's sake. This was no beach, was nothing like a beach. Nothing like the Caribbean, or Thailand, or even the south of France. How utterly disappointing. Her teeth chattered a little, and a little girl appeared to her left. The girl had a face like hers, but a little darker, a little more angular. The little girl reached out at once to touch her face. Serene slapped it away. Reflexes. The girl recoiled, with large, untrusting eyes.

"Sorry," said Serene,
because the girl had a forlorn way about her, which Serene felt
as if it came from inside herself.

It looked like her inner and Abbé's outer, for reference.
"I'm Serene," she offered, to the air between them.
"That's my mum's name," said the girl.
Somehow, Serene knew this already.

The girl had a lovely, lovely name. As seven-year-old girls in the same sandpit are wont to do, they made friends in the space of an hour. In the dream, there was a time lapse, because dreams don't know how to respect time. She and the girl in the sandpit made firm friends, over and over again. They told each other secrets about how they had come to be. The girl had a sister, she said, but Serene knew this already, too. The girl looked at her in a way in which she had never been looked at before, and it gave her a strange feeling in her bowels and lower stomach, somewhere between excitement and a sharp, inexplicable fear. She found that she needed to test the girl. She needed to be sure that the girl was hers to keep. "Let's be naughty," she said in the best seven-year-old voice she could manage. "See that kid over there?"

The girl, whose name, she had said, was Clara, followed Serene's eye towards a pale boy with his leg in a cast, sitting on the swing by his mother.

"Take this stone," said Serene. "Take this stone. Hit him. Hard."

Without as much as a beat between, Clara aimed and did not miss.

When Serene woke up from this collage of instances, Abbé was gone, but this was nothing new. Next to her mouth, a green line of vomit and foam. Again, nothing new. But there was a feeling she had never felt quite so clearly before. A feeling that perhaps there was another thing happening. The sensation was almost translucent, like a fading fingerprint, a vanishing map. Such thoughts are common when you have just woken up from a dream, she told herself. But when you have understood a new truth, when you have taken it into your heart, there's no fooling yourself. The next time Serene wanted to be somewhere else, she didn't worry so much. When Abbé came round to the house and handed her the baggie, she took the drugs and landed. She felt her entire consciousness shifting, placed inside a body that was neither hers, nor someone else's, a peculiar mid feeling, dulled and liminal. And yet she knew this body, no? The dry skin covering the neck and elbows, the sag at the waist?

At the other side of a dark room,
a man stood at the door.

"Look," he was saying, "I have no interest in little girls. I'm just saying, make a decision."

She didn't know what it was all about, but the body she was in seemed frightened and confused and willing and everything else. Being in a body like this was new and yet understood. It was a shorter, more invisible body. A body less sure of itself, prone to ill treatment. When she watched the girl watching herself in the mirror, she had to urge herself not to turn away.

You're alright, she mouthed to the reflection, knowing that the body so needed those words.

You're perfect just as you are. You don't have to be anyone else, not now, not ever. But even in the night, she knew that she couldn't make herself or the body believe it. She thought about revealing herself, in her own image, announcing herself, making herself known in the deep, dark room, but thought better of it. There was a fragile sense about the girl. She needed help. Without invitation, Serene took to her new body.

The following night on her travels, she went back to the same dark room, back into the small, sad body. She heard movement from the next room, so she rose from her bed and followed the sound. The man from the night before was sleeping, wheezing a little, smelling of Brut or Old Spice. Life felt terribly, terribly desperate. *You have to secure your love,* she thought. *You have to do your bit.* She climbed into Kendrick's bed, did what she thought best.

A LIST TRYING TO MAKE SENSE OF THINGS BY DEMPSEY NICHELLE ELIZABETH CAMPBELL

"Okay," I tell my dazed sister, who is lying in the bed, annoyed that I dared to try opening her bedroom curtains at 9:30 a.m. On my phone I read the notes I've been making through the night. Clara covers her head with the duvet. I sit on the bed, placing a hand on what I think is the curve of her back.

"Okay now Clara," I begin. "If the mother in the book is the woman here on earth, we know that she is

1. Not to be trusted
2. ~~A little bit selfish; will think nothing of leaving us behind.~~ extremely selfish. Very self-serving
3. Preys on the weak ~~and unassuming~~
4. Visits them in the night and threatens them and makes them write books.
5. Has a violent streak, like her oldest twin. We all know who I'm talking about.
6. Will stop at nothing to get what she wants, which remains

unknown? Money? Clothes? Control? Love? Fame? Stability? ~~World peace?~~ JOKING

7. ~~Will take your friend from right underneath you, that's for sure~~

8. Might be a climber, aka a leech.

9. and not be sorry about it

10. Though unreliable, is quite good at her job. It is as Veronica says, she can put her mind to anything. She can also

11. turn on her charm and turn it right off, and when the light goes off she is Awful, plain and simple.

"Bleurgh," goes my sister, with her puffy morning face. "Pass me the phone. I'm ordering food. Want anything?" We pause while I try to find a non-greasy option from the café up the road, and then I resume the summation of my findings.

"If Abbé in the book is Marcus," I go,

"we know that he

1. Is an Aquarius. A triple air sign has all the tendencies, including

2. thinking he's not of this world and detaching, detaching, detaching

3. is a total enigma, and it's irritating and weird and quite selfish and evil

4. can only be seen through clouded screen doors

5. is battling a pretty serious addiction

6. has never hung out with me sober

7. likes to people please which according to Rayna Panelli is the ultimate form of manipulation."

The food arrives. I chose poached eggs with a little spinach. Clara has ordered two rashers of bacon, two rounds of white buttered toast, and two helpings of baked beans. When we plate up the food, Clara makes a soggy bean sandwich with the toast.

I wonder how I'm going to broach the subject of Kendrick with my sister, since I barely want to think about it myself. She wrote it in a book for all to see. I should be angry. I should punch her in the face. But all I can think is, *She sees me. She knows. Someone else knows.* Perhaps I feel lighter. I take a deep breath.

"How did you know about the night with Kendrick in the doorway, and what happened the night after? How did it find its way into your book?"

My sister looks at me, concern in her eyes. Then suddenly catching it, and with her usual bravado says, "It's like I said. I was visited. Inspired."

"Like those people who wrote the Bible?" I quip.

"Like that," says my sister, without any sense of irony. She's impossible. I decide not to press things further, since I can feel a familiar rage brewing in me.

"I believe we are dealing with a ghost," I tell her. "But I don't know if the ghost is the mother in the book, and further, I don't know if the woman in the book is the woman here on earth."

"Mmm," goes my sister, splattering bean sauce on the table.

I wonder how I'm going to let her know why I insisted on the passport, or my dealings with a possibly crackpot psychic, but figure that if I can believe my sister in all of this fantastical madness, my sister could at very least believe me.

"Clara," I say, setting my phone down. "There's someone I need you to meet."

THE BOTTOM
OF THINGS

"As far as I can see," says Veronica the Sangoma, setting down her cup of tea and pausing for dramatic effect, "there is absolutely no question, no question at all, that Serene is your mother, travelled back to you via another means. If you look at the charts it is all present and correct. And check out this bloody passport! Your mother's full name! NOT a fake! I could feel the energy field around it. The only thing that does not make sense is that she should be here so soon."

Veronica makes a gurgling sound with her throat and if you didn't know better you might be forgiven for thinking she is pulling a prank on us. Her babies are in the cot again, kicking up their little feet. Veronica's place looks even dustier and more cramped than the first time, but I wonder if I only feel more conscious about it because my sister is here.

"But judging by your ages, she shouldn't have arrived yet—you're both twenty-five, right?"

"No," says that sister of mine, looking caught out. "It says that on Google, but, you know."

Veronica the Sangoma stifles a grin. "Thirty?"

"Then it matches up. It all tracks. You're thirty. She was thirty! When she . . . you know."

We stare at each other.

"The dark odds have a bad rap," Veronica continues, smoking her weed and the petals we brought as an offering. She blows a steady plume

of smoke in Clara's direction. Clara looks unconvinced, but engaged.
She gulps down the dark brown sludge that Veronica is offering.

"People think seers are evil, but we're not at all. You ever heard of a
twinning spirit?"

We shake our heads.

"Okay," says Veronica. "How to explain? Oooohh girls," Veronica
exclaims. "It's deep, y'know!"

She pulls out a lavender A4 sketch pad and a purple fine-tip marker.
"Basically, as you know. Twins are anomalies."

"Yes," I say. "We are."

"There could be a glitch," Veronica says. "A lot of people who have
twins are capable of this glitch. A recessive trait. We have more to talk
about. So much more, but . . ."

Baby Two starts hollering, then screaming out her little lungs. Veronica hurries over and goes about changing the little one, who squeals at
her mother(?)'s touch. I want to ask if these multiracial babies are hers,
but it might be seen as rude. The smell of fresh baby poop fills the air.

"Not to rush you out the door," Vee says, "but as you can see, both
my hands are full. Letmegetmyheadaroundthis. I'll deliver you a report
next week, next week. Also, Clara . . . got any more copies of your book
lying around at home? Could you sign one for my ex-husband? He absolutely, absolutely loves you." Veronica swings a soiled nappy in the air,
this being the cue for us to leave.

DANCING ALL AROUND IT

Unfortunately for me, I too have now seen Kendrick's penis. He wouldn't drop the insistence on an immediate phone call to put his mind at rest, he being a *PUBLIC FIGURE AND ALL. ME TOO*, I wanted to say, but instead I wrote, *WELL WHY DO YOU USE YOUR REAL PHOTOS?*

EASY ENOUGH TO CLAIM PHOTO THEFT, he stated. Sometimes the need to Fuck Around outweighs the Fear of Being Found Out. In lieu of the phone call, we settled on multiple photos of body parts. I like my body parts a lot, and consider showing them a public service. Also, I wasn't ready for him to recognize me yet. Sadly I hadn't bet on Kendrick feeling the need to reciprocate. Nobody needs to see *that*. I steal a sideways glance at my sister, who is watching a vegan cooking show on TV while eating fresh walnuts very carefully, one by one from a glass mason jar. I wonder about the real live details that happened with her and Kendrick, all those years ago. I suppose that when writing about the thing in the book, I hadn't really understood the weight of all I was saying. It had felt like fiction. I'd been caught up by a certain malevolent spirit of creation that rushed through me, but hadn't once stopped to consider the implications. Did I retraumatize her? Did I even stop to think about how she would feel reading it? Did I know it was real? I wish I could have been a better sister when we were eighteen. I wish I could have let her know it wasn't her fault.

Dempsey is now taking down notes for a vegan casserole that looks like shit. Each to their own. Without looking at me, she says, "Meat slows you down, you know. It's scientifically proven."

"Whatever," I say, waving her away. "We're at the top of the food chain. It's the circle of life."

I think back to the meal we had in Bermondsey, how Serene and I gobbled down our meat and rice as though we were one and the same.

> "*Simeon needs me to finish a little project,*" Serene had said, "*one last bit of ongoing work with him.*"

Was the one last project Dempsey and me? Was the one last project this elaborate scam?	"Depends where you are," my sister is saying. "You wouldn't be saying that in the jungle."

"Serene is a scammer, for sure," I tell my sister. "But I'm not sure to what extent. And so was our mother. So *is* our mother, oh . . . I don't know." I groan. Dempsey stands up.

"I think you're going to laugh at me for this," she says, "but sometimes I get stuck and stuck on a thing. It's like I fixate. And the only thing that can get me out of it is dancing."

She turns on some channel on YouTube with a lot of half-naked people prancing about with what looks like fake tribal paint on their faces. My sister is so fucking unintentionally funny sometimes that I can't believe it. I often think she's joking, but she rarely is.

"What the fuck is this?" I say, but Dempsey has already risen to her feet, is swaying around the room with her eyes closed.

"It's ecstatic dance," she says, dreamily.

"You like this?" I ask her, though I'm not sure why I'm surprised.

"Pay attention to the message," my sister warns, "not the messengers."

So I ignore the sun-burned hippies on the screen, concentrating only on my sister, who looks to be in a world of bliss, smiling, letting the music wash over her. I watch, mesmerized by the way she moves her hips, her wide, toothy smile. I watch my sister for a long time. In the dim light of the room, she almost looks like a real dancer. The music is nothing I've ever heard before, synthy, hypnotic. She opens her eyes and looks right at me, unafraid, offering me her hands. I take both of them, and we move together. She doesn't take her eyes off me and despite myself I'm smiling too. Before I know it, I'm matching her movements, almost carefree. Almost. I love her but I hate her. I *all the things* her. She is me, in part, and I can't make that alright with myself. She reminds me of the forest, of pinewood, burning trees, sweat, sweet, burning sap. She pulls me into a slow dance. Kendrick Lewis will fucking pay.

VOICENOTE ABOUT
YOUR MOTHER

(sorry I hate writing hahaha)

FROM VERONICA THE PRIVATE
INVESTIGATOR / SANGOMA
18 SEP 2025

I am following your mother, as requested, as promised. When she is order-ing an English Breakfast cuppa she likes white bread toast with jam. She drinks milk—real milk like a cat! She uses margarine, girls! Who even makes margarine anymore? She doesn't know or care what gluten is and says things like low fat, which no one says anymore, right? There is some tiny webbing on her (yes very beautiful) long fingers. It's hard to notice but if you know you know. They would have called her a witch in the old days. Clara I gave your book a second and third read. God you're good. Spooky stuff, but it all follows. Mate—I think she's the Ghost you speak of. Mate you wrote her alive! Men love her. Go proper mad for her. I've seen her walk into places and walk out, not having paid for her wares! Peo-ple forget themselves and end up giving things and themselves over and over again. Strange then, that her life often appears from the outside, as a run of oppressive, very bad luck. It didn't have to be like this. Girls, here's tough news. I think your mother might be living on the street. Even for an esteemed private investigator like myself (I'm older than I look hahaha don't tell anyone hahahah) she slips out of view, into trees, into the air, beside bodies of water. Streams, and the like. She evaporates into dull rain. Plus—your mother is ever the opportunist. On Tuesday evening, when the sun was going down, I saw her in a café drinking pea green soup with a man who looked like a punter, let's just call it what it is—I'm extremely sex worker positive by the way—you'll find no judgement here. I myself have lived a life. Anyway, he went to the bathroom leaving his briefcase (who carries a briefcase these days lol) and no word of a lie, she popped it open, just like that! Idiot that he is, he had notes in there and she helped herself to a whole wad of them. Suffice it to say, I've watched her steal all manner of things, from a piece of lean steak wrapped up at the butchers to a red woollen dress. And she loves a nice watch. Sound familiar?

I hate to sound cliché but on Tuesday morning she popped into House of Fraser, leaving with a coat in her hand. She was able to walk out without paying, just like that. When the police ran back the video they found no sign of her—like she knew where the cameras were. Small potatoes, though; what a waste of gorgeous, unbreakable talent. She could be/could have been anything she wanted, I reckon. Okay that's a bit of judgement maybe—no one's PERFECT. In the morning she takes a walk in the local park and looks out at the swans on the lake. She watches them meet each other. There is a sign that says please don't feed the birds, and she feeds them anyway, rebel that she is. Sometimes she meets Marcus on the corner (your Marcus, Dempsey, sorry girl) and they go for a drink, and she knocks them back like you do Clara. It's a family disease, girl.

Another theory opened itself up to me. It's mostly about numbers, which I'll admit are not my strong suit. Are either of you any good at maths? Can you come and see me on Wednesday? It is a distinct matter of Urgency.

THE DISTINCT MATTER
OF URGENCY

"Okay girls, hold yer hats," says Veronica. "Developments. Thanks for bringing dinner."

"It's only takeaway," Clara says, tossing Veronica her silver box. "I don't cook."

"Who cooks?!" spits Vee, but we don't know if she's joking. We're back in Veronica's little bedsit. Her hair is half bum-length purple braids and the other half is her afro. She is holding a baby, who is not Baby One nor Baby Two, but a different baby, light-skinned with a ginger afro.

"The thing is," says Veronica, spooning some curry chicken from the foil into a bowl.

"I planned my whole family on the numbers system, so I know what I'm talkin' about, know what I mean? I just had to get my fella to corroborate because I always count the wrong numbers twice, and it's a problem." Clara gives Veronica a mistrustful look. I sip my miso soup, trying not to see.

"Can you break this down in layperson terms please," Clara says.

"Serene's about to get pregnant, basically," says Vee.

"We know," Clara says between mouthfuls. "We worked it out."

"Wait a minute," I say. "I didn't make the connection . . ."

"It's going exactly as the book says," Clara interrupts.

"Basically," confirms Veronica. "I have a theory."

"Can you stop saying basically," goes Clara, "since there's nothing basic about this."

Vee ignores this outburst, picking at her teeth. "You say you're all thirty, right? So if you're thirty and she's thirty, there's a mirroring happened. You guys are thirty, she appears on your thirtieth—the plot thickens, girls! I think you're about to get conceived."

Vee throws us a sheet of printer paper with some dates scrawled on it. She reads from the paper. Her pointy nails are blue today.

"Here are the dates. The middle two dates being the most likely, the others peripheral. Thursday, September 29, 1994; Friday, September 30, 1994; **Saturday, October 1, 1994** . . . See that one's in bold. As is **Sunday, October 2, 1994**; then there's Monday, October 3, 1994; Tuesday, October 4, 1994."

"But how," I ask, "will we know which of these we need to act on?"

Vee takes back the paper. "So we're thirty years later. But look at the dates. Look what week we're in."

"Shit," says my sister softly. "We're heading toward danger week."

I look at my sister and Veronica, who are exchanging knowing glances. I hate being out of the loop. The radiator in the far corner of the room hisses and sizzles and I wonder why we're taking advice from a madwoman, a charlatan, a woman who can't even clean her flat when expecting company. My sister, too, could be described by some as unstable. Am I aiding and abetting? Also, where are the other babies today?

"The babies," says Vee as though hearing me, "are with their dads."

"Are you sure?" I wonder how best to phrase what's coming next. "Are you sure . . . that we should be basing the whole thing on a thing you devised, Clara?"

"What else do we have to go on? Everything else is working out the way it did in *Evidence*."

"What about Marcus's name?"

"I've already told you my theory on that. Even the twins' names have been changed. The only person whose name I saved was Serene's."

"And Simeon's," I put in.

"Ah, yeah," says Clara. "Honestly, that one slipped through the net."

I feel a tinge of pity, then, for Simeon, who wasn't even considered important enough to be made anonymous. But then I remember that he charged Clara fifteen thousand for the privilege of breaking her heart.

"What else is there to think?" Vee says. "You're what we call a prophet, Clara. A visionary."

Clara nods, unphased, crunching on a spring roll. "Yeah. I mean I can't argue with that."

"I really need to know," says Veronica, "that there's no way you two might already have been conceived."

"She means has she fucked him yet," says Clara.

"I know what it means," I say, sharply. "Clara, I do understand how the world works, you know."

"Alright, alright," says my sister. "But if the dates correspond as they did in the past and they do in the book, we need to cover all our bases. What if they've fucked already? We need to stop it from happening again. What if we're inside her already, beginning?"

"Can't have done," I say confidently. "She only met him last week."

"What's that got to do with anything," says Clara, meanly. "You can meet someone in a second, and boom!" Clara makes an uncouth slapping sound with her hand, and I feel my entire body burn. "Can't you, Dempsey?" she grins. I actually want to strangle her. I give her a look that says, *Can you take it down a notch?*

"I hear nothing," says Vee, waving her hand at me. "Don't mind me. At least forty-five spirit people and unknown entities are trying to make contact with me right now so I'm not particularly invested in what either of you are saying."

"Weird that you've been spying on our dad like this," says Clara, who can never resist an opportunity to make me feel less than. "To think you've spied on him all this time without putting two and two together."

I've had enough of Clara's shit today.

"Weird that you're obsessed with our so-called mum, who can do no wrong," I retort. My sister points at me, narrowing her eyes.

"If you have a crush on him . . . ," Clara wrinkles up her nose. "If you have, I can't even . . ."

"Not everything is about sex, Clara!" I snap. "And anyway, I'm not the one crawling around on restaurant floors, am I? Serene told me all about that. *What* was that about?"

Clara's face falls and we squabble a little until Veronica starts to speak over us.

"You two are cute," she says, which pisses us both off. A lot.

"She hasn't even been to his flat yet," I say.

"Not true," says Clara, her mouth full of rice. "In the book they meet on the bus and then she goes back to his house."

"The same day?" Veronica asks her.

"No, not the same day," says Clara. "A few days later . . . let me think?

"No one," I say, "has been at the flat. I rarely go out myself."

"Dempsey," puts in Vee. "You really think you know all the comings and goings in your building?"

"I think it's unlikely," I say, feeling somewhat flustered. "It's highly unlikely. I would know. I swear I would know." But then I think about the night at my house. Serene leaving. Next, the voices above my head. On my watch? Could we have been made on my watch?

"This is serious, Dempsey," Clara says, her brow furrowed. "If you've got it wrong and we're already beginning, there's a chance this might not work. We're supposed to stop them from having a baby. Two babies."

"Cockblock," I say, out of nowhere, and Clara bursts into laughter, but when we look at Veronica again she's dead serious.

"Basically, yeah," she says. "Stop 'em from getting together. You guys need to be on it."

"We'll just have to have them not meet up," I say.

"Well, it's too late for that," says Clara, looking accusingly in my direction. "They met at the park."

"No, on the bus, first," I correct. "You're forgetting your own story, Clara."

"Remember," says Vee. "The forces of this timeline are going to work against you. You've got to use all your combined might." Clara giggles. "Are you drunk?" says Veronica, casting me a worried look. "Girl. Have some filtered water."

Clara drinks the water gulp by gulp, until she's downed three quarters of a liter and counting. I notice the distinct similarity between her and the woman she is calling our mother, their rude, unquenchable thirst. While Clara is glug glug glugging Veronica goes on, unperturbed.

"Girls. I think you might need reinforcements."

We look at her as she crosses the room to a dresser with silver star stickers all over it, the everyday kind you get from the stationer's. The kind you use to reward children in their school exercise books for high marks. Veronica pulls out three vials containing an amber liquid. Two of them are test tube–shaped and one is shaped like a naked lady. We look on.

"Let's say I wanted to incapacitate someone," she goes. "Just . . . let's say I did. I'd use redlace. Takes you out cold for a good twelve hours."

"What is redlace?" we ask.

Vee flashes a wicked smile. "A really amazing sedative. People come out of it as though from the best sleep ever."

"You're sure it's not dangerous?" I say. "'Cause it sounds like poison."

Veronica looks at Clara. Clara looks at Veronica.

"Nah," she says. "It'll just quieten someone down for twenty-four hours or so. I'm just saying. You might need it, is all."

"You just said twelve hours."

"Twelve if you're a six-foot-four regular man with locs."

She pours some of the solution from the naked lady decanter into a beaker with a lid and hands it to my sister, who accepts it with relish.

"Now it is imperative," says Veronica, "that you not allow these possible probable potential parents together. By doing so you'll create yourselves again."

"And we all know how that turned out," I say.

"Well," says Veronica. "Exactly."

My sister gives her a look.

"There's something else," says Veronica. Her face, usually cheerful and glowing, has become solemn.

"So, girls, if you prevent that timeline, I can't say how it affects the other, you know? Like the one that we're standing in."

"Say more," says my sister, looking intently at Vee.

"What I can't tell from this . . . I've never seen . . . I mean the thing is, I don't think I know how the timelines link. There could be a possibility . . . well I think you might . . ."

"Spit it out," says Clara, losing patience. "Come on, Vee."

I study my sister's nostrils, which are flared like a newborn. Vee, unperturbed by any of this, goes on.

"There's a possibility, and a strong one, that you could erase yourselves. I know it sounds a bit mad, but hear me out. Like if you are not conceived, you may not have been born then, either."

"Wait," I say. "Wait wait a min. Soooo cancelling the conception means cancelling ourselves?"

"The problem is," Veronica says, "there's no way of knowing."

"How convenient," says Clara, strangely chipper. "Still, a challenge, right?"

Veronica looks genuinely troubled. "I wish I knew more. It's just that the maths . . . it's all conjecture, you know?"

"So Vee," says Clara, who weirdly appears to somehow be enjoying this, "what you mean is, if we do as you've suggested, you might be sending us to our deaths?"

"Not to scare you," says Vee, "but yeah. Basically."

An odd sense of calm fills the room.

"Right then," laughs Clara. "Russian Roulette."

••

Once we have driven off, I turn to my sister. "Clara. You sure about this? Vee . . . doesn't she seem a bit . . . well . . . off? I mean I met her sitting outside with her boobs out, she has all these babies of varying races . . . now she's talking about timelines and erasing ourselves. What if Vee's the con woman? And don't you think it's a bit far-fetched that the moment of conception is next week?"

"Dempsey," says Clara. "It's all far-fetched." She turns up the music loud. After a few long minutes, she pulls over the car next to a children's playground, squinting into the sandpit, as if willing some mirage to appear.

"Dem," she says, softly, after a while. "Would you say you were happy? Like, ever?"

"No," I say. "I didn't think we needed to be."

I think of Jack Spratt and Chrissie Wang and Rayna and Raymond and Kendrick and Claudette and Sunny.

"Like, is anyone? Happy?"

"I think we could be," says Clara. "I think it could be possible, in the end."

I say nothing, understanding a little and then not really understanding again.

"You're beautiful," I tell her, or am I pleading? "You're successful. People love you. People want to *be* you. It's a big risk."

Clara looks at me, something in her eyes. "Dem." Her voice croaks.

"What?" I say. "What?"

"What the fuck does any of that have to do with me?"

"People love YOU. People want to be YOU."

"Oh, don't be so disappointing," Clara says, rubbing her eyes. She winds down the window and spits in the direction of the playground. "Stop projecting. None of that matters if you don't feel it. I don't *feel* it."

"Okay," I say, after a while. "I think I understand."

"Sometimes I feel like my heart is missing," says my sister, "like not *my heart* in a cliché way—more like the thing in the centre of me. The thing that keeps us alive, keeps us marching toward . . . I don't know, *more life*. A vital organ . . . if not a heart, another important part of one-self that everyone else has and needs, like a liver, or a spleen. Sometimes I think that a long time ago, someone might have stolen it away from me in the night. And then in other moods I realise that perhaps I never had it. Perhaps I never had a chance."

I know I'm supposed to have a counter for this, but I don't. The truth is that I know exactly what she means. I need to make some speech right now to save her, to save us. So why don't I have the words?

"What I mean to say," she goes on, "is that I'm fine with whatever happens. I'm satisfied. I don't think any of this is real anyway. Our mother should have gone away and stayed away, but she didn't. She kept coming back. Sometimes I think she lived whole years as me. Like when I think back, I can't remember them. Like my twenties? Do you *really* remember your twenties?"

I wonder if I should remind her about the amount she drinks, but this doesn't feel like the appropriate time, and really, when I come to think of it, I realise that I, too, do not remember much of the last decade. I close my eyes, and I don't remember anything at all special, or relevant.

"After losing our parents, there was never, ever going to be any real peace, Dem. Not really. I want peace. Dempsey, don't you want a little peace?"

"I do. I want peace," I say.

• •

That night, I sleep in bed with my sister again and my sister sleeps in bed with me again and I don't even mind that she snores and gurgles, loud and open-mouthed. It is the thickest, most powerful sleep I've had in a while. I close my eyes, and all of a sudden I'm in the New World. All night we share dream-space, swap information. In the mid-morning, we wake up, sleep in our eyes. She pads down the stairs in her silly white camisole, talking away to herself as though there's a camera following her around. She gets back in bed with two sparkling clear drinks and she hands me the nonalcoholic version, she says, with limes in it. We talk about Kendrick and Claudette and other related things and she holds me as I cry. Then we make a little pact, we do.

NAUGHTY LYING SHITTY SCUMBAG GIRLS

I am already leaned, hands resting against the dinner table, just as planned, when Claudette saunters in. She is wearing a powder-blue tunic and matching trousers. She has her hair wrapped, and I can just make out the grey ringlets at the root.

"Claudie," says her husband. "You have visitors."

Behind us, my sister takes a sharp breath, watching Claudette.

Claudette places her steely gaze on me, and I try to meet her eye. Claudette is still tall, still ramrod straight. Her eyes are cloudier than I remember. She does not go over to greet Clara, but stops, just a foot away from me.

"Good to see you, Dempsey," she tells me. "You look nice today. This is good hair for you."

"Natural," says her husband. "The only way to do it."

I touch my curls. I feel a swell of pride at this. I do. Somewhere behind me, I feel my sister bristling.

"Now," says Claudette, "to what do I owe this visit?"

"We were in the area," I say. "Sorry. I might have called first."

"You might have," she says, and watches me a little more. She nods to herself then, as though I've passed some kind of private test. "But it's fine. Would you like to have some tea?"

"I'm not stopping long," I say, "I mean we aren't stopping long."

Claudette still hasn't acknowledged Clara, who looks to be fast disappearing into the floral wall behind her.

"*Staying*," corrects Claudette. "You mean you aren't staying long. Good to see you together, anyway."

"Yes." I nod. "But Claudette . . ."

"What is it, my love," says Claudette, now fussing around with the kettle in the open-plan kitchen.

"I just wanted to know," I say, eyes fixed on the dashiki what's-his-name is wearing. It is orange with pale blue and red chevrons embroidered on the perimeter of the neckline and sleeves. I notice, then, that Claudette's outfit contains the same common pattern. In the periphery of my vision, my sister sways—or do I imagine it?

"Yes, Dempsey?"

From across the room, Claudette blinks at me, expectantly. I did, after all, come here for a reason. Clara says that today is all about CLOSURE. To do this, I need to be my full, assertive, realised self. I need to be thirty-year-old Dempsey with Natural Hair who is certain of her life and what she is choosing to do, and why. Though I have not been invited to do so, I pull out a dining chair, taking a heavy seat at the table.

Claudette comes over, takes the seat beside me. She fixes her cloudy eyes on my face, my nose, my hairline. Everything in me wants to jump up, to run away. But this is for US. My sister and me. I feel my voice tremble.

"I mean, I just never understood, that's all . . . like, Claudette, like, why didn't you call the police?"

Claudette leans towards me, a puzzled look on her face.

"Why didn't I call the . . . who?"

"The police," I say, still using Eye Contact, still remembering that's what you need to do.

I've never looked Claudette directly in the eye before. It is a daring act that takes everything I have inside me. I feel my scalp tingling, an understanding from long ago slipping into place. Suddenly I can breathe. I watch Claudette register this change in me. Something about it causes her to falter slightly. Her husband, noticing this, stands up.

"Look, what's this all about?" says the man, getting in between me and his wife.

"I think you know what I mean, Claudette? *That* time."

"Dempsey," says Claudette, slowly. "I really have no idea what *time* you're referring to. I . . ."

"The day you burned all my hair," I interrupt.

"The day I . . . oh . . . ," Claudette puts a hand to her mouth. A tinkle of something. "Oh, you were allergic. Your dad got very excited, didn't he?"

Behind him my sister—who I'd damn near forgotten was in the room—lets out a snarl.

I daren't look back to catch her eye. Claudette and the husband ignore her.

"He isn't my dad," I say.

"But speaking of Kendrick," I say, my voice curling around his name. "Why didn't you call the police? On Kendrick?"

Claudette wrinkles her nose in a very Clara way. Now I know where Clara got it from.

"Since you thought I wasn't safe with him?"

"I don't remember saying that," she says, touching her narrow neck.

Tears begin to come, before I have time to control them. This is a mess. Clara says nothing. Hunches over. Begins tapping her nails on the countertop impatiently.

"It wasn't my concern," says Claudette.

At this I watch my sister slowly start to hum a tune . . . something far away, something I heard from our giant, shared dream. My sister takes a while on the action. She glides over to where the kettle is boiling, has clicked shut.

I wonder if she's going to attend to the teapot, the waiting cups, but I know that would be fiction;

and then I see my sister walk on her hands
but then when I look back she is walking normally
and I made the whole thing up.

What I mean to say is that I see her walk on her feet, right over to Claudette.

No one else seems concerned. Knowing, knowing, knowing too well what my sister just might be capable of, I spring to my feet.

"I think we'd better go," I say, right as my sister raises the kettle, right over Claudette's head.

Claudette registers the move, a grim recognition flooding her features. She turns, slowly, to face my sister, as if daring her. Clara, my hands now gently guiding her, places the kettle gently back on the stovetop.

"She was going to scald me," says Claudette, softly.

A moment, then, "What the hell—Get out! Get out, get out!" Kwesi is screaming. But no one is listening. We three women regard each other matter-of-factly. Claudette remains unperturbed. Is watching my sister.

"Well, well, well," says Claudette.

"I'm not joking about this, Kallis," says Kwesi. "Think of your career."

"I'm going to have you arrested," Claudette says, her voice seeming even, devoid of any feeling. "You've always been a lost cause. Sometimes I think . . ."

"That's enough," Kwesi cuts in.

Claudette makes a swatting motion with her hand. Kwesi looks scolded.

"Sometimes I think we took in the wrong one."

Clara, who has not fully let go of the kettle, lunges for Claudette again. Kwesi lifts my sister up, roughly. The kettle and its contents skid over the floor. Hot steam rises everywhere.

"Call the police then, bitch," screams Clara over his shoulder, as Kwesi curses, having stepped in the water in his socks. "We'll be long gone!"

"CallthefuckinpoliceIfuckindareyou!"

"Ugly," says Claudette. "Ugly, ugly work."

Kwesi throws us out of the house. I look at my sister, who is trembling on the front porch. I think of all the nights I went to bed willing my life to be less like mine and more like hers. I take off my cardigan and place it on her shoulders, which are heaving up and down.

"Come on," I whisper, "let's leave this place."

"Dempsey," she says back to me, looking out at the road ahead. "Can you please relax? And take this disgusting thing off me."

••

We go back to the Italian restaurant where I can eat practically nothing off the menu (it's all pure allergens!) and Clara gorges on carbs and red wine. In the end I settle on octopus on a bed of green, buttery spinach, though I'm sure the butter will hurt my stomach. We eat in silence and Clara pays with a heavy silver credit card. Back in the car, my sister throws her head back and will do nothing but giggle, putting her foot down, driving faster and faster.

"We're going to the Rose and Crown!" is all she will tell me, only I don't know what the Rose and Crown is. Clara pulls into a parking lot, without slowing down to take the curve.

"They do the best whisky sours," she tells me, panting, "And I fucking need a whisky sour."

The Rose and Crown is taken over by an event. Everywhere I look, there are banners and neon posters for a night called "Naughty Lying Shitty Scumbag Girls." I gasp at the name, and Clara throws her head back, guffawing. "What's all this?" she asks a cool-looking blonde at the bar.

"It's a monthly women- and femme-presenting-only night in which people go up onstage and talk about their wildest exploits and greatest fears," she says, as though this is a well-rehearsed spiel. "The fears have to be funny. The funnies have to be close to the bone. Our host, Alexis, is everything!"

Clara downs what I assume is a whisky sour and some pint of something (gross) and says she thinks I'll be a natural. Before I can stop her, she has marked my name down on a list of comedy hopefuls. I tell her there's no way I'm doing that; forget it. But my sister is on one. She kisses my head, pulls back, and gives me the *loveliest* smile. My heart threatens to explode.

"Dem, you have to," she tells me. "You're fucking brilliant."

A row of fireworks happens in my stomach. Well, okay. Today I looked someone in the eyes and CONFRONTED THAT PERSON! How much harder could it be to make jokes about my life? Still, I'm hardly a comedian. There are at least ten names ahead of mine, enough time to cry off or disappear.

Alexis explains to us that it's a show that celebrates being bad. Someone gets onstage and talks about their "complicated homelife" on finding out their parents were both sleeping with the neighbours, unbeknownst to each other.

A girl talks about life in a death cult, only all they did was make moonshine and have sex with each other. It sounds better than my first children's home, to be honest.

Someone is speaking about life with three mothers and two dads and how when it's good it's great, but when they all start to squabble and play games it's like "the Gulf War," they say, which is not politically correct, even I know that. *Bitch*, I think, *all those people who love you.*

Other people go onstage one by one, and I note their patter, their intonations, and make the decision to at least go for it. My sister watches them, a familiar blankness in her eyes. I recognize it as the thing that appeared, tight in the middle of Claudette's face, when I said the things I said. My sister is a product of her environment. Only that. I decide that if it comes to me and I actually do it, the whole bit will be about how nervous I am every minute of the day, and why. How my entire chemical makeup changes when I leave the house, and everything is fearful and outsized. How deathly afraid I am of the very beautiful, but only if they are women. I look over at my sister. *Am I really one of two? Part of her?*

Then Alexis calls the name of the girl before me, who suddenly is nowhere to be found.

"Ooooookiieeee then," says Alexis. "Dempsey? *Dempsey*, you there?"

My sister points to me, "She's here!" she calls to Alexis, and the room. "She's here!"

"Let's give Dempsey some encouragement, people," shouts Alexis from the stage, reading my expression—the sign of a great host. Everyone roars and claps. I climb to my feet, legs buckling below me. Then I'm up on the stage, with a lot of loud, appreciative half-drunk people smiling up at me. It's a kind of ready love I could get used to—a benign, easily pleased blanket of safety. More safe, indeed, than the wild outdoors. The lights are hot on my face. I feel a me that is not me, could not surely be me . . . riffing on tales of old and tales of now. There is the essence of my sister about me, searching the crowd, courting the crowd. I think I even wink at a girl looking shyly at me from down, down and to the left. I do a spin, showing off my very mediocre outfit. I tell them about my pains getting makeup to actually stay on my face.

I tell them about Kendrick and the birthday cards, and the hair-relaxing fiasco. Then I go for broke and launch into the thing about the porn. As if it were not me with the very unconventional kink problem. As if it were a girl I was watching from the corner of the room. The audience whoops and hoops and hollers, in awe and recognition, and I feel not so alone. I feel like an army. I feel more me than myself, more like me than I have ever felt. Me without the constant worry and the living upstream. Me without the fighting and whatnot. I keep going on about my nervous tics and all the times I have wet myself in public—even the dribbles. The more the audience listens and laughs, the better I feel. The more calm I feel. I look down and to the back of the audience, where my sister is looking up at me for maybe the first time ever. And she is laughing. Really, really laughing, not the deranged car laughter, nor the affected, self-aware chuckle when she's drunk on stage, posed and preened like a prize cat. She is hitting the wooden table in front of her and stamping her feet, and now, in this moment, I feel as though anything could be possible. I start in on my sister, specifically about the differences between us.

I say, "People . . . do you realise—I'm the identical twin of that one there?"

Clara staggers roughly to her feet, takes a bow.

The audience go awwwww for me, and giggle, and scream, and my sister laughs the most, throwing back her head, and smiling with those slightly too white pricey teeth of hers. Those teeth of hers that catch the light and gleam—teeth of the rich, the successful.

There are three clear liquids in shot glasses that my sister has lined up in front of her. They are gleaming too! Clara carries one of them over, downs two of them herself. The liquid is sharp and awful, but it warms my throat. After the show people come up to me and tell me I'm funny as fuck. Thing is, I've never really known I was funny before. Alexis invites me to do another show. Clara says I should go for it, without thinking, and then we remember the possible outcome and grow a little more quiet, a blank space where it pertains to The Future of Us Both. There are times when I think about what I could have done when I was younger, with all of this time, stretching out for days and years, if only shame hadn't held me under.

A PARTING GIFT

Claudette did not, as she promised, call the police. Kwesi must have calmed her down. That or she never truly felt threatened, not for a minute. She might have known Clara would not have been able to scald her.

On Wednesday morning I clean out all my browsing history. I clean off the porn and all my deep-dive searches on Jack Spratt, Chrissie Wang, Marie Antionette the Style Kween and everybody else. I think about ditching the entire laptop in the river, but don't really know about doing that with the way the planet is going and everything. I'd feel guilty about the ducks.

Today, Clara picks me up, music on loud, hair short and pretty, and we drive to get breakfast pastries. We reach the Nobu Hotel. My sister parks the car and turns off the ignition and sits there a while playing with my hair, practically brimming with excitement.

"Okay Dem," she says, a dangerous look playing across her face, "I have a present for you. It's in the lobby. Let's go."

Before I understand what is happening, she has grabbed her bag and jumped out of the car to meet me at the other side.

"Let's go," she says again, head angled toward the sun. "Please don't worry, okay?"

I follow her, a little afraid of the last thing she said. Why would I be worried about breakfast? Should I be worried about breakfast? I follow her into the black and gold lobby, which makes me think a little of Rayna and all the calls I've been ignoring. Feeling a pang of doom, I look round, wondering where the restaurant is.

There's a guy with green eyes resting like a large cat in the corner sofa. He looks like an influencer from now or a model from the early 2000s. He watches as my sister leads us over, standing up to greet us.

"It's good to meet you, Dempsey," he says, smiling, "like really great."

Full. Deep. Pink. Lips. Wow. My sister laughs and nudges me, and it's then that I realise I'm just standing there, gawking.

"You look like you should be on TV," I blurt out. "Like, you look quite familiar . . . to me."

"Funnily enough," he says, "I am! On TV. Sometimes."

"Oh my God. What are you in?" I breathe, a little light-headed.

Clara gives me a sideways look, shaking her head.

"I'm sorry," I say, regaining myself. "It must get really annoying to get asked that."

"Nah," says the man. "I'm an actor. Trust me, I need it."

We all sit down and I listen, spellbound, as the beautiful boy named Cristian talks about two shows I have never ever heard of in my life. One's for a cable network that they only play in Sweden, but, good for him.

I try to sound really interested and tapped in but I'm more worried about what I'll say next and why we're here, and whether I'm being natural and what my sister is thinking and what he must be thinking. Clara shifts on her seat blowing air out of her mouth, as though Cristian is talking too slowly for her liking. It's quite uncomfortable. Eventually Cristian does a sort of nervous laugh and asks, "Do you want to go upstairs and talk some more?"

"Don't mind me," says my sister, who has been nose deep in her phone, already getting to her feet.

"I have somewhere else to be, anyway. One more stop to make before we find her!"

She almost sings the words. I've never heard my sister so giddy before. She takes one of the brightly coloured macarons on the small marble table and pops it into her mouth, then touches my cheek in an almost kind manner and leaves.

Oh no. Oh no. I can't speak. Oh, my God. I try to gather myself, to catch my own breath. So this is what it is? My sister really believes that it's going to happen, just like that? Cristian looks at me. My head suddenly starts to feel a bit light again. My skin starts to feel like it's on fire.

"Uh, yeah. You wanna get a cup of tea?" I ask him, once Clara has skipped away.

"I can make you a chamomile if you want," says Cristian. "Upstairs? Up to you."

I cannot meet his eye.

In the end, I follow Cristian to room number 30, because what else can I do? When we get into the hotel room, I'm so bloody nervous that I can't stop talking about L-theanine and ashwagandha and he's talking to me about red maca until, almost lovingly, he places a large hand on my shoulder. Before I know it, we're standing very close to each other. I can feel his pulse, which is racing.

"So," I say, taking his hand off me, though I'm not sure I want to. "What *is* this?"

Cristian doesn't answer, is busy looking for the kettle thing, which he finally locates in a drawer.

"Foundya!" he says, in a kiddie voice. He looks up at me a little shyly.

"Did your sister talk to you about this?"

"No," I tell him, wanting to be truthful. "She just kind of dropped me off and here you were."

"Okay," he says. "Okay, well *that's* awkward."

But I have changed since going onstage, since baring my soul. Since calling out Claudette. I can make this how I want it. I can run this thing. He's my gift, after all. All I need is some . . . what would Rayna say, or do?

I arch my back a bit. I touch my curls. I invite Rayna Panelli into my body.

"I don't know that it has to be," I say, smoothly, I think, making sure not to break eye contact. At this, Cristian's shoulders relax a little. He leans back on the considerable bed, squinting up at me.

"You seem really nice," says Cristian. "Really sweet. I'm relieved."

Not the desired effect but, anyway.

We make chamomile in tiny pewter cups.

"Are you hungry at all?" says Cristian. "It's actually all on your sister. She left her credit card. Are you close?"

"Not hungry," I say. "Not close."

I'm starting to feel that this might not be right. He pats the space beside him and I settle down on the bed.

"I'm a bit of a superfan," he admits. I realise then that if I'm bad at flirting, Cristian is terrible. I don't know much about dating, but I know that when you're trying to seduce someone, talking about her sister is not the thing. Still, he's so beautiful, he's already forgiven.

"So . . . an actor?" is all I can think of to say. "For how long?"

"Forever. It's the only thing I'm good at really."

"Well, you look like you might be good at sport."

He drains his water bottle, drinking the tea in tandem.

"Nah not really," he says. "I'm just very vain. Work hard at it." He looks at me, a long look, while I scramble for more things to say. Cristian's eyes are a danger-grey, but he doesn't seem dangerous at all. I start to imagine all manner of things. Things from the specialist porn site that I won't speak of. I think then that I'm not waxed, and all the girls on the specialist porn site are waxed and hairless and small.

"I'm hairy," I say, out loud. Cristian smiles.

"I'd really love to touch you," he says, in a movie kind of fashion. If I wasn't so scared I might laugh at him. He seems so comical, so non-real, that suddenly I feel a bit guilty.

"Are *you* sure?" I ask him. "I mean, I know she . . . my sister put you up to this and I . . . I just want you to know . . . Because you definitely, definitely don't have to." A new thought occurs to me. "Oh my God, she didn't pay you to do this did she? Did she?"

Cristian takes my face in one of his hands and kisses me gently, and most of my blood rushes to my head, and all the rest rushes to you know where. Next he pulls me into his hard body and begins to breathe a little too hard and a little too theatrically. It's all very YouTube web series. No, all very soft porn if the soft porn was Netflix circa 2019. I put a hand on his chest to stop him. It's all moving a little too fast for me.

"Can we watch one of your shows?" I ask him.

"What did you say?"

Cristian lights up from the inside out, emitting a full-on glow. It seems a lot more real than the person I met downstairs.

I decide to massage his ego a little. It looks as though he needs it.

"I'm just saying. I'd love to see you on screen."

"Oh," he says, looking genuinely confused. "Do you mean that, Dempsey?"

"Of course I do! I'd love to see you in your element," I say. "I bet you're wonderful."

He stares at the carpet for a few beats. "Well I've nothing currently on the TV," he says, "but . . ."

"Yeah?"

"I have my showreel on my website, but that's a bit . . . it's a bit silly, having you watch that."

He looks up at me through his brown lashes. I notice a smattering of very cute freckles across the bridge of his nose.

"I'd *love* to see that!" I say, sounding every inch the actor myself. His pale brown face scrunches a little, as if he's trying to work me out. He rummages around in his nonironic tote. It says *GYMBOX* all over it. He pulls out his phone.

"It's just," he is saying, "not something most people ask of me."

We lie back on the bed, one of his gorgeous muscular arms draped over me, and on his phone, we watch twenty-seven minutes of scenes by Cristian Rimmer of the Gattison Partnership.

In scene one he's a lifeguard, doing a questionable Californian accent, which I don't comment on. Best not to, since there are no good words for such a performance. In the second, third, and fourth clips, he's an impossibly hot policeman, chasing some kind of dangerous criminal (it's truly hard to decipher the context).

In the fifth clip he's a dangerous villain, which is kind of improbable. The role doesn't suit him. In the last scene, he's a father of eight-year-old twins. This does it. Him as a kind, kind father. I feel the very first stirrings of arousal. As if sensing this, Cristian moves in, starts to nuzzle my neck. I feel the nub of myself hardening against my underwear. My legs stiffen. I feel myself clenching a little. Then, I'm removing my shirt and he's removing his.

"I can go slow," he says, when we're both completely naked.

He is staring at my belly, I think. I pull in, as he places a hand gently on it.

"I'd rather you didn't," I say, bolstered by the hungry way he is staring at me.

"You want to stop?"

"No!" I say. "Just not the belly, okay? Leave the belly alone."

"Okay. But I think it's lovely. You're lovely."

We try a kiss.

His mouth is softer than I imagined; perhaps softer than mine. With my tongue, I explore the entire width of it. He breathes as I kiss him, a subtle, relaxed sigh, which feels like the most delicious thing I have ever experienced. We lay each other down, and he tries different things with his hands. I tell him what feels good. Then he gets on top of me. I let him touch my inner thighs for a long, long time. What follows is metal, is bread, is clay, is liquid and light, is both sharp and soft. I swear I see a faint glimmer on everything, as though I've invented the whole room, the whole bloody orbit. When I orgasm, I feel the whole room tilt as if on its side. I make a low, animal sound, so much so that he playfully places a hand on my mouth, which drives me even crazier to tell the truth. When it finishes, and I'm sure it can no longer do anymore, he places his mouth where he just finished and I nearly collapse with the exertion of the second one. When I reach my apex the room goes silent.

"Wow," he says, "you're really special." But his voice comes to me from another place. My ears aren't working so well.

"So are you," I say, patting his head.

"I mean it," he says, "you might be the warmest person I ever met."

In that case, I feel sorry for him.

He goes to the bathroom, leaving me wondering if that was one of his lines from his show or something.

When he comes back, he keeps staring into my eyes like someone who really cares about me, so I do the same back, as though we are old lovers. We start his showreel again, from the beginning because I tell him I'd quite like to offer feedback.

"Should we order dinner instead?" he says, quickly. "Need some protein. Immediately. I'm on a timer." He shows me all his timers for his nutrition intake, which I think is the coolest thing ever.

I text my sister and tell her we'll be a while. We attack the menu. Cristian is as excited as me. We order only the healthiest things.

THE IMPENDING DOWNFALL
OF COUNCILOR
KENDRICK LEWIS

Kendrick is glued to the cricket when I let myself in through the side door. I'm getting good at this thing. I could have been a thief in another life. He's wearing glasses on the end of his nose and he's thinner than he used to be. His beard, which was always oiled and gleaming, is now almost completely white.

I take in the features of the living room, nasty rattan furniture, some free weights in the corner. The carpet, a stale blue.

As I approach, Kendrick jumps to his feet. He is shorter than I remember. Or I'm taller. Or both. It takes a while for his face to register me, and then,

"Oh my God!" he says, "Is it . . . oh my God Clara, it's you!"

"It's me," I say. "It's me. It's me. It's me."

Kendrick turns to look into the hallway, and then down toward the back of the house.

"Did you let yourself in?"

"Dempsey's old key," I tell him. "You never changed the locks?"

"Well okay," says Kendrick, rubbing his neck. "Okay, okay . . ."

"Can I sit down?" I ask him. I sit down anyway on the suede sofa, positioning myself exactly opposite his armchair.

Kendrick hovers in the doorway. "Is Dempsey coming?" the man has the nerve to ask. I shake my head no.

He looks to the door, then back at me.

"The thing is," says Kendrick, hovering, "I'm kind of expecting some-one. I honestly don't mean to rush you out. I'd really like to reconnect . . ."

"Hello," I say, in a deeper voice, shaking out my wonderful, expen-sive hair.

"I'm Davina Doll," I say. "We've been talking on AdultFriendFinder."

It takes longer than it should for him to understand.

"So . . . wait," Kendrick says, slowly. "Let me get this right. I've been talking to you? You're Davina . . . ?"

"Yeah," I say. "That's what's I'm telling you. Yes."

"What's the meaning of this?" says Kendrick. "Is this a joke or . . ."

"It's no joke. Famous authors need to get laid too."

Kendrick looks like he doesn't believe me.

"I've never been on a dating site," he says. "I mean I have, but not adult . . ."

"Oh, come on," I groan. "Let's not pretend. And between us—there's always been a thing."

It's worth a try. I've barely seen him enough in my life to have had any kind of *thing*, but you can tell some people anything.

Kendrick still isn't doing anything, so I strip to my underwear, right there in the living room, to let him know I'm not joking. This kind of thing always works.

"Okay," he says, "you're serious. Alright."

"As I've ever been." I train my eyes on the wiry white chest hair pro-truding from his polo shirt.

He comes up to me. Sniffs at my armpits in brutish fashion.

"Kendrick!" I exclaim, not bothering to hide my surprise. I giggle, one hand covering my mouth.

"You smell a bit wild," he says. "Busy day, was it?"

"I like it," he says.

I turn away to him and to the window, squeezing my eyes shut. I will not give myself permission to feel sick now. I'm going to stay and see this through. When I turn back to him, I replace my disgust with a raised eyebrow, a suggestion of a pout.

"It has been said."

"I like it," he says again, sniffing the air, the pervert.

"Do you have anything to drink in this place!" I demand.

He gives me a look, as if weighing me up. "Wait there," he says, and runs out of the room.

"Scotch okay?" he calls from the kitchen.

"I'll drink anything, me," I tell him.

He comes back with only one glass, and the bottle, which will not do.

"Drink with me?" I say, in as bratty a voice as I can muster.

He gives me a look to say, *you've twisted my arm*, and goes back to the kitchen, during which time I have poured myself a significant amount, downed half of it, and refilled it—half scotch, half redlace. He sets the new glass down and I pour myself a drink, handing him the one I made. I watch as he sips.

For his age and everything he seems quite nervous, a little fumbly. We curl up on the sofa together, watching white-clad men run up and down on the green as I nibble his sweaty earlobe, waiting for the medicine to kick in.

"What's this?" I coo into one ear.

"Just the cricket," he whispers.

I pretend to be interested in whatever this is, while Kendrick, taking my cue, tickles my ear with his horrible beard. This goes on for fifteen long minutes.

Finally I hear him draw a breath. Now he turns to me, slurring a little. "Do you want to go up and lie down, then?"

I want to laugh. "Thought you'd never ask."

Upstairs, Kendrick's bedroom smells of old man cologne and Febreze. His bedsheets are the polyester kind of thing people might have had some years ago; there's a light sheen to them. I watch, unimpressed, as he clumsily swipes at my bra.

"Let's get in bed first," I tell him.

The fact that I'm nearly naked is sticking a little. Strange, I didn't expect to have much of a problem with this part of it.

"I wanna see you," slurs Kendrick. "All of you."

I fix an eye on him.

"Did you fuck my sister?" I ask him, as he makes his way over.

His face melts into—well, I'm not sure what.

I am quiet, then.

Kendrick grasps for the words. Finally, he arrives at this: "She . . . she wanted it."

I didn't expect to feel the bile that rises. "What the fuck did you just say?"

Must calm myself. Mustn't flip out.

"Do you know," I say, pointing to my phone that I have leaned up on the bedside table, "do you know that you're live on camera right now?"

He looks at my phone, which, to be honest, might even be switched off, but he doesn't know that.

"Oh it's a blackout app," I tell him. "You can't see them, but they can see you."

"You aren't serious," he says, going for the phone. "You're lying."

But I'm too quick for him. I snatch up the phone, pointing it at his face. For a second, I remember the fact that I came in here without any kind of weapon and no fear, none at all, for my safety. Nobody knows I'm here right now. Not even Dempsey.

But Kendrick is incapacitated, is saying things that don't make sense.

"I think this is what they call a leak," I say. "You're on a live video call to everyone who works at Bermondsey City Council, everyone. I invited them to all to watch."

I kneel up on the bed, motioning him to look at the lens.

"Abusing a girl in your care. But why?"

"It was what she wanted," he says, his eyes pleading. "She was eighteen! She was over age. I mean . . . what I mean is . . . It was eighteen years ago! She was eighteen."

"Kendrick," I say, suddenly bored. "Kendrick. You need better boundaries."

I point the camera at his face and his crotch.

I make like I'm recording his crummy old body.

"Don't you want to hit me?" I ask him. "Don't you want to knock me out?"

Kendrick begins to cry. I watch him, thinking only of Dempsey. The room around me shifts, begins to feel hyper-real. I feel the type of blue energy emerging. I wonder if maybe he'll hit me. I wonder if I'll taste blood.

"You really hurt her, you know." A wash of red comes over me. "You really hurt my daughter."

"Hell are you talking about?" he sputters, eyes rolling back in his head.

> Something feels amiss,
> is slipping out of place.

An upstairs window in my head goes black. I wonder if I'm having some kind of aneurysm. I clutch the side of my head.

"You . . . you know what I mean."

Kendrick stares toward the fake people watching from my phone.

"I didn't do anything with any young girl! I want you to know I'm being blackmailed!" Kendrick tries to hide his face with his floppy hands.

I throw my head back and laugh, and laugh.

And then, Kendrick's eyes begin to bulge, and he won't make sense.

"Whaddya doo?" he says.

In the corner of my eye I see Kendrick's belts hanging up on the wardrobe. I feel as though anything might be possible. Kendrick follows my eyeline.

"Noooooo," he says. "Pleeeee."

I look at him, easy meat. "I could give you eighteen lashes," I say, feeling somewhat of a thrill. But this is for Dempsey, not for me. I mime the action of slapping him on the bottom. Kendrick flinches.

"Ah relax," I hiss. "Stop whimpering, I'm not going to fucking whip you. I reckon you'd like that anyway. I reckon you'd be rock hard, Kendrick!"

Kendrick is gesticulating. Kendrick is crying.

"My sister could have been adopted by someone decent . . ."

". . . them raised you . . . ," he is slurring, drool pooling at the edges of his lips.

"You'll leave my sister alone. No more birthdays."

"No birthdays," he slurs. "No. . . ." Silence. Kendrick is *out*.

I pat his round belly just above his crotch, where his erection, of course, is up like a tent pole.

"Okay then, you," I smile. "Can't stay and chat. I really need to get off."

I take four intimate pictures of him, for good measure, just in case I change my mind about things, and leave, using the front door, which I leave wide open.

I dance down towards the garden gate, and outside, to my car.

••

I pull up to the hotel to see my sister standing outside, looking renewed and freshly fucked. She gets in my car smiling. I don't want to ask her what is what.

"You changed your hair," she says, then doesn't ask me what is what. We put on the radio. "I'm A Kid" by Jadu Heart is playing.

DEBREIFING

"Well?" Clara wants to know when I get in the car. "How was it?" I squint my eyes at her, weighing her up. She looks beside-herself happy, nearly manic.

"It was good, I think."

"You *think*?"

"I had fun," I say, embarrassed. "What d'you want me to do, draw you diagrams?"

"He's great, isn't he," says Clara, settling in her seat, her voice hoarse. "Yes, I thought you'd like him."

A small, unsettling thought clicks in my mind, attaches itself to the base of my spine.

"Clara," I groan. "You didn't! Did you?"

"Did I what?" says Clara.

"Have you like . . . did you sleep with him before, or something?" I say.

"Oh no," says Clara, backing out of the hotel car park. "No. That one's for you."

I sit back in my seat, relieved. You never know with her. No boundaries.

"He's soooo handsome," I admit to her. "And he was very into it. I'm surprised."

My sister looks genuinely bemused. "What do you mean, surprised?"

"Clara, I'm hardly you am I? I'm surprised he could . . . you know . . . perform. What I mean is, I know I'm not commercially beautiful."

My sister looks crestfallen. "Dem. I'm sorry for the terrible things I said. That night with Serene."

"It's okay," I say, wanting to talk about anything else. I stare outside the car window at a brunette woman in the car to our right who is singing away, smiling away, singing away.

"I don't really believe those things," I hear my sister say.

"Yes you do," I say, before I have time to stop myself. "But it's okay. It's really okay."

Clara puts a hand on me but she doesn't argue.

"I'm awful aren't I?" she says, after some time. "You can admit it, Dem."

"Sometimes," I say. "But you're my only sister."

Looking away, Clara tugs on my jacket sleeve.

"I don't know. I think that makes it worse."

"When We Were Young" by Adele comes on. I love the song and everything, but the moment is too cliché and thankfully we both laugh, breaking this awkwardness. We stay, hands rested on each other, until Adele finishes singing.

Clara sighs. "Are you ready?"

Now is the time to state my case, if ever there was. I think about everything there is to do. I think about pleasure, and experiences like today, and what we could be if we were better, if we were more.

"Clara, are you sure it makes sense? It doesn't make sense."

My sister grips the wheel, presses on the accelerator. Around us the sky, navy blue.

"Every day since I was a kid, I have wanted this, in a way."

I'm not sure I understand what she's saying here. "Do you mean that every day you've wanted to die?"

"Not die," she says. "Just to . . . I don't know . . . disappear off into the ether somehow. I would like to not have happened, you know."

"Some might call that dying."

"Some might. I prefer *unexist*."

We pull up to a stoplight, and the shapes of two small children run across the street.

"Wait," I say. "Not suicidal, are you?"

Clara takes a long breath, looking out and past the window. "Time After Time" by Cyndi Lauper is playing now. "Isn't everyone a little bit suicidal?" says my sister, staring at the hill in the distance. The dip and bow before our eyes, the streets a moving diorama. My sister has this incredible quality of saying the most out-of-this-world thing and making you consider it. Even if it's a deep, dark thought, bigger and badder than anything you could have brought to mind. It's why she's such a persuasive and effective public speaker. She says it like it is and like it isn't, can present the fact and sell any truth. I'm not suicidal. Am I? Am I? I squeeze my eyes together, trying to do some kind of mathematical sum.

"I'm not suicidal," I say to her, finally, as though I've arrived at a thought.

"That's good," she says.

The other honest thought escapes my mouth before I get a chance to hold it in. "But I'm not *not* suicidal," I say. Also the truth.

"Gotcha sis," she says, looking over at me in the passenger seat. It sounds unnatural, the way she says "sis." For a second, she kind of looks like her mother. Not the birth mother, the adopted one. Claudette.

"I've come to a bit of a realisation," my sister is saying, "but Dempsey, you might not like the details."

I look at her, squinting, trying to guess what might be coming. For some reason, I put on her sunglasses, which rest just under the dashboard. I check myself in the sideview mirror. They turn up at the sides and they actually suit me. I've always thought I didn't have the face for glasses, but this shape works so well. I spread a thick line of tinted lip gloss, the clean strawberry-flavored Boots brand that I have always used. I have a feeling about where her mind is going. But the thing about being a twin to someone is that decisions that must be made must be made together. Someone must always concede.

"Try me," I say, feeling daring. "Go on, *sis*."

WE'RE ABOUT TO BE FAMOUS, JUST YOU WATCH

Emma brings her baby onto the Zoom link, parading her around like a pink prized doll. The baby is nothing to speak of, to tell the truth. She is a round shiny ball of perfect goodness, I suppose, and when her face catches the light, there's a cherub's cleft in the chin. Cute, if you like that kind of thing. The baby bobs her head around, as though nothing is wrong with the world. Her face is almost a mirror image of her mother; relieved, pink, benign. It is a look that makes me want to reach into the iMac screen and drag Emma back to her reality—to the star in question, me. She has no idea what she might lose if she doesn't pay a little more attention. But no, Emma is more interested in her fat, demanding baby and the dribble and poo. I understand it though. What does she owe me, really? Good for her. I should hope she has other bestsellers lined up. I'm beginning to feel bitterish, then almost sad, but then the baby's face fills Emma's screen and I don't know how to be any of those things.

"Sorry," laughs Emma. "Sorry everyone."

"We would like to option *Evidence* for TV," says one of the thin women in another box on the screen, "and we have a ton of suggestions for writers to adapt it. Before that, though, we were wondering if you had any interest in a cowrite."

I squint at them all, trying to separate what is good from what is more work. I find my expensive smile.

"That's wonderful news," I hear myself saying. "She'll love that. Serene will love that."

In the bottom rectangle, Emma looks horrified for a moment, then fixes her face. I smile about what I've been able to write into existence. What a manifester I am. I told my mother we'd be famous and look at us now. I told Dempsey to believe I write true stories, of the past and the future—well look at me now. Perhaps I am a dark witch, a person for whom all might be possible.

"Not even a movie script," I say, "even better. Everybody likes TV."

The seven women laugh politely.

"I told my mother," I say, "and by doing that I made it happen!"

The women stare and stare at me and smile and smile at me.

"Absolutely, yes you did," says Statement Necklace.

"Yes, yes," says Emma, trying to cover up my outburst, as usual. "A wonderful opportunity," says Emma, bouncing the baby, a little hard. "We're all totally over the moon! You'll celebrate tonight I'll bet, Clara!"

Everyone starts talking about logistics and money. And then they talk a little about motherhood 'cause, guess what, they're all mothers.

"Yeah," I tell them all. "I'm going to kidnap my mother and stop her from making me and Dempsey."

But everyone is saying goodbye, talking over each other. That and the baby is whining, mewling, dissonant.

"Good good," says Emma. "Have one for me! Have sooooo much fun, okay? Byeee everyone, byeeee."

The screen blinks out. Everyone has gone. Gone.

Were I to write this book again, Dempsey and I would feature a lot more heavily. We would have less of our mother the scammer. I would call it *The Catch*—because there is always a catch—and in it, there would be several distinct chances to do everything right.

DEMPSEY & MARCUS
TAKE A DAY-DRINK

I spend so much time on my makeup this late afternoon. I make sure that I'm getting it just right this time. I contour my cheeks for a good twenty minutes. I take time blending out the powder, as though my life depends on it. I stick gemstones on the corner of each eye so I look like Gen Z. I use a highlighter on the places I want to see the bones. When I'm finished, I survey myself with an awesome wonder. I am so incandescent. I'm a cool space girl. People would want to be near me today, because they choose to and for no other reason. I can hear Marcus moving upstairs, so any moment now. I'm still marvelling at my craftwork, lost in a whirlwind of self-congratulation when my buzzer screeches in a way that I don't like so much. I'm alarmed, because that sound hardly ever happens, except for the Amazon courier or the postman.

"Ho . . . hi?" I call into the speaker.

"It's Raymond," says the clear, raspy voice. "Raymond Panelli."

"Fuck!" I hear myself say. "Fuck! Fuck! Fuck!"

Unfortunately I say this part into the intercom, too. "Erm, Raymond," I tell him, trying to gather myself. "It's not really a good time."

And it isn't. Clara and I have timed this to the minute. It's a quarter to six. In fifteen minutes I need to go upstairs and intercept whatever Marcus is doing.

"Well, it won't take too long," Raymond's voice calls out. "Just dropping by.."

I think about moving away from the intercom, ignoring the unwanted caller, but wonder how it'll look to Rayna when her husband reports back. Grudgingly, I press down the open-door buzzer, and before I know it, the man is standing in my doorway, taking up all the space.

"Dempsey," he says, leaning forward in an unnerving fashion. "We haven't heard from you in a while, that's all."

"I know," I tell him. "I'm sorry, I've been so, so busy."

Raymond walks right in, thinks, then spreads himself on my sofa like some kind of oversized lizard, looking around at my peeling walls, his growing disgust palpable. He squints at my bed, which makes me feel exposed.

"I'm sure," he says, in a very sarcastic fashion. "Can we cut to the chase a bit, my dear?" Leaning against my door, I get a shooting pain in my temple. Raymond makes a smacking noise with his lips. "I'm afraid," he tells me, folding his arms, "that Rayna is in a complete state. Over everything. She feels quite abandoned by you."

"Oh no," I say, looking at the phone clock. "I'm so, so sorry to hear that."

"I'm sorry too," says her husband, stony faced. This is awful, so awful.

I decide I'm going to have to break it to him.

"Listen," I tell him. "The girls have totally stopped talking to me. You . . . you can still totally trust me . . ."

Raymond lifts a finger to shut me up. He really is quite rude.

"I have another plan . . ."

"Okay," I say, dramatically looking at the clock again so Raymond will take the hint. As it happens, he does.

"All dressed up. Do you have somewhere to be?" he says, as though the thought is preposterous.

"I do," I tell him. "I have a date."

"Oh wow," he says, smiling in a way I do not like, not a bit. "The world goes on, doesn't it?"

"It does," I say, not smiling.

Raymond leans back, laces both hands behind his head, with all the moves of someone who isn't planning on going anywhere, not for a while.

"I'll get to it then. Your sister . . ."

"My sister?"

"She might have the influence we need. If she could make some kind of statement in support of Rayna . . . just amplifying one of her books or something, just an itty-bitty POV." He squints at my painted face, takes me in a little more. "That would help us a lot. We need someone to come out in a public endorsement of Rayna and all the work she's done for women. That's all."

I can't believe this man. The absolute fucking nerve. Not content with pressuring me and offering to pay off the Womb-Men, he now wants to use my sister's reputation to make things alright for them? I pull myself off the wall and take a single step toward him.

"You're saying," I tell him, in a slightly raised voice, "that you want my sister to use her self-curated, self-made platform to support your wife, who—not going to lie—did orchestrate a group masturbation session? We were all consenting, but the truth is . . ."

Raymond is casting me a withering look. I hold on to my head.

"The truth is that it *did* happen. And it was great! Like, why can't she just admit to it?"

"You *know* why," says Raymond, his voice rising. "Oh, Dempsey, come on. You know the internet. I know," he says leaning in closer, "how much you know the internet. You . . . you LOVE the internet. All corners of it. Don't you, Dempsey?"

I pale, imagining the things I've shared with Rayna all these months. All of it. So much for confidentiality. She isn't even a real doctor.

"Your wife," I tell him, eyes narrowed, "isn't even a qualified psychologist. And I'd much rather be having this conversation with her. Now can you leave? It's just that I have . . ."

Raymond doesn't move.

"I mean it," I tell him. "My father lives upstairs, and I'm about to call him."

"You don't *have* a father," snarls Raymond.

"Everyone has a father," I tell him.

"Go on then." Raymond bangs on my table, sending my magazines flying. "Call him. Call your daddy down."

Great, Raymond. You asked for it. Two birds. One stone. I get out my phone and text Marcus that there's an emergency happening downstairs.

Can you come?
Come now.

There's a rumbling above my head, like some large power getting to its feet. A hero, a long dark fairy tale I summoned.

In about ten seconds, there's a loud knock on my door. Raymond's eyebrows shoot up. He leaps to his feet.

"Wait . . ."

"Just a second, Dad!" I call out, leaving Raymond looking on, perplexed. I answer the door to a skittish-looking Marcus, who towers over me, red-eyed.

"You okay, girl?" he all but slurs into my face. He looks past me at the wall, ceiling, floors.

I do a nod thing towards the couch to Raymond. Marcus stalks past me.

"Is there a problem?" he goes, moving towards Raymond, who looks from Marcus to me and back again, making a quick assessment.

"Was just leaving, mate," says Raymond.

"Alright then," says Marcus, "you were, you were."

He walks Raymond to the door wordlessly, wringing his hands, and Raymond slinks out.

"I'll see you again, Dem," the man has the nerve to threaten.

When Raymond has gone, Marcus throws himself on my couch, lengthwise. Vibrating with something. He seems animated, a little jumpy.

"Thank-you" I say, nearly panting.

"Whadda creep," goes Marcus, and jerks his head at me. "So Serene needs me to get there a little earlier. Press pictures and stuff. We're meeting at the pub."

I pretend not to remember. "Where are you meant to be going?"

"A party," he says. "In central. She knows people."

"I thought we could pop open a drink?" I say, wondering if that's how ordinary drinkers phrase things.

"Good idea," says Marcus. "Got the shakes. Need a layer to get me in the game."

I nod. "I know."

Easy enough. There is work to do, a fire bolt to extinguish.

"Got less than an hour to get ready," Marcus explains.

"I have wine." I lie.

"Get it going, girl!" he says, clasping his hands together.

I pour two thirds of the redlace into a beaker of cranberry juice and give him the drink. Marcus accepts it readily, doing a thing on his phone, and we sit in a kind of uncomfortable silence for a bit. He stares at the drink, which looks nothing at all like wine—even to me—and gulps the thing down.

"Got any good music?" I ask him.

Marcus puts something somber and grungy on, some crooner with a dirty beat.

••

"I think I met someone," he says, as we are dancing.

"It's my friend, isn't it?" I venture. "It's Serene."

Marcus looks a little caught out, like someone working out how to play this. "I mean . . ." he says. "I mean . . . I had already met her *before* the park, you know. We met on a bus."

How to warn him? How to tell him Serene is a witch, or dead, or something worse?

"Look, Marcus," I begin. "There are a few things you might want to know about this person."

Marcus's face glazes over, and I see the party started way before me. Oh dear. His breath is kind of labored now.

"Marcus, you alright?"

"Oh," says Marcus. "Sorry. I'm a little high. I've been feeling a little anxious. Going to be socializing, and all that."

"Yeah," I tell him. "I get it. I'm anxious all the time, honestly. I'm anxious every day."

Marcus visibly relaxes. He says something ever so softly, out of the corner of his mouth.

Mirroring his movements, I have a thought that stops me. I should very much like to know more of this man. I would like very much for him not to be trying to launch a music career. I should like it if his only reason to be in the world were to see me grow and thrive. And I would *love* it if he loved me. I suddenly wonder if there's a new way to do this without all the risk. Why lose everything now?

But my phone rings, cutting through my thoughts. It's my sister. I know she'll be impatient and likely rude, and I'm not at all keen to pick up. But a pact is a pact is a pact. My sister needs care too. I have to be there for her. I answer my phone.

"Can't talk now," I say, in a low voice, trying to be pointed about it. "I'm *drinking* with a friend."

"You're still home?" hisses my sister. "I need you here! This was supposed to be a super-quick thing. It's getting late. We've only got an hour and a half."

"Well excuse me," I hiss. "I've never poisoned anyone before!"

"*That girl is poison*," sings Marcus in the background. He giggles, and his head dips a little.

"Stop pissing about," says Clara's voice. "Get on with it, we've got shit to do."

The bitch hangs up. The music continues. Marcus is the easiest person in the world, I reckon, to put to sleep.

Marcus flops down onto my couch with no clue in the world about what's about to happen. What if we have it all wrong, including the dosage, and I'm about to commit murder? What if it's a bad mix with whatever he's taken? It'll be in the papers and people like Jen and Sally will shake their heads and people like Sunny will say that they always imagined it of me.

"Do you want a line?" he is saying. I shake my head no, wondering why I never really noticed before what a mess he was.

"Black girls don't never want cocaine," says Marcus and laughs.

"That's not true," I tell him, "I feel like my sister loves it."

"I have to meet her!" says Marcus.

"Be careful," I warn. "I don't think cocaine and wine . . ."

But Marcus is already shaking out some white powder, right there on my table.

"I feel so so good," says Marcus, and immediately sags. I sit down next to him. But then Marcus alarms me by jolting upright.

"The thing is," he says out of the blue, seconds later, "she's a good kid. She's just rough around the edges. I really think I could love her. She's different alright."

"You're not even making sense," I tell him. "Who are you talking about?"

"Make me make sense then," sings Marcus, wrapping his long arm round me.

"Marcus, I really need to know if you've . . . you know. With Serene?"

Marcus thrashes back his head and I wondered if I made it too obvious.

"Need to know!" he sings. "Need to know need to know need to know." It is hard, at this point, to know whether he's feeling the amber solution or just feeling himself.

"My father was called Abaso Sill," sings Marcus, fighting against the liquid. "He lived on giant boat you know. My mummy couldn't never find him."

"I'm sure," I tell him. "I'm sure"

"Can I tell you about the boat?" goes Marcus. "It runs in the lining of your coat."

Oh no, I think. *I did this too early.*

I want to hear about the coat lining from Marcus, who has no way read Clara's book. Right?

"What boat." I demand. "What. Boat?"

"I met a girl who balanced on the seas," Marcus says, in full Trinidadian voice. "Between the lines of what is good and acceptable. She doesn't know what love is, having never learned . . ."

Marcus is starting to slur.

"Go on," I urge, holding his face and trying to rouse him. "Go on about the boat."

"The boat became a bus."

"We met on a bus going nowhere," sings Marcus, in delicious baritone. He struggles to his feet, holds on to the wall.

"Yes, yes, go on," I plead, wishing Clara were here to corroborate fact and evidence.

"Your friend," he says, eyes closed, "will want to be rid of me, but I'm a catch. Dempsey, I'm a goddamn catch!"

"Serene?" Now we're getting somewhere. "You are," I say. "You are."

He smiles down at me, and does at little hiccup.

"Marcus," I say, as gently as 1 can. "Did you sleep with her? She's bad news."

"I just want to be your friend," says Marcus, looking straight at me now. "I don't love you that way."

"That's fine, Marcus, but did you sleep with Serene yet?"

"Oh no," goes Marcus, getting dreamy-eyed. "Oh noooooooo." His eyes roll back in his head. "A gentleman never tells," he concludes.

For a brief moment I wonder if Marcus is actually sober, and just fucking with me, but then he loses his footing and lands face down on my bed.

I can't leave him like that. People have been known to choke on their own vomit and that's how they leave the world, and I can't be responsible for that. I lean over him, trying to pull him into a more breathable position. Marcus, his face close, takes my face in his strong hands. My body grows warm. Vulnerable.

"We're just friends, okay?" whispers Marcus into my ear, holding my head. "You and me. I care about you." I wonder what my father does with things he cares about. I hold Marcus's dark, long fingers in mine, letting the feeling wash over me. I turn his fingers over, watching the perfect little crescent shapes on his cuticles. Marcus retrieves a roll-up from his jacket pocket, sits up a little straighter. He's says nothing as I click on my phone, which is ringing again.

"Don't fucking tell me you're still in there," says my sister's angered, shrill voice. "What the fuck are you waiting for?"

"I couldn't help it!" I tell her. "Raymond came over. It's just . . . I'm a bit behind."

"Who the fuck is Raymond?" goes my sister. "Listen, are you with our father or not?"

"We're just chilling," I say. "Drinking. As in . . . we're *drunk*."

"Good. Now get out of there," says Clara, "before someone sees you."

"Is that my baby?" Marcus slurs.

On the other side of the phone, my sister gasps.

Marcus's breathing slows. As his warm hands grope around for mine, I feel my shoulders relax.

"I think it might be working," I say. "Look at him," I say, clicking on FaceTime.

My sister's head and shoulders appear on the screen, dressed in an army cap and slick black bob.

"Handsome," she says. "Quite."

"But is it him?" I ask. "Is it our father?"

"He could definitely be the man in my story," says Clara. "And I'm not going to go on about it, but all this might have been caught earlier if you'd read my fucking book. You would have known the signs to watch for. Some of this might even have been preventable."

"Not according to Veronica. Look, can we talk about it later?"

Marcus is drifting, floating upstream.

"Are you sure that he'll be alright?"

"Sure you dosed him enough?" my sister says, looking doubtful. "He looks even bigger than I imagined."

"I'm not sure," I tell her. "I think he's sleeping."

"Hurry up and get the fuck out," she says finally, and hangs up.

I stay there a while, watching my father sleep.

And then his eyes flicker open.

"Wwaaiiit . . ." he appears to be saying. "Wwww, I gott . . ."

"I love you," I assure the bobbing head. "I love you so much!"

He makes a move as if to get up again, and falls right back this time, thankfully in a more breathable position.

"So sorry about this!" I shout out to him, before backing out of the door. "You'll be alright. It'll wear off, eventually, promise!"

Despite his best efforts, Marcus begins to deep-snooze. I take one last look at the man in my flat. He looks so peaceful. For a moment I want to be nowhere else but with him. Curled up with our palms touching. I blow a kiss into the room as I leave.

I BROUGHT YOU INTO
THIS WORLD,
IMMA TAKE YOU OUT

CLARA

10:50 p.m. Still the same long day. The last possible day of conception, if that Veronica is to be believed. My sister and I stand, a little way up on the Hidden Beach, just behind the Old Justice Pub, waiting for Serene to appear. She's headed to an industry party, two whole hours late. The kind of party where people who make things happen make things happen. She thinks she's taking Marcus. Only Marcus is drugged at Dempsey's. Surprise! We've only waited our entire lives. The moon is fuller than usual, and beating blue, all this blue. Not the bad blue, either.

Earlier, Dempsey nearly gave me a heart attack. I thought I'd been abandoned. I thought I'd be left to do the whole thing myself. Dempsey, ever the fashion maverick, approached wearing what can only be described as fishing garb. Her makeup, though, is perfect. Iridescent. She's gotten so much better. She actually looks pretty good. It's like a glass skin wet look vibe. It's only taken her thirty years. The tide is choppy, fast moving. The ripples in the water, intricate and divine.

DEMPSEY

"I thought we might need some layers," I say, brandishing one of my sister's more expensive cream jackets. "It's colder than I thought it might be."

"No it isn't," says Clara, who has to argue with absolutely everything, even now. I shrug, happy to be covered up. We stand there, looking at the water. Since she won't take her jacket off or wear it, I put it on myself.

"I ran into Sunny," my sister offers, and grins.

"How in the hell did you run across Sunny?" I say. "Clara, what did you do?"

"You and our mother," says my sister, "are not the only ones who can hunt a person down. I listen. I heard about what you said onstage."

"What happened?" I want to know, but all Clara will say is, "Your doctor is a bit of a fraud, girl. She's actually like, obsessed with recruiting people for her and her husband to have sex with."

I'm about to start bawling, I think. My sister clocks this and, to my great surprise, squeezes my thigh.

"I know what that's like," she says, nodding sagely. She raises her arms with a wry smile.

"I mean, look at where we are. I found my dead mother shoplifting in a department store and then we discovered that life is magic and she's our age stuck in our timeline somehow and she has no regard for us, and we have to track her down and stop ourselves from being born. Oh, and we might even die tonight. Hahahaha."

CLARA

Hahahaha.
We laugh a while,
We laugh, covering our very different mouths.
We laugh and we laugh and we laugh and laugh. If you look at
    the word "laugh" long enough,
You will notice that it is spelled very weirdly. It should not be
    English, but is anything purely English?

DEMPSEY

"We all have ways of getting what we need," says Clara. "By hook or by crook we get what we need," says Clara the Sage. Clara the Sangoma. Sometimes I'd swear that my sister is three to six different people, I'm telling you.

"What do you think our mother needs?" I ask her.

A rustling nearby, through the trees.

"Your guess is as good as mine. Let's ask her."

Because there, stumbling a little, darkening the secluded road that we walked to get here, is none other than our mother. The very same. Serene is dressed head to toe in black, a lint-covered dress, hair every-where, eyes darting around furtively.

I do it.

I walk out, intercepting my mother's path. Her eyes grow large as I place a hand over her mouth. Then my sister and I back her down to the steps toward the river wall where the water meets the pebbly stretch. Once in the shadows on the deserted beach, I pull away my hand. My mother looks vaguely irritated, but not at all scared. Not even.

"Unnecessary," she says. "What's this then? Where's Abbé?"

"Marcus," I tell her. "His name is Marcus."

"Whatever," Serene snaps, and turns around, eyes fixed on Clara. "You paid Simeon for my fucking passport? Oh, he loved telling me all about that. You do know that he can knock those things up out of nowhere, right? He's a scammer."

"It takes one to know one. You need to leave my friend alone," I say, standing as tall as I can. "Marcus needs help. It's clear he just needs help."

"He's fine," says our mother. "He's just messy. Spoiled. Did you know his parents are millionaires?"

I think of Marcus's piano and his copper pans and his top-floor apartment and no job and all the rich white girls with their floral dresses, and then it begins to track.

"Sorry about *Marcus*," says my mother, "but it is what is it, okay? I'm helping him with a music thing tonight. He needs direction. He has no hustle!"

"Let me guess," cuts in my sister, using a sweet and nasty cadence. "You're going to be his *manager. You're going to do his PR.*"

"As it happens," sings Serene, "you're dead right."

Serene goes to push past us in the direction of the pub, but I hold my own, using the size of my short body as a barricade.

"You won't be going anywhere," I say, in the way I have been practicing. My sister smiles at me approvingly.

"I like *this* Dempsey," Clara says. "Where've you been all my life?"

She touches my shoulder, and we feel close and complete, some out-of-this world pair. My heart double jumps. Our mother rolls her eyes.

"You both fucking serious? If this is over a man, I don't know what to tell you. It isn't worth it, girls. It never is."

"How many times do I have to say it! He's. My. Friend!" I tell her, stamping my foot like a three-year-old.

"No," says our mother, slowing down her voice as though she's speaking to the same three-year-old. "He's not. You don't know him any more than I know him. He only feels sorry for you. Oh God, you have to know that? You do know that, right?" She's cruel, alright. My sister takes a long breath. She steps ahead of me and in front of Serene, blocking the secluded path.

"Don't talk to her like that, Serene."

Our mum twists a corner of her mouth. "Or what?"

"I swear to god, Serene . . ."

"I'm not scared of either of you," says Serene. "I've hit you before, remember how that went?"

Clara just looks at her. I look at her. We, each of us, stare hard at the other.

"I want my fucking stuff," says our mother. "Give me my ID at least?"

"I don't have it with me," says my sister. "And you've some explaining to do. I'll throw your shit in the Thames. You'll have to go in there and fish it out."

Our mother stares out ahead of the water, sighs. Then she tries a different tack. She has to.

She turns her head; puts on a new face—the pretty one, from the photos. The one that looks like us. Behind her, the water laps at her heels.

"Look," she says, her tone now a softer shade of something. "I swear I haven't been trying to fuck with you. Either of you."

"We just want to get this straight," goes Clara, "then we'll let you go wherever you need to be getting to. We'll get lost."

"Okay, fine," our mother says, quickly.

"Who. Are. You?" Clara asks, her voice thin against the wind.

"And why do you have the exact same name and body as our mother?"

"Because my mother, *Diana*, named me that. And lots of people look like other people."

"You're lying!" I put in, even though I don't know if that's necessarily true.

"Serene," says my sister, trying to be patient. "Are we to believe that your mother is the same as the mother in my book? Our grandmother, dearly departed? Same, same, same? Are we to believe that your house is the same as the house in the photos? What do you take us for?"

My sister is an incredible actress, sensational, in fact, because as she speaks these very words I understand that yes, she absolutely, absolutely believes them. She believed in Serene. She believes Serene. She believes Serene is our mother.

Serene raises her eyes skyward, clapping between every word. "I. DID. NOT. READ. YOUR. FUCKING. BOOK. LISTEN, IT'S 2025. WHO HAS TIME TO READ A LONG FUCKING BOOK?"

Clara steps back at once, digesting this, her face a picture of immediate despair.

"I want to know about the boat," I say, quickly.

"What the fuck are you talking about?" goes our mother.

I look down at my watch.

"Look, we haven't got all night," I tell them both, growing frustrated.

••

The standoff continues. It's almost twelve a.m. A quarter to, in fact. Neither one of us has moved. All of this colour has appeared in the sky. There are bright lines everywhere, like a TV screen going bad. There's a static to the air all around, and something not quite lightning. But almost. Almost.

"What about all the money you cost Clara?" I demand.

"It doesn't matter," says Clara quickly, just at the exact time that Serene says, "What about all the work I did? And as for Marcus," she snorts, "take him."

"It isn't like that between us," I say, flecks of spit making their way out of my mouth. "But I don't expect *you* to understand."

I fold my arms, stick out my lip. My sister looks at me as if to say *stop acting up*. Without thinking much of anything, I stick my tongue out at her. Clara says nothing in response to this, her eyes becoming glassy.

"For what it's worth," she says, to our mother person, "I do think you were worth it. I really do."

There's another sound in the distance, but these sounds are getting hard to identify.

It's like I can feel them inside me, as vibrations, as colour, as taste. Serene starts to say something.

"Can I call you mother?" my sister interrupts.

"This again?" sighs the person we love. "I can't with this. Listen, girls, what do you people want? I'm really late."

"That won't be happening, I'm afraid," says Clara, looking almost apologetic. "You won't arrive at the party, Mummy."

"I have to get there," says Serene through her teeth. "He has important people coming. He's performing. He won't be able to handle it himself."

"Why is it so important to help him and not us?" I say.

"I keep hearing my mother's voice," says Serene, holding her head. "She says I have to complete it. Complete the circle. Since I pretended to read your weird book, I haven't been right. I've been thrown off."

"If you didn't read it?" says my sister. "How do you know that it's weird?"

Our mother has no answer to that.

"I'm homeless because of you," is all she says, into the turning sky. "I lost the orange house."

We all watch each other.

Suddenly our mother lets up. Like all the fight she has left in her body gives way.

"Sure," says Serene. "If it's what it takes to let me go, call me *mother*. Go on, psycho, knock yourself out."

There is a cawing from far away, crows circling in the dark sky above. My sister places a hand on her mother's face. Then, I hear a loud whack—and when I turn round Serene is standing over Clara, who is on the ground. My sister cowers, confused and docile, looking up at the mother with all the hurt of a child—and for a second I don't know what to do. Just for a second, though. Only for a second, because naturally, I'm not having that.

I don't know how I do it, but I do it. I grab our mother by the shoulder and force her back, back over the riverbed, the stones of the rocky beach crunching under our feet. She trips over a lone object on the beach, and by the time she gets back to her feet, my twin has appeared beside me. We both stalk our mother, who is backed onto the gloomy water's edge, the weeds framing her in a perilous border. She seems older by the faraway light of the city buildings. For a flicker of a moment I wonder if this is really our mother, or someone else's haggard long-lost relative, but we know better, for we have Evidence.

And as if in agreement,
the clock strikes twelve.

"Okay, listen girls," Serene croaks, doubled over. "I didn't know it was that deep."

"You didn't come back, Mum." I whisper. "You made us tonight and then you had us and then you left us." Clara grabs hold of Serene's neck with both hands. I put my hands around her small body and squeeze with all my might. Everyone is shouting at everyone. Globules of spit are going everywhere and then my mother raises her dulling, transparent nails to Clara's face and swoops. Someone begins to sob hysterically. Loudly. Crying like I never heard before. It makes you want to murder someone, the person who caused this mess. The person at the start of it all, if there's indeed a start.

It makes you want to end her
if only you didn't love her.

The clock strikes twelve for the second time tonight, or this morning. A highly unlikely phenomenon.

DISSIPATING,
OR
BLACK TIME

O r . . . wait.

Dempsey, chill the fuck out.

Perhaps we don't strangle her. Perhaps not just yet. It's 11:11, and then it's midnight already. The sky, filled with colour.

Our mother backs into the water, more uncertain now as Dempsey and I close in on her. "Listen, girls," she is saying. "I didn't mean anything by it, okay? I didn't know it was that deep!"

My sister and I exchange a knowing look. Still, we keep moving towards her, closing the gap.

"I swear. I . . . I wasn't trying to fuck with you. I promise. I didn't know. I didn't know," Serene keeps saying, as though they are the words that will save her life. She almost trips on some cloth-like material on the ground. Something yellow.

"What are you trying to do here?" she demands. "Look, can you just let me go?"

Of course Serene does not know, cannot know, that we are not here to harm her. We are here to save her. She turns to stare at the water behind her, the cruel wind crashing on the waves beyond.

"Girls! What do you want?" Our mother is shouting, shivering, defiant. Getting a little desperate now. "Fine! I owe you all the fucking

money back. I need to get going, okay? I really need to help him out with
the stuff tonight. He's gonna pay me. He's rich!"

We want to tell her it'll be okay. We want to put our hands on her
face and comfort her and kiss her and warm her. It's getting quite cold,
and the clock strikes, and then, it begins. This strange sensation in my
toes. I can't help it. I feel the light in me changing. A force like electricity warming my knees and inner elbows. It feels like coming up on a
pill or when you mix your controlled substances right. It is suddenly
after twelve. It is the next doomed day. I look at my sister and see she
is not crying as I thought, but laughing, as though a ridiculous thing
has occurred. An impossible thing. Everything has suddenly become
hilarious. I match her hysterics immediately. Imagine. We think this
is funny. The funniest. My sister and I in unison. My breathing is getting shallow. I begin to feel light as air. All at once, I see my mother's
face change. She is watching Dempsey, or she is watching me, a look of
naked horror on her face. I look round at my sister and see the night
happening underneath her skin. Dempsey—still laughing, with everything she has.

"What's happening?" our mother is saying, rubbing her eyes. "What
the fuck's happening?" Feeling twinkles of euphoria, I grab at my own
hands, through which now I can see the streetlights, the reflection of
distant lights. Oh, it is working. Praise Vee. Praise Vee. The twin-spell-
thing is working! I look again at my sister, who is all outline, all London
city at night, all moving traffic and colour and wheels. "Clara," she is
saying. "I feel all warm. I feel amazing, Clara." Her voice sounds deeper
now, deeper than it ever has, some textural quality to it. She sounds a
lot like me. "Dempsey," I say, sounding less like me and more like her. "I
think we did it, Dempsey!" I look down at my slender, borrowed limbs,
staring at the light travelling my body. I hold my sister close and feel
like a person put together again. Two grown, giggling girls fighting their
mum on the water. Two girls zeroed in on their mother. Two girls caught
their mother. Two girls dissolve into one open, scared girl. One girl
fighting on the riverbed. Fighting to stay here. Fighting an unrelenting
timeline. Our mother alone,

fighting no one. Or fighting *her* mother, dead but never gone. Or fighting herself, like someone possessed. You've seen those in the street who fight with people no one else can see. You know how it is. Our mother has fallen silent, and she watches the proceedings, crouched on the ground, open mouthed. We turn to her from somewhere not sky, not land. We smile and we wave goodbye for now. We spill, all the best and worst parts of us, into the brilliant dark. Then we are floating, up into the atmosphere, down, down towards the smiling black sea. The moon breaks everything up into colour. The moon; new and ancient at the same damn time. My sister and I are seeking new air. We hit the black at long last;

and so Become,

and so End.

Two parts, held at last by the warm, deep light. We know this place. We have lived underwater forever. We hold each other's bodies and sink.

We sink. We hit the darling water.

THE END
(only joking)

EPILOGUE: WHAT SHE DOES NEXT

A person walks briskly away from the scene, feeling as though she has lost something, lost two things, perhaps.

As she approaches the water's surface, her memory completely edits itself, clouds over itself like a dream, disappearing just a little more with every second. But the fingerprint is there, alright. Serene felt sure they were going to kill her for what she did to them. People have wanted to do worse to her for less. She hadn't intended things to go the way they had. It's a little mean to prey on the vulnerable, but it is what it is. That's government. That's optimisation. That's self-actualisation. That's commercialism. It's survival. It's making a few good quid. It's staying relevant even when your circumstances are plotting against you. It's making a way out of no way. It's gorgeous. It's totally brutish. It's *seven seconds away*. It's *just as long as I stay*. There are things that might have been true, depending on how you look at things, that are no longer obstacles. She feels lighter, somehow,

as though ~~something~~

~~some things from~~

something(s) parallel but not quite here have released her. There she stands, Serene Marie Nkem Droste, on the left bank of the Thames somehow naked, breathing and full of purpose, as though she learned to swim overnight. There she arrives on the left bank of the Thames, shivering a little. There she goes, there she walks on the life banks of the

Thames. There she sees her clothes folded and ready to wear. But who wears boot-cut jeans anymore? Omg! Her yellow Wu-Tang sweater, from 1992! She hasn't seen this thing in years . . . but . . .

this might have to dissolve too,

anyway, she walks through the streets. And are the streets as she remembers? Didn't there used to be a bingo hall there? Wasn't ASDA right here, and the working man's club, and the park with the skinheads, with the thick black lace-ups? The scene appears to have been replaced by a block of flats, a complex, and all these coffee shops. There she walks, passing the rows of the city at night. It is seven a.m., time to get ready for the biggest event of her life so far.

She lets the legs that she is walking on top of carry her around a while. She allows it, because if left to her, she won't know where the hell she belongs.

She goes home to a new house. She goes home to a different timeline, a place that she vaguely remembers as her home. Emma has attached the words U GO GIRL to the dress that has been couriered, which is irksome and just . . . ugh but it's Emma. Emma does this kind of thing, but she's a very good agent, very current, very *now*, so we have to let it go. We have to play the game.

JUST OVER A WEEK LATER, EVERYTHING IS ALMOST NORMAL

S erene ignores her stomach and the smell-memory, puts on the
purple dress,
a purple dress that is on loan from the designer,
a dress that cinches in the waist
a dress that is not too serious or too impractical
yes, a dress both appropriate and eye-catching. Today, taped to the
fridge, is a letter.

a letter to our mother, from The Girls Underwater
(well, now on the shore but let's not get technical)

Enjoy the house and the shower and the lipstick and your vin-
tage T-shirt—which, now I am thinking about it, might have
been yours to begin with, depending on how this timeline thing
works. Isn't that a head fuck. Oh! Enjoy the TV deal. Remember
to read all the small print. Remember not to give up the story
writing credit - if you're not careful, you could lose the entire story
to someone else, which would be nothing short of ironic, and your
ancestors didn't die for that lol black fist emoji. If you are reading
this, then it's true, I have gone, and my sister is gone with me. You
have taken our place. Fantasy is a family disease, and so also is
the willingness to escape, to draw new circumstances from a bum

lot. You did not love us. How could you? You were not able, and it is not your fault. We, on the other hand, wanted you. How much we wanted you, our mother. We loved you so fiercely and so completely that we could not survive it, and as such, we chose not to. Well what was the point? In a sense, we were never meant to be, and so we returned to the place where you left us. The place where our father loved to escape. Anyway, on a lighter note, how about that TV script option?! It's all about your life, so well bloody done! Don't let it pull you under. By order of kin, the credit belongs to you. May we meet again. We hope it's soon.

Clever, clever. The note the twins have left; an exact replica of the penultimate chapter of *Evidence*. Nicely played, Clara. Excellent work. Now, what came first, egg or hen?

also wtf did they mean by *now on the shore?*
They'd better be gone.

THE CAMBERWELL EVENING NEWS BLOG, BY SELENA MARTINA NELLIE DONALDSON

(staff writer at *The Daily Word*)

12 OCTOBER 2025

TWO BODIES FOUND ON THE SHORE THURSDAY MORNING

Identified as Clarissa and Delaney Brown, two identical(ish) twins from Bermondsey who escaped the Mayflower Centre for the criminally insane. No one knows how the girls got out. There was some kind of electrical fault, where all the lights in the doomed Centre went out and everyone fell asleep after eating their dinner and drinking their hot cocoa. Everyone fell deep into an unrousing slumber, I shit you not. Pure fairytale stuff. Prior to this, the girls hotfooted it to Dulwich, where they attacked one woman in her house and kidnapped one man before drowning themselves in some kind of "suicide pact." Both victims are unhurt; the woman is being treated for shock, and the man has stepped down from his post as the Councilor of the borough of South Bermondsey citing complex PTSD and a heavy workload. He was said to be inconsolable, when learning of the "suicide." The woman said nothing much, just nodded and thanked the police for letting her know. (All hearsay, but your girl has her ear to the ground; I gotcha.)

Back to the girls in question. Both unemployed. Clarissa was an aspiring writer, 30. Delaney unemployed, 30. The story gets weirder from here. It does. They left a strange note for their mother, also deceased (thirty years ago to the day). They are not reliable witnesses/victims. Of course. Police are not treating the deaths as suspicious. We wonder why.

#justiceforBlackwomen2025

ALTERNATE BLOODY ENDINGS
BY VERONICA THE SANGOMA

a) The twins jump in the water aged eight and eight, one month after the Hair Relaxing Fiasco. They find the place where their mother disappeared, hold each other's little girl hands, and splash . . . like that, they are gone.

b) The mother comes back from the party on a comedown to find the girls are missing. Turns out the wayward babysitter just took them to ASDA supermarket. See, nothing to worry about. The father overdosed the following week but everyone else is fine. Everyone else has to get on with things. We move!

c) The mother kills the girls then kills herself. Simple. Shocking. Effective. Of course, the papers print full page pictures of the (beautiful) Black woman who did the unthinkable. Beautiful is always, always relevant. More relevant, even, than Black, in some circles.

d) That sixteen-year-old babysitter drowned the girls! She gets locked up for murder. Murder! The mum then gets admitted into a psychiatric unit because her 2 Reasons To Be have both been extinguished, basically. Snuffed out.

e) ~~The girls basically have a mother shaped hole inside them and live their lives in the shadow of the loss. They are as good as estranged, but come together when Clara sights~~

their mother in Selfridges, in 2025. Deciding that they need to give their mother another chance at life they.....wait a minute...

f)   no one found the twin girls, till it was too late—not least the scheduled babysitter who was very used to finding them alone but in fact never showed up for work because she took a bad ecstacy pill and had to be rushed to hospital. The baby twins expire from cold and hunger (I hate this one the most, for obvious reasons, I'm a mum!)

g)   The girls die in a nursing home, both aged 90, their mother beside them, also 90. It is a strange phenomenon and nothing like this has happened since a case of the St Louis twins in 1856. You can look it up, mate. The scientists have a field day, but people think it's myth. (This one is cute.) It's in the paper and people are fascinated with it for about two weeks, until everyone loses interest and moves on to the next juicy story. A man gave birth to a non-human sea urchin last week. Now everyone's on about that.

h)   Nothing of the sort happens or has happened. Clara made the whole thing up. She doesn't even have a sister. She's deep in Peru with that advance money, changing her life, getting free, doing Ayahuasca for the very first time and this is what came up. This is what the medicine told her.

i)   Dempsey, ever the dreamer, made the whole, entire thing up, can ya believe it? She doesn't even have a twin! She's a girl from a council estate in need of some friends and a Life. What an imagination. With jokes like this, she should be on the stage. So she does. Go on the stage, and does quite well out of it.

j)   The whole thing is a mess. The book never came out because it never got finished, because the girl who was writing it plagiarized the narrative and had to pay her whole advance back to the publishers. Ah, she loved a party, that one. She's in rehab at the moment - best place for her. There will be more authors, more books. More spells. More drama. There will always be more, you get me?

k) nothing, nothing no-one. everyone is unreliable. no one, really, can be trusted, not even me. Stay awake. Hold your head above water level.

BONUS CHAPTER: MOTHERLAND

Oh,

it's the curse of being a woman, Serene tells herself. You always second guess yourself, even when you're not the one in the wrong. You can't help it. There's always what you chose and what you should have chosen, and what you might have chosen if you'd been thinking, and what you could have chosen if you were being unselfish. Then there's what you may have chosen if, for once, you were being kind to yourself, if you decided *for* yourself rather than against. Anyway, how does a person plagiarize their own life? It simply isn't possible. As the twins confirmed in the letter, Clara wrote the book, but *Serene* inspired Clara to write the book, and anyway, Clara stole her story, the whole thing, all the darkness and the light and the magic. So isn't the story hers, being about her? Well that depends; is not the ghost writer the true author of the book? But Serene is subject material. None of this could ever exist without her. Serene can answer any question anyone has; surely that's the point of the argument. Yes, here are the closing statements.

It's the curse of being a woman, she tells herself.

As if she's a human, and not an undead demon.

As if she is anything other than something pretending to be something pretending to be something else. Emma grins at her from the green room.

"Go get 'em" says Emma, as if anyone talks like that.

••

It is hot for the beginning of October. Too hot, too hot. All wrong for a British autumn. The organizer is doing the thing that people do when they are trying to do too much. When a Black woman walks into a room and there's all this pomp and circumstance, all of this (very coded) deference, all of this pandering. OMG coo's the organizer. Quuueeeeen. Queeeen. You absolute Queeeeeeeen. OMG your haiiiirrrrrr. OMG your skkiiiiiin, so dewy! SO glowy! So wet and incandescent! With a gracious nod, our mother circumvents the foolishness. She goes to the bathroom, checks herself in the mirror. Looks at her reflection, which is always pleasing to her, even in more difficult moments. Especially in her desperate moments. She smiles and smiles as the room fills up, taking in the velvet furniture. Thank God she had the courage to write what she felt even when it felt like ramblings. Even when it didn't make sense. Professor Gene Harris did not know what he was talking about. Even if he *was* just a voice in her head, he was wrong, wrong, wrong. All of a sudden, she cannot put her finger on it. Who wrote about Gene first? Was it her imagination or did someone in some story actually meet him? Her inner critic took the form of a doubting old English academic who tried to have sex with her; how quaint. People are holding her book to the light and smiling. It is a book of the hottest, most unapologetic pink. On the back a picture of her looking as good as she's never looked. Serene smiles so hard her insides are hurting. Makes a large joke about the venue. Everyone laughs, or so it is written. Someone is asking a question about "imposter syndrome." Someone is asking a question about the length of time a book takes. Blah. Someone is almost crying. New motherhood is really, really getting to her. What a conundrum.

"Sorry. That was quite long-winded. Sorry," the person says, staring up at her with awe. "Not at all, not at all," says Serene, feeling magnanimous, taking a long sip of water. Someone asks how she came upon this cruel, never-ending story. Only instead of saying cruel and never-ending, they say Classic Retelling!

"I was visited," Serene tells the crowd, "by ancestors or something, twin-like things. Perhaps a nod to a parallel life, who knows? In the writing of this I spoke to my own demons. I made a kind of bargain with them, my own kind of peace. Whatever happened, they saved me. I was depressed as hell; for a while I even thought I was losing it or might have to go to rehab or something, and then they came here, and I will tell you this, they walked me all the way through it."

"But *who* were they?" someone wants to know, and someone else says, "Were the girls analogies, or . . . ?"

Serene takes her time with the question; chews on it a while. She makes a squishing sound with her mouth.

"Metaphors," she tells them, finally, crunching the letter from this morning in her pocket.

"Literary devices who haunted me and chased me around and would not stop. When I tried to leave, they brought me back. When I tried to end it all, they saved me."

There she goes again sounding like quite the eccentric.

She does not say that they already lived, once.

She will not say that they walked the earth behind her, alongside her, on top of her.

Nor does she say that she dreamed them up.

She does not say that, in one draft, she left them in the house that day for anyone to find.

In another draft, she left them with a prepubescent babysitter. Or on the riverbank, ready to do the unthinkable to save her life. She will not say that she had them go to the bottom of the river last night for anyone to find. She does not say that in one mood she escaped underwater. She will not say that she chose herself, that she will *always* choose herself. And how can it ever,

ever be a crime to choose yourself?

When you're a mother?

Who wouldn't choose the realm where they win the game?

A good enough mother?

"I have a question," a person in a pretty green dress or a pretty person in a green dress is asking. It is the kind of dress she would have chosen, if she hadn't felt dead set on this purple thing. The purple was unanimous. The purple was prewritten. The dress is not her style, not at all; but look, the purple was fate, was always supposed to be. Head cocked to one side, she wonders for a brief second if the person in green might be trying to upstage her. Women do this kind of thing from time to time. It's like wearing white to someone else's wedding, which was a no-go in her day.

In. Her. Day. She has to stop saying that. She needs to melt into the Now, which is all everyone else is doing anyway. She belongs to here, and only here.

THIS IS HER DAY. THIS IS HER NIGHT.

This is an evening with Serene Marie Nkem Droste.

Green Dress stands up,
in the corner;

"How hard was it to leave your *metaphorical* daughters? It must have been hard, I think?" Serene does a double take. The person looks a little or a lot like Clara, but cannot possibly be, because Clara and her sister threw themselves in the *never ever happened* a whole—was it a week ago?—and in the note, they promised her they would be gone. Still, the resemblance is uncanny. She could be the sister of Clara, and the someone sitting beside her, the smaller person, could be the cousin of Dempsey. The smaller person stands up beside her, backing her sisterfriend up.

"Do you miss them at all?" the smaller one wants to know.

No, no that's all wrong. They actually look more like the twins she read about online, the twins who have absolutely nothing to do with Serene. Nothing at all. You get confused when you tell stories for a living, especially dark fairy tales. No, these two have nothing to do with her. Those lost girls belonged to someone else, didn't they? What a shocking, awful story. Clarissa and Delaney Brown, two twins . . . or were they simply sisters? Two women from Bermondsey aged thirty, who went ahead and who drowned themselves in some kind of desperate suicide pact? The unfortunate thing is that no one looked for them for days. Neither one was missed, you see.

Serene can understand their plight, even from a distance. Yes, she might have a loose, vague understanding. Some days she feels like she'd rather not be here. Some days you cough all of these terribles up, and when you look down there's your very own part of the black sea, looming, bleak, decadent.

Back to the matter(s) in hand. Serene needs to get a grip. Serene needs to clean herself up. Serene and Marcus-Abbé need God, or rehab or similar. Serene holds on to the podium with her bunch of notes. She grips the wood so tightly that the hands that she is using start to burn. She stares intently at the two women, neither of whom appears to be breathing, or is that just fantasy? Is this just a tiny, tiny horror? Two dark girls, Black as the galaxy, and glistening blue. Not identical, but twins, for sure; you can tell from a mile off. The taller twin is striking, the shorter one is cute. They are dressed in material that touches the floor, material that catches the light, all seafoam and turquoise and what not. They look at her so long, and so hard and so full of a thing like love—or is it awe? That's the thing about being on a stage. Everyone looks up, up at you and it can skew things. It can have you believing the hype. The small girl begins to drip, drip from her head. Her twin attends to her with a pink towel that seems to have materialized from—the air?

"Come again?" says Serene, feeling bothered by this fluffy detail. How is no one in the audience catching this? Why doesn't someone save her? Why can't Marcus, deep in the throes of whatever comedown he's in, shield her from the past and take her home, where none of this exists? All she can see is twins, and the pink, pink book.

The tall girl opens her mouth, coughs
and water comes out.

The audience, watching this whole scene occur, sits in the hard-backed chairs, captivated. Serene raises her hand to her brow, which is by now soaking wet too. Everyone's full of nothing but water. It's how the tall tale goes.

Oh, it is too hot for autumn. Oh, we've messed up the planet. That's what everyone is saying, at least. All this talk of climate change, which was news to her. Hadn't she seen it for herself, though, under the water? The cumulative effects of all our wrongdoings? All the coral reefs are deformed these days. Up close, they're crumbling. All the sewage is turning all things sour. She freezes, aghast at the sudden memory. What else did she see where the River Thames entered the North Sea? What did she find in the bottom? The memory comes to her. The memory lodges itself in her throat. A coughing fit ensues.

"Sorry everyone," says Serene, struggling to get her breath. "I'm so sorry. Bit of a . . . bit of a cough."

She needs to get a grip; this is ridiculous. The girls are two normal, regular girls, devout fans of her and her writing, nothing to do with her girls in the book. Nothing at all to do with the girls, in the *Camberwell Evening News*, who took the easy way out last week. Serene Marie Nkem Droste is a fighter; she cannot possibly relate. She stops coughing now. The two friends look awkwardly at each other. They both seem bookish, young, nonthreatening. They peer at her, one under her wet bangs, totally in awe, awaiting her action. Serene stares them out. So this is how they want to play. She isn't about to go out like this. She's going to remind them who won.

"I think Serene just wanted to be herself," says our mother, doubling down. "She didn't want to be caught up, you know? She has things to do. Things to prove. You don't get long enough on this earth. You have to seize your opportunity. You have to be a pirate."

The girl nods, and nods, seemingly inspired, seemingly satisfied. The other one, for fuck's sake, seems to have another question.

"Go on then," says Serene, trying not to sound annoyed. "Let's hear it. Try to be quick, because other people want to ask questions."

There is a murmur in the crowd and a flicker of embarrassment in the smaller one's face, but she gets on with it like a champ.

"I just wanted to know," she begins with her reedy, snotty voice. "What was the significance of the father and the boats? Is he a real man?"

Serene looks to the front row and to the left, where Marcus is sitting, looking at his phone.

"He's on a different planet," says Serene. "He's in his own world. It's just a nice way of saying it, I suppose."

The girls sit down, satisfied, horribly in unison. Sure, they seem less interested in her right now, thank God, and more interested in what is going on, what is all round, who is wearing what, what timeline they are sitting in, that kind of thing. Serene will ignore them for the rest of the evening, and if they try anything funny after the show—if they try to get an autograph or selfie—she'll have Emma remove them STAT. Emma—busy breastfeeding in the office, as though there's no one around, thinks Serene, feeling a patch of judgement. She's a feminist and everything, but some people take it too far. Some people almost *will* you to say something. It's inappropriate. Anyway, all that looks painful, she observes, with a shudder. It looks sore. Her body stiffens at a certain memory.

Other people stand up and ask questions, and then it is as if the girls are just regular twins, and its fine—it was just her paranoid mind, of course.

"*Metaphors,*" she says again, for anyone who didn't hear. Loudly, for *us* two at the back. And wait, there is no letter in her pocket anymore. It disappeared,

or she ripped it up earlier and flushed it down the green-room toilet. Either way, it is safely underwater. She only needed to get rid of the evidence, to make us untrue. So we girls sit down, and she answers more questions about Form, and being a Woman Writer in the World, and about if she thinks AI writers are going to take over the industry and even though she's hungover and kind of spinning a bit, she has quite a lot to say about *that*.

> After the event,
> the sky is pink,
> daylight drips away.

A girl comes up to her with a shock of red hair. The girl's very hot boy-friend hangs back in the distance, looking all starstruck. Serene watches him. He is watching her. Serene needs to get out, out, the walls are clos-ing in on her and she has a man-baby to deal with.

Serene takes the book, smiling, and poses for the picture. If Marcus weren't hanging around somewhere acting all forlorn, she might have snuck away with the hot boyfriend. But she's on her best behaviour. With all the newness gifted, she cannot let it slip, slip away. Must control impulses because HARM REDUCTION. Must act normal, which means BEHAVE. She shudders under the weight of the act, and does a smile thing back at the red-haired woman, and it's time to sign even more hot-pink books, which swims along easily, on account of the brandy to take the edge off things.

Marcus-Abbé Wilson, the unsigned, unmanaged, largely unman-ageable RnB/techno wizard, is waiting in the green room after the show, sullen because today isn't about him. It would have been too much to tell him not to come but he's about to be dropped. Eleven days ago, he didn't know it would be the last time, but oh, it was. Men get so attached, on the quiet. It was like that with Simeon; if you want to get into it. Diana said a man can be an anvil if he isn't directly involved in your betterment. Diana said a man can be an anchor, though not quite in the way you want. You have to shake them off, or they'll drag you down and under-neath. They take all your best parts and years and leave you bereft, too wizened and waterlogged to make better choices, and with this second chance at existing, she doesn't feel much like risking it. No, the blond will have to stay exactly where he is.

Marcus looks visibly distressed, but that's nothing new. His locs are tied back from his stately face with a piece of golden thread. We follow them out on the street, where a car service and driver await them. Serene launches forward, a new grip of nausea upon her. Next to her, Marcus nearly stumbles over an odd dip in the pavement.

"What's up?" our mother says to our father, irritated. "You hung over or something?"

"Must be. I still feel groggy," he complains, clutching the side of his head. "Shit! I haven't had a migraine like this in months!"

"Well can you at least try not to look like you're dying?"

"It was that girl from downstairs," he says almost stumbling again, this time over our two discarded EVIDENCE BY SERENE MARIE NKEM DROSTE event goody bags. "I thought it was wine. She told me it was orange wine! I haven't been right since!"

"You're having a thing with the girl downstairs?" our mother says, in a rote fashion, as though she cares. Marcus, not catching this, rubs away at both of his eyes.

"I think it was ketamine. I'm not even joking. That was the feeling. That's how it felt."

"You're saying that the girl from downstairs drugged you and tried to have her way with you?"

"It isn't like that," Marcus moans. "She's just a friend."

"Who slipped you ket when you weren't looking? She must really have wanted your body. Anyway, it was over a week ago now."

"Feels like last night," he complains, still looking dream-dumb, not catching our mother's sarcasm one inch. "And . . . I don't know. Good trip, though."

Serene gives him a bombastic side eye. Marcus smiles, and his beautiful black mouth gives her that telltale weakness, beneath the knees, rubs the empty dad-spot, the thing that ruins women who are on the way to something great. But Diana's terrible rage runs through her, countering that, shattering any threat to her ambition. It is, quite frankly, a huge relief if Marcus is messing with someone else. She needs to do the same thing. Marcus acts as though he doesn't have a home to go to, has all but set up camp in her new, inherited house. Feet firmly under the table, that kind of thing. Marcus, who gets his rent paid for him and has moneyed, worried parents sending him funds all the way from Trinidad to support a self-imposed habit. Must be nice, thinks our mother, hating and hating and hating our father.

No, our mother knows she deserves more than this. She isn't a natural nurturer—not at all, not a bit, and here comes a whole grown man trying to rely on her. She's never had a whole, new house to herself before. She wants this new, whole house to herself. The book money has placed her in a higher echelon now. No leeches around, no dark, heavy things that stick. A new and different way to work with all the new chances that have suddenly arranged themselves into view. But there are rules to this new assignment. One false move and everything might be stolen away. In short, she might still drown. She may still fall into a river. Any time.

"You need to check yourself in somewhere," says our mother, who, now that she is standing still, is feeling not too well again. She threw up hard, the other week on the banks of the Thames, alone and coming to. The vomiting was so violent, emptied her belly right out. Turns out there was nothing in her stomach to be sick with; only water and weeds. It happened when the smell of things in the river met the air. That river smelled deep and sickly, just like her. It felt familiar and secret; like a low thing that you did once.

It has happened every morning since, for ten whole days. This morning was no exception; she vomited again as soon as she put on the dress. Mourning. Mourning.

Sickness. Sickness.

~~She remembers thinking that maybe she has had this feeling before.~~
~~She knows what this is~~
She has never had this feeling before.
She is gritting her teeth right now and thinking something
    along the lines of

"not if I can help it."
But she will not (help it, we mean),
and that is the thing about destiny. She comes and it comes and
    we come around.

THE
END

Acknowledgments

The very first person who understood what this story could be is Kwame Kwei-Armah. Because of you, because you know how to embrace the first embers of a story, humor your mentees, and draw the best out of them, the novel lives. I am in awe of you and your work—and most of all, of who you are.

Dionne Edwards for loving this book from the beginning, in its tiny baby and toddler stages. Your love kept my problem sisters going.

Marya Spence, for your brilliance, for what you see and understand and your beautiful mind. Thank you as always, as ever, and thank you Mackenzie Williams!

Gina Iaquinta—thank you for your incredible attention to detail. I have been honored to be doing this alongside you. Your keen, kind eye and encouraging words kept me going during the twilight of this book.

Glory Edim—thank you for all that you do. I'm so very excited about our beginnings! Thank you for seeing what you saw in this book.

Thank you to Maria Connors, Janet McDonald, and the whole team at Liveright.

Thank you to Joelle Owusu and the entire team at Merky Books, I am overjoyed to be doing this with you!

To Eloghosa Osunde, for your intoxicating words and sounds—thank you for being my first enthusiastic reader!

To Lefterrible Lefteris, for your dimensions and gorgeous attention to literature and beauty, in all its forms. Thank you for holding my infant chapters. You are loved.

To the real-life Alexis G. Zall, who *does* have a night called Naughty

Lying Shitty Scumbag Girls, which I frequent—thank you for being a star and so captivating on the stage and page! Thank you, thank you Leone Rose, for your light, and you.

And to my dear, dear siblings—my readers who have lost one parent or the other(s) . . . they remain. Inside and around us, they keep coming back.

"**Well-Read Black Girl Books** is a collection of magnetic debut fiction that invites readers to explore powerful narratives rooted in diverse cultural experiences. These stories offer readers an opportunity to step into new worlds, expand their horizons, and experience the transformative power of fiction. Just as the Well-Read Black Girl community celebrates literature that resonates deeply, these books are crafted to not only be read but cherished, shared, and revisited for years to come—characters that stay with you long after the final page."

—**Glory Edim**, founder of Well-Read Black Girl